Praise for S

"A sexy, fun, cat-and-m_____ page one!"

—**Jennifer Prob**_____
Bestsellin_____

"The minute I finishe_____ *g*
Mr. Right, I started _____ k
is! I laughed, I cried, and I fell totally in love with Grant
Emerson and Penelope Blue, one of the most fascinating
book couples I've ever read."

—**Sandra Owens**, author of the bestselling
K2 Special Services series

"Tamara Morgan has masterminded the perfect heist of
the heart."

—**Katie Lane**, *USA Today* bestselling author

"A rollicking romp that packs a surprising emotional
punch."

—**Jenny Holiday**, author of *The Engagement Game*

"This sexy cat-and-mouse game between an FBI agent
and a jewel thief had me furiously flipping the pages
until the very end."

—**A.J. Pine**, author of *The One That Got Away*

STEALING MR. RIGHT

TAMARA MORGAN

Published by Sourcebooks Casablanca, an imprint of Sourcebooks, Inc.
P.O. Box 4410, Naperville, Illinois 60567-4410
(630) 961-3900
Fax: (630) 961-2168
www.sourcebooks.com

Printed and bound in Canada.
MBP 10 9 8 7 6 5 4 3 2 1

For Travis. There's no one I'd rather plan heists with.

THE HEIST

1

WHOEVER SAID CONFRONTING YOUR FEARS HEAD-ON IS the best way to get over them obviously never had to spend eight hours wedged inside an air duct.

It wouldn't be so terrible if I was on a temporary journey, pushing my way through the metal like a tube of lipstick. I might even be able to handle it if the fan at one end turned on and started sucking me toward an untimely demise. At least then I'd know my agony would soon be over—a rainbow of human parts awaiting me at the end.

No such luck. Not only am I well and truly wedged, but I have to *remain* wedged until I get my cue to move.

The only thing keeping me company in the meantime is my fear of confined spaces. Well, my fear of confined spaces and a bladder so full, it's drowning my other internal organs, one by one. I indulge in the luxury of a quick peek at the phone I was issued this morning, but it doesn't help. Only ten minutes have passed since the last time I looked.

Ten long minutes. Ten painful minutes. Ten minutes drawn into a time warp and stretched into infinity.

Tight spaces have a way of magnifying everything that way: time, fears, sounds. It's that last one that accounts for my being in here at all. If it were possible for me to climb through the ducts and get in place without sounding like a stampede of elephants, I might actually enjoy my job. As it is, I have to be in place long before business opens for the day.

Watching. Waiting. Wondering why I ever thought a career as the world's most claustrophobic jewel thief was a reasonable life choice.

Since I already have my phone out, I decide to distract myself with my favorite pastime. My fingers fly over the touchscreen as I text my coconspirator. Tell me a joke.

It takes all of fifteen seconds for Riker to respond. Stop clogging the communication lines. What's your status?

A quick glance through the slats of the vent currently serving as my veranda allows me to size up the situation below. Two clerks behind the counter. A security guard posted at the door, his vigilance waning as the afternoon wears on and his protruding stomach digests his lunch. Three shoppers overall—two men in nice suits, looking at matching gold watches, and one young woman with a knockoff scarf, gazing wistfully at engagement rings.

I want to tell her not to bother—to buy herself a nice cat and take up knitting instead—but not at the cost of giving my position away. Sometime in the next half hour, they're going to open the safe in the basement and bring out a diamond necklace worth two million dollars.

That young woman's happiness is important, but not at the cost of a cool two million.

I'm not saying anything until you tell me a joke, I text back.

We count three shoppers inside. Can you confirm?

I shift a little too much inside my metal prison, and my elbow hits the side with a clang. For a second, I think I'm made, that I'm going to have to haul out of there like a rat driven by smoke, but the lilting background music that's been playing on repeat all day covers the sound.

Relieved—and sweating out only mild profusions of anxiety—I text back, Even a knock-knock joke will do. I'm bored.

All I get this time is a series of random letters and numbers, which means Riker either smashed the phone against his forehead in irritation or gave up entirely and chucked it out the window. It's easy for him to be full of righteous anger. He and our getaway driver, Oz, are comfortably set up in a utility truck down the street, with room to stretch their legs and pee into a coffee cup, should the need arise.

Relax, I text. It's all going according to plan. What do you call a sleepwalking nun?

He won't respond, of course. Riker doesn't approve of humor on the job—or anytime, really. Cracking a smile might mean someone will mistake him for a human being, which is something he actively strives to avoid.

A roamin' Catholic. I wait a second. Get it? She's roamin'? Roman?

Still nothing. It's too bad these temporary cell phones won't let you download Candy Crush or something. I'm dying in here.

The sound of movement down below stops me before I make the mistake of sending Riker my favorite limericks line by line. The young woman has given up on her pursuit of the perfect emerald-cut diamond, and the two men have finally decided on a pair of Concords that look like gold bricks. Clerk A moves to help them while Clerk B picks up the phone and casts an anxious look toward the back of the shop. His adrenaline spikes so much, I can almost feel the shift in the air, all of it drawn up into my vent.

Not that I'm judging him, mind you. He has every right to be nervous. Today is the first time in a decade that necklace will see the light of day, and it's an anniversary we intend to mark in a big way.

When seen at a distance, Paulson Jewelers isn't all that impressive. It has a small, lackluster inventory compared to its more upscale competitors in Manhattan's diamond district. The building is crowded between a Laundromat and a discount shoe store, which doesn't do much to boost its overall aesthetic. In fact, if it weren't for the small, overlooked detail that it's built on top of a former bank vault, it wouldn't have anything to offer.

But, oh, that bank vault is worth notice. Hidden below the city streets and wiped from official records during Prohibition so it could be used as a distillery, that vault has been the secret hiding place of *the necklace* since it went missing after a botched heist ten years ago.

It wasn't *my* botched heist. I was only fifteen at the time. Still, I've got what you might call a personal tie to the original thief. I've spent many long nights thinking about that necklace, dreaming of it, picturing what my life might have been like if someone had left that signature twenty-carat stone deep in the cavern it came from. I like to think there'd be ponies and wide open fields. Maybe even an Italian villa or two.

Since turning back the hands of time is outside my skill set, I'm stuck with option B—all two million dollars of it. It's the only reason I've allowed myself to be crammed into this tin can like a human nut loaf. I mentally go over the plan in an attempt to distract myself.

As soon as the necklace is removed from the safe and brought upstairs to be picked up by its owner—a woman by the name of Erica Dupont—Paulson Jewelers will be plunged into a blackout. No cameras, no emergency generators, no phones. The doors will automatically lock, and the metal screens will crash down over the windows. This kind of safety feature means no one can come in, but it means no one gets out, either. A closed crime scene, the police like to call it.

With my trusty night vision goggles in place— they're on top of my head, waiting for me to drop them over my eyes—it'll be easy for me to lift the vent away. The screws have been undone for hours, waiting in my pocket for a quick return. I'll slip down, snag the jewels, and be back inside my air duct before the sleepy security guard manages to locate his flashlight.

The best part is I get to hightail it out of this vent without regard for the clatter of escape. Jordan, our detonation expert and my best friend, is standing across the street, getting ready to set off a chain of firecrackers in a garbage can. She considers firecrackers the lowest form of explosive, and she almost cried when we told her she couldn't bring out her homemade C-4 or flash bombs, but we don't need the big explosives for this job. All we require is some noise to scare the clerks and security guard into thinking there's a gunfight going on outside. They'll be so busy trying to figure out what's happening in the street, they won't notice a few extra thumps as I make my escape.

And then? Freedom. Air. Two million dollars shoved down the front of my bra. It's practically foolproof.

My heart picks up as a sleek town car comes to a stop in front of the jewelry store. Because of how narrow the storefront is, the car blocks the entire view out the window, and I can't tell if Jordan is in place or if Oz is performing his requisite drive-by before Riker cuts all the electricity on the block.

I can, however, see a regal-looking woman in her seventies emerging from the backseat. Erica Dupont looks exactly how a person who owns a two-million-dollar necklace and buries it in obscurity for ten years should look—rich. Overdone from the delicate pink of her pantsuit to the leather handbag clutched at her side, this woman's wealth is such an ingrained part of her, she could probably have necklaces hidden all over the city and never notice their loss.

It's hard to imagine that kind of existence—to have so much money, it simply stops mattering. Most of my life has revolved around the idea that there never has been and never will be enough. Oh, I started out just fine, mind you, clothed and shod and poised to follow in the footsteps of one of the most successful jewel thieves this world has ever seen, but you could say there's something about this particular career choice that breeds instability. All it takes is one bad job to change everything.

A new text flashes across the screen, stopping me before I fall too deep into the pit of my past.

Erica is on the move, Riker's message says. Unnecessarily, I might add. I'm not the brains of this operation, but I'm not an idiot either. *And she appears to be accompanied.*

That's also well within my powers of deduction. I can't make out the face of the large male figure opening the door and ushering her inside, but he must be some kind of bodyguard she's decided to bring along for security purposes. Which isn't surprising, really. We'd half expected her to show up with an armored truck and a fleet of hired guns in tow, but she's been making this really easy on us.

In fact, everything about this job has been easy so far. Fortuitous, I like to think—karma coming around and playing fair for a change. From the moment Riker heard about the necklace finally resurfacing after all these years—and managed to land us a two-million-dollar contract from a highly motivated buyer—this whole process has been like a series of dominoes falling into place.

Can you handle him?

Big means slow, and the nice suit he's wearing means he isn't expecting any action. I can handle him.

No sweat, I text back. *The necklace is on its way up.*

Good. Blackout in T minus two minutes. Cutting cell contact now.

That's all I need to start my internal countdown. Two minutes should give the couple enough time to approach the counter. The clerks will be obsequious and distracted as they prepare to hand over the necklace. The security guard at the door will be busy keeping the shoppers off to one side, his eyes on the door for signs of any suspicious characters.

That leaves only me, ready to swoop in like, well, a suspicious character.

"Would you look at that?" A low whistle fills the air as the couple comes to a halt below me. "I knew it was an impressive piece of craftsmanship, but the pictures hardly do it justice."

I almost drop my phone in my attempt to tuck it away in my belt pack. *No*. It can't be. I must be hearing things.

"If I turn it like this, I can actually see my reflection in the big center stone. Do you think everyone looks this good in twenty carats?"

I'm delirious. Dehydrated and cramped. Losing my goddamned mind.

"We might as well have you wear it out. One thing I've noticed in the course of my career is it's much harder to steal something from around a neck than you think. Necks and socks. Those are the best hiding spots. No one ever wants to go for the toes. Too afraid of fungus."

There's no doubt in my mind now. Only one person in the world has those kinds of inane theories. I fumble for the phone. ABORT, I text, even though I know Riker is no longer plugged in. Still, I have to try. ABORT NOW.

An ominous blank screen is my only reply. There's nothing left for me to do but snap my eyes closed and wince as my internal clock hits the two-minute mark. Shutting my eyes against the inevitable is an awful lot like pulling the blankets over my head and hoping the monsters under the bed can't find me, but it's all I can do, short of tumbling out of the vent and turning myself in.

The man releases a showy catcall, and I can only assume he's managed to put the heap of stones around Erica's neck for an admiring glimpse against her décolletage. But even obscenely wealthy breasts aren't visible in the dark, which means...

Cautiously, optimistically, I open one eye. Riker must have gotten my message, thank God, and I can finally pay enough attention to make out the features of the muscle-bound bodyguard below.

Dirty-blond hair, worn a little too long so it curls at the ends like a surfer after a day in the sun.

Rough features, with a broken crook to his nose and a heaviness to his brow that makes him look like he's deep in concentration, even when he sleeps.

Large, deep-set eyes the inky-brown of coffee, with crinkling lines that extend outward whenever he laughs or smiles.

And the lips. I don't need to see the lips to know what they look like. Feel like. Taste like. Grant's lips have always been his best feature—the one soft spot in the thickheaded, hard-bodied exterior I know so well.

"What I wouldn't give to let my wife catch a glimpse of that beauty." Grant shakes his head at the stones around Erica's neck. "She'd love it. She has a thing for diamonds like you wouldn't believe—can't seem to get enough of them."

I have to close my throat around the rising sound of irritation. *Of course* I have a thing for diamonds. I especially covet the diamonds that caused my father to disappear from my miserable fifteen-year-old existence, leaving me for all intents and purposes alone in the world. One might even call it an obsession.

"Does she?"

"Absolutely. I'm more of an invest-my-money-in-real-estate sort of guy, but I can see how a necklace like this might have its advantages. I've always loved the curve of a woman's neck right there."

I almost tumble out of my duct again, but this time, it's because I'm straining to catch a glimpse of what part he's talking about. Unfortunately, all I can see is his broad back and the warning lights of a panic attack in my peripheral vision.

"You know what?" Erica says. "If she likes diamonds so much, you should buy her a bauble while we're here. We can delay a few minutes if you want to shop around."

"Really? You don't mind?"

"Why not?" She releases a tinkling laugh, the sound like champagne flutes clinking against gold coins. "I'm not in a hurry, and you said yourself there haven't been any signs of trouble."

"If you're sure." Grant leans casually over one of the jewelry cases. "I'd like to get her something special. Believe me when I tell you—she has it coming."

Oh, I have something coming, all right, but I seriously doubt it's that pair of earrings he's lingering over. Not that it matters about five seconds later, when the whirring click of the air turns off behind me.

Air. One.

Music. Two.

Lights. Three.

With that, the entire jewelry store plunges into a vacuum of electricity—just like we planned. So much for aborting the mission. Riker's sense of timing has always been worthless.

On cue, explosions sound from the street outside, spurring me to action and filling my ears with the ringing clatter of crashing metal and shouting. I don't bother to hide my groan as I drop the night vision goggles into place. As much as I'd love to see this job through, there's no way I can safely nab that necklace. Not now. Not if my husband is standing between me and Erica Dupont's neck.

The vent takes on an eerie green glow through my goggles, but I don't wait around for my eyes to adjust. Quick—so quick I almost lodge my shoulders sideways—I manage to get myself turned around. On my stomach, I wriggle as fast as I can in the opposite direction.

Even though this duct is used for cooling purposes only, I swear I can feel the metal heating underneath me as I worm my way through. In my panic, I'm also convinced Grant is right behind me—rattling the vent panel, climbing in, grabbing me by the ankle and giving a firm tug...

The duct still echoes with the sound of my escape as I make it to the exterior panel. Even though I know—*I know*—it's only my imagination holding fast to my foot, a creeping numbness invades the limb. Which is why, by the time I finally push aside the metal cover and pull myself into the blinding night-vision-enhanced sunlight, I end up sprawled face-first on the rooftop tar, my foot twisted unnaturally underneath me and a sharp stab shooting through my ankle.

"Ow. Ouch. Ow." I tuck into a neat ball and roll up on one leg, forcing myself to keep hopping, keep going, keep moving. Failed jewel thieves don't have the luxury of wallowing in their pain.

Especially not failed jewel thieves whose husbands might come flying up the fire escape at any moment.

Even though our plans originally called for me to jump down to the back alley, where a dumpster full of padded garbage bags awaits, I decide it's too risky to be anywhere near street level. Gauging the distance between me and the discount shoe store rooftop with a cringe, I put as much weight on my ankle as I can. It's not much, but it's enough to give me the running start I need.

With a quick prayer to the gods who watch over the desperate and determined, I leap.

So much for my foolproof plan.

⬥

I'm limping, exhausted, and starving by the time I arrive at Bryant Park.

"Food." I drop to the round, café-style table with a sigh, ignoring the sounds of ping-pong taking place across the lawn. My ankle is throbbing inside the black jazz shoes I always wear when I'm working, but I don't dare take them off. Based on the swelling currently ballooning inside my skin, I can't risk releasing the pressure, or I'll never get them back on again. "And water. And *food*."

"Give me the necklace first," Riker says. He's looking rested and well-fed, two characteristics that don't endear him to me at the moment.

"Don't mess with me right now. I'm so hungry, I could eat this table, bird droppings and all."

He drapes his arm more firmly over the picnic basket he brought along, tempting me with its signature red checks. Not that there's anything delicious in there. If this were a *real* picnic, there'd be roast beef sandwiches, plates of cheese, and cake in a rainbow of colors. Sadly, this is no friendly meal for two. It's a rendezvous between one tattered, exhausted jewel thief and the handsome bastard of a man who tells her what to do.

"Seriously, Riker." My stomach growls a warning that practically echoes through the park. "I haven't eaten in, like, ten hours. Please tell me you brought cookies."

He slides the basket across the table and lifts the lid. "You know the deal. Drop off first."

It's with an unhappy sigh that I begin tossing in the paraphernalia from the running belt strapped to my waist. The night vision goggles, cracked and useless and with several clumps of my reddish-blond hair caught in the band. The cell phone, which Riker will dispose of by mysterious means. The now-empty energy gel pack that was supposed to sustain me during my long, cramped stay in air-duct-ville. And finally, the screws to the vent, which I was unfortunately unable to replace in my mad dash to get outside in one piece.

"The necklace?"

I shake my head.

"You don't have it?"

I shake it again, more forcefully this time. This whole thing is his fault in the first place—even the twisted ankle, though making a rational argument for that one will be hard. "I take it you didn't get my text message?"

"Which one? You spent half the day sending me terrible jokes." He pauses, only the right side of his mouth scowling. It's a common trick of his—he's always had these freakishly weird lips that twist in opposite directions depending on his mood. The left side smiles. The right side scowls. You'd think such a quirk would make him appear disfigured, but it suits his dark, angular features to perfection—brings a touch of human to his otherwise flawless exterior. Seriously. I know super-models who weep over the shape of his cheekbones.

"Pen, you're starting to freak me out. I'm sorry it took so long for the lights to go down—I missed one of the wires—but that shouldn't have been a deal breaker. Just a delay. What happened?"

"I didn't get the necklace, that's what happened," I say. "I'd go into more detail, but my blood sugar is too low. I feel a faint coming on."

"Please. You've never fainted a day in your life. You have an iron head and a titanium stomach."

"Exactly my point."

Finally—finally—he takes pity and hands me a banana from among the discarded tech in the picnic basket. A *banana*, of all things. Riker is paranoid I'm going to gain weight and ruin all his plans to squeeze me inside air ducts and garbage cans, so he polices my diet accordingly. Still, I peel it greedily, not pausing to chew before I swallow.

"There, you're fed. If you don't have the necklace, where is it?"

I hand him the peel. "I assume it's back in the vault. As soon as the lights went out, I got out of there as fast as I could."

"But everything was going according to plan!"

"Um, not everything. Did you happen to see who was helping that woman out of the car?"

"A guard. Hired help. You said he wasn't a problem."

"He *wasn't* a problem. At least, not until I recognized him."

Riker's eyes flare in a moment of alarm, and that's when I know he understands. "No."

"Afraid so. I should have known the moment he walked in. Shoulders like that could only belong to Grant."

As if conjured by my husband's name, Jordan appears out of nowhere, sliding into the seat opposite me and smelling like her usual mix of sulfur and candy. She's still wearing the jean shorts layered over ripped leggings she donned for the job—an unquestionably punk outfit to go with the juvenile antics of setting off fireworks in a garbage can. In her everyday life, Jordan is much more likely to wear sweater sets and neatly ironed linen dresses, but she's found that an impeccably attired, twentysomething black woman setting off explosives in broad daylight draws much more attention than a slouchy, underdressed teenager doing the same. How's that for societal expectations?

"*Grant*-Grant?" she asks, not missing a beat.

"Grant-*Grant*-Grant," I confirm. I peek inside the picnic basket, but unless I want to start munching electronics, I'm going to have to wait until I get home. "I guess the FBI must have received a tip-off the necklace was being moved and decided to get there first."

"What do you mean, you *guess* the FBI must have received a tip-off?" Riker asks.

"I mean, based on the day's events, which conspired to place my *very own husband* at the scene of our crime, I can only assume he was on the job. We always said it seemed too good to be true, the way the necklace was being transported with almost no security. Now we know it was. He's probably been in on it from the start."

"But how could you not have seen this coming?" Riker demands. "He never mentioned stopping by a jewelry store this afternoon?"

I don't like his tone. "Of course not."

"And you didn't accidentally indulge in a little pillow talk one night?"

Now I don't like his words, either. "What exactly are you accusing me of here, Riker? I just spent *all day* trapped inside an air vent. *Months* planning this with you guys. Do you honestly think I'd have gone through with everything if I had any idea Grant would be there?"

"It's one monster of a coincidence. Are you sure he isn't having you followed?"

"Of course I'm sure!" I'm on my feet now, glaring at him across the table. "You're the one in charge of details. If we're going to make accusations, why don't we point fingers at your mysterious underworld buyer and his two-million-dollar promises? I thought you said you vetted this guy before you agreed to the job."

"His name is Blackrock, and I *did* vet him. The man is infallible, a god among thieves."

One thing I know for sure: gods and thieves rarely play well together. "You must have overlooked something."

"I didn't overlook anything."

"Well, you underlooked, then. Grant was *there*, Riker. So close I could have touched him."

"You're yelling, Pen." Jordan speaks calmly, ending our argument before it has a chance to get started. For a woman who loves a good explosion, she's always been a remarkable diplomat.

She's also right. I *am* yelling, and I have to force myself to take a deep breath and relax, focusing on the careful rise and fall of my chest. It's the technique I resort to whenever the walls start closing in on me—metaphorically speaking—and it comes in handy at times like this. Whatever else I might be able to say about him, Riker is good for my oxygen saturation levels.

"I'm sorry we didn't get the necklace," I say and mean it. This makes two times someone in my family has failed to get their hands on those diamonds, but at least I haven't disappeared into thin air as a result. *Yet*. "And I'm sorry for yelling. I didn't want to lash out at you, but I'm hungry and cranky, and I hurt my ankle climbing out of the vent."

Riker's scowl lifts. "Apology accepted."

True to form, he doesn't offer one in return. Before I can drop a hint that one would be welcomed—deserved, even—Jordan takes over, her natural tact smoothing over the rough spots. "There. Now that you have it out of your system, you two can be friends again."

Friends. As if that word contains the depth needed to describe the complex, tangled, soul-deep relationship I share with this man. It would be like calling Federal Agent Grant Emerson my *husband*. Sometimes, mere semantics aren't enough.

Jordan further proves the inefficacy of the human language with a quick hand gesture that neither Riker nor I can decipher. I recognize it only as a signal to Oz, which she makes using a weird sign language the two of them created when they were foster kids together. Those two are so emotionally connected, they can practically write Shakespeare in a few twitches of the wrist. It's freaky.

It's also a sign of how good a master of disguise Oz is, because I didn't even see him standing over there by the entrance to the library. Medium height, medium build, average features, eyes that aren't really any one color—when Oz isn't in some kind of prearranged uniform, even I have a hard time spotting him in a crowd, and I've known the man for just about forever.

"Oz thinks we should take a few days." Her eyes squint as she tries to read his hand movements from afar. "That way, we can decompress and cool off. It's not a bad idea. We'll regroup later this weekend and do the postmortem then. I think we're all feeling disappointed, and it's not going to do us any good to take it out on each other."

Before I have a chance to agree—it *is* a good idea to take a few days away from the people I love most and least in the world—Riker shakes his head. "Nope. It won't work. We can't meet this weekend."

Oh, for the love of everything. Would it kill him to be conciliatory for once? It's not like any of us wanted things to turn out this way. Besides, he knows how much that necklace means to me. Few people get a chance to cash in on the unlucky talisman that ruined their lives. I know my cut of the money won't make up for the loss of my dad—and it won't even begin to cover the huge fortune that disappeared with him—but it's a decent start.

"Come on, Riker," I say. "Your hot dates and big plans are going to have to wait. Figuring out what went wrong is more important than your personal life."

"Too bad it's not my personal life that's the issue here." He pushes back from the table. His movements are jerky, a clear sign he's trying—not very successfully—to hide his emotions.

That's when it hits me.

"In case you've forgotten," he says, "tomorrow is your anniversary."

My anniversary.

Well...*crap*.

THE HUSBAND

2

(Later that Night)

"I KNOW IT'S A DAY EARLY, BUT I GOT YOU SOMETHING."

I don't make a sound as the low timbre of my husband's voice surprises me from the bathroom doorway—that's two decades of on-the-job training put to good use right there—but I do fumble with the razor I'd been drawing over my leg. I see the nick before I feel it.

"Jesus, Grant." I twist my leg to keep the sudden welling of blood from dripping all over the claw-foot tub. "Give a girl a little warning, will you? I think I might need stitches."

"No, you don't. Stitches are only for wounds of depth—not breadth. There's nothing there to stitch."

It's a fair assessment, but I'm not about to let him bury my gaping leg wound under his practical streak. Grant has the annoying habit of FBI agents everywhere in believing that an injury isn't worth note unless it's a gunshot wound sustained in the line of duty. He and Riker share that in common, actually. My pain is a matter of complete indifference to them. I could be hit by a car, and both of them would expect me to remember to sit up and jot down the license plate number before it got away.

"Are you going to give me a first aid lecture while I bleed all over the bathroom floor?"

"If your plan is to sit there until you pass out, then yes. It sounds like you might need one."

"What I need is sympathy, you jerk."

He complies in an instant. "Of course you do, poor baby. Let me see it."

He passes silently from the doorway to my side, where I'm perched on the edge of the tub, my leg extended at an awkward angle and propped by the tiled wall. It baffles me that a six-foot-two former Virginia Tech quarterback can walk around without making a sound, but he's always had an uncanny ability to move on a cloud of air.

I want to protest as he perches himself on the toilet seat and draws my naked leg into his lap, but, well, my naked leg is in his lap. Nudity has a way of taking over every other consideration, and I'm reminded that the rest of me is also quite bare, wrapped up in a fluffy white towel and nothing more. He's aware of it, too, his eyes following the line of my thigh up to where it disappears into the terry cloth.

It's all I can do not to melt into a puddle alongside the overspray from my shower. Even though tomorrow will signal an entire year of wedded bliss, I haven't yet figured out how to be naked in a room with my husband without being all too aware of my body's discrete parts. I'm all skin and nipples and legs, my nerve endings pricking to awareness thanks to his proximity alone.

His proximity is, unfortunately, impossible to ignore. Although it's been a good eight years since he played football, he hasn't lost a fiber of the well-formed muscle from his athletic youth. I should know. I've seen the pictures. I've *studied* the pictures—not to mention the school reports, his recruitment to the FBI, an obscene list of professional accolades, childhood immunization records, and even an article from when he was twelve and won the Pinewood Derby.

In short, I've discovered just about everything there is to know about this man, but I still couldn't tell you how he knew I was going to be at that jewelry store today.

And he knew. There's not a doubt in my mind that Grant planned today's botched job down to the last frantic second.

He's too good not to. That man sees, hears, and knows all. Let me tell you—there's nothing worse than a husband who's always right. Unless, of course, he also happens to be your mortal enemy.

"I think you're going to live." Grant's gentle smile mocks me, but that doesn't make it any less powerful an aphrodisiac. His movements are careful as he pulls out a box of Band-Aids from under the sink, and he even goes so far as to blow on my shin before putting the bandage in place. His breath is hot and cold at the same time, and even though admiration is the last thing I should be feeling for him right now, I can't help but appreciate the way his generous lips form a familiar and enticing shape.

Dammit. I lied before. There *is* something worse than a lover-slash-enemy who knows too much. If there was any justice in this world, he'd at least refrain from being a heap of masculine perfection in shirtsleeves. I swear, someone beyond the pearly gates must be laughing it up at my expense. I hope they're enjoying the show.

Fortunately for my sanity and self-control, his hand brushes my ankle as he tosses the wrapper in the garbage. Even that slight contact shoots fire up my leg. Since I know I'm not going to get any sympathy from Grant unless I can magically transform a twisted ankle into a bullet wound, I bite my lip to keep from crying out.

Conversely, my stoicism brings out the nurturer in him. "Oh, Penelope Blue—what did you do?"

I should point out that Grant is the only person in the world I allow to call me by my full name. He infuses it with a playful, singsong quality that *should* make me annoyed but doesn't. There's something about a large, arrogant man falling into sudden outbursts of rhyme that gets to me.

He moves his hand over the eggplant-colored bruise running parallel to the arch of my foot, his touch featherlight and almost reverent. "What happened? Were the kids hard on you today? Lots of pirouettes gone wrong?"

Now, this is where things get tricky. In case you aren't confused enough, my cover story is that my professional goals extend no further than teaching dance to a group of four-year-olds at a midtown rec center—something I actually do a few days out of the week to lend credence to the lie that is my life. But there is no class on Fridays, and Grant knows it. I know Grant knows it, but I'm not sure if Grant knows that I know he knows it.

See? Tricky.

"It's nothing—I just fell when I was leaving." I stick to reality as much as possible in situations like these. One thing I've learned in the past year is that it's much easier to keep up a strong cover story if there's an element of truth to it.

"Always so clumsy." Grant makes a tsking sound. "Tripping up when I least expect it."

My heart picks up, and I steal a peek at his expression. His eyes—always so innocent in their wide, sleepy way—*seem* sincere, but I'm unable to keep from testing him just to be sure. It's a problem of mine, this not knowing when to stop. I push when I should back away, argue when I should agree, get married to an FBI agent when I should be running as fast and as far as my feet will take me.

"I'm not clumsy," I say with a prim lift of my nose. "Everything I do is carefully arranged ahead of time. You could say it's all part of my master plan."

His eyes crinkle in what I *think* is amusement. "Is that right?"

"Yes. I just want you to believe I'm accident-prone. That way, when I dazzle you with my acrobatic grace and contortionist abilities, you won't know what hit you."

"Acrobatic grace?"

"*And* contortionist abilities."

This proves too much for his gravity. His lips twitch. "I know you're flexible, but don't you think contortionist is taking things a step too far?"

I don't even blink. "I could fit inside that bathroom cupboard and stay there all night without breaking a sweat."

He laughs out loud at that, his chuckle deep and rich. I feel it tingling in places better left unmentioned. "Nice try, but I know how you get inside small spaces. You can't even look at an elevator without cringing."

Instead of making me feel comforted, his words only throw me into greater disorder. I never know what to think when he makes statements like that—so sure of himself, so sure of *me*. Yes, he knows I get a touch claustrophobic from time to time, but either he believes me to be a jewel thief capable of sitting in an air duct for eight hours, or he doesn't. There isn't a middle ground.

If he notices how flustered I am, he doesn't let it show as he once again turns his attention to my ankle. "Do we need to have this looked at?"

"You're the first aid expert. You tell me."

He studies my foot for a moment, his brow furrowed in concentration as he gives the limb a delicate twist. I have to laugh at how serious he looks—as if he has X-ray vision on top of all his other superhuman capabilities.

Then I stop laughing, because there's a good chance he *does*. Seriously. I wouldn't put anything past this man. Secret government experiments and all that.

"You'll live," he asserts. "As much as I'd like to keep you chained up here for the rest of your life, you'll be back up and dancing in no time."

Dancing. Right. That's what he's afraid of.

I'm about to make the major mistake of saying more, of feeling him out on the subject of today's events, but he lifts my foot to his lips and drops a kiss on the bruise. Gone are all thoughts of pain. No more do I care if he knows my secrets and intends to reveal them to the proper authorities. That foot is now the center of my entire being, linked to a million coils of sensation firing like pistons between my legs.

He's *that* dangerous. If his lips moved a few inches higher, the pistons would start hammering so hard, I'd end up confessing everything.

Which is why I clear my throat and delicately take my limb back. Now is not the time for leg pistons. I obviously need to get a grip on myself. "First things first. I thought I heard you say something about a present?"

"Always so greedy." He flicks my cheek with his forefinger before reaching into his back pocket and extracting a long, flat package wrapped in white paper. "It's a good thing you're so cute, or I'd have divorced you months ago."

Sticking my tongue out at him is as good a response as any—especially since words are having a hard time rising to the surface.

"And be careful. You're going to want to be gentle with this one. It's expensive."

My first thought is of the jewelry store and Grant's declaration that I deserve something nice, as if I'm some sweet, docile lamb of a spouse who works with children and cooks regular meals. But this is clearly not a jewelry box, and the package is heavy—much heavier than I expected.

I look up, startled, but Grant's expression is unreadable. "Happy anniversary. Here's to another eighty incredible years."

Damn him. He knows exactly what to say to make me feel as if the room has tipped on its side. "But I didn't get you anything."

"You don't have to get me anything." His fingers graze my bottom lip for the briefest touch before his entire hand—a big, capable, ex-football-player's hand—cups the side of my face. I turn into it like a cat. "Being married to you is enough."

He's about two seconds away from kissing me and rendering the towel barrier between us null and void, so I crinkle the package and give it my full attention instead. In true man fashion, the wrapping job is clumsy and clumpy, and I have to unroll the paper for what seems like five yards before I finally reach the item inside.

And then I drop it.

Fast—too fast, his reflexes on the ready—Grant catches the necklace before it has a chance to hit the tiles below. I want to act normal, as if being presented with a two-million-dollar necklace for one's anniversary is a girlish delight rather than a shock of ice water over the head, but I can barely breathe, let alone squeal.

"What the hell?" I can't bring myself to touch it again. God, those diamonds were heavy. I mean, I've held diamonds before—uncut stones and gleaming, polished jewelry sets and once, an entire velvet bag full of gems—but never anything like this. Four people's futures could fit inside these rocks. One little girl's dream could be brought back to life. "Why are you giving me this?"

"It's customary to give one's wife a gift on an anniversary." His tone is level and unreadable. His smile gives nothing away. "Or so I've been told. You don't like it?"

I reach for it again, but my hand stops about halfway between our bodies. *A trap*. This has to be some kind of trap. He wants me to get my fingerprints on the necklace so he can plant the evidence somewhere. He's going to put the stones around my neck and strangle me with them the second my guard is down. *Something*.

"It's...lovely."

"Lovely? Are you sure? That's what women usually say when they're disappointed."

"Gorgeous," I hastily amend.

"That's better, but a little generic, don't you think?"

"Too much," is my final answer.

His expression gentles. "Nothing is too much for you, Penelope Blue."

He makes a motion as if he wants to hang the necklace around my neck, but I'm still stuck in place, glued by paranoia. I'm usually better able to parry with my favorite adversary, but this is what they call a killing blow. Nothing about this situation makes sense.

"Aren't you going to say anything?"

All I have to offer is a feeble, "I don't get it." If it were possible to understate an understatement, I just accomplished it in four words. Yay me.

"No, you don't get it," he agrees. "Not permanently, anyway. This one's just on loan. I've been asked to babysit it for a few days."

"Babysit?" At that, I dip my head, drawing myself closer to the necklace. I can't help it. There's so much shiny coming my way. Besides, given the fact that I'm naked and trapped with a man who could bench press me two times over, playing along seems the safest course of action.

"Yeah. It was the craziest thing." His hands are on my neck now, close enough to strangle me, though, of course, he doesn't. Those aren't murder hands— they're seduction hands, and they linger on the slope of my clavicle as he fastens the necklace in place. A shiver works down my spine and covers me in goose bumps, the way it does when someone supposedly steps over the site of your future grave. "I was assigned to help a woman pick it up from a jewelry store today. It was supposed to be an easy task—no one in their right mind would try to steal a necklace like this in broad daylight—but someone actually made the attempt."

My mouth goes dry at the full weight of his words. Of course I'm not in my right mind. If I was, I'd hit him over the head with our industrial-sized shampoo bottle and make my escape out the bathroom window—nudity be damned—without another moment's hesitation.

But I stay in place, the biggest rock in the center of the necklace settling on my chest, right over my pounding heart.

"Really?" I say, feigning shock—and doing a decent job of it, if you ask me. "How exciting. I'd love to hear how you managed to save the day."

Is it my imagination, or is that a gleam of appreciation in his eyes? "Well, there I was, keeping an eye on all the exits, the owner getting ready to pick up her package, and *BAM*"—I jump a little—"out go all the lights. It's pitch dark. The security bars come crashing down over the windows, and there are no emergency backup generators coming on to bring the lights back up."

"Sounds like maybe it was an electrical problem."

"That's what I thought, too, but then we heard the gunfire outside."

Good old Jordan. "There was gunfire?"

"Heading straight for me. I barely made it out alive."

I know it behooves me to fall into a ladylike swoon at

this point. A *good* wife—heck, even a barely competent one—would show at least a little concern for her spouse being caught in the crossfire of a major jewelry heist. But of all the lies that are lodged between us, my being a *good wife* has never been one of them.

"How could the gunfire have been heading straight for you if you were locked inside the jewelry store?"

"I was speaking metaphorically, of course."

"It was *metaphoric* gunfire endangering your life?"

"Gunfire is gunfire. If you'd ever been shot before, you'd show proper deference to the dangers of firearms."

See? I told you. Gunshot wounds trump everything else. It's like no other injury even exists for these guys.

"I'm sorry, you poor, highly trained field operative," I say, since he's obviously in search of some wifely sympathy. "You must have been so frightened. Whatever did you do?"

"Brat." His fingers pinch my chin, forcing me to glance up and find his deep, brown eyes searching mine. "You wouldn't care if I was killed in the crossfire, would you?"

My pulse leaps, but I'm not about to be coerced into a confession. Not when I have no idea how much he actually *knows*. "Well, we do have that lovely life insurance policy."

"Lovely, huh? You keep using that word against me—I don't think you realize how much it stings." I'm saved from having to reply when Grant releases his hold on me and shrugs, his careful nonchalance back in place. "Anyway, nothing happened after that. The lights came back on, but no jewelry was stolen. Not even a wallet or a purse. We aren't sure yet what happened—maybe the perps got spooked—but my section chief thinks the woman's home is the most likely place they'll hit next, so I'm supposed to keep a watch on the necklace for her. It's a pretty brilliant plan, don't you think? No one would suspect the underpaid sap in a federal suit is the chosen keeper of a piece like this. Our house is the last place they'll think to look for it."

I open my mouth and immediately close it again, unsure what to say or even what to think. His boss is absolutely right. Our house, located about an hour north of the city in good ol' suburban Rye, *would* be the last place I'd think to look for it…if Grant hadn't just given away the whole show by placing it against my heart.

"Are you sure my neck is the safest place to keep it right now?" I can't help asking. "How do you know I won't run off to Mexico with it the second your back is turned?"

"I guess I'll have to trust you, won't I?" is his glib response. "Besides, I couldn't resist the temptation. It's a beautiful piece of craftsmanship. I spent most of my day imagining what you'd look like wearing that necklace."

There's no mistaking the rumble in his voice or the way my body responds to it, every part sitting up and taking notice at once. We're no longer talking about firing pistons over here. The whole engine is up and running.

"Well?" I give my head a playful toss, exposing all my neck's curves so he can choose his favorite one. From the looks of it, he prefers the softly beating pulse in the hollow of my throat. The sensitive spot. The weak spot.

My breath catches, my body poised for fight or flight. That pulse is the only sound in the room. I wonder if this is what an animal hears right before it's clamped in the wolf's jaws, or if the world goes black first.

Either way, he's clearly waiting for me to say something—anything—so I manage a feeble, "What's the final verdict? How do I look?"

That's all Grant needs to hear to get moving again. His eyes kindle a dark warning as he pulls the towel from around my body, and that's when I know he plans to elicit a lot more than my fluttering pulse—and that neither flight nor fight is an option anymore.

"Actually, I spent most of my day imagining how you'd look wearing *only* that necklace."

THE
GUARD DOG

3

(Nineteen Months Ago)

"WE'VE GOT A PROBLEM." RIKER SLID INTO THE BOOTH where Jordan and I sat having lunch, the pair of us lingering over expensive coffee and miniature desserts, trying to eke out as much time as we could from a single shot glass of crème brûlée.

The overpriced bistro with metal stools instead of chairs wasn't an ideal setting for a long-term stakeout—as my butt could attest—but it had one important benefit. The view of the high-rise apartment building across the street was crystal clear. Oz currently stood balanced on a rope-suspended scaffold outside the fourteenth floor, pretending to wash windows as he snapped photos of the interior.

His job was hard; ours was easy. He was in charge of reconnaissance, risking life and limb for a glimpse of the apartment layout. All Jordan and I had to do was create a diversion if anyone in a position of authority happened to notice an out-of-place window washer and decided to call it in.

Diversions have always been my favorite part of the job, even though I rarely get to do them. The secret is to make sure there's plenty of backstory in place in case someone ends up asking questions they shouldn't. In this particular instance, I was prepared to run outside and start pulling Jordan's hair in a catfight over a cheating boyfriend we'd decided to call Manfred. Manfred was a jerk of the highest degree, a verbally abusive manwhore, but he was a football player, so we could hardly be blamed for our infatuation. Women have been known to make silly decisions over that particular brand of athlete.

As I would soon come to learn.

"Is that you, Manfred?" I asked. Riker didn't look at all like a football player, with his formfitting jeans and cut-glass cheekbones, but we'd been sitting there for two hours and were mightily bored. "How dare you show your face at a time like this? We're on to your double-timing schemes."

"I'm serious, Pen. I was just scouting the catering company so I could check up on things, and guess who was there?"

"Were you the one who invited this bastard to lunch?" I ignored him, turning my attention to Jordan instead. "I should have known you'd go back on our mutual vow of chastity. It was a ploy to keep him to yourself all along, wasn't it?"

Jordan just compressed her lips to hide a smile and shook her head. She knew better than to poke Riker when he was in a high-and-mighty mood—or to indulge me when I did the poking—so she made the wise choice to back away slowly. It helped that her level of tolerance for us was at an all-time high at that point. She and Oz had been with our team for just a few weeks, so Riker and I were still charming instead of annoying.

We'd known Jordan and Oz for years, of course, but we'd only recently reconnected to indulge in some light larceny together. These sorts of things happened all the time in the criminal world, believe it or not. *We'd* been after a certain gold-plated statue; *they'd* been after a certain gold-plated statue… In the end, it was deemed wisest to split the profits four ways and form a partnership.

I know. It might seem odd at first, this implicit trust among thieves, but you have to understand that the four of us had practically grown up together. Oz and Jordan ran away from their foster home when they were about thirteen. I found myself abandoned and broke at the tender age of fifteen. And Riker was pretty much born on the streets. To hear him tell the tale, he'd been raised by feral cats in a back alley somewhere.

The homeless teen crowd in New York is a surprisingly small and tight-knit group. Like an unprepared militia called up for war, we went through the same kinds of rites and hardships, suffered the same injustices. You didn't come out of that sort of thing unchanged. *We* certainly didn't.

"Would you stop playing around for five minutes and listen to me?" Riker asked. "We're going to have to call it off. You-know-who was there."

I felt a flutter in my stomach that had little to do with the five cups of espresso I'd just consumed. "Oh, really?"

"Yes, really. And he was asking all kinds of nosy questions."

"Maybe he needs a caterer."

"Right. Which was why he wanted to know how they transport the food, arrival and departure times tonight, if he could look at the list of waiters they have on payroll…" He trailed off ominously. Riker has always loved to do things ominously.

Jordan made the motion of a question mark with her spoon.

"Don't ask," I suggested, but of course she did.

"Who are we talking about?"

Riker savored the moment of suspense, extending his pause while a bored waitress refilled our coffees and shuffled off again. "Agent Emerson." He nodded as if those two words were all that was needed to incite riots of fear and panic across the globe. "Our nemesis."

One of Jordan's brows lifted as she glanced back and forth between us, playing into Riker's drama like she was born to it. "We have a nemesis? How has this not come up before?"

"We don't like to talk about him," Riker said.

Oh, for crying out loud. I could have sworn that inside his hard-edged exterior lived a little girl who never got enough attention from her father. Since I've *been* a little girl who never got enough attention from her father, I'm allowed to make qualifications like that.

"*Nemesis* might be pushing things. Are you sure that's the word you want to use?"

He set his jaw. "Yes."

"Don't listen to him. Agent Emerson isn't that bad.

He's more like an annoying puppy who keeps getting in the way."

Then I pictured him, that mountain of a man who'd become our shadow, the heady rush of adrenaline I got when I realized he was once again on our trail, and I added an amendment. "Okay. Maybe he's more like a guard dog—one of those K-9 units they use to sniff out bombs. Yeah, that's better. He's a big, strapping K-9 unit who could destroy us using only the force of his pecs."

I could practically feel Riker's nostrils flaring at me from across the table. Whatever. He was just mad I never complimented *his* pecs.

"We have a big, strapping guard dog?" Jordan's other brow came up to join its neighbor. I probably should have mentioned that—Jordan has the most expressive eyebrows I've ever seen. She could hold entire conversations using them, like Groucho Marx with a better wax job. "I repeat—how has this not come up before?"

"He's hardly a guard dog. He's a federal agent. One, I might add, who has the uncanny ability to know exactly when and where we plan on striking next." Riker looked at me as he spoke, as if I were personally responsible for the slip in our security, simply because I'd noticed the man had Batman-suit-quality musculature.

It wasn't my fault. I dared any hot-blooded woman *not* to notice.

"Stop overreacting."

"I'm not." Riker shook his head. "We've been made. There's nothing we can do but pull out."

At that, Jordan's eyebrows plummeted, my confidence doing much the same. As fun as it was to rile Riker up by pretending not to care about our federal tail, I wasn't keen on losing Jordan before we had a chance to give this partnership a real test run. It was great having an explosives expert—as in, really great, a sign of us moving up in the world—but even better was the female companionship.

Jordan was so calm, so nice, so *real*. Already, she'd taken me shopping two times and showed me a secret chemical formula for peeling paint off walls. I didn't have so many girlfriends in my life that I could afford to throw them away.

"How long has he been following you guys?" she asked.

I waved my hand airily, hoping to assuage her fears. "Oh, just a few months. He's not as big a deal as Riker is making him out to be. You have my word on that."

Riker smacked my hand away. "Don't listen to her. Pen has always refused to see what's right in front of her face. It's like she has a pit where common sense should be."

"I have common sense, thank you very much. I'm practically drowning in it."

"Oh please," Riker said. "You didn't even know how to tie your shoes until you reached puberty."

Sadly, that was true. "I've always preferred slip-ons."

"You thought the hazards of mixing bleach and ammonia was an urban myth."

Unfortunately, also true. "They're both cleaning solutions! I assumed it would double the potency."

Riker took that as proof positive of my incompetency, which was mean of him, if you asked me. He knew very well my childhood hadn't been a conventional one. When other kids had been chanting *bunny ears, bunny ears, playing by a tree* as they learned to loop their shoelaces, I'd been out lifting wallets and breaking into safes with my dad. Instead of a kind, gentle mother teaching me which cleansers worked best on bathroom tile, I'd had an evil stepmother who cared so little about me, she'd bailed less than a month after my dad disappeared.

Forgive me for having a few lapses in my soft skills.

Riker leaned over the table to focus on Jordan. "The best we can tell, Emerson's been after us for about a year. He first got onto our rig after we botched a job down on the wharf last summer."

By *we*, of course, he meant *me*, which was totally unfair, given the circumstances. We'd miscalculated the tide coming in, and even though Riker swore I wasn't in any danger of drowning inside a cargo box at the edge of the dock, I still had occasional flashbacks whenever I passed by a sushi restaurant.

"He wasn't *onto* us then," I countered. "I'm pretty sure he was there for a drug bust the next warehouse over. If you ask me, those docks are becoming an unsavory place to do business."

Jordan tried not to laugh, hiding her smile behind her hand.

Riker wasn't so easily amused. "Regardless of how long he's been following us, it's too dangerous to keep going with this job. If we're being watched, the Jaeger-LeCoultre isn't worth sending you up there."

On the contrary, the half-million-dollar watch *was* worth sending me up there, which was why we planned to steal it in the first place. The man currently in possession of the diamond-encrusted timepiece was an egotistical windbag and even more of a criminal than we were. If he was stupid enough to throw a tax evasion party up on the fourteenth floor while wearing his new pride and joy, then he deserved to be relieved of its burdensome weight.

"Would you relax? I'm sure Emerson's presence has nothing to do with us—there's no way the FBI knows or even cares about our plans. If anything, they're after the bastard we're robbing. The FBI loves catching bad guys on IRS charges. It makes them feel like they're bringing down Al Capone all over again."

"You're so naive," Riker said, but his heart wasn't in it the way it had been a few minutes ago. He obviously hadn't thought of that before—there being better, higher-profile criminals for Agent Emerson to pursue. "If he's after the host of the party, why bother with the caterers at all? He could just waltz up there with a warrant and call it a day."

There was some truth to that. We'd gotten Oz hired as a bartender for the night so he could smuggle me upstairs inside an empty beer keg, making us the most likely targets of Emerson's investigation. Still, I didn't think this was the catastrophe Riker made it out to be. There was no reason for the FBI to expend this kind of manpower to hunt us down. I was pretty sure I had about twenty parking tickets they could have hauled me in on had they really wanted to.

Jordan was looking pretty worried by this time, her eyebrows doing a wobbly dance of alarm, so I decided to pull the clincher.

"Think about it, Riker. If the men in black had actual hard evidence, they'd be doing everything in their power to stay out of the way today. They'd let us get the heist all set up, have Oz send me upstairs in a barrel, and arrest us only *after* we had the goods in hand. The fact that Emerson's there, snooping around in plain sight? That's good news, not bad. He doesn't know who or what he's looking for. He's just guessing."

My triumph was stolen by a sudden burst of movement at the apartment building across the street. We turned to watch as Oz finished with his reconnaissance and lowered his rig so he could wash the thirteenth-floor windows in earnest. Part of his amazing ability to blend in was his commitment to the cover story. He wouldn't stop until the entire building gleamed.

"I should go tell him not to bother," Riker said, mostly to himself. "Damn. We really needed this win."

We *did* need this win, and I was convinced there was no reason why we couldn't still have it. The day I let one measly FBI agent dictate my actions was the day I gave up a life of crime. I was born to this kind of thing. Literally.

"Don't say anything to Oz. Not yet." I slid off the stool and surveyed my attire. I was already in the tight black leggings and running bra I favored when I had to bend my body into a pretzel for a few hours, which would serve my purposes just fine. "I want to check something first."

Riker rose in an attempt to regain his height advantage. "What are you going to do? This isn't a good idea. We need to lay low, maybe even move to Chicago or D.C. for a bit. New York is too hot for us."

On the contrary, it was the exact temperature I preferred: a little warm, a little sultry. "Give me two hours, that's all I'm asking. I want to find our little puppy dog and say hello."

"You are not talking to that man. He'll arrest you."

"It's not illegal to flirt."

"I swear to God, Penelope, no good can come of this."

"Wanna bet?"

Jordan's eyebrows were high as she took in the sight of Riker and me squaring off in the middle of the bistro, but there was nothing to be afraid of. Not now. Not when I'd already won.

And I'd won. There was no question of that.

Poor Riker. Few things were worse than having your weaknesses laid out for the world to see, to know that one word would have you ricocheting off in a tailspin. All that man had to do was hear the word *bet*, and all bets were off. Last I'd heard, he owed about twenty thousand dollars to a loan shark who operated out of something called the Wire Cage.

It was wrong of me to take advantage of him like that, pushing him even closer to the brink, but I had limited options. If Riker walked away from this job, it could be months before we managed to pull together another one. We'd lose Jordan. We'd lose Oz. We'd lose the small bit of momentum we had, and I was so freaking tired of losing all the time. My mom, when I was born. My dad, so many times when the next big job took priority over me. My world, my life, my future, when he disappeared for good.

Just once, it would have been nice if someone stuck around long enough to matter.

"What are the stakes?" Riker asked. He transitioned from surly harbinger of doom to efficient junkie in less time than it took Jordan to blink. "I've got five thousand that says you get arrested the second you saunter up to him and bat your eyelashes."

"You don't have five thousand. I doubt you even have five hundred. How about we make this a gentleman's bet instead? A wager of pride?"

Some of the light went out of his eyes. "You're not a gentleman."

"Neither are you."

"At least I have the right parts."

"Then use them for a change and man up." From the look on Jordan's face, concern and regret binding her brows into a firm line, I could tell I needed to make this count. "How's this? If I can't succeed at wooing Agent Emerson with my feminine wiles, then we'll end the job here. No bartending, no beer keg, no five-hundred-thousand-dollar watch."

"And if you succeed?"

"Easy. If I succeed—*and I will*—he'll be asking me out for dinner and drinks tonight as far uptown from this place as we can get. It's going to break his pec-popping little heart when I turn out to be a no-show, but at least we'll know he's not about to make the bust of his life."

It wasn't Riker's favorite kind of bet—he wasn't happy unless someone's kneecaps were into danger of being broken—but it was clear he was wavering.

"We've got nothing to lose at this point," I added. "Either he knows enough to throw a wrench in our plans from here on out, or he doesn't. I say it's better if we find out now."

I knew I was in when Riker's scowl almost took over his entire mouth. "What makes you so sure you can seduce him, anyway? Maybe you're not his type. No man wants to be saddled with a thieving hellcat who can't take anything seriously."

I laughed out loud at that. "Are you sure? I remember a time it worked just fine for you."

Riker snorted as Jordan muffled a laugh. That's when I knew I'd won, for better or for worse.

Funny how these things turn out.

THE
CELEBRATION

4

(Present Day)

JORDAN LETS OUT A LOW WHISTLE AS SHE ALLOWS THE necklace to slip through her fingers, feeling the incredible weight and luxury of ten of the most beautiful diamonds in the world. "And he really put it around your neck, just like that?"

"Yep."

"Walked in the door, said, 'honey, I'm home,' and handed over the exact same piece of jewelry we were trying to steal a few hours earlier?"

"Yep." I'm having a hard time meeting Jordan's eye. Or Riker's. They're both sitting in my living room, goggling at the precious gems that have been left in my care while Grant is picking up groceries for dinner. I have no idea if he expects it—or me—to be here when he gets back.

"And then what?" Jordan is itching to try it on, I can

tell. I know the feeling, tingling up from your toes and making your fingers curl into a pair of ineffectual claws. It's not too different from a mind-blowing kiss, actually. "Did you wear it all night? I'd wear it until he pried it from my cold, dead hands."

"Oh yeah." I sigh, remembering Grant's reverent touch, the way he traced the outline of the stones against my body with his tongue, not stopping until the impression of each one had been permanently sealed on my skin. I'd half expected to wake up and find a brand still there. "He wanted me to keep it on while we had sex."

Jordan flings the necklace away as though it's suddenly gained serpentine features. "Geez, Pen. Open with that kind of thing, would you?" Her head tilts as she glances at where it lands. "Did you do it?"

"Oh, I did it."

She squeals. "Well?"

"It's worth every penny of its two million dollars, and that's all I'm saying on the subject." I hobble over on my still-swollen ankle to collect the necklace and return it to the shoebox that has become its temporary holding case. Riker's eyes are on me as I push aside the abstract flea market painting covering our safe, but I angle my body so he can't see the code—or my expression, which I'm afraid is rather moony.

I know we were supposed to take a few days off from one another to collect our thoughts, but I begged them to trek up here the second Grant headed out for the afternoon. This is kind of an emergency, and I'm not sure how much longer I can maintain a careful front where he's concerned. There are too many coincidences and too many kisses happening inside these four walls. I can usually handle one of those things at a time, but together?

Yeah. I'm useless. And until you've been tossed to the bed by a man like Grant and told you're not getting up until you scream his name, I'll kindly ask you to refrain from passing judgment.

I adjust the painting so it's back in its customary position, waiting for the inevitable blast from Riker.

"Well, I guess it'll be easy to steal this time," he finally says, his voice even. I think for a second he's going to react in a rare moment of levelheadedness, but then he adds, "We can stage a home invasion the next time the insatiable Mr. Romance brings out the necklace and demands his marital rights. When do you think that will be, Pen? Five minutes after he gets home? Ten? Can he wait a whole hour at a time?"

I ignore his acid tone, which, if handled improperly, will end up burning us all. From the moment I initiated that bet about seducing Grant, Riker has never been able to get on board. He's always been a little grouchy—it's part of his charm—but the past year has seen him spiraling toward the dark side at an alarming rate. In fact, the only time I've seen him even slightly happy was when he was planning the necklace heist.

For a while there, it had almost been like seeing the boy I once knew resurfacing for air. More left-side smiles than right-side scowls, a kind of latent energy crackling underneath his thorny surface. I could almost picture the two of us on the streets again, living by our wits and my ability to pick any kind of lock.

That feeling is gone now. Squashed by failure and… conjugal relations.

"He's not as depraved as you're making him out to be," I say in defense of my husband. "And it doesn't matter anyway. We're not taking the necklace."

Riker sits up in his chair—or, to put it more accurately, Grant's chair. In the manner of aggressively male, law-abiding husbands everywhere, Grant comes home every day to a well-worn leather recliner that somehow smells like cigars even though neither one of us smokes.

"No way," Riker says. "We're not letting an opportunity like this pass. We could grab it right now, get it to Blackrock, and be out of the country by nightfall."

I cross my arms. "We're not taking it."

"It does seem like an awfully good opportunity." Jordan glances longingly toward the safe. "I can hear it calling to me."

"Resist it. I'm not changing my mind."

Jordan and Riker share a *look*, one that reminds me how far out of the inner circle I've grown as of late. I'm glad Oz isn't present at our little meeting, or I might not be able to hold the team back from voting to finish the job right here and now.

Riker and Jordan are too much a part of my life to be a secret from Grant—in fact, Jordan was a bridesmaid at our wedding—so although it might be odd for them to come over with a bouquet of flowers and a happy anniversary balloon, it's not unheard of. Oz, however, is a secret we intend to keep for as long as possible. There are times when we need to be able to come and go under Grant's watchful eye, and it's better for all of us if no one can positively identify Oz in the aftermath. I think he might be the gardener with the turned-up collar and ball cap trimming the next-door neighbor's hedges right now, but I couldn't say for sure. That gardener seems a little too tall.

"So help us, Pen," Riker says. "If you're developing *feelings* for this man…"

"This has nothing to do with my feelings, thank you very much."

"Really? You could have fooled me. We want to steal the necklace *you* have personal ties to, from a man *you* live with, in hopes of getting some of the closure *you* never got as a kid. Tell me again how your feelings aren't weighing in on your ability to make sound decisions?"

My marriage is and always has been the one topic of conversation I'm not willing to compromise on. It has to be. Once we fall down the rabbit hole to that murky place where logic and emotion intersect, we aren't likely to find our way out again.

"I'm not a complete idiot. I know what I'm doing." That's not even a little bit true, but I forge on. "C'mon, Riker. Think for once. It has to do with that ever-elusive common sense you're always going on about."

"Right."

"Which is something I have an abundance of, even if *some* people don't think so."

"Sure."

I throw up my hands. "Would you step back and look at this clearly? If we disappear the same day as that necklace, there won't be a doubt in anyone's mind that we're the culprits—and you can bet your ass Grant won't rest until he tracks us down. He'd scour the earth on hands and knees before he'd be made a laughingstock like that. Do you want to go into hiding for the rest of your life? Is that your goal?"

"Of course not," he says sullenly.

"You know the saying. 'It's not just about getting the goods. It's about getting *away* with the goods.'" I'm hit with a pang of nostalgia as I repeat the words my father so often said, the family mantra drilled into me from birth. *Getting away with it* had been something of his specialty. In his lifetime, he reportedly amassed more than a hundred million dollars' worth of diamonds, gold, jewels, and plain old cash.

So, yeah. I'm kind of an heiress. Or rather, I *would* be, if anyone had any idea where that treasure is. Unfortunately, there's been no sign of it since he went missing. My dad was always careful about keeping his money where no thief could find it—which, as it turns out, includes me.

"I appreciate all your hard work on this so far, I really do, but we have to tread lightly moving forward." Even though I'm pretty sure I've already won the argument, I feel compelled to add, "If we wanted to get in the smash-and-grab circuit, we could have done it years ago and saved ourselves a heck of a lot of trouble."

Riker casts a pointed look around the living room I share with Grant—at the woven blanket tossed over the couch and the bookshelves overflowing with antique knickknacks, at the smiling photo of the two of us in scuba gear from our trip to Costa Rica last winter. "I don't know. Maybe we underestimated the benefits of the smash-and-grab circuit. There's something to be said for being able to make a quick getaway."

I shake my head, as much to avoid making eye contact with him as to disagree. There are a lot of things wrong with this situation—the genuine happiness reflected in my eyes in that Costa Rican picture among them—but it's not like there's anything we can do about it now. My bed has been made, rumpled, and heartily used.

"We have to watch our steps from here on out." I drop the facade with a sigh. "I know it's hard for the two of you to believe, but this isn't me acting rashly. This is me trying to do the careful thing for once."

Riker's facade also slips away, leaving the pair of us vulnerable and exposed. It's been a long time since we were together in a sexual way—seven years, in fact—but that doesn't make this any easier.

"You said this wasn't a long-term plan, Pen. You said it wasn't forever."

"It's not forever," I say, my tone gentling. "Everything is still set to go. We'll take the necklace, get it to Blackrock, and split the proceeds. I just need a little more time to figure out what kind of game Grant is playing first, that's all. I don't like the way the pieces are set."

I can tell Riker wants to say more—complain about the delays and extra costs, about how unprofessional it makes him appear to ask for more time—but he refrains, his mouth set in a firm line. Gratitude and guilt surge through me, and it's hard to tell which emotion is stronger.

See, Riker's not a bad person, no matter how much he pretends to be. In fact, if I had to pick which one of us was more selfish, more stubborn, more demanding, I'd pull ahead as the clear winner. Sure, he has a bit of a gambling addiction that requires a regular cash influx, but *I'm* the one who keeps pushing us to steal more and steal larger. *I'm* the one who digs in her heels and refuses to listen to others. *I'm* the one who married a man she didn't love in hopes of finding answers.

"This stupid necklace is one of the only things I have left of my dad." My voice cracks. "I know it's silly to put so much stock in finishing a job he started half a lifetime ago, but I need to find out what it is about this necklace that made him risk everything for it. I need to feel like there's a reason he left me all alone."

There it is. The sad truth. I'm just another desperate, lonely little girl struggling with her daddy issues. The only thing that makes me remotely unique is that my father's long-lost legacy—all estimated one hundred million dollars of it—means other parties are just as interested in discovering the truth about his disappearance.

The FBI, for example. Just look at the lengths they've gone to. I'm pretty sure Grant's part in our marriage is what's known as *deep undercover*.

"Time, guys. That's all I'm asking for."

"Then we leave the necklace there for now," Jordan says firmly. She wants to hug me, I can tell, but she knows how bad I am at handling physical affection when I'm teetering on the edge like this. "This is Pen's life and Pen's house. She decides when we make the next move."

I flash her a thankful, albeit watery, smile. "It's not just my emotions doing the thinking here, I swear. It's all too convenient. I can't help thinking this is an elaborate plot Grant is setting up to test me."

Jordan nods in agreement, but Riker stays uncharacteristically quiet, his thoughts turned inward for once. I open my mouth to ask what's wrong, but the sound of a key in the front door signals Grant's return and stops me short.

We share a quick glance of understanding before

turning off all thoughts of thievery. To look at us, you'd think we were nothing more than lifelong besties enjoying a chat and some midafternoon lemonade. Seriously. We've done this for so long—pretending to be upstanding citizens—it's almost like a curtain rising. We're the actors, and we're all on cue.

Grant pushes open the door, unsurprised to find the three of us sitting there determinedly *not* staring at the canvas block of red and orange on the wall. His arms are full of leafy greens since he plans on cooking our anniversary dinner tonight, which is sweet of him and only fifty percent likely to contain poison.

"I thought I heard voices in here," he says as soon as he spots Jordan and Riker. "You guys didn't have to stop by. Oh, and you brought flowers. How nice."

If you're wondering what role Grant plays in this little stage drama of ours, it's not that of an innocent audience member. Oh no. He's the star of this particular show. There's not a glimmer of suspicion in his dark-brown eyes, no sign of disingenuousness in the pearly white of his smile. You'd think nothing would make him happier than to share his anniversary weekend with his wife's felonious friends.

"Hey, Grant. We meant to be long gone before you got back." Jordan rises to her feet in an elegant sweeping motion and heads toward the door, eager to get out of the crossfire. Of all of us, she's the most uncomfortable with the deception we've put Grant through. She doesn't mind blowing up the occasional parked car, but she hates hurting other people's feelings. "Four's a definite crowd on a day like this."

"Don't be silly—you two should stay." Grant leans

forward to drop a kiss on my neck, his lips hitting the exact spot where my pulse pounds. I know for sure now what part of a woman's neck he favors, and I shiver despite the fact that it's seventy degrees in here. "I have more than enough food for everyone. We can make it an anniversary party." He moves to put the groceries away.

Riker doesn't bother hiding his scowl. He's never been a big fan of public displays of affection—not even when he was the one doing the neck-kissing—and he takes it as a personal affront that Grant doesn't share his qualms. "I think I can tell when I've overstayed my welcome. We'll get out of your way."

Grant pauses. His wide, unblinking stare settles on Riker. "Uh-oh."

Riker steps back, his hands up. "No. Just…no."

"It sounds to me like someone is having a bad day."

"I'm fine, Grant. Really. It's nothing."

Grant isn't dismayed by Riker's tone or the way he looks right now, like Satan finding out his entire flock has been forgiven and let in upstairs. You could say he's come to expect this reaction—Riker's scowl and the antipathy it carries is male aggression in its purest form. Grant's also found a surefire way to combat it.

He lifts his arms toward Riker in a now-familiar gesture of gently mocking compassion. "Do you need to cry a little?"

"What I need is to go home. I have really important things to do today."

"Are you sure we shouldn't do a heart hug first?"

"We should never do any kind of hug. Ever."

His arms still up, Grant makes his move. "Bring it in, buddy. Bring it in."

Jordan and I share a grin as Grant makes good on his threat, wrapping his enormous bear arms around Riker's more compact form and holding him there. Forcibly.

"Shh," Grant says soothingly, his voice low—the better to get under Riker's skin, I'm sure. "See how your pulse is lowering already? We'll just stay here, locked and loaded, for as long as you need it."

"This isn't funny."

"It's not supposed to be funny. You should be more in touch with your emotions. It's not healthy to keep it all in." His voice is perfectly dry.

"Let me go, Emerson."

"Nope. Not until your heart starts to feel it."

"I mean it. Let go." But there's nothing Riker can do except *feel* it, an agony he tries to impart to me over Grant's wide shoulders. Not even I can help him at this point. Riker isn't strong enough to physically break Grant's hold, and any low-handed tactics like kneeing him in the groin would be immediately counteracted by Grant's years of field training.

I'm sure *heart hugs* weren't part of that training, but there's no doubt it's one of the most effective tools that man has in his arsenal. Grant could easily take Riker to the ground with one punch. He could tell him off and ask him never to come back. He could pull his gun and haul him off to his FBI buddies on any flimsy pretext he wanted.

But he doesn't. Instead…this. It throws Riker off like you wouldn't believe—causes him to fluster and bluster and make mistakes, which, let's face it, is probably Grant's objective. He's trying to dismantle us both with a pair of strong arms and strategically timed declarations of affection.

I let him try, my body relaxing in his presence in ways Riker's never will. Going with the flow has never been one of Riker's skills, but I've learned to enjoy the turbulence of this particular ride. We lost out on the necklace score, yes, but that doesn't mean the game is over. Until we have a chance to figure out what comes next, all we can do is keep playing along.

"My heart is good now," Riker says stiffly. "It's all puppies and rainbows over here. I promise."

Grant claps him on the back and releases him. "Want to talk about it?"

"No. I don't want to talk about it."

"I'm sure Penelope won't mind. You're part of our family—and that's what today's all about, right? Family? We'll eat. Play charades. Toast each other's good health."

I can see Riker wavering, the two sides of his mouth working up and down. Even though Riker hates Grant—can barely contain his irritation at the sports talk they always end up sharing over cheap beer and cheesy snack foods—he hates the idea of leaving me here to deal with things even more.

I think that's been the hardest part of all this for him: letting me have control and trusting me to handle my husband in my own way. It was just the two of us for so long, and always with him in the lead, so he has no framework for not having someone to boss around. He's always decided what we steal and why. He's arranged the back-alley deals without giving me any kind of say. To call him a dictator might be pushing things a bit, but there are definite autocratic undertones to his personality.

"It'll be fun," Grant adds. "I'm making scallops."

Riker starts. "I'm deathly allergic to shellfish."

He's not kidding. He can't even be in the same room as a lobster without breaking out in hives. He hates the ocean for fear its mollusk bounty will taint the air he breathes, but Grant doesn't know that.

At least, I don't *think* he does.

"My mistake." Grant turns his easy smile Jordan's way. "What about you?"

"Not allergic, but definitely not staying. You two kids have fun. I'm sure you have lots of excitement planned without us."

My gaze—a traitorous, wanton thing I can't seem to control—turns Grant's way, and a flare of longing coils up from my belly as his smile shifts from friendly to intense. I don't know *what* he has planned, but I'm not so sure I can handle another night like the last one.

"I guess it'll just be the two of us." His voice is rumbly with meaning, and it's all I can do to nod in reply. Two is a very cozy number.

Riker starts making furtive movements toward the front door, and I know he wants me to accompany him so he can give me some last-minute instructions regarding the necklace. But I'm not going to steal it right now, no matter what he demands, so I pointedly ignore the hints.

"Pen, I wonder if you could help me—" he begins, but the sound of Grant's phone ringing fills the room. It's a ringtone I know well—that call to action in the middle of his weekend off, the sound of interrupted dinners and date nights cut short.

Grant's face flashes with what appears to be genuine disappointment before he lifts the phone in apology. "I need to take this."

"Oh, I know the drill," I say airily, waving him off as he heads toward the kitchen. Sometimes, I make an attempt to listen in when he gets calls—for intelligence-gathering purposes, of course—but this time, I let him go off without resorting to my usual skulking. "Sorry, guys," I say. "The duties of an illustrious crime fighter never end."

"Do you think it's about the necklace?" Jordan asks as soon as Grant is out of earshot. "They could be making plans for transport."

"It doesn't matter. You heard the lady. She's canceling the job. Her husband wouldn't like it." The way Riker says *husband* practically drips with disdain.

"I'm not canceling anything. I'm adapting. It's different. I can't promise I'll find anything else out tonight, but I'll try my best."

"Maybe you should do that special thing with your tongue," Riker suggests. "That always did the trick for me."

"Out." There's no mistaking my command this time.

"I was just trying to help."

"No, Riker—you're trying to make me feel guilty. It's not necessary, okay? I promise I feel plenty of guilt about this already."

"There is one easy way to make it all disappear…" Riker begins, but I stop him with a stare. His way includes either a divorce or a body bag—both of which he contemplates with equal amounts of enthusiasm.

"That's not funny," I say, but he's partially right. Ignoring this problem won't make it go away. The sooner we figure out what Grant's up to, the sooner we can come up with a concrete plan to move that necklace. "Okay, fine. How's this for compromise? I'll keep an eye on him as much as I can at home, but I can't follow him everywhere without drawing suspicion. If you're careful, you guys should be able to tail him the rest of the time and gather information about what he's doing and why. Jordan, can you get Oz on it?"

Riker shakes his head before she can agree. "There's no need. I'll do it."

"But Oz can—"

"I said I'll do it, and I will." He clamps his jaw. "Believe me. Nothing will make me happier than finding dirt on that bastard."

It's not dirt I want so much as evidence, but Grant's already been gone longer than I expected, so there isn't time to discuss it further. With a sigh of begrudging assent, I close the door behind them, pushing my back to it with relief. I always dislike it when Riker and Grant are in the same room together. The undercurrent of tension that charges the air almost chokes me. I know Riker isn't interested in me like that—not in a romantic way, not in a *soft* way—but he has strong protective instincts. Add Grant's predatory nature into the mix, and you can see the problem. One of these days, those two are going to lock horns and kill each other.

Hopefully, giving Riker this task will keep him busy long enough to forestall the inevitable.

"Damn. They're gone." Grant enters the living room, a frown etched on his face as he surveys our surroundings. The room is quiet with the buzz of conversation suddenly halted, and there's not even the gardener outside the window to alleviate the burden of tranquility. "I was hoping they might still be here."

"Nope. It's just us."

"Just us…" He frowns again.

It's strange for Grant to be so unguarded—he usually takes painstaking care to wear his cheerful husband facade around me at all times—so I force a smile to make up for it. "They can't be far. I can always call them back."

"Only if you want the company. I'm so sorry, my love. I have to go in to work tonight."

Although I should be thankful to have this moment of reprieve handed to me, the first emotion to wash through me is one of unmitigated disappointment. Grant sees it and reaches for me, but he stops halfway, his arm dropping heavy at his side.

That arm falling feels like a guillotine. My heart lurches. "What happened? Is it something bad?"

"No. Yes. Maybe." His frown, mysterious and alarming, remains in place. "I can't tell yet. Can we try this again later tonight?"

"Of course. Go to work. Have a good time. I'll just order a pizza and suck all the helium out of these balloons. I should be entertained for hours." It's a lie, but one thing Grant has always been upfront with me about: when the work bell sounds, he'll drop everything to heed it. A Saturday afternoon call like this means he's probably going to be gone for the rest of the weekend, leaving me alone with that necklace and a growing sense of unease.

He manages a small smile, but it's obvious his thoughts are already far away. On duty, on obligation, on the career that will always be a barrier between us.

My unease only increases as he grabs his keys and heads out the door without anything more than a last look in my direction. It's not even a loving look—tinged with distraction, it's clear I'm the last thing on his mind right now.

Well, crap. This can't be good. My husband might be putting arsenic in my oatmeal and plotting my eventual downfall, but he always, *always* remembers to kiss me good-bye.

THE 5 GAME

(Eighteen Months, Thirty Days, and About Twenty-Two Hours Ago)

FINDING AGENT EMERSON TO WIN MY BET WAS A LOT EASIER than it should have been, when all was said and done.

I'd prepared myself to make a lengthy survey of the city streets, jogging past the catering company and the high-rise apartment we planned on hitting, stopping to ask various female passersby if they happened to notice a rugged god in a dark, well-cut suit walking among them.

As it was, I hadn't had to ask a single one. Turns out that freakishly large, athletic men standing around staring at their feet were kind of an eyesore in the constant movement and noise of the city. It only took me thirty minutes to find him, situated two blocks from the apartment building, his look of deep concentration fixed on a sewer grate.

Tearing his attention away from that sewer grate was another matter entirely. By the fourth time I jaunted past him, purposefully running on the balls of my feet to maximize gluteal vibrations, I realized I was up against a man not easily swayed by bouncy females.

Huh. It seemed I would have to play a more direct game with this guard dog of ours—and I couldn't help a smile from spreading at the thought. A direct game was going to make this so much more fun.

I stopped a few feet away from him and took my time stretching my inner thighs. It was a good pose, my roundest body parts projecting in all the right places, but not even the prospect of a carefully jutting hip elicited the desired response. In the end, I had to make my way in by clearing my throat and offering a not-so-clever, "It's a nice sidewalk, don't you think?"

As stupid as the words sounded once they left my mouth, they did the trick. Grant finally looked up at me, his expression one of complete surprise. For five suspended seconds, I thought I'd just made the biggest mistake of my career, not counting the time I'd sampled a nauseatingly floral perfume before crawling into a washing machine for three hours. That look on his face—a look I haven't seen to that degree since—told tales.

And they weren't the sort of tales a girl liked to hear on a tranquil fall afternoon like this one. Those unguarded eyes knew me by sight. That relaxed hinge of his jaw recognized me as the thief he'd been tracking for months. The perplexed pucker to his brow told me I was about to spend the rest of my life behind bars.

But all he said was, "I beg your pardon?"

His voice was softer than I expected: low but controlled, the sound of an authority figure who knows he doesn't have to shout to be heard. I've since realized that's the most dangerous kind of man to go up against in a fight. He didn't bluster and yell the way Riker did, and he didn't speak in terse rebukes, the way I remember my dad doing when I made an error in the middle of a job. Grant was all control and manners.

I hadn't expected manners.

"I've never seen a man so intrigued by concrete before," I said, less polite but still within the bounds of friendliness. "I've run past you a total of four times now, and you never once glanced up to check me out."

The surprise faded to amusement. "Is that a fact?"

"Yes. And I thought for sure three times would do it."

Since it appeared he wasn't about to book me for fifty counts of conspiracy, I took a moment to appreciate him up close. From a distance, packed into a dark suit, always on the scent of something we didn't want him to be, he really was more like a ferocious guard dog than anything else. But up close? *Unf.* There was nothing canine about him, and fear wasn't my primary reaction. He was a behemoth, taller than me by at least a foot, his build not powerful so much as overpowering. He wasn't handsome—at least, not in a clean-cut, underwear ad sort of way—but he was incredibly attractive. It's possible for a man to be a perfectly assembled collection of model parts and invoke nothing more than a mild appreciation, like looking at a sculpture or a really nice diamond tiara. It's equally possible for a man to boast coarse features, oversized limbs, and a rugged smile—and make a girl want to take off her clothes on the spot.

Happily, I refrained.

"How do you know I didn't watch your ass as you

ran past?" he asked, picking up my flirtation with ease. I should have been disappointed that he was sharp enough to follow along—a slow, stupid nemesis is always preferable to a fast-witted one—but all I felt was a warm feeling of pleasure. "Maybe I was being discreet."

"You didn't," I said smugly and switched to stretching the other leg. "If you had, you would've stopped me ten minutes ago and asked for my number."

"Maybe I'm in a relationship."

"You're not. Otherwise, you wouldn't be watching my ass now."

He laughed but didn't relax. I only noted this because men have a universal way of dropping their shoulders and opening their stance once they realize they're being hit on. Women probably do it, too—you can almost see the walls coming down around their hearts—but Grant's wide shoulders remained firmly in place.

I stuck out my hand, hoping physical contact would do the trick.

"I'm Penelope," I said, not bothering with an alias. That was one lie I'd never had any use for. I was born a thief, raised a thief, and would probably die one. A fake name wouldn't benefit me any more than changing spots would a leopard. "Penelope Blue."

That look of surprise moved across Grant's face again, but he managed to quell it long enough to take my hand and shake.

It would have been pushing things to say there was a tingle of electricity, or that my life flashed before my eyes as the rough texture of his palm grazed mine, but there was no mistaking how strong his grip was. With just the flick of his wrist, he could have broken the bones in my hand, conquered me right then and there. Instead of being alarmed by his physical mastery, I felt no sense of danger. Only wonder.

This man could crush me, I thought. *But he won't.*

"Grant," he said. "Grant Emerson."

If I'd been operating at the top of my game, my attention not so fixated on what other feats those hands might be capable of, I'd have said something outrageous and provocative to keep the flirtation going. As it was, I found myself staring down at the same sewer grate that had held his attention for so long.

"Did you drop something down there?" I asked.

"I beg your pardon?" he asked again. This time, I noticed there was almost a twang in his voice, a touch of the Southern gentleman coming out to play. I'd later learn that's exactly what it *was*—his West Virginia upbringing not yet quashed by the big city. For the moment, all I felt was charmed.

"The sewer. You seemed transfixed. Did you lose your keys down there or something? Maybe I can help—I have weirdly skinny fingers."

That was when his shoulders came down. I don't know what I said or did to bring on the sudden transformation, but one second, he was all FBI business in his well-cut suit and linebacker stance; the next, he was a friendly, interested male I knew I'd won over.

Hopefully, it wasn't the skinny fingers that did it. That was one fetish I wasn't so keen to explore.

"Actually, you *can* help me." He took a step back and ran an appraising gaze over my body, bringing a flush to the surface of my already heated skin. "You're a small person."

"Gee, thanks. The words every girl longs to hear."

He laughed again. I liked the sound of it, deep and rich and with an almost forceful undertone, as if it made its way out of his throat whether he wanted it to or not. "My apologies. You're small and well-formed. Is that better?"

I held up my fingers in the approximation of an inch. "*Well-formed* is something people use to describe a horse."

"Your ass is top-notch?"

"Wait a minute…"

"I can say that with absolute sincerity, since I made an intense study of it every time you passed by. I thought at first you might be lost."

Aha! So he *had* been watching. "How modest of you. Most men would assume I was trying to get their attention."

"The thought did cross my mind. I also suspected you of casing the bank across the street."

I won't lower myself to describe how erratically my pulse leapt at that confession, but there was a definite off-the-charts moment happening inside my rib cage. There was no reason for it, since I was completely inno-cent for once. I hadn't even *noticed* there was a bank across the street—and that kind of institution isn't our style, anyway. Banks and vaults are way above our pay grade. Access to them is a lot more complicated than putting on a disguise and rolling up an elevator in a beer keg. Fancier, if you will. Much more my father's style.

"I've always thought jogging would make an excel-lent excuse for that," he added by way of explanation. "Everyone notices a beautiful woman running by, but her motives are never suspect. Not even when she goes by several times."

It was too good an opportunity to pass up. "Does that

mean you're suspecting my motives? How astute. I'm actually here to rob *you*, not the bank. Stick 'em up."

His smile started at his eyes, a crinkle of skin and a flash of humor that worked its way down to his lips. Oh, but that was a good smile, all the more so because he seemed to mean it. When Riker smiled, there were always strings attached—usually ones that pulled me places I didn't want to go.

"Unless you're hiding a gun inside your bra, I'd like to know how you plan on following through on that threat. Your small, well-formed body doesn't stand a chance against me."

My small, well-formed body was well aware of that fact. It was also tingling most unbecomingly at the prospect of a tussle with a man of his impressive…stature.

"Maybe I have an accomplice with a gun pointed at your head right now," I said. "He's a sniper, and he's very good."

"Nice try. In order to hit me at this angle, he'd have to be on the eighth floor in the bank building—which, you'll note, is impossible, since it's only seven stories high—or hiding inside that office undergoing renovations. Which is possible but not likely, since they've got an asbestos removal team in there today."

My blank stare must have been obvious, because he chuckled and added, "Security at a national bank might be tough, but security when they're dealing with potential mesothelioma lawsuits? Forget about it. No one's getting in there without a hazmat suit and six levels of clearance. This is officially a snipe-free zone."

Damn. He was better at this than I thought. Our guard dog would have to be upgraded to a wolf, at the very least.

"You seem to know an awful lot about bullet trajectories," I noted.

"Occupational hazard. Are you flexible?"

My head whirled with his fast-paced conversation, his proximity, and the fact that those two things made it hard for me to remember what I'd come here to do.

Flirt. I was here to flirt and capture his interest, and I knew only one lie that would make that a certainty. "Why, yes. Yes, I am. I teach dance at a rec center a few blocks from here."

One of his eyebrows lifted in pure masculine interest. "Really?"

"Would you like me to hook my knee behind my head and prove it?"

"Very much, but that's beside the point." He nodded at the sewer grate. "As a small person with dance teacher levels of flexibility, what would you say is the likelihood you could slip inside and crawl two blocks north of here?"

I caught his meaning instantly. Sewer lines were second only to air ducts for sneaking inside buildings undetected. If I wanted to get into that apartment building without drawing unwarranted attention, that'd be one way to do it.

Which, by the way? Gross. I'll squeeze into a lot of unpleasant places in the line of duty, but I draw the line at anything containing human waste.

"The likelihood that I *could* do it? High. The likelihood that I *would* do it?" I gave a ladylike shudder. "There'd have to be a pretty big incentive waiting for me at the end. What kind of incentive is there, Grant Emerson, man of strange sewer questions and scary amounts of knowledge about gunfire aerodynamics?"

"That depends on what motivates you, Penelope Blue."

It was the first time he used my full name in a mocking rhyme, as well as the first time I let him—with a smile and a pitter-patter of my heart. Ten minutes into the meeting, and he'd already been granted a right not even Riker could lay claim to.

I should have known then that I was up against a foe more dangerous than a dedicated FBI agent onto all our tricks. Oh yes. I was up against an attractive man with catastrophic levels of charm.

This was what wiser people might consider *the beginning of the end*.

"I suppose I might make the trek to save someone I love," I said, feigning thoughtfulness. "Though I'd have to love them an awful lot."

"An admirable response, but I was thinking more along the line of monetary gain."

"I just told you I teach dance to small children for a living. If monetary gain was one of my primary life goals, I think I could have come up with a much better use for my flexibility, don't you?"

"I wonder what kind of use that might be," he mused, head cocked.

"Oh, you know. Running away with the circus. Pole dancing," I said. That rakish tilt to his head proved too much for my always questionable self-restraint. "Maybe even breaking and entering."

Well, I'd done it now. Once the truth—that slippery, seductive beast—fell out into the open, there was no taking it back. It could only sit there, waiting for one of us to pick it up again.

"Go out with me," Grant said.

I blinked. "Um…what?"

"Go out with me." There was more command in his voice that time, and he punctuated his statement by grabbing my hand and running his thumb over the back, as though testing to make sure I was real. "Tonight. Meet me for drinks and dinner. There's this great Italian place about an hour upstate I'd love to take you to."

In a fit of alarm, I tried taking my hand back, but he held it firm—proof of his physical superiority. How easy it would have been for him to twist my arm behind my back and push me to the ground, to slap me in a pair of handcuffs and haul me away.

But he didn't, and for the first of many times to come, I wondered why. He *must* have had that bistro bugged earlier and overheard my entire boast to Riker that I could woo him away from the scene of the crime. There was no way he'd just make that offer on his own. He had nothing to gain from it.

Even though this outcome was exactly what I'd angled for, I released a nervous laugh. "I hardly think it's a good idea for me to leave the city with a man who knows as much about snipers as you do. Call it maidenly reserve."

He gave me his devastatingly powerful crinkly-eyed smile. He wasn't the least bit put off by being put off. "Somewhere closer, then? Do you know the Whiskey Room?"

Okay, now things were getting freaky. The Whiskey Room was well-known as a favorite FBI haunt, situated as it was across the street from the New York field office.

"I'm familiar with it, yes," I hedged.

"What if we met there instead?" He dropped my hand

and lifted his fingers in a Boy Scout salute. "There's nowhere safer to meet a perfect stranger, I swear. My coworkers and I meet there after work all the time. You'll be surrounded by badges."

"Badges?" Was he about to admit to being an FBI agent?

"Yeah. Want to see mine?" He didn't wait for a response as he fished into his interior jacket pocket and flashed me the shiny gold of his authority as an upholder of the law. "I probably should have mentioned it earlier. There's a reason I know so much about bullets and casing banks. I'm not as creepy as I seem."

I reached out to touch the badge, though I wasn't able to make full contact. Despite years of close calls with the law, I'd never been that close to a badge before. I was half-afraid it would burn my skin, like holy water scalding a vampire.

"Aren't you supposed to keep it a secret?" I dropped my fingers and shoved them uncomfortably behind my back. "So, like, bad guys can't sniff you out?"

"But then how would I impress attractive women on the street?"

"I guess it's no worse than accidentally flashing a wallet full of hundred-dollar bills," I allowed after only a brief moment of panic. "Or casually mentioning how hard it is for you to find condoms that fit without cutting off vital blood flow."

"No way. Men don't really say that kind of thing."

"Oh, aren't you so sweet and naive? Don't worry. I'm suitably impressed by your credentials."

"I also have a hard time finding condoms that fit without cutting off vital blood flow, if it helps," he added.

In that moment, with his adorable smile and crinkled

eyes pointed dead-on at me, I almost wished I *was* a
dance teacher who had nothing but free time to cavort
with dangerously attractive officers of the law. What
kind of a life would that be—so ordinary, so comfortable, so sane?

Not mine, that was for sure.

"Okay, FBI Agent Grant Emerson." I took a deep
breath. This was not a moment for vague dreams or fan-
ciful what-ifs. It was all or nothing. Go big or go home.
"You won me over with that last one. Let's go to your
upstate restaurant for dinner and/or murder."

"Really?" His smile went from adorable to lady-
slaying powerful. "I can pick you up around six or so?"

"I'm not *that* won over. A girl always needs an escape
route. How about you give me the address and I'll take a
Zipcar instead? Say, around seven?"

His eyes clouded over for the briefest moment, disappointment mingled with something darker, before
he pulled out a business card and scrawled an address
on the back. "You sure you aren't going to make me
drive all the way out there to sit alone at a table?" he
asked. Cannily, I thought. "A trick like that might end
up breaking my heart."

"I'll be there," I lied. It was a tough one to get out,
even for a woman like me, accustomed to half-truths and
misdeeds. "I'm not so easy to get rid of. I have this way
of worming into the least likely places."

At that, he took my hand and kissed it like a knight of
old. The action almost killed me on the spot, especially
when he didn't relinquish his hold right away. He peered
at me over the top of my fingers instead. "I have a feeling that's true, Penelope Blue."

Oh man. He was rhyming again.

"And I have no reason to get rid of you just yet," he added with a wink. "In fact, I have a feeling we're about to become *very* good friends."

THE 6 CALL

(Present Day)

DESPITE MY BEST EFFORTS, FIGURING OUT THE MOTIVES OF A highly suspicious FBI agent turns out to be no easy task.

On the first day of surveillance, all I get from Riker is a text informing me that he can see straight into our living room from the tree across the street, prompting me to install new blinds and consider chopping down the oak for firewood. The second day is equally unproductive since I don't hear from Riker at all. In a panic, I call Jordan, thinking he's been caught and is currently in FBI holding, but she assures me that all is well.

"He told us to sit tight. He thinks he might have a lead."

"What kind of lead?"

"He wouldn't say."

Which isn't surprising, considering how much Riker loves to be mysterious. It matches his dark hair and broody outlook. That man was a magician in a past life, I'm sure of it.

Unfortunately, day three isn't proving itself all that helpful, either. Riker refuses to pick up his phone, and Grant has been the soul of cheerful husbandly ardor, present in body but distant in mind.

"Hey, Pen?" Marta, the woman who runs the activities department at the dance studio where I work, pokes her head through the door. Since I have to stick to my regular routine as much as possible, I'm currently in the middle of one of my sessions teaching beginners' ballet to a bunch of four-year-olds in multicolored tutus. And by *beginners*, I mean the hyperactive kids who mostly need a place with four walls and a semiresponsible adult until their parents get out of work. No one else cares for this job, which is the primary reason I'm allowed to do it, but I also like the disorganized chaos. These little princess terrors are my kind of people.

I should probably mention that I don't get paid to work here. My position is and always has been done on a strictly volunteer basis—though I do use their printer to make fake pay stubs every month. I'm nothing if not thorough.

"What's up?" I ask. "If it's about my foot, I promise I'm not putting any more weight on it than necessary. There will be no lawsuits or workman's comp claims, on my honor."

Marta, a thin-lipped woman whose face always seems to be pulled back as tightly as her hair, doesn't smile. My charm has never had much effect on her. "Very funny. You have a phone call. It's your husband."

An adorable pixie of a girl wearing a neon-green tutu

swirls past me, and I find myself transfixed by the revolutions of that unearthly color over the faded wood floor.

"My husband?" I ask. "Are you sure?"

"Well, that's what he called himself. Do you want me to take a message?"

It's a simple question—and an even simpler situation—but I have no idea how to respond. I *never* get phone calls at work. In fact, I've made a point to reinforce that the rec center's budget is so low that they rarely pay the phone bill. The last thing I need is one of those relationships where Grant and I regularly check in with each other at work. *Sorry, dear. Can't talk now. Jordan's about to choke a security guard with a smoke bomb. Want me to grab some Thai for later?*

"Hello? Pen?"

"Sorry. Of course. I'll go talk to him." I blink myself into focus, suddenly struck with the thought that maybe I should grab some Thai for later. Grant's been working almost nonstop since our failed anniversary night, and in my panic about the necklace, I haven't had a chance to get him a gift. "Would you mind watching the kids for a few minutes?" I ask.

Marta waves me off, her face relaxing as she claps the girls into a semblance of order. Poor dears. Like most of the people in my life, they'd be better off having someone skilled and, you know, noncriminal to depend on. I slip out quietly so as not to disturb the lesson.

Even though the front desk isn't the most private place to have a conversation, no one seems to notice or care when I pick up the beige plastic receiver with a tentative, "Hello?"

"Oh, good. You're there."

In terms of romantic effusion, Grant's greeting could use a little work, but the subtext—that he wasn't sure I could be trusted to appear at work during my regular hours—gave my heart enough of a pitter-patter to make up for it. "Yes, I'm here. Is everything okay? Have you been shot or something?"

"Is that the only reason I can call you?"

"You have, haven't you? You took a bullet." I'm only half joking—I can't think of any other reason for this unprecedented phone call unless it's part of this sneaky test of his to see if I'll take the necklace. "How long do you have to live?"

He hesitates. "If I were to tell you I only have five minutes, what would you do?"

"Five minutes exactly, or five minutes ballpark figure?"

"It doesn't matter. I'm dying. What would you say to me if you knew it was the last thing I'd ever hear?"

Romance might not be my forte, but I know the answer to that question. It's *I love you*. No matter what's happening or whose life is on the line, a wife should always send her husband to the great beyond with at least that much.

But Grant isn't dying, and I'm not sure I care to deal with the repercussions of that claim. In all our time together, that's the one lie we've both managed to avoid. "Um…I promise to wear black every day for a year after you're gone?"

"You already wear black every day."

"I'll add a veil."

He sighs. "You would, too, just so you could say you held up your end of the bargain."

I open and close my mouth, unsure how to proceed. He actually sounds hurt that I didn't follow the script.

Fortunately—or not—there's no time to backtrack. "I know you're busy today, but do you know where my passport is?" he asks.

I do. It's right next to my passport, the pair of them entertaining one another inside the sanctity of our safe. They're probably discoing under the bright lights cast by the multimillion-dollar necklace.

"Um, yes? I think it's at home where it always is."

"Perfect. I know it's out of your way, but can you swing it by the Bureau this afternoon?"

I pull the receiver away from my ear and stare at it, tempted to give it a shake. Is he kidding? He wants me to open the safe I've been studiously avoiding since Saturday *and* journey to the wolf's lair?

"It's kind of urgent, so sooner is better," I hear him say from a distance.

I put the phone back to my ear with a start. "What? Why? Are you going somewhere?"

"No, no—nothing like that. It's just this new thing I'm trying out."

"What kind of thing?"

"A top secret thing." He pauses, and I can hear a clipped voice of authority in the distance. I strain to make out the words, listening for anything that might sound like *diamonds* or *necklace*, but the voices are too far away. As usual, he gives me just enough to raise suspicion—never enough to cast it aside. "Listen, I've got to run, but you'll come by later with that passport?"

"I just have to get all the way home and open the safe first…" I say, hoping he might give me more to go on.

He doesn't. "I knew you wouldn't let me down. Good ol' dependable Pen."

Good ol' dependable Pen, my ass. I'm the least trust-worthy human on the planet, and he knows it. Either he's trying to butter me up so he can slam me with some new curveball, or there are darker forces at work. Not for the first time, I wish I had the ability to cut through his smiles and compliments, chuck aside his flattery, to see the real man below. There are times, like when he was in that jewelry store with *my* necklace, that I'm sure he's my enemy.

There are also times, like this moment, when I suspect he might be more.

"Grant, before you go—"

"Yeah? Have you decided what your last words will be before I succumb to all this blood loss?"

My chest constricts at the image of Grant actually bleeding out, all that life and vitality trickling away. The stubborn man takes so many risks on the job and always with a kind of cheerful unconcern for his own well-being. It's not that much of a stretch to picture it.

"It's just…" My voice wavers enough that I have to take a deep breath before continuing. "Would it be okay if I stop by a little later with the passport, maybe closer to six? I was thinking I might bring takeout with me, if you think you could spare half an hour."

Whether it's the cheap handset or the profound silence of his hesitance, I hear nothing but buzzing for a full ten seconds.

"You want to have dinner with me tonight?" he eventually says.

He's so surprised by the offer that I feel like I've accidentally announced my darkest secrets. "Only if you're not too busy," I rush. "I was thinking Thai sounds good."

"Thai does sound good." His voice is warmer than before, and even though the noises in his office pick up, he doesn't hang up right away. "In fact, Thai sounds great."

THE NE7CKLACE

(The Next Day)

"IS IT POSSIBLE TO INVENT A MURDER NECKLACE?"

Jordan looks up from the table where she's working, goggles over her eyes and some sort of makeshift chemist's lab set up in front of her. There's a burner and a milky-white liquid bubbling in a flask, which I figure has equal chances of being an explosive or a recipe for a chai latte.

"Are you asking about my capabilities or soliciting my professional opinion?" she asks.

With a kick of my foot, I manage to slam her apartment door shut behind me. I've got *actual* chai lattes balanced in my hands, which makes navigating the security locks a bit tricky. I'm only supposed to use her spare key in emergencies, but this is. An emergency, I mean. I'm pretty sure I'm dying.

"Professional opinion." I set the cups down, as far

away from her experiment as possible, and shrug off my messenger bag. "If you wanted to kill someone, could you put poison in the metal or invent some kind of incredible shrinking gold that slowly tightened in a choke hold?"

She flips the switch on her burner, the flame dying from a healthy blue to an orange whimper. "Is this about the diamond necklace?"

I wish. The diamond necklace might be causing me sleepless nights and panic-inducing anxiety, but it's the one currently around my neck I'm really worried about. Yesterday, it was passports and Thai food. Today, *this*. I don't know how much more I can take.

"I can't get it off." I twist my head to reveal the slinky gilded chain pressed against my throat. It's probably too soon for the poison to be taking effect, but I swear I can feel my skin burning away in a neat circle. "He welded the clasp shut or something. I'm trapped, and only the jaws of death will save me."

The goggles come down, which is good, because they were making Jordan's eyes freakishly large. "Holy smokes, Pen. That's some necklace."

"Don't start."

"No—I'm serious." She draws closer for a better look. This time, she smells like chloroform and candy instead of sulfur and candy. It's still oddly appealing. "I think I might like it better than the one we were trying to steal. It's beautiful."

"I *know* it's beautiful." I give it a tug, but the thing is made of kryptonite or something. "No one is questioning its beauty. What I'm questioning is its lethality."

"Hold still a minute." Her fingers are warm as she

pushes my hair aside to work the clasp, a task that takes her all of five seconds before the chain slips from around my neck and pools into her waiting palm. "You're so dramatic sometimes. It's got a security clasp, that's all. So it won't fall off or get stolen by a light-fingered thief."

"Oh."

She doesn't say anything more, just examines the newest piece of jewelry that's been introduced to throw my life into disorder. This one isn't nearly as big or expensive, but Jordan is right about how stunning it is. It's a delicate gold chain, twisted in the center to show-case a perfect infinity knot. Exactly my style and an ideal complement to my simple wardrobe. "I guess Mr. Romance wasn't done with the anniversary celebrations yet, huh?"

I glance sharply up. "Don't call him that."

Jordan blinks at me in surprise.

"I'm sorry. It's just…" I trail off, shifting on the balls of my feet, and reach for one of the cups of tea. I'm not really thirsty, but if I don't bring some kind of snack or beverage to Jordan's house, she always feels a motherly urge to feed me. Instead of drinking, I toy with the lid. "I don't like it when you guys call him Mr. Romance, that's all. It's not like that between us."

"Okay."

"Okay?"

"Okay." She nods. I'm so used to fighting Riker over every little thing that it feels almost wrong to have someone respect my boundaries without question. "It is from Grant, though, right?"

"Oh, it's from Grant. He took me back to Paulson's today."

Jordan laughs, the sound of it so genuine and warm that I feel better in an instant. It's exactly what I need to sort my feelings, to know that I'm not going crazy all alone. "Did you hear that, Oz? Pen paid a visit to our favorite jeweler today."

Oz pokes up from the couch in the living room like a meerkat.

Although I once again manage to subdue the worst of my alarm, I stagger back a step at the sight of his tousled head appearing as if from nowhere. I swear, if that man were an assassin, I'd be dead ten times over by now.

"Jesus, Oz. Have you been here this whole time?" I ask.

He shrugs and makes a vague gesture toward the door. "Girl talk?"

I pick up on his meaning right away. It's nice of him to offer to leave so I can have a chance to chat with Jordan alone, but there's not much of a point. As much as I wish I could keep things close to the heart the way he does, I've always been the hang-your-dirty-laundry-out-for-all-the-world-to-judge type. Ladylike mystery is for much classier women than I.

"He's keeping me company while I try out this new compound," Jordan says. "It was supposed to be a liquid explosive that neutralizes itself after a few minutes, but I got some of the components wrong. Here. Smell it."

"Will it kill me?"

"Probably not. Oz and I are still here."

I give her concoction a sniff—and then immediately regret it. It smells kind of like that bleach and ammonia mixture Riker mocked me for. I press my sleeve to my nose. "God, that's awful. What's in it?"

"Do you really want me to list the chemicals?"

Not really. I only got as far as the ninth grade in school, way too early for chemistry classes. Jordan might be a scientific genius who trained herself—and has the burns on her arms to prove it—but I never really bothered furthering my own education. Not the formal kind, anyway.

"As long as you know what you're doing," I say.

"Let's hope so." She lifts the flask to her lips and takes a deep drink. I'm ready to make a dive to save her from her own folly, but Oz just chuckles from across the living room. If he's not worried, then I probably shouldn't be. That man would cut off his own limbs to save her from getting a paper cut. She swirls the flask and sips again. "Huh. It's kind of fruity. I didn't expect that."

"Are you going to turn into the Hulk now?"

"Nah. It neutralized itself exactly the way I wanted it to. It's just the explosion part that's missing."

"I'm still not drinking any," I warn.

"Fair enough." She flaps some kind of hand message to Oz, and even though I honestly don't mind if he sticks around—who's he going to blab all my secrets to?—he takes himself off to the bedroom. The door clicks quietly shut behind him.

"What's he going to do in there?" I wonder aloud. Oz doesn't strike me as a snooper, but it's not like Jordan has board games or even a TV. Sitting around staring at the walls has to get boring after a while, even for him.

"Escape out the window and come back later, probably." Jordan sets her flask aside and settles her full attention on me instead. "Grant really took you to Paulson's? With the diamonds still in the safe at home? That man must have nerves of steel."

He has *something* made of steel, but I'm much more inclined to believe he keeps them in his pants. "It was awful. I thought for sure I was done for. He left work early to pick me up and everything. He said he wanted to get me something special."

"That's sweet."

No. It wasn't sweet at all. It was some kind of ploy to get me to break down. He'd used the exact same words from the failed heist, startling me right out of my skin. *I want to get you something special*, he'd said and pulled me into his arms. *You deserve it.*

There was nothing I could do to stop him. He'd been so eager, whisking me away to the jewelry store, forcing me to stand there while he tried different necklaces on me, his hands touching, roaming, caressing... It's getting to the point where I can't even *think* about a necklace without my thighs turning liquid. Things could get embarrassing if we ever go to one of those fancy dress FBI balls.

"Has Riker reported in to you yet?" I ask, mostly to distract myself. "I spied him yesterday outside the field office, but I didn't see him while we were at the jewelry store today."

She shakes her head, her lips compressed in a tight line. "I haven't heard anything, but he's been purposefully vague ever since he started tailing Grant, so it doesn't mean much. It's weird. I think maybe..."

I wait patiently for her to finish her thought, but she remains silent. Probably because what she thinks isn't something I want to hear. It's hard for her to say hurtful things, even when they're not her fault.

"You think he's planning a secret backdoor heist to

take the necklace from that safe, don't you?" I ask, only half kidding.

She's not amused. "Riker would never do that to you, Pen."

No, I guess he wouldn't. But that necklace being so close at hand—*all* these necklaces being so close at hand—is making me crazy. It wouldn't be so bad if I could just get my hands on evidence of what Grant's planning. As it is, all I have are theories and conjectures and a whole lot of nothing. "Then what is it? What has Riker discovered that's so important he can't take five minutes to check in?"

"I don't..." She draws a deep breath. "I don't know the details, but be prepared for anything, okay? He said something the last time we talked, something about Grant's deception going much deeper than we all suspected. I'm afraid things might get worse before they get better."

Personally, I don't see how that's possible. Things feel pretty awful already.

"Well, I guess you better clasp the stupid thing back on me, then." I gesture at the necklace. "Until Riker can be bothered to resurface, all we can do is keep playing along."

"What about the poisonous metal?"

"I almost hope it does kill me. At least then I could relax again. I swear, Jordan, it's like Grant *wants* me to steal the diamond necklace—almost as much as Riker does. Why else would he keep drawing my attention to it?"

She doesn't have an answer, so she holds the chain up. I dip my head to accept it, the noose slipping back on—except it doesn't feel like a noose, and the ring of burned skin now tingles with a different kind of warmth.

Infinity. Forever. Me and you, Penelope Blue. Grant wasn't much for flowery words, but I'd remember those for a long time.

"Leaving the necklace unattended in your safe could be his way of letting you know how much he trusts you," Jordan says gently. "A man who showers you with jewels and affection isn't the worst thing in the world, you know. Maybe you should just accept defeat and take the life he's offering you."

"And what about the rest? What about my dad's fortune? What about you and Oz and Riker? I can't leave you guys behind."

She laughs. "It just so happens we know where to find a highly unguarded two-million-dollar necklace. If you do end up abandoning us, I think we'll be fine."

THE 8 SAFE

WHEN I WOKE UP THIS MORNING, THERE WAS A NOTE ON the fridge from Grant telling me he got called out of town for the next few days.

I guess I needed my passport after all, he wrote. *Take care of the safe's contents for me while I'm gone, would you?*

I'm pretty sure he's just screwing with me now.

THE LIBRARY

(Eighteen Months and Twenty-Four Days Ago)

"YOU STOOD ME UP."

The scream that left my throat at the sound of those words is impossible for me to look back on without shame. In my line of work, the most important quality a girl can possess is a cool head in moments of surprise. Even if a flock of birds flies straight at your face while you hang precariously by your toes over a pot of boiling tar, you don't show even a mild spasm of alarm.

But I showed a major spasm of alarm. I screamed and then felt a warm, glowing joy that I'm also rather ashamed to admit to now.

"Grant!" I shoved the book I'd been holding deep in my bag. It wasn't really a hardback copy of *In Cold Blood* I was reading—it wasn't a hardback copy of anything. A clever invention of Oz's design, the book had been hollowed out to allow me to smuggle snacks into the library.

It wasn't as strange as it sounds. Libraries are crazy strict when it comes to crumbs getting inside their rare books room, so much so that they actually check your bag before you head in. It's the height of irony that I could have easily squeezed myself in through the vent and stolen every last book in the room, but woe to the woman who tried to eat a Twix anywhere near a first edition Dickens.

"How did—? What are—?" I looked around for a quick escape route, but unless I was willing to squeeze through the aforementioned vent, I was out of luck. "Um. Wow. Hi."

Grant wasn't dressed for work this time, the dark suit having been replaced by worn jeans and a tight long-sleeved T-shirt that did amazing things for his pectoral muscles. He was also growing some weekend stubble, indulging in a scrape of golden hair along his chiseled jaw.

More than anything else in that moment, I wanted to rub myself on that stubble like a cat. I wanted to feel it abrade my skin until I was raw and clean and new again.

Happily, I refrained from that, too—but it was a close call. I would have to seriously watch myself around this man.

To make matters worse—or better, depending on your perspective—his face contained nothing but a smile, his eyes twinkling as they appraised me in my moment of nonglory. I'd had nonglorious moments before, of course—slews of them—but my audience usually consisted of my friends.

"Hold still," Grant ordered.

For the briefest of moments, I considered putting my

arms up in surrender, so powerful was his aura of command. But then his hand came at me, and all I could do was remain affixed to the chair. My whole body froze in place as I croaked, "Whaaa—?"

"You've got something right here."

I remained still as his palm cupped my chin. He brought a thumb to my lips to wipe away what I could only assume was a smear of cookie and chocolate.

I won't tell you how close I was to sucking his thumb into my mouth in a move wholly inappropriate to the time, place, and man. All I will say is that it was a good thing I couldn't move.

"Eating in the library?" He made a deep tsking sound. "Shame on you, Penelope Blue. You're lucky I don't turn you in to the authorities."

I relaxed ever so slightly. He wasn't arresting me. He was *flirting* with me.

"You can't prove a thing," I said quickly. "I swallowed the evidence."

His eyes deepened in color until they were almost black. "Now that's something I like to hear."

There was nothing to do after that but accept that I was trapped. I had no idea how he'd tracked me down here—my monthly sojourn to the New York Public Library wasn't widely publicized—but I suppose it could have been worse. If he'd caught me last week with Riker, for example, where a certain Jaeger-LeCoultre watch had changed hands, things might have been really uncomfortable.

"You stood me up," he said again, and this time, I didn't scream. I only gulped and tried to collect the wits that had scattered to the four corners of the room. "I sat at that restaurant for an hour, taking up the best table in the place while dozens of hungry patrons glared at me from the lobby."

"I got lost," I lied, thinking fast.

"You could have called. I would have given you directions."

"My cell phone didn't get service out there."

"I know for a fact there are two gas stations on the main stretch of highway that still have pay phones."

"I have an unnatural fear of using pay phones. I read a study once about how many germs collect on the handsets. They should really take those out in the name of public health safety."

The twinkle in his eyes dimmed just enough to make me feel like a jerk. I'd never stood up a man for a date before, and the vision of him sitting there alone, with pain in his puppy dog eyes, made my stomach churn. It was as unfamiliar as it was unpleasant.

Guilt. That's what it was. I was feeling guilt.

"I was really hoping you'd be there," he said.

"If it was at all possible, I would have been." I meant it as lip service, a lie to cover my tracks, but as I spoke, I realized I meant every word. It wasn't because Oz had almost rolled the keg I'd been hiding in down five flights of stairs, or that I'd only just gotten the lingering smell of beer out of my hair that morning. A meal with this man would have been…educational, to say the least. "I'm sorry, Grant. I wanted to be there more than you know."

He studied me for a long, careful minute, as if weighing the sincerity of my apology. It would have been an ideal time for me to come up with an *actual* story in my defense—something about getting hit with a twenty-four-hour bug or a grandmother languishing in the hospital—but that seemed worse. I hadn't met him for dinner because I'd sent him on a fool's errand so I could rob an unsuspecting—if slightly crooked—man of his favorite wristwatch.

The truth was bad enough. I wouldn't compound my sins by adding even more lies.

"Okay." He pulled out the chair opposite mine and lowered himself into it. There was something strangely erotic about the action, this lowering of his massive body to a chair of normal human proportions. He moved so carefully, containing his strength for my benefit. "Let's try this again, then, shall we? What brings you and your snack foods to this dark hole in the library? Are you doing research?"

"I think the better question is, what brings *you* to this dark hole in the library?" I countered. "Were you following me? Cashing in on your fancy FBI connections to hunt me down?"

Even more of the light went out of his eyes, and I cursed my clumsiness. This was a case where I needed to tread lightly and parry swiftly. Flirtation was all well and good, but there was more at play here than a man suffering from a bruised ego. He'd known something was going down at that party last week. Something *had* gone down at that party last week, and I may or may not have been his primary suspect for that something.

Direct confrontation would only bring the questions and answers to a head—which was the last thing I wanted.

String him along. See what I could discover. *Play.* That's what I needed to do here.

"I've always wondered about that, actually." I gave my hair a toss and leaned over the table, showcasing pure, feminine interest—as well as a healthy glimpse of cleavage. I had wiles. I could backtrack. "About whether you guys use your fancy FBI connections to woo the ladies."

A smile played on his lips, there and gone again. "What do you mean by that?"

"Oh, just that you could be pretty dangerous if you put your mind to it. You could look into my records, find all my weaknesses, handcuff me somewhere dark and secluded. You know—if you wanted to."

"You think I want to handcuff you somewhere dark and secluded?"

I didn't have to feign the sexual interest that rumbled low in my throat and in my belly. "Don't you?"

He didn't answer. "You come to this library every month and have for at least the past two years," he said, his voice disappointingly businesslike. "You sign in at the front desk and usually stay for about three hours. The librarians know you bring in food, but they like you, so they pretend to look the other way. You should be more respectful of their restrictions, though. Rules exist for a reason."

Holy crap. He *was* following me, and for a lot longer than I'd realized.

He was also blocking the door. Even though it didn't look like he was carrying a gun, he could easily overpower me with the bulge of just one of those muscles he was packing.

A familiar panic surged through me. I was trapped—in more ways than one.

"You have a bad poker face, you know that?" Grant said. He leaned over the table and touched my lips, this time with the press of three fingers. I shivered. "You look like I just accused you of murder. Relax—I'm not following you. I saw you come in and asked at the front desk which direction you'd gone. The woman was very helpful."

Oh, I bet she was. "Did you flash her your badge or your smile?"

He pretended to be offended.

"The badge?" I echoed. "Or the smile?"

He showed me the full force of the latter: the crooked pull of lips over teeth, the crinkles of his eyes blending into his hairline. "Which one do you think?"

Dammit. I couldn't even be mad after that. I'd have given *myself* up for that smile.

"Well? I'll admit to being curious. What's in here?" He looked around to see what might entertain me in a twenty-by-twenty room that smelled like old leather and dust despite the high-tech air filtration system that kept all the paper at peak temperature and humidity. Books with various faded colors lined the walls; several older tomes were kept behind glass for greater protection. There was even an intern at the door, posted to make sure no one came in without the proper authorization first.

"Books," I said.

"I see that. Is there a particular one that interests you?"

"Not in this room."

"No?"

"Too fancy for me. I like those mysteries with cats and bakeries in them—preferably the ones that come in paperback form. I don't approve of books you can't take into the bathtub with you."

He lifted a brow at that. "Not even the ones worth tens of thousands of dollars? Some of the books in here are incredibly valuable."

There was an insult in there, I was sure of it. I was tempted to defend myself against the accusation that I stole from underfunded public institutions—I'm a thief, not a monster—but I had just enough common sense to realize he was still fishing.

It was that realization—the creeping certainty that Grant didn't know nearly as much about my activities as he claimed to—that goaded me to speak next.

"Oh, I know how valuable they are. I've been systematically stealing the entire library, one book at a time, replacing each item with a reproduction as I go." I pointed toward the back of the room, where the library kept an assortment of foreign language manuscripts. "I started with the French translations, in case you're wondering."

And then I almost gave away the whole show by laughing. The pucker of Grant's brow was just worried enough to indicate that he believed me—or, rather, that he believed me enough to send a guy or two in here to investigate.

Looking back, I'd have to say that was the moment everything changed for us. Oz got a job that very night as part of the library's nighttime custodial staff, and he gleefully informed us that a team of FBI experts showed up to inspect the rare books room every night for the next week. It was a monumental waste of government time and resources, but I'd done nothing illegal that Grant could arrest me for. Only a small white lie, a playful flirtation with the man they sent to spy on me.

I like to think that was the moment Grant and I declared war, our swords crossed, our wills engaged. One of us was going to come out of this triumphant, and I had a pretty good feeling it would be me.

"*Parlez-vous la langue de l'amour?*" he asked. Clearly, he wasn't yet aware of my mastery on the battlefield. "*Merveilleux. Vous êtes une femme de la profondeur.*"

It was a nice recovery, especially if you factored in the way gruff French syllables melted off his tongue and turned everything in the room to liquid along with it. Unfortunately, my French was limited to words like *croissant* and *baguette* and other tasty carbohydrates.

"You speak French?" I asked instead. It wasn't hard to infuse my question with the appropriate amount of doe-eyed wonder to build up his vanity. I was beginning to suspect there was nothing this man *couldn't* do. "Intelligent as well as gorgeous. Geez — some men have all the luck. Then again, some women are lucky enough to have a chance to appreciate it."

"Some women don't seem to care about that chance," he said pointedly. "You stood me up, remember?"

Dammit. We needed to move on from that. There was no way I'd be able to convince him that date had been anything but a ploy to get rid of him, which meant it was better if I didn't try.

"I'm actually just here to think," I said by way of distraction.

He blinked. "I'm sorry?"

I gestured around. "I don't read the books, but I like being surrounded by them. I like that this room is big enough to feel spacious but small enough that I can always keep my eye on the exits. It's a nice place to think."

I could tell he wasn't ready to write off the book-stealing theory, but his interest was definitely piqued. "What do you think about?" he asked.

Whatever we planned to steal, most of the time, but I wouldn't admit to that one out loud. "Oh, you know—things. Life. Death. The existentialism of mankind. My dad."

I wasn't sure how that last one slipped in there, but it was the most accurate of all. My existentialism was about as good as my French.

"Your dad?" Grant reached for my hand and began playing with my fingers. It was hard to describe exactly what he was doing or why. He ran the pad of his index finger along the slope of each one of my digits, as though measuring them before moving to play with the underside. I had to wonder if there was some kind of sneaky FBI trick behind it—like he was secretly scanning my fingerprints—but all he had to do was dust the table after I left for that.

Whatever his motivation, I was distracted enough that I didn't think to temper my response. In hindsight, that was also something I should have paid more attention to from the start. Whenever Grant touched me, even if it was only a teasing handhold on top of a table in full view of the public, I had a tendency to lose control of myself. Hands, lips, fingers; later on, when we'd move to more interesting parts like thighs and the spaces contained between them...it was more than a caress.

It was an attack.

"He used to come here all the time when I was young." I stared at our hands as I spoke. "He called it his quiet place, his thinking place."

I wasn't sure if Grant believed me or not, but he played along for the moment. "Did you come here with him?"

"No. He used to tell me children weren't allowed inside this room—that was why he chose it. It was the only way he could get any alone time. Up until a few years ago, I thought you had to be twenty-one to enter. He was that adamant about getting away from me."

"You must have been one hell of an obnoxious kid."

I laughed out loud, caught unaware. "I'm sure I was. It worked, though. A bar or a strip club I might have been willing to break into to get near him, but this place?" I shook my head. The way my dad felt about this library was almost religious. "It might as well have been Fort Knox."

"I'm surprised you'd let that stop you."

Was that a dig at my criminal tendencies? Rude. "I would've tried, but I have a healthy respect for librarians."

He watched me with that inscrutable look in his eyes for a moment longer. He no longer played with my fingers but kept his hand on my wrist, almost as though he was checking my pulse. It was probably some kind of truth-telling test—which, for the record, I would have passed in full—so I didn't pull away.

"Where's your dad now?" Grant asked.

Wouldn't he like to know? *Wouldn't I?*

I'd decided some time ago that the only possible answer was that he was killed—either in an attempt to get that necklace or in the hours immediately following. Not because I'd had one of those dark epiphanies where I felt his loss in a physical way, and not because I had any hard evidence, but because I wasn't sure I could accept any other option.

Fifteen is awfully young to be thrust upon the world without a penny to your name. Yes, I was a bit more worldly-wise than most, possessing a skill set that would always ensure my survival. And yes, I had a stepmother who could have theoretically provided for my care, but circumstance hadn't favored me then any more than it did now. Tara and I had butted heads right from the start of their marriage. She'd been only five years my senior and much more interested in becoming my father's protégé than taking care of his *actual* protégé—a fact she never attempted to hide from either of us.

When my dad failed to come home that first night, we fought. When he didn't come home the next day, we panicked. When he didn't come home the next week, we scoured all his regular haunts, looking for the supposed treasure he'd amassed.

When a month went by and the hotel we'd been living in finally kicked us out, Tara gave up. She disclaimed any interest in being saddled with a brat of my ilk, especially if there wasn't an inheritance to soften the blow, which meant this ilky brat was left to fend for herself.

I felt a long-buried surge of emotion move through me at the memory. It was anger and despair, a sense of vulnerability that made me want to encase myself in diamond-crusted armor and stay there forever.

My father had to be dead. He had to. The alternatives that presented themselves over the years—that he'd taken his treasure and assumed a new identity, that he'd been caught by the feds and coerced into cutting a deal and retreating into witness protection, that he couldn't face the infamy of having been caught doing something so amateur as triggering the alarm on the Dupont family safe—would have worked perfectly well, assuming he hadn't left me to face the aftermath alone. But he *had*, and that was all the proof I needed. No shame was too great, no deal so sweet, that you'd sentence a kid to a life on the streets.

Death was the only thing I could believe. I couldn't handle it otherwise.

"I'm sorry," Grant said when I didn't answer right away. A portion of my thoughts must have shown on my face, because he tightened his grip on my hand. "Is it hard for you to talk about?"

"No, that's not it. I just…" I stared at that hand, so warm, so comforting, and slipped even further under his spell. "I haven't seen him for a long time, and coming here is my way of connecting. I miss him."

"I know the feeling," he said. "I miss my dad, too."

I glanced up, sure he was patronizing me, but a wistful expression had taken over his features. He looked boyish.

"You have a dad?" It was an incredibly stupid thing to say—of course he had a dad—but he caught my meaning with a smile. *You have a dad who's gone? You have a dad who paved the way for a broken heart?*

"He left my mom when I was pretty young. I don't have many memories of him, but the ones I managed to hold onto are all good. We were happy together, you know? Throwing a football, fishing, going to baseball games. Man stuff."

"Man stuff," I echoed. Could this guy be any more virile? He was probably tossing the pigskin before he could talk.

"I know he was technically a jerk—he left for a younger woman and never looked back or sent a dime in child support—but I still feel like he was a good guy under it all. A bad person doesn't spend hours teaching his five-year-old how to dig for the best worms or patiently answer all his questions about the seventh inning stretch."

That showed what he knew. Bad people could pretend to do almost anything.

"It's a talent of mine, actually: cutting through the bullshit and getting an accurate read on a person." His dark gaze swallowed mine. "Well, it used to be. So, how about you?"

I blinked, breaking the spell. "How about me what?"

"Your dad? Was it a divorce situation like mine, or did he pass away?"

In context, it was a perfectly normal question to ask. When a woman sat in an empty room that reminded her of her father, growing morose and lost in her reflections, it was polite to inquire about the circumstances. Expected, even.

But most women weren't descended from the elusive Blue Fox. Most women weren't considered the last living human to set eyes on his one-hundred-million-dollar fortune. And most women weren't respectable jewel thieves in their own right.

Which begged the question: Why was Grant Emerson, FBI agent and guard dog extraordinaire, so interested in my father? And why the hell was I sitting here, feeding him answers?

Amateur. Idiot. Fool. Take your pick—the insult fit, and I deserved each one.

"I have to go," I said and pulled my hand back. I got to my feet and slung my bag over my shoulder. More than anything else, I needed to get away from Grant's persuasive fingers and a room that was starting to feel very small.

"Go where? Maybe I can take you. I'm parked not far from here, and government-issued cars are pretty nice, if I do say so myself."

Right. He probably expected me to ride in the back, where the doors locked from the outside and the only way out was with a full confession.

"Thanks, but I'll pass." I moved toward the door, but I stopped and turned before I got halfway. My emotion had made me even more reckless than usual. "And for the record? This is low. Even for the FBI."

"Penelope Blue, what did I do?" Even now, he played with the way he said my name and made me question everything. The deep V between his brows looked so damn *sincere*. "Don't leave like this. I'm sorry. It was an insensitive thing to ask."

It wasn't insensitive. It was dangerous.

But no way was I sticking around to explain the difference.

THE BOMBSHELL

10

(Present Day)

TO THE OUTSIDE WORLD, IT LOOKS LIKE I'M MEETING MY
friends at the steps of Bethesda Terrace for a picnic. A
real picnic this time, with a basket full of actual food, a
blanket to sit on, and a Frisbee to toss around, should the
urge arise. The sky is bright and sunny—one of those
days that finds New Yorkers gladly taking refuge behind
dark sunglasses—and there's even a class of schoolchil-
dren out on a field trip. They ooh and aah over the foun-
tain they've probably seen eighty times already.

Anyone paying attention, however, would notice
how unnaturally still I am, lounging next to Jordan and
Oz, waiting for Riker to arrive. Whereas other people
get twitchy and restless when they're nervous, I turn to
stone. It's another side effect of the job. We wouldn't
want me thumping around every time I start to feel
qualms about my life choices.

I'm feeling them right now. Grant got home from his trip a few days ago, fully intact and with no explanation for his absence. The necklace is still in the safe, mocking me with its proximity. No attempt has been made to retrieve or move it—either by Riker or the FBI. And Grant won't stop looking at me when he thinks I'm not paying attention.

It'd be one thing if his gaze followed me with love or desire—hatred would even make sense—but I mostly feel like a lab rat dropped into a maze. He watched me throughout the movie we saw last night, his scrutiny so intense, I couldn't tell you what the film was about. He watched me this morning at breakfast, his eyes following the movement of the spoon to my mouth like a starving man. And he watched me as I packed up this picnic a few hours ago, offering to help with the sandwiches or run to the store to pick up additional supplies.

It's weird. It's weird and it's not like him and it's seriously freaking me out. Only this promised meeting with Riker saved me from doing something rash.

"Hey, guys." Riker appears from around the corner, his mouth in a moment of rare balance. Neither smiling nor scowling, his lips form a perfectly straight line. In all the years I've known him, I'm not sure I've seen that line before, and I don't like it. "Thanks for meeting me. Are we clear to talk?"

Oz flashes him a thumbs-up while I fight the urge to stand up and yell at him for making this so much more difficult than it needs to be.

"What's the matter with you?" I hiss instead, finding the susurration almost as soothing as a good scream. "Do you have any idea how worried we've been? How confused? Why couldn't you pick up a phone and let us know what's going on?"

No glimmer of contrition crosses his face as he turns toward me. "I wanted to be sure before I said anything."

"Sure about what?" I demand and then don't bother waiting for an answer. "Did you follow Grant out of town? Where did he go? What's he up to? What are his plans for the necklace?"

Riker only pays attention to the last question. "As far as I can tell, he doesn't have any plans for the necklace. He didn't do anything or go anywhere to indicate he cared about it. You could take it tomorrow, and I doubt he'd notice. In fact, I think that's exactly what we should do. Open the safe and make a break for it. You in?"

There's an expectancy about the request, a weight that feels uncomfortable in the current circumstances.

"What are you talking about?" I ask.

"You and me, Pen," he says. "Oz and Jordan. Two million dollars. I told you before, the best course of action is to take the necklace and run. Nothing has happened to change that."

"But…" I search his face, looking for clues. What's the big news? The mysterious truth? What's he been doing with himself for the past week? To look at him, you'd think he'd just asked if I want cream in my coffee.

"But nothing. I'm giving you one last chance. Let's grab it and go, leave all this mess behind."

Ultimatums have never set well with me. "You know I can't just take the necklace," I say irritably. I swear, it's like he's willfully misunderstanding the delicacy of this situation. Grant is my *husband*, not some random mark. I can't walk away from him like that. "We're talking about two million dollars Grant is personally responsible for. He won't just blink and let us go."

"That's what you think. What's two million dollars compared to love?"

My heart expands to twice its size before clamping down on itself. "What does love have to do with it?"

"More than you think. It took me a few days, but I discovered a little something about that dear husband of yours. Something that puts a definite kink in your lovelorn refusal to cross him."

"I told you already," I say. "I'm not lovelorn. I'm being cautious."

"Good." Riker's expression lifts, a smile settling in place of that uncanny line. "Then you won't be upset when I tell you that the reason Mr. Romance has been acting so strange lately is because he's having an affair."

◆

"Under no circumstances are you coming in with me." I block the doorway with my arms crossed and my legs shoulder-width apart, refusing to let Riker past. "Go back to the train station and gloat with Oz and Jordan. I can handle this on my own."

"I'm not gloating," Riker gloats.

"He's not having an affair."

"Says you."

"It's probably just a work colleague."

"In snakeskin pants?"

"Maybe she's undercover." Even as I stand here at the door to the house I share with my supposed beloved, defending him against Riker's slurs, I realize how ridiculous I sound. So what if Grant is stepping out on me?

Our marriage is hardly a conventional one. We're more like cat-and-mouse lovers than anything else. When Judgment Day comes and we're asked to stack up our sins for comparative analysis, infidelity isn't likely to stand out above any of the others.

Or so I keep telling myself. The spike ripping open my throat seems to indicate otherwise. The delicate gold chain of the infinity necklace isn't nearly strong enough to hold it closed.

"Pen, you know you can't do this by yourself." Riker falls into a rare moment of concern, all those angles of his face less jagged, less likely to cut. "If you spy on him and end up seeing what I saw, you'll get emotional and blow everything."

"I won't get emotional. I'm a calm, levelheaded businesswoman making calm, levelheaded plans for the future."

His look of disbelief is worth a thousand words. "This is a *good* thing. Now we can start building a legitimate foundation for divorce. We'll hire a private detective, set it up so you look like a woman scorned, and make it so even the FBI can't question your motives. Hell, you might even manage to score alimony out of the deal. That'll annoy him."

He reaches for my hand in a show of solidarity. It's been so long since we touched for any reason other than absolute necessity that I almost don't remember what it's like. There's unquestionable strength in those long fingers. *A thief's strength. A thief's hands.*

He squeezes. "I think it's time we pull out from the project, with or without the goddamned necklace. Don't you?"

I glance at our hands and back up at his face, sure
I'm imagining things. This has to be the first time I've
heard Riker willingly offer to walk away from money.
He loves to act like this whole situation with Grant is
my doing, my obsession, my fault, but that's not fair.
He never complained when I used my position to lure
Grant away from the crime scene, never asked twice
when Grant let something slip about his investigation
into my dad's disappearance. As long as the funds and
information flowed freely, he was happy to turn his
scowl the other way.

Which is why I'm so floored now. "Without the
necklace? You'd really do that?"

"Absofuckinglutely. Let's make this a clean break, Pen.
Let's end this. Let's go back to the way it was before."

Before. It's hard to tell what he means by that.
Before, as in before I made contact with Grant? Before,
as in our youthful attempt to be more than friends?
Before, as in those hand-to-mouth days when our meals
were never guaranteed?

In the end, it doesn't matter what he means, because
I can't do it. There's nothing clean about this scenario—in fact, I feel dirtier now than I have for all the
other parts of this arrangement. Grant and I might exist
on opposite ends of the law, and our marriage might
have been doomed from the start, but I've never once
considered sleeping with another man the entire time
we've been together.

Call me sentimental, but that means something.

"I'm sorry, Riker." His hand stiffens, and even
though I know he can tell what's coming next, I say it
anyway. "I can't just let it go. This isn't how things are

supposed to end. *We* use *him*, remember? We uncover the truth. We win."

"There's still time. We'll find another way to win."

No. That's not how this works. I've never been less triumphant in my life. I feel like I've collapsed just a few feet shy of the finish line, and I won't ever get up and walk again.

"It's no good," I say, my voice cracking. "I have to see this through. He doesn't get to make me feel like this."

He doesn't get to break my heart.

Riker's arms are around me before I know what's happening. It's familiar here, wrapped up in his solid embrace, my head fitting perfectly in the crook of his neck. I almost forgot what he's like in his softer moods, how much I like him when he's able to turn off the demons of his past and let himself connect with another human being.

Our problem is that we could never sustain this kind of connection for very long. It's only a matter of time before he remembers how much he owes his bookie or I say something flippant about his hair. I wish I could make him the love of my life—how much easier everything would be then—but some relationships are simply never meant to be. We're too explosive, too volatile, to be anything but a mistake.

"If it makes you feel any better, she's not nearly as pretty as you are," Riker says.

I release a watery laugh. "That doesn't help."

"She's older, too. Thirty, at the very least."

"That's not older." I pull away and slug him in the arm. "That's a woman in the prime of her life."

"What are you going to do?"

The fact that he's even asking shows how much he cares. "I'm not going to confront him, if that's what you're afraid of. I'm not going to steal the necklace and skip town with you either, so you can wipe that excited smile off your face."

"What's keeping us, Pen? I mean, *really* keeping us? In an entire year, we've discovered nothing about your dad we couldn't have found out somewhere else, made no real progress toward any of our goals. What are we waiting for?"

I don't have an easy answer. Part of me wants to do exactly what Riker says, to draw up the divorce papers and put this whole mess behind us. Another part wants to march inside, take the necklace, and damn the consequences. But the last part—an admittedly large one— wants something else, something so elusive, I'm not sure what it is anymore.

"I'll handle Grant," is all I say.

It's clearly not the answer he's looking for, and our moment of affinity is gone as quickly as it came. "So that's it? You'll get tested for STDs and turn the other cheek? Keep pretending you love that man for the sake of a few solid leads? What kind of plan is that? What kind of life?"

I recoil against the chilly anger in his voice, drawing into the warmth of my house instead. "*My* life, Riker. That's what kind it is."

"Is it? Is it really? Because from where I stand, there are three other people whose lives you affect by hanging on like this. Keep it up, and we'll all come crashing down together."

It's all I can do not to slam the door in his face. I

know that. I know I owe him and Jordan and Oz so much more than I'll ever be able to repay. My entire life has been a burden other people are forced to carry. My dad didn't have time for me. My stepmom didn't want me. My friends have to put up with me. And Grant…

I bite my lip so hard, I can taste the metallic tang of blood rushing into my mouth.

Grant is worse than all the rest. He thinks I have something he wants, but the second he finds out I'm as clueless about the whereabouts of my dad's fortune as he is, it's obvious he'll have no problems moving on.

Oh, Penelope Blue, what are you going to do?

"If this is about the money, I'll buy your share out," I say coldly, knowing—and hoping—the words will send him running. I'm not sure how much more of this day I can take. "I have lots saved up from the last few jobs we pulled. Tell Oz and Jordan, too. I'll make sure everyone gets a fair cut before you leave."

"Fuck you, Pen," he says, pulling away. "This isn't about the money at all. If you ask me, you and Mr. Infidelity deserve each other."

THE WHISKEY ROOM

11

(Eighteen and a Half Months Ago)

AT FIRST GLANCE, THE WHISKEY ROOM WAS THE LEAST intimidating watering hole in all of Manhattan. There was something about a pub-style bar amid all the bass-thumping, overpriced social clubs that made me feel instantly welcome. It might have been the sticky wood-grain bar top, the beer taps that splashed foam all over the glass, or the way people walked through the door and immediately loosened their belts.

Literally. Ties were unknotted and jackets shrugged off. Shirtsleeves were pushed to the elbow, and high heels dangled from toes. The men and women inside this bar were clearly coming down from a hard day at work and looking to drown their problems.

I could respect that. I didn't necessarily agree with it, but I could respect it.

Then I noticed how many of those jackets came off to

reveal shoulder holsters and heard the guffaws of a pair of men crowing over a successful five-hour standoff. A girl could be blinded by the glint of so much honor and good intentions collected under one roof.

"Are we sure this is the wisest decision right now? I thought we were supposed to hide from the FBI, not seek them out." Jordan looked much more at home here than I did. She wore a pencil skirt and a silky red blouse, and she could probably pass as just another agent-at-arms ready to wind down for the night. Me, I'd opted for black leggings and a black T-shirt—all I needed was a dark beanie, and I'd look like every criminal these guys ever bagged. My entire wardrobe was, unfortunately, a product of my career choice. It was either this or my jogging gear again.

At least the shirt plunged in a deep V at the front and was fitted to my body. I noticed a look of approval or two on the way in.

"Oh, it's a terrible idea," I agreed and ushered her toward a booth in the back. It was fairly isolated and gave us a good view of the door, which suited my purposes just fine. I had a man to catch, but I didn't necessarily need an audience while I did it. "You were a fool to come with me. There's a fifty-fifty chance we'll walk out of here in handcuffs. More like sixty-forty, if I'm being honest."

Jordan slid into the seat opposite me, one brow raised in concern. "Is that supposed to make me feel better?"

Not really, but I liked being upfront about our chances of success. "What's that saying? Keep your friends close and your enemies closer? Look around. You can't get any closer to the enemy than this."

The brow stayed firmly raised, and she didn't take me up on the offer to peruse the bar's impressively fit clientele, causing a healthy chunk of my confidence to slough away. She was wavering, I could tell—questioning the wisdom of entering an FBI bar, of being part of my team, of continuing an acquaintance with me, period. I couldn't blame her—that was the worst part. I wouldn't have stuck by me, either.

"It's okay if you want to go." I tried not to let my voice sound as wobbly as it felt. "Riker didn't bother to hide his feelings about this idea, and there's no guarantee Grant will show up anyway. He only mentioned the bar in passing that one time."

"But you think he'll come?"

I did. I couldn't have said exactly why I thought he'd be here, waiting for me, expecting me, but the feeling was unshakeable. *He* was unshakeable. I saw him everywhere I went these days—not in real life, of course, but you know what I mean. A flash of his broad shoulders here, the low timbre of his voice there, the image of him shirtless all over the place.

What? An imagination can be a tricky thing if you let it in the driver's seat, and my imagination had shoved me out of the car days ago.

After the initial debacle at the library, my reaction was to go into hiding. My whole body thrummed as I realized what—or rather, who—I was dealing with. An FBI agent, yes, but more importantly, a man who knew things about my past. Dangerous things. Profitable things. See, Grant wasn't interested in me as a person. Oh, I think he liked flirting with me, and I was sure it suited his masculine pride to know that all he had to do was smile and touch my lips to make my insides turn to mush, but other than that? I was a conduit, a source of information. Nothing more.

He wanted my dad's fortune, not me. No one ever wanted me.

That was when I realized I had nothing to fear from him, imaginary or otherwise. The jerk thought I might know something about the whereabouts of my father's long-lost treasure, and he'd hit on the idea that a love affair was the fastest way to access it. He was that low. He'd use his charming wit and disarming smile to try and take the one thing from me that no one had gotten over the years.

People had tried—believe me, they'd tried. My step-mom, friends of my father who cared more about the money than whether or not I had somewhere to sleep, so-called friends who chatted me up only to drop me when it turned out I wasn't sleeping with diamonds under my mattress... My entire life was a testament to the allure of cold, hard cash.

Well, fine. Two could play this game. I could smile wide and bat my eyes, too. I could lower his defenses and probe for information. He wasn't the only one who wanted to know where the Blue Fox hid his fortune—and he wasn't the only one willing to go to unscrupulous lengths to find out.

We'd see how he liked it when I turned *his* insides to mush.

"He'll be here," I said firmly.

"And you really want to do this?" Jordan asked. "You want to start this war with this particular man?"

Yes. Absolutely. Without question.

In fact, my heart picked up as I pictured him saunter-ing through the bar door, at how smoothly he'd assimi-late me sitting here so he gave nothing away, at how quickly I'd let him. He was the professional, but I had street smarts. He held the cards, but I called the game.

Damn, but it was going to be fun seeing which of us would eventually come out on top.

"I know it's crazy, but yes, I do. I've never been this close to someone who might have hard evidence about my dad's disappearance. I think I might actually be able to make this work."

Jordan's head tilted as she examined me. It was one of her long, silent looks, the kind that made me squirm and feel like I was about to be sent to my room without dinner. But when she finally spoke, she surprised me. "Do you remember that time we almost got arrested outside the courthouse?"

"Which time?" Unless I was mistaken, there'd been more than one.

"Um…the first? It was early on. We must have been sixteen or seventeen at the time. Riker was going through his emo phase, so his nails were all painted black."

Oh yes. That was a phase I wouldn't soon forget. It had suited him. "*We* were seventeen, which means *you* must have been only fourteen or so. God, you were cute back then."

She wrinkled her nose at me. She was *still* cute, and we both knew it. Life had been cruel to her in more ways than one, but from the outside, you'd think she was raised behind a white picket fence instead of institution bars. "That cop kept telling us to leave, but you and Riker wanted to wait for the hot dog vendor to make his rounds."

I remembered it well, and so did my salivary glands. "Oh man. His hot dogs were the best. I think it was because he never changed the water he cooked them in. It was like ten years of flavor in every bite."

She ignored my reminiscences with a grimace. "You told the cop that exact same thing, so he asked to see the money we intended to use to buy our food."

"Of course we didn't have any." I grinned. We never had any back then. We used to pay for each meal with our wits. "Do you still remember how it all went down?"

"Of course I do. You told him exactly how we planned to get our hands on the food."

It had been a simple but beautiful plan, as all of ours were. Jordan was set to run across the street and start a garbage can on fire while Oz dropped something metal into a stranger's pocket to set off the courthouse security alarms. The cop would have to choose which problem to check out, which would leave Riker free to harass the vendor while I slipped up from behind and took all the sweet, semitoxic hot dogs my arms could hold.

"It was a good plan," I said with a sigh.

"It was a *great* plan," Jordan agreed. "And I was sure you'd blown it by outlining all the details in advance, mocking that cop to his face. You were always doing that—breaking the rules, riling up authorities."

I could see where she was going with this. "That was the most successful job we've ever pulled, I think. That poor guy had no idea what to do when the cart arrived and you sauntered across the street, setting not just one, but three garbage cans on fire. He couldn't believe your audacity."

"That was technically an accident," Jordan said. "I only meant to do the one."

It didn't matter. The results were the same. The cop knew very well that all four of us were in on it—thanks to my handy tip ahead of time—but he couldn't arrest us all. In his hesitation deciding which one to go after, we all got away.

Teamwork, that's what that was. The one advantage we've always had.

Even though it was a good memory—a happy one— Jordan's brows came down in a moment of gravity. "After that, I thought you were the bravest and luckiest girl I'd ever known. I still do. No matter how dire the circumstances, you always manage to make them work in your favor. You were born to do this stuff."

I knew what came next. This was the part where she pulled the plug. This was the part where she told me the hazards of my friendship were too high, that she was leaving just like everyone else.

"But?" I prompted.

Her moment of hesitation seemed to go on forever, giving me plenty of time to go through all the sensations of loss and despair, the two so familiar by now that I almost welcomed the numbing lash of them.

"But nothing." She shrugged. "I trusted you then, and I'm trusting you now. Taunt your cop and tell me where to set the fires, Pen. Oz and I have your back. We always will."

The prick of oncoming tears had me blinking rapidly and pinching the bridge of my nose. I wasn't sure anyone had given me such a nice compliment before, recognized that my ability to survive was one of the only things I had to offer the world.

To save myself from the embarrassment of breaking

down, I mumbled something about needing a better view and approached the bar, my smile brittle and my determination to see this thing with Grant through even stronger. Jordan was right. The trick when dealing with officers of the law was to throw them off their game. In the general balance of the world, they held all the power. They were so sure of their position, their superiority, their ability to stay on the straight and narrow and come out triumphant. It never occurred to them to question what they'd do if they suddenly found themselves in a thick and tangled brush. Whereas my kind of people had nothing at all. No power, no superiority, no path. We hid in the shadows and grew impervious to thorns. Most importantly, we had each other.

I dared Grant to try and scratch me now.

"Hello, bartender," I said with a bright smile, made all the brighter by the glitter of tears I refused to let fall. "I'd like a tonic water with a twist of lemon, please."

Jordan joined me, her presence at my elbow palpable and comforting.

So of course, I ruined it. "And my friend here would love nothing more than an Irish Car Bomb to get her going."

Jordan grimaced, but she accepted the Guinness-Bailey's-Jameson boilermaker the bartender handed her in good form. "You're hilarious, Pen. You should say that a little bit louder next time."

"Relax." I hooked my foot on the barstool and appraised the crowd of people playing pool and chatting at tables, none of them paying us the least heed. "These are stout-drinking folk. They're used to it."

We sipped our drinks for a minute—well, I sipped while Jordan did her best to stop the overflow of alcohol spilling out of her glass—as I renewed my appraisal of the crowd. Ordinary guard dog, ordinary guard dog, ordinary guard dog…not a single K-9 unit in sight.

"Still no sign?" Jordan asked.

"I don't see him." I placed my drink down with a sigh. "He's probably stuck doing paperwork for that failed library job, poor man."

Jordan laughed and then immediately covered her mouth, as if finding my stunt funny was cause for arrest. "Aren't you afraid he'll be angry about that when he sees you again?"

Nope. Not even a little. He was too good an actor—too good at playing this game—to let something like anger get in the way of winning. I may not have known him long, but I knew that much for sure.

"I can handle Grant Emerson," I said firmly.

"That's good to hear," Jordan said and nodded at the door. "Because I think he just arrived."

Every nerve ending wanted me to turn around and glance in the direction she indicated, but I was determined to play it cool. "Oh yeah? What makes you think it's him?"

She grinned. "Because he's heading right for us."

◆

"Well, well, well. You do know where the Whiskey Room is."

I could tell the exact moment when Grant reached us. Not by the sound of his voice—that low rumble of his almost-but-not-quite-Southern twang, the vibrations shaking me to my core—but because he leaned in, placed a hand on the small of my back, and dropped a kiss on my cheek.

A *kiss*, of all things. This man I barely knew and didn't trust, this man I'd fled from last week as if my life depended on it, had the nerve to put his lips on my skin. Not in a creepy way, either. It was friendly, gentlemanly, one of those gestures only polite and incredibly confident men can pull off.

If that weren't bad enough, there was also just enough stubble on his jaw to remind me that he might have been friendly and gentlemanly, but he was also very much a man. All my senses spiraled outward at once. I was still trying to find my balance when he gestured at the agent standing behind him.

"I don't believe you've met my friend and partner yet," he said with a casual air.

Well, crap. They were multiplying. "Um...no. I don't believe I have."

"Then let me introduce Simon Sterling. Simon, this is Penelope Blue—the woman I was telling you about."

Oh, I bet he had. I could just picture the two of them standing by one of those boards where they try to figure out crimes, my face and my father's face connected by a red string. That's how official the two of them looked side by side. Simon had the wide shoulders and cocky stance I'd come to expect from this particular breed of man, but he was more urbane than Grant—and that wasn't a compliment. I couldn't say if it was the severity of his necktie, pulled tight like a noose, or the way his cold, blue eyes glittered like ice as they took me in, but this was clearly a man who considered himself above his company and had no intention of being charmed by my quirky criminal ways.

Good. I had no intention of being charmed by him,

either. One FBI agent whose smile stopped my heart was enough.

"I'm sure it was all wonderful things," I said and extended a calm hand. I also congratulated myself on my foresight in bringing Jordan along. It hadn't been my intention to make her play wingman, but if anyone could get somewhere with this uptight man of the law, it was her. Unpleasant, fastidious men like him loved her tender ways. "This is my friend, Jordan."

Based on the twinkle in Grant's eye as he politely expressed a greeting, I could tell he knew her name already. "Wonderful," he said and meant it.

Simon wasn't quite as excited at the prospect, but some kind of secret message passed between the men, and they arranged themselves in a divide-and-conquer stance. Obviously, Simon was to take Jordan aside and pump her for details, while I was to be assigned Grant's undivided attention.

I was more concerned for myself than for her. Jordan was like a vault—she'd learned a long time ago to hide her true feelings from the authority figures in her life, foster parents and FBI agents alike—and she could handle herself. Me, on the other hand, I wasn't so sure about. Already I could feel myself basking in the warm, soft glow of Grant's gaze, leaning into his strength as if it could carry me across mountains.

"I thought for sure I scared you away last week," Grant said, his expression neutral. "I can't tell you how happy I am to discover I was wrong."

With that, the game was back on. I *wasn't* scared—and he'd soon come to learn that he was wrong about a heck of a lot of things.

Jordan picked up her cue in an instant, putting a hand on Simon's arm. "And I can't tell you how happy I am to meet someone of your expertise. I have so many questions I want to ask."

Simon looked down at her hand as though it might burn him. "About crime?"

"Oh, no. I know enough about that already." I thought I heard Grant choke a little at Jordan's honesty, but it might have been my imagination. "What I'm really curious about is a movie I was watching on TV the other night. There was this FBI agent scaling the side of the Empire State Building using nothing but suction cups, but based on my understanding of air pressure and surface tension…"

Her voice trailed off as she directed him toward the booth we'd been sitting in earlier. I had to bite on my lip to keep from laughing out loud. I was wrong about the tenderness in Jordan keeping Simon busy. Her inquisitive mind would more than take care of that. I doubt Simon could teach her anything she didn't already know, but she'd at least make sure he tried.

"You have good taste in friends, I'll give you that," Grant said as soon as they moved out of earshot. "I like her."

So did I. "I hope your partner can be trusted with her. He seems…" By the book? Straitlaced? Unpleasant? "Serious."

Grant twisted his head to look at me. "He *is* serious. But he's also been my partner for a long time. I can safely promise you that no harm will come to her through his hands."

Much as I hated to admit it, I would have to trust this

man enough to take him at his word. Of course, that didn't mean I failed to notice that he fully reserved the right to cause harm through his own hands. I wasn't stupid.

I smiled to show my blessing. Grant smiled back to accept my blessing. And that was that.

"Excellent," he said and turned his attention to the bar. "I'll have what the lady's having. And get her another."

"Make mine a double this time, bartender."

The bartender winked at me and carefully poured out two glasses of tonic water. Grant took his in hand with an almost perplexed look on his face.

"Sorry to ruin your big moment," I said. "But I don't drink."

"Ever?"

"Not since I was about eighteen years old." I shrugged an apology and set to work squeezing my lemon. It behooved me to tread lightly moving forward—especially regarding my tales of the past—but if I wanted to get answers out of this man, I would have to open up enough to keep him interested. Give and take, push and pull. Nothing in this world was free. "I drank a lot of malt liquor and bottom-shelf vodka when I was young—and I mean *a lot*."

"Fake ID?"

"Five-fingered discount."

Grant's eyes flashed in an expression of interest, the same way they always did when I surprised him with the truth. "Ah, youthful dissipation. I know it well."

Somehow, I doubted that. "Oh yeah? You hit up a lot of liquor stores when you were a kid, Agent Emerson?"

He laughed and loosened the knot of his tie, just

like every other lackey in the place. Unlike everyone else, however, there was a sensuality about the action, a man allowing himself to come undone at just the throat. A flash of that vulnerable spot, taut with muscles and sprinkled with hair, was all that he released to me.

Oh, dear God. It was enough.

"I wasn't always an officer and a gentleman. I had my fair share of youthful shenanigans."

"If you called them *shenanigans*, I promise you had no such thing."

This time, his laugh was a rumble, that force of nature not even his massive strength could hold back. "You're a fascinating woman, you know that? The stories I bet you could tell…"

He had no freaking idea.

Or maybe he did.

"You're probably wondering what I'm doing here." I changed the subject with a smile, fishing around in my bag. My fingers sought the peace offering I'd brought with me. "I came to apologize for storming out on you the other day, and to give you this."

"This?"

I handed over a carefully wrapped box the size of his palm. "I've got a few connections. It's probably better if you don't ask."

His face revealed absolutely nothing as he took the gift in hand, but I could tell he was surprised. Three times I'd encountered this man, and I was already beginning to figure him out. His laughter was genuine, his smile devastating, his sense of humor perfectly intact. He was also phenomenally good at hiding any emotion other than that. Amusement and interest were allowed to run free, but the rest of it—the suspicion and the alarm, the fact that he genuinely thought I just handed him a stolen piece of jewelry or drugs in the middle of a federal agent's bar—was quashed before it had a chance to surface.

He was good. He was very, very good.

But I was better.

"It's a bit early in our relationship for presents, don't you think?" he asked, but he tugged at the ribbon, his movements as methodical as if he were unwrapping a bomb. "I'd have gotten one for you, but I don't know anything about you."

"You know my name, what I do for work, and that I have deep-seated daddy issues. What more is there?"

He paused in the middle of sliding open one end of the paper. "Why did you bring your friend Jordan with you today?"

Well, well. He wasn't wasting any time, was he? Fine, then. Neither would I.

"She insisted. My friends are very protective, especially when it comes to things like this." I shrugged to show I wasn't intimidated by him. "Besides, I didn't want to come in alone only to be bombarded by federal agents trying to pick me up. They have this strange thing for me."

"They do, huh?"

"Can't seem to get enough. Sometimes, it feels like there's one waiting for me every time I turn around."

His grin deepened so much, there was actually a hint of a dimple. "I wonder why that is?"

"I suspect it's my weirdly skinny fingers." I nodded at the present. "It takes you a really long time to open things."

"Sorry. It's my grandma's fault. She always liked

to save the wrapping paper so she could reuse it. That woman never threw anything away."

I could tell by the way he paused that he wanted me to offer a tidbit of my own in exchange, but I couldn't have told him anything about my grandparents if I wanted to. My dad's parents died when he was young—hence the life of crime—and we never talked about my mom at all. I could count the things I knew about her on two hands.

She'd been beautiful and funny and *good*. Her family disowned her when she married my dad. She died giving birth to me less than a year later. And the one time I asked about any aunts or uncles or cousins I might have floating around out there, my dad shut down so quickly that I'd never had the courage to bring it up again.

I'd had to be content with the two of us. Until, of course, he'd remarried and changed everything.

"Um...my stepmom was the opposite?" There. That would have to be enough to satiate the beast. "Unless it had substantial resale value, she threw everything away."

He paused long enough for me to realize I'd made a huge error. "You have a stepmom?"

Shit. Crap. Damn. I'd assumed the FBI would have been diligent enough to find all the records of my father's past—including the courthouse wedding that tied him to a woman young enough to be his daughter. But if they'd somehow missed that one, I'd just handed them a whole new lead on a silver platter.

"Well, *mom* is pushing it," I said quickly, hoping to make light of my mistake. Maybe if I didn't draw attention to it, he wouldn't realize I'd spoken without thinking. Maybe he'd believe it to be another plant. "She wasn't really the maternal type. Her idea of bonding

time was to take me shopping with her. I had to pretend
to steal something and keep the security guards busy
while she got out with ten times as many goods."

There. Hopefully, that would keep him busy for a
while. Nothing I'd just said was a secret—there were
several juvenile arrests on my record to attest to it—and
I was establishing a foundation of trust.

"More shenanigans?" Grant asked, but he didn't comment further. He might have, but he finally opened the
package to reveal a box of extra-extra-large condoms.
His laugh was all I needed to assure me I'd made the
right choice.

I pointed at the slogan on the front of the box.
"Guaranteed not to inhibit blood flow."

When he looked up, his eyes were fully crinkled.
"You have connections, huh?"

"I told you not to ask."

"Oh, I won't." He held up three fingers in a Boy
Scout salute. "I also won't push my luck by asking if
you'd like to take these out for a test drive."

A twinge of regret took up residence alongside the
desire in my gut. I mean, it wasn't like I was actually
going to sleep with the guy, but he could have at least
made a push for it. It would have been fun to turn
him down.

"So, what now?" I asked. "I tracked you down. I
apologized. I introduced sexual tension into our relationship. What comes next?"

He dropped a few bills on the bar to cover our drinks
and rose. His movements were silent but assured, and
when he extended a hand to help me to my feet, I took it.

"You didn't introduce the sexual tension." He didn't

relinquish his hold on my hand. If anything, his grip grew tighter, determined to shackle me to his side. "That's been there a lot longer than you realize."

Not true. I knew this man was going to be a problem the first time I laid eyes on him, standing on the other side of those docks as I hyperventilated inside a cargo box. Now, as then, I couldn't seem to ignore the thrill of being near him. The hard, heated wall of his body pressing against mine was doing dangerous things to my self-control.

"As to what we do next, I was thinking we should abandon Simon and Jordan and head out to dinner," he said.

"Dinner?"

"Absolutely. Dinner, dessert, and one of those heart-felt conversations that goes long into the night." He lifted a hand to my cheek, brushing my skin so gently, it almost didn't count as a touch.

But it did. It counted big time.

"I can't wait to learn everything there is to know about you, Penelope Blue. Shenanigans, evil step-mother, and all."

Of course he couldn't, the sneak.

"Will you come?" he asked. Anxiously, I thought.

I cast a look over at Jordan and Simon, the former chatting animatedly away as she scribbled what I could only assume were complex chemical equations on a cocktail napkin, the latter with that look of overwhelmed incomprehension men always got when Jordan talked shop. Oz was the only man I'd seen who accepted that side of her without so much as a blink.

"I meant what I said before." Grant's voice was

earnest. "Simon won't hurt her. You have my word on that."

"Oh, it's not her I'm worried about," I said. And I wasn't. As I accepted Grant's hand and invitation, I knew damn well that I was the one who was going to need all the help I could get.

THE OTHER WOMAN

(Present Day)

IT'S THE HEIGHT OF IRONY THAT I END UP HIDING IN A linen closet to find my cheating husband out.

It's not my most elegant moment, crouched as I am underneath the bottom shelf, the scent of neatly folded sheets and towels rendering the air thick with domesticity. There are at least a dozen better hiding places in our house, but I panicked.

For the past twenty-four hours, I've been scouring the house while Grant's away at work, searching for some sign of infidelity. What that sign might be, I'm not quite sure. I hardly expect to find used condom wrappers or receipts for shady hotels lying around the house—especially when we're talking about a highly trained liar—but I don't know what else to do. I'm not used to this kind of deception.

Yes, my friends and I steal things for a living. And

yes, I've spent the better part of my life breaking laws and lying to get my way. But I've never set out to purposefully hurt another human being—at least, not without them knowing about it ahead of time. Grant and I have always operated under a set of unspoken rules that bind us: we don't talk about work, we don't talk about my father, and we definitely don't talk about what the future holds for us.

The idea that Grant could hold me in his arms, kiss nonsense words into my neck and hair, claim my body with his over and over again…only to do the same with another woman?

No. A cold chill works through my body, a slice of icy fear that has nothing to do with my cramped conditions. That part was real. That part was safe. That part was *ours*.

The front door opens and closes again, signaling Grant's return home in the middle of a workday. That's the reason for my mad dash into the linen closet in the first place. I only noticed his sleek FBI-issued car pulling into the driveway with enough warning to dive into the first hiding place I could find.

Grant doesn't come home early from work if he can possibly help it. That man lives and breathes for the FBI, spends more time with Simon than he's ever lavished on me. In fact, I bought them a pair of His and His coffee mugs last Christmas. Grant thought it was hilarious. I'm pretty sure Simon smashed his with a hammer.

"My wife shouldn't get back for a few more hours," Grant says, his voice distant in a muffled sort of way. "She's at the rec center today, and she almost always stays late afterward to make sure all the kids get picked up."

"That's nice. She has good maternal instincts." A

throaty female response does little to improve the current state of affairs—pun intended. "Do you have any?"

"Maternal instincts? Can't say that I do."

She laughs. Predictably, it's one of those phony, oh-you're-so-funny-you-big-strong-man sounds I'd like to throttle at its source. "Of course not, dummy. I meant, do the two of you have any kids?"

"Not yet. But there's plenty of time for that."

It's all I can do not to spring out of my hiding place right then and there. Not yet? *Not yet?* What the heck is that supposed to mean? Not only is it highly unusual for a man to discuss his future procreative plans with his mistress, but I can't imagine what would possess him to introduce children into our relationship. He works eighty hours a week, and I have all the benevolence of a scorpion. Riker would make a better parent than us.

"If we're not in a hurry, do you want to have drinks or something first?"

Grant pauses. "Nah. We should make this fast. I want a chance to get everything cleaned up before she gets back."

"We could always do it later, if you want. I'd hate to get you in any trouble with the missus."

"Don't worry. I can handle her."

I beg your pardon. I'm not a trick pony whose reins he can pick up anytime he feels like it. I'd like to see him try handling me after this.

"You're sure she won't mind? I don't want to step on her turf or anything."

"I'm sure." His voice is grim. "If there's one thing Penelope has made very clear to me, it's that she doesn't care about what I have to offer."

My chest clenches tightly, squeezing my heart and cracking a few ribs along the way. That isn't true. I do care. Maybe not the way other women care, and maybe not enough to overlook the fact that I'm a hardened criminal, but I've done the best I can.

"Now turn around," Grant says. "I'm going in."

The firm way he commands her is familiar, almost primitive, and I'm hit with an overpowering urge to well up in tears at the sound of it. Which is bad, because as soon as my tear ducts start working, I feel a tickle building up in my nose. It's the combination of emotion and all the fabric softener in the close air of the closet.

"You mean I can't watch? You're a bit of a tease."

"We do this my way, or we don't do it at all."

"A man of decision. I like it."

The pressure behind my eyes is so strong now that I have to crinkle my nose and bite my fist to keep from giving away my position. If I'd known he planned on bringing her *here*, to our home, testing the springs on the antique couch we bought together before we were married, I never would've put myself in such a prime eavesdropping position. The last thing I want to do is sit here listening to the muffled sounds of my marriage ending. In fact, I don't think I can do it without making myself sick.

I risk peeking under the crack in the door to evaluate the topography of retreat. The hallway is set back enough from the living room that there isn't a clear line of sight to my hiding place. I might be able to sneak across the hall to our bedroom and escape out the window. It's not a great plan, but it's all I have. I shift on my haunches.

I'm about to edge the door open when Grant speaks

again. "I should probably warn you—it's a lot bigger than you think. Penelope had a hard time believing it was real at first."

My skull cracks the shelf with a start. There's no way to hide the sound, but I can't move right away. I'm too rattled, too confused. Grant wouldn't talk about the details of our sex life with another woman—with another *lover*—like that.

Would he?

"Do you have a dog?" the woman asks. She sounds less throaty this time, as if she's alarmed instead of trying too hard to be seductive, and something about it registers with me.

I've heard that voice before. I *know* that voice.

"We don't have any pets. Penelope doesn't like animals."

That's not true. I like animals just fine, but mine wasn't a childhood of chocolate chip cookies and camping trips with the family golden retriever. I don't exactly have a framework for that sort of thing. Unfortunately, I don't have time to quibble over the details. This is clearly another *abort, abort now* moment, only I don't have the promise of Riker's plunge into darkness to count on.

Without wasting another second, I slip the door the rest of the way open and roll neatly to the master bedroom across the hall. Equal parts ballet, gymnastics, and desperation, it's an impressive feat. I wish there was enough time to scramble out the huge window overlooking the back porch, but the sound of footsteps makes me reevaluate my plans.

They're her footsteps, in case you were wondering.

The clack of high heels on our newly varnished wood floors is a foreign sound, since the tallest shoes I own are my thick-soled winter boots, but at least it's more of a warning than I get from Grant. As always, it's impossible to hear him coming.

I flip my head down to infuse a sleepy red color to my face and pull my loose T-shirt from one shoulder. As a last-second gesture, I also tug the blankets from the bed to make them look as if I was in there. I've always been a light, restless sleeper—something Grant knows all too well. I warned him early on in our marriage that the only way he'd get any rest at night was if we kicked it old school and got separate twin beds, but he just grunted at me and threw his massive arms and legs over my side. It turns out a girl literally *can't* be restless with almost two hundred pounds of man-muscle pinning her to the bed.

I always sleep best when he's with me, anchoring me in place.

Faking a bleary-eyed look isn't necessary after that. As Grant rounds the corner and looks into the room, I dash a hand against my eyes. To anyone seeing me for the first time, it probably seems like nothing more than a gesture of wakefulness.

"Penelope!" Grant doesn't have time to hide his surprise or come up with a clever excuse. His mouth opens and closes again as he takes in the room at a glance. "What are you doing home?"

"I've had a massive headache all day." It's only a partial lie. *Something* certainly feels like it's about to rip me in two. "I was taking a nap."

"But you never sleep during the day."

I'm saved from having to respond as his bit of arm

candy totters up behind him. Her shiny silver heels distract me enough that I start at the bottom and work my way up, my heart sinking with every inch of finely crafted female skin. I'm a dancer—ostensibly—and Riker makes me jog three miles every day to stay in shape, so I have fairly decent legs, but this woman could crush me with one flex of her calves. There's nothing but miles of taut, creamy skin, all of it leading up to a tight red dress that might have functioned as a Band-Aid in a past life.

Its primary function now is to lift. Ass, waist, boobs—there isn't a part of that woman that sags the way God and nature intended.

I know, in that moment, that what I need more than a diamond necklace, more than a better hideout than the linen closet—more, even, than a husband who doesn't love me—is a red dress like that one.

Then I see her face.

Maybe it's the fact that I just tipped my head upside down, so there's an abnormal amount of blood trapped there, or maybe it's the overwhelming sensation of too many surprises, but the second I notice the wide-set eyes and perfectly sloping nose, the platinum hair flowing like the mane of a lioness, I lose all sense of my surroundings.

I'm no longer standing in the bedroom of a house I share with my enemy. My husband isn't cheating on me with a gorgeous blond wearing a Band-Aid. I'm rushing blood and a sensation of hot-cold-hot-cold on rotation. I'm weak in the knees and about to slump to the floor.

I'm out like a—

"I think she's coming to. Do you want me to grab her a glass of wine or something?"

"She doesn't drink. Water will be fine."

"Doesn't drink? That's odd. I remember—"

Even though I'm comfortably ensconced in Grant's lap and still feeling light-headed, I snap my eyes open before Tara has a chance to say what she remembers. The summation of her worldly knowledge is something I have a profound interest in, but I'm not about to ask her to spill it while my husband sits here, running his palm in a soothing pattern over my forehead.

In fact…

I struggle to sit up, scooting a few inches away from Grant as I go. I don't want his gentle caresses and warm lap right now. I don't know where that lap has been…or rather, *I do*, and that's the problem.

He can tell in an instant what I'm thinking, because he wraps his arms around me and holds me tight, refusing me the benefit of space. It's not a hug—it's more of a choke hold—but I can already feel my body betraying me.

He's so warm, so solid, so comfortable. And *strong*. I'm pretty sure he's not straining so much as a fiber of muscle to keep me pressed against him.

"Let me go, you bastard." I struggle against that strength, feeling better when the swell of his muscles tenses and he's forced to exert a little effort to hold me in place.

"Not until you calm down."

Oh, he does *not* get to tell me to calm down right now. "I'll scream. I'll scream so loud, they'll hear me in Queens."

"This isn't what you think, Penelope."

How does he know? I glare. "You have no idea what's going through my head right now."

"If the look on your face before you passed out was anything to go by, I have a pretty good idea." He drops his mouth so close to my ear that I can feel the vibrations of his breath. Like a tuning fork, my entire spine tingles its response. "Stop fighting, my love. I'm not going to release you until you let me explain."

Despite those tingles—or perhaps because of them—I glare harder. He doesn't even have the decency to look ashamed of himself.

"You can't force me to listen to you," I say. "Is this why you left our anniversary dinner early? Is *she* the reason you went out of town?"

I try a quick bending twist, hoping I can outmaneuver him by being slippery, but he anticipates the action and pins me with some kind of wrestling move. Now it's not just his arms or his lap trying to lull me into a state of complicity—it's his whole body, all those pounds of him pressing down on my softest parts. Breasts and thighs, the thrust of pelvises fitting neatly together. He uses that pressure, the laws of gravity and human nature, to try and subdue me even more.

He's not being very gentle with a woman who just passed out—a fact that's finally borne on him when he manages to stop my wriggling, his leg pinned between mine and his forearm across my throat. "I've never seen you pass out like that before. Are you okay?"

It's almost impossible to speak while he crushes my windpipe and slowly presses the oxygen out of my lungs, but I manage to croak out a credible, "I just found out you bring women to the house when I'm not here, and now you're trying to murder me to hide the evidence. Do you *think* I'm okay?"

His expression goes from concerned to pleased, which, I can promise you, doesn't push me toward forgiveness. "Are you jealous?"

Jealous is not the right word for what I'm feeling. Angry, maybe. Livid, probably. Hurt, for sure. It's one thing to step out on me with a hot woman in a flashy red dress. It's another to step out on me with that *particular* woman. Even though she's aged a good ten years, I remember all too well the last time we shared breathing space.

She'd stolen the man in my life that time, too.

"Of course I'm not jealous. I'm suffocating."

He releases me from his death grip and rocks back on his heels, his lips still turned up in a smile. "You're not suffocating."

"I'm not *now*." I rub the front of my neck—an action that was supposed to highlight my near-death injury—but my fingers brush against the infinity knot of my necklace instead, and I drop my hand like it's on fire. "Stop smiling at me. You're a cheating bastard, and you can't charm your way out of this one."

He obeys my command—for what has to be the first time in his life—but he replaces his smile with a gentle expression that unsettles me even more. "I'm not cheating on you, Penelope Blue. I decided a long time ago that I was going to have you or no one."

Gah. Now is not the time for singsong antics and sweetly sexy voice rumbles. Tara will be back here with a glass of water any second, and I need to figure out whether I'm supposed to recognize her.

*Why, no, Grant. I've never seen this woman before.
You might want to run a background check, though. She
has the cheap look of a con artist, don't you think?*

*The reason I passed out isn't because you're a two-
timing jerk, Grant. It's because the woman you decided
to cheat on me with happens to be my stepmother. How
long have you two known each other?*

Neither of those options holds much appeal, but I'm
a woman floundering in the deep end over here—and I
don't know how much longer I'm going to be able to
keep my head up.

"She's a business associate," he says, his voice low
enough that only the two of us can hear. Any lingering
playfulness is gone. "That's all."

As I'm fully aware of her line of business—making
men fall in love with her and ruining their lives a few
short months before they disappear into thin air—that
doesn't bring me much comfort.

"She's in the FBI?" I ask incredulously. "The physical standards must be slipping over at the Bureau."

"She's a contact. Contacts aren't required to pass the
physical, or we'd be in a hell of a lot of trouble. Not
everyone can stay in this kind of shape, you know."

I ignore the provocation. "What kind of contact?"

"The usual kind. Slightly shady but useful enough for
the good to outweigh the bad. You of all people should
know how lenient the government can be about that sort
of thing." His dark gaze doesn't leave mine, and I swallow heavily. "I had to call her in when my other plans
fell through. My first choice refused to take the bait, so
I was forced to resort to extreme measures."

That's all I'm able to get out of him, because the

woman of the hour totters back in, a glass of water extended in one hand.

"She looks like she's feeling better," Tara says when Grant twists to glance up at her. "Drink this, honey. It'll help."

"I'm not your honey," I grumble.

I don't want to drink her water, and I don't want her to slip back into this ridiculous *Mommie Dearest* role—the same one she fooled me with all those years ago. Tara had only been nineteen years old to my fourteen when she married my dad, but those five years might as well have been fifty for all it had mattered to me. I'd wanted to like her. Love her, even. She knew things—practical things, common sense things—that had eluded me for years. Makeup, tampons, that always tricky question of how to shave your legs without ripping off all the skin. I'd thought she was some sort of goddess sent to soothe my adolescent woes.

The feelings hadn't been reciprocated. Tara had hated me on sight—not that she would have done anything to let my dad know. To hear her tell the tale, all she'd wanted was for me to be her dear, sweet stepdaughter, but my surly attitude kept her away.

I was fourteen, motherless, and had taken up a life of crime mostly to get closer to my absent father. Of course I'd been surly.

"She's right." Grant holds the glass to my lips. "Drink this."

I do, but begrudgingly, glaring at him all the while. Grant pulls me to my feet and takes a look at the two of us—his angry, disheveled wife and the siren business associate—as if deciding how best to proceed in this tangled web of his making.

Tara takes the guesswork out of it. She extends her perfectly manicured hand and smiles, a familiar flash of teeth that makes what's left of my heart turn to lead. "I'm Tara. Tara Lewis. So pleased to meet you."

Lewis, huh? When she married my dad, she took on the Blue surname. The fact that she returned to her maiden name—or what she always told us was her maiden name—speaks volumes. Also, it seems we're pretending not to know each other. How interesting.

"Penelope Blue," I reply and shake.

Her brow lifts once she realizes that I, too, am using my real name at a time like this. It's almost funny, actually. If I think it's weird that she's working with an FBI agent, she must be losing her shit over the fact that I married one.

Well, too bad. What did she think would happen, abandoning me to the streets without a penny to my name? If it weren't for Riker, my life could have ended up a lot worse than this. Marrying Grant might not have been the smartest decision I've ever made, but at least I'm still alive.

Though probably not for much longer. The next words out of my mouth are designed to irritate everyone in my immediate proximity.

"So, Tara," I say, "what do you do for the FBI that requires you to dress up like a hooker and go to strange men's houses?"

"Penelope!" Grant says sharply—more sharply than I've heard him speak before—but I won't be swayed. I'm suddenly very tired. All the lying and sneaking around, the double speaking and near-misses. For once in my poor, twisted life, I'd like to say what I'm thinking: *I'm not so sure I want to play anymore.*

"What?" I ask, the surliness of my youth rising anew.

"That was uncalled for."

Uncalled for it might have been, but Tara just laughs, the sound deep and rich and evidence of the chain-smoking I remember from my youth. She actually used one of those cigarette holders from the forties when she indulged in the habit—all part of her man-catching charm.

"No, no. It's a perfectly fair question." She casts him a sly smile. "I don't blame her for keeping a tight leash on you. If you were my husband, I wouldn't let you out of my sight."

I scowl. More doublespeak. She means, of course, that the only reason I married him was to keep close tabs on his movements and leverage the relationship for my own purposes.

Whatever. It takes one to know one.

"In fact, I agree with her," Tara continues, blithe as can be. "I think you should tell her what I'm doing here. That way, we can prep her on what to say if they bring her in for questioning."

"If they bring her in for questioning, we're screwed either way. Penelope can't lie to save her life."

"Hey!" I protest. "I'll have you know I'm an excellent liar. I lie to you all the time."

His expression, when he turns it my way, is grim. "What makes you think I don't know that?"

I'm flummoxed enough, I can't reply right away.

"You're right, though," Grant says to Tara. "We have to do something with her. She's too much of a wild card to leave hanging."

"But I thought you said she won't play along."

"She won't—that's the problem. She's always hated

doing anything that might make my life easier. What she needs is plausible deniability."

"I'm standing right here," I say. "I can hear you."

Grant turns to me with a half grimace, a twist of his mouth I can't quite read. If I didn't suspect this is all part of some secret government plot to drive me over the edge, I'd think he was almost remorseful.

Well, if he's not remorseful now, he will be soon. I told him once that it was hard to get rid of me. He'd see how much I meant it. He'd discover I had no intention of letting him walk out of my life without a fight.

"Whatever you do to me, I'll hunt you down," I warn. "I'll track you and follow you and run all your carefully laid plans right into the ground."

He studies me carefully. "Is that a promise?"

I glare. "Absolutely."

"Deal." He nods once. "You heard the lady. We'll have to do this the hard way. She's not going to rest until she has my head on a platter."

"That's not the part of you I plan on carving."

He's surprised into a chuckle. "This might actually work in our favor, now that I think about it. If we can make them believe I turned on my own wife—"

"You *are* turning on your own wife."

He casually ignores me. "That should erase any lingering doubts about my intentions. It's not how I prefer to do things, but that's usually the case where Penelope is concerned. I can only take what she gives me. Which, unfortunately, is never as much as I want."

"I still think it would be easier to just tell her—"

"No. Trust me. It's better like this. I know how she works."

Not true. If he did, he'd realize how close he is to being murdered right now.

Tara casts her reluctance aside with a shrug. "It's your funeral. Let's tie her up so we can get on with it."

"Agreed."

"Hey, now." I take a step back, my hands up. "I think you two have had enough fun. There's no need to make empty threats."

"It's not an empty threat. I *am* going to tie you up."

"Grant—you wouldn't."

"I don't have any other choice. You brought this on yourself." He lunges for me, but what I noticed the other day while I was hiding in the jewelry store air vent is true. Big means slow, and small means fast. I duck before he's able to get a grip.

It's half a victory, because now I'm trapped in the hallway. The only door at this end leads to the bathroom, and even though a window exit isn't out of the question, there's no way I'll have enough time to slip out before I'm caught.

Grant knows it, too. He takes a step toward me, using his wide shoulders to create a blockade. Instinct has me glancing toward Tara in hopes of finding an ally, but she's conveniently disappeared.

"I won't hurt you," he says. "It'll only be for a few minutes."

"Don't come near me. I'll lock myself in the bathroom."

"I'll break down the door."

"Not before I escape out the window."

"The latch sticks. You won't make it in time."

He draws closer and closer with each word. A sense

of danger has heightened my awareness of him, making him appear to grow to epic proportions as he draws near, his body heat lulling me into complicity.

I fight it with the only thing I have left. "Stop. Wait. You know who that woman is, don't you?"

"I do, actually," he says. "Someone dear to me once dropped a helpful tip about her."

I'm the one who stops. I'm the one who waits. I think we all know who that someone was.

"Tara Lewis, one of the most sought-after cat burglars in the world." Grant appears pensive as he mentally brings up her file. "Put on the FBI watch list before she was legally allowed to vote, married the Blue Fox before she was legally allowed to drink, and believed to be responsible for over fifty million dollars in theft in the United States alone, including the attempt on the Mint back in '09. She's the second-best jewel thief I know."

There it is. He knows. He knows this woman is my stepmother, knows what she did to me, and he still considers her an asset. He's still choosing her over me.

Grant lunges again. I don't put up a fight this time, and he catches me easily. It's a heady feeling, being overpowered and held to his chest, especially when he scoops me into his arms. His heart beats faster against mine—evidence of the adrenaline of the chase—but he's not the least bit winded by my weight.

If anything, he's made more confident by my struggle, and he drops a kiss on the side of my mouth. It's a brief touch, but it's enough for the impression of his lips to mark mine, for the slightly minty taste of him to linger.

"Don't be angry," he croons. "I don't like this any more than you do."

That jolts me enough to fight back, but it's too late. Grant has no intention of letting me go, and he hoists me over his shoulder as he enters the living room. There are only so many times I can wriggle and ineffectively punch at the strong breadth of his back before I give up.

"There's a length of rope in the toolbox under the sink," he says to Tara as soon as the struggle ends.

"Rope is taking things kind of far, don't you think?" she asks.

"No. Rope is exactly what's called for."

"I hate you," I say, but no one listens to me.

Grant swings me off his shoulder and onto his favorite leather chair, which deflates with a whoosh as my weight hits. He looms over the top of me, quickly quashing any thought of escape. His legs hit mine, pinning me against the chair, and his arms crash down on either side of me. His lips are inches from mine. It's a very erotic position—possessive and domineering—but he doesn't make a move to kiss me.

"What I'm doing isn't as terrible as you think," he says, his voice low. "Can't you find it somewhere in your black, thieving little heart to trust me?"

My black, thieving little heart pounds, taking up residence somewhere in my throat. He knows everything. He has all the power. He's won.

"Trust you? Please." He's still too near, too earnest, so I force myself to focus on reality. This man works for an organization that would happily put me and everyone I love behind bars, even after all we've been through together. There are black hearts, and then there are black souls. "I'd sooner trust a snake."

"One year we've been married. One year I've never done anything to hurt you—and believe me, you've done plenty to provoke it. Don't you think I deserve some of your confidence by now?"

I provoke *him*? I set my jaw. "No."

He sighs and lifts one of his jail-bar arms long enough to run his finger along my cheek. It's a mocking gesture, condescending in the extreme, but his expression doesn't match. His mouth is a flat line; his eyes carry the look of a wounded animal. "You really do think I'm the enemy here, don't you?"

Of course I do. That's what he is.

"If only you knew how much I—" he begins and draws a deep breath, shaking his head.

I hold perfectly still, waiting for him to finish, but there's no time. Tara returns with a coiled rope under one arm and a handful of zip ties in the other.

"I thought these might be more humane," she suggests, indicating the latter.

"I don't want humane." Grant takes the rope and begins unwinding it with fearful efficiency. This clearly isn't his first time tying up a woman. "We need it to look real. A little rope burn goes a long way in situations like these."

"If you so much as bruise one of my wrists…"

"I'll kiss it and make it better later, I promise."

If Grant and I were the only ones in the room, I like to think I would have fought more. I'm not a woman who goes along quietly, and he deserves to have his eyes scratched out for how tight he makes the ropes across my chest and over my thighs—two areas he's never going to come near again, if I have anything to say about it. But there's something undignified about engaging in a marital squabble with another person present, so I sit with quiet loathing while he goes to work instead.

That decision turns out to be a good one, since it allows me a moment to observe Tara without my husband's watchful eyes on me. As expected, time has been good to her, settling her with poise and confidence in addition to her phenomenal good looks. She was always a little coltish when I first knew her, as if she hadn't yet grown into her skin, but she's definitely grown into it now. There isn't a cell in her body she's not acutely aware of and working to the max.

I can tell she's performing a similar assessment on me. Whatever she finds isn't nearly as complimentary, because an expression of aversion moves over her, drawing at her perfectly arched brows like the strings of a curtain.

Well, too bad. Maybe I would have done a better job glamming it up if she hadn't run off and left me for dead. I hope she gets wrinkles from all that disgust.

Grant tugs on a knot and steps back, a look of appreciation on his face as he appraises me strapped to his favorite chair in true *shibari* fashion. I refuse to give him the satisfaction of wriggling in discomfort, so I settle in with the same forced calm I use when I'm trapped in an air vent. This man has no idea how long I can sit without twitching a muscle.

Or maybe he does. I'm so confused right now.

"Okay," Grant says and gestures toward the safe, which I realize is wide open. "Tara, you can go ahead and grab the necklace. Make sure you leave lots of fin-gerprints. I need there to be no doubt you're involved."

"We've been seen around town for days now. I'm pretty sure everyone knows we're involved."

Grant leans close to me. "Not *that* kind of involved, in case you're worried."

"I'm not."

"You were worried before."

"I was angry. It's different."

"This isn't how I wanted things to turn out," he says, and then, with what I'm sure is feigned concern, "Do you want another glass of water?"

"No, I don't want any stupid water. What I want is a divorce."

His jaw tightens. "Too bad," he says and promptly ignores me to watch Tara plant clumsy evidence all over the safe's exterior and lift the necklace out of its shoebox.

"Holy shit," she says, holding it up to herself. Seeing the necklace on her perfectly sculpted neck rankles me even more than being tied to a chair, but I don't have time to protest, because Grant grows equally rigid at the sight of it. He's at her side in an instant.

"Don't get any funny ideas," he chides and slips the necklace into his pocket. "For the time being, this beauty belongs to me. No one else is getting their hands on it until I say so." He casts a look at me as he speaks, and I can feel my cheeks burn under the intensity of his regard. God, I hope he ends up dropping that stupid necklace off a cliff.

Tara just sighs. "You're in charge, I guess. So what do we do now?"

"We proceed as planned."

Tara's eyes widen. "But what about Pen? We can't just leave her there."

"Yes, actually. We can." Grant leans in to kiss me, but I snap my teeth at him. He settles for a softly planted press of his lips on top of my hair instead. "Sorry, my love, but you leave me no other choice. You've always left me no other choice."

"I swear to all that is good and holy, if you walk out that door without untying me from this chair…" I have a full speech prepared, buckets of names to call him, lawyers to contact to start the divorce proceedings—but it's no use.

He and Tara are out the door without so much as a good-bye, carrying my necklace and all hope of escape with them.

And *that's* when I start to kick and scream and struggle against the ropes that bind me.

THE DATE

13

(Eighteen Months Ago)

"I'M GOING TO KISS YOU AT THE END OF OUR DATE TONIGHT."

I paused in the middle of pulling open the door to greet Grant. My hair was only halfway curled, one of my eyeballs was bloodshot and raw from the clump of mascara I got in there, and I was still figuring out how to use the iron to get the wrinkles out of my dress, so I was wearing sweatpants.

In other words, it wasn't my most glamorous moment—as opposed to Agent Ridiculously Handsome standing in the decrepit hallway to my apartment.

"I just wanted to get that clear, right from the start," he said when I didn't respond. "If you have any objections to that plan, for any reason whatsoever, now's a good time to let me know. There's no telling what I'll do once this thing gets underway."

As if I was in any position to stop him. He leaned

against the frame of the doorway, filling it with his wide shoulders and the tightly fitting sweater he had pushed to the elbows. His lips were turned up in a smile, his hair was perfectly curled at the ends, and I could see the bulge of a gun at his side. It was a heady combination—this law man and sex god rolled up into one.

I found my tongue. "That kind of takes the fun out of it, don't you think?"

"On the contrary." His smile deepened, cementing itself somewhere in my loins. "Now we both have something to look forward to."

Like a true Southern gentleman—or a vampire—he waited until I invited him in before he crossed the threshold. I could understand why vampires had that rule when he brushed past me, sending jolts of electricity through my sweatpants and up my spine. My apartment, already a minuscule studio whose only valuable feature was a bay window that took up most of one wall, seemed to shrink to nothing once he filled it.

And now that he'd planted the idea of kissing inside my head, I could only imagine what other spaces he might be willing to fill with his massive bulk.

Dammit. This was going to be a long freaking date.

"I'm sorry I'm not ready yet. I need maybe ten more minutes?" I made a vague gesture around the apartment. "Make yourself at home. There might be some expired milk in the fridge if you get desperate."

He spun in a slow circle, offering me a long, leisurely glimpse at the taut globes of his ass filling his jeans—a sight that didn't help boost my own self-confidence. This was our third date, and I'd officially run out of cute outfits to wear to them. Any more of these, and I would have to answer the door naked.

When he finished the revolution, there was a line down the center of his brow. "Were you recently robbed?"

"Um...I don't think so?" I followed the path of his gaze, skimming over the empty walls. A lone futon made up my bed and couch in one, and a folding chair was pushed to one side in the rare event I had company. "Although I guess anything is possible in this neighborhood. Whoever the thief was, they were probably disappointed. I'll leave them something next time."

"This is your home." He didn't phrase it as a question.

"I warned you it wasn't much."

"You literally own two pieces of furniture."

"I told you that already." My apartment wasn't *that* bad. I mean, there weren't any rats or cockroaches, at least. "You're the one who wanted to pick me up here 'like normal people on dates do.'"

He turned his attention from the bleak walls to my not-much-better, sweatpants-wearing self. "I thought maybe you were lying."

I was about to ask what on earth would possess me to lie about living in semisqualor when I realized I already knew the answer. According to the story we'd set up between us, I was supposed to be a rec center dance teacher, not a successful jewel thief. A poorly furnished apartment in a bad neighborhood would only make sense for the former. Unless, of course, the successful jewel thief in question spent most of her money bailing her good friend Riker out of debt and squirreled the rest away.

But he didn't know that part.

I knew, though. The sole reason he'd wanted to pick me up was to get a look at my digs, to probe even further into my life. He was fishing again.

I wanted to be mad—throw him out in a fit of indignation, even—but I had to admire his technique. I also couldn't help but remember the reward waiting for me at the end of this date, that declaration of intent offered by a man so backwardly honorable, he'd lie and sneak and follow me around town and then draw the line at taking advantage of his position without my consent.

There was nothing else to do. I could hardly let him go without at least *sampling* that kiss.

"What do you know about ironing women's dresses?" I asked, changing the direction of our conversation a full one-eighty.

"As in, the theories of?"

"As in, I borrowed both a dress and an iron from Jordan, but I have no idea how to work it. You could make yourself useful while I finish getting ready."

He blinked. "You don't know how to iron?"

Not even a little. It was yet another in a long line of common sense, real-life skills that had never crossed my path before. The number of everyday tasks I didn't know how to do was much longer than this man would ever realize.

"No. I don't know how to iron. I also don't know how to cook, how to bowl, how to ride a bicycle, what the square root of any number is, or how to break down the thematic elements of *The Catcher in the Rye*. Do you want me to keep going? I've got all night."

His lips pressed in a firm line to hold the laughter at bay. "A bicycle? Really?"

"Listen up, Emerson. You can stand there judging my life choices, or you can speed things along so we can get this date started." I pointed to where the iron sat in a corner, mysterious and filled with water—which made no sense to me, because I thought water and electricity equaled immediate peril. "The sooner it starts, the sooner it ends, if you know what I mean."

He knew what I meant. "Go get me the damn dress."

"Okay, okay. Now it's my turn," I said, sitting back in my chair. I was drunk on laughter and chocolate cake, growing sleepy with the lights of the restaurant dimmed so low, we had to eat by candlelight. "What's your most prized possession?"

Grant drummed his fingers on the tabletop, either thinking about the question or pretending to think about it—I couldn't tell which. I couldn't tell much of anything at that moment, to be honest. Either this man had studied my profile so deeply that he knew how to plan an absolutely flawless date from start to finish, or this game of who-can-outsmart-the-other was going to be better than I'd thought possible.

The sheepish way he shrugged highlighted his sincerity and his sex appeal in equal proportions, doing little to help me make sense of it all. "Will I sound like a total tool if I say it's a painting I found at a flea market a few years ago?"

"A little." I smiled to show I meant no harm. He could have told me it was his gun or a knife he planned to hold to my throat later, and I'd probably have gone along with it, foolish smile and all. I was that far under his spell. "What's the painting of?"

"This is going to make me sound even worse, but it's not really *of* anything—that's why I like it. It's in the style of Willem de Kooning, though, of course, it's not the real deal. He's out of my price range."

Art was yet another thing I knew virtually nothing about, right up there with philosophy and literature and all the other classical arts. My dad used to talk about stepping up our game and making the shift from jewelry to art; I could remember a few afternoons spent wandering the Met, scouring the walls and coming up with exit strategies under the guise of scholarship, but I never learned anything other than the rotation schedule of the security guards.

Like most ambitious men, my dad had always stuck to one very narrow, very crooked path, which meant that art mattered only insofar as it could line our pockets. We stopped going to the museum after a few weeks, and when I asked if we were ever going back, he just tugged on my ponytail and told me he had other plans. Thus ended the artistic education of Penelope Blue.

"Don't tell me you're an art connoisseur on top of everything else," I said with a groan. It was becoming impossible to keep up with this man. "You're starting to give me a serious inferiority complex. Let me guess— you're a painter and poet in your spare time."

He tilted his head and looked at me with one of those long, penetrating stares, a scope straight to my soul. I tried my best not to squirm under the intensity of it.

"It's a fairly recent interest," he said cautiously. "One I originally picked up for work."

"Ooh, was it a big art heist?"

"Something like that."

I relaxed. For once, I wasn't worried by the innuendo in his tone. If he was fishing to find out if my team
planned to hit up the MoMA next, he'd need a different
kind of bait. Like I said—that sort of thing was above
our typical pay grade.

"Well, I recognize the name, but not much else," I
admitted. "What's he done?"

Grant's head didn't move from its cocked position.
"Abstract stuff, mostly—the one I have is a complicated
mass of orange and red, which is why it reminds me of
him. He used a lot of bright colors."

I felt like he was searching for a specific response, but
I'd always thought abstract art was kind of silly—like
something a five-year-old could do. So I did what any
woman trying to impress her date would in that situation:
I lied. "Oh yeah. Now I know who you're talking about.
His stuff is pretty."

Just like that, Grant's head moved back into place.
His easy smile once again warmed the table. "Now that
I've admitted my secret and shameful love of Dutch
abstract painters, it's your turn. Quick. Save my reputa-
tion and tell me your most valuable possession is something worse, like handcrafted doilies."

I didn't have to think very hard about it, but I took
my time anyway, enjoying our surroundings and the
fact that I was having an honest-to-goodness fantastic
time without even trying. Grant didn't tell me where
this magical third date of ours was going to take place,
but he'd decided to bring us to that great Italian place
an hour upstate where I'd stood him up the first time.
I understood the implication—*ha-ha, very funny*—but

he actually had the audacity to pull over at both of the telephone booths along the way to point out the various times at which I could have called to let him know I was lost.

You'd think that him being so obvious and mocking would place a damper on the evening—put up walls and encourage us to retreat behind them—but it turned out to do the exact opposite. *It's okay. I know you're an under-handed sneak, but I like you anyway*, Grant seemed to say. *Now try this pasta.*

And the pasta was good. The pasta was *amazing*.

Even more amazing was the fact that he'd had the restaurant cleared for the night. I didn't know how or why he'd pulled out all the stops, but we were alone in the cozy Tuscan-inspired interior, save for a discreet waiter who'd occasionally bring more food before retreating back to the kitchen.

Yeah. Not my typical date, if you'd believe it. In fact, the only other time I'd done anything remotely like this was when Riker and I broke into a Spaghetti Warehouse in the middle of the night and swiped a party-sized tiramisu.

"You've seen my apartment, so you know I'm not one to hold on to things," I warned.

Grant leaned over the table ever so slightly—a man hanging off my every word, though I couldn't say whether it was because he found me fascinatingly attrac-tive or because he thought my answer would be some-thing like the pair of Fabergé cufflinks my dad lifted off the French prime minister in the eighties. He'd been on a run of high-profile thefts at the time. You know, before I was born and ruined everything.

"The one thing I really love is this Sgt. Pepper

album that belonged to my dad." There. See? Maybe it wasn't jewelry or art, but it was enough information about my father to keep Grant interested. I knew how to play the game—and it just so happened I was also telling the truth.

His brow lifted. "You a big Beatles fan?"

"Not really. But 'Lucy in the Sky with Diamonds' was kind of our song." As was the entire *Diamond Dogs* album by David Bowie, the Rolling Stones' "Ruby Tuesday," and "Diamond Girl" by Seals and Crofts. "He had this great portable record player, and he'd put that song on over and over again. It's silly, but it's the only thing I still have of him."

I hadn't intended to get so maudlin, but I could almost see my dad grabbing the record and putting it on, taking me by the hands to twirl around the living room. When I was really little, I'd stand on his feet while he showed me the steps. As I got older, I mostly wanted to run and hide whenever he pulled out the vinyl. It was the only dorky-dad thing I remember him doing. *If things ever get tough, baby doll, you'll always have our song*, he'd say.

I still did, technically. But just the one record, the one song, stashed inside a kitchen cupboard for lack of a better place to put it.

"That's all he gave you?"

I shrugged in an attempt to deflect further questioning. It *was* the only thing I had of him—God, how much easier my life might have been if he'd left more—but I didn't want Grant to know that. If he didn't think I could lead him to my father's mythical fortune, he wouldn't have a reason to keep seeing me.

Pathetic, right? I warned you what kind of trouble an ex-football player can get you into.

"It's all I *have*," I said, emphasizing the last part. In reality, there'd been clothes and a watch I'd pawned, a few more records and personal belongings that helped ease my way. None of it had lasted much beyond the first few months. "I'll show it to you sometime. Maybe you can even rustle me up a record player so we can listen to it."

"I'd like that," he said. Now he definitely leaned across the table, interest kindling in his eyes. "I like *you*, Penelope Blue."

Oh God. I liked him, too. Liked him so much I was afraid to tell Riker and the rest of my team the truth—that I enjoyed his company to dangerously unhealthy levels. I was going to have to reevaluate my motives—and soon.

But not at that moment. Just then, with the lights down low, our stomachs full and our hearts open, his lips parting as they angled toward mine, I wanted nothing more than the kiss he promised me. And I was going to get it, too.

Or so I thought.

"I see what you're trying to do here, and it won't work." His mouth was close enough to mine that I could feel the vibrations of his voice, warm and enticing, but he placed a finger on my lips before I could make contact. "Shame on you. I said at the end of the date, and I meant at the end of the date. I hope to make you realize I'm a man of my word."

"That's the funny thing about men of their words. Eventually, they have to stop talking."

"And then what do they do, I wonder?"

I didn't wonder. I knew. They left.

But that wasn't the game we were playing, and I didn't want to ruin the moment by being morose. I was about to answer with a saucy remark about the other things he could do with his mouth, but a cell phone went off with a shrill break in the air.

"Goddammit." Grant groaned and sat back in his chair, looking grumpy at the interruption and no less appealing because of it. There's something about an unsated and clearly driven man that gets to me every time. "I'm sorry. I have to answer this."

It was the first of many such interruptions, and I acted then as I have every time since. With a wave of my hand and a forced smile, I let him at it.

Predictably, he rose from the table to take the call somewhere private, leaving me alone with crusty breadsticks and congealing alfredo sauce. I picked at the crumbs silently, doing my best to overhear the strains of conversation coming from the bathrooms. But just as Grant could move around in complete silence, so too could he drop his voice to indistinguishable levels.

It was something I'd need to remember for the future.

There were *several* things I needed to remember for the future—including the fact that Grant was doing a much better job of ferreting out my secrets than I was of his. So far, all I knew was that he had a professional interest in the Blue Fox, he was aware of my relationship to the man, and he was willing to go to highly unethical means to get information.

Warning bells should have been clanging loud and

clear, but the only thing I could think was that I hoped his ethics grew very, very thin. So thin, in fact, they'd practically be naked.

When Grant returned, I could tell any chances of that happening were gone. The relaxed, playful mood we'd been in for most of the evening had vanished, replaced by a wide step and a straight back. His mouth was set in a grim line. I'd have been lying if I said that version of Grant—man of action, FBI agent to the core—wasn't as much of a turn-on as the softer one.

"I hope you're the kind of woman who doesn't get mad when her date walks out halfway through," he said. There wasn't nearly as much apology in his voice as I'd have liked, but something about the anxious expression that replaced the crinkles around his eyes put me in a forgiving mood.

"I don't know what kind of woman I am in that situation. I've never had a date walk out on me before."

The anxious expression lightened a touch, and a surge of pleasure moved through me at having lifted it myself. "Do you feel a strong urge to throw that plate of fettuccini at me?"

I toyed with my fork. "Surprisingly, no."

"How about the water? Is there a chance it'll end up in my face?"

"Such juvenile tactics you resort to in times of anger." I made a soft tsking sound. "If I wanted to seek retribution for the outrage I've suffered at your hands, I'd be much more subtle than that. My revenge would be years in the making."

I got a flash of his teeth, a *real* smile, before he carefully tucked it away. "That I believe. The bill's taken care of, and you can feel free to order more dessert while you wait. The cab should be here in about fifteen minutes."

"Wait—you're not going to drive me back to town?"

He winced. "I'm really sorry, but I can't. I shouldn't even be taking this long to get on my way. We'll pause the date, okay? Pick up again later?"

Pause the date? Was that even allowed?

Some of my annoyance must have shown on my face, because he took two massive strides and pulled me out of my chair, holding me so close, our chests bumped and tingled. Well, his bumped; mine tingled. I'd never wanted any man to touch me as much as I wanted Grant to touch me in that moment. It was impossible not to imagine how the solid weight of his hand would feel sliding between our bodies, skimming my curves, settling on the softest, roundest parts, and staying there for hours.

Something told me that Grant was a thorough man in this, as in all things.

To my shivering delight, his hand did come up, but only to cup the side of my face. His thumb grazed my lips just long enough to trace the outline before falling away again. I couldn't say for sure, but I'm pretty sure a groan of my frustration escaped before he finished.

Then again, the sound could have just as easily come from him.

"I'm sorry. As much as I'd like to bring this date to an end the proper way, I have to run."

"You aren't going to tell me why?" I asked.

"You know how it goes. I *could* tell you, but…" He didn't have to finish. *Then I'd have to kill you.*

Despite my frustration—a mounting feeling lodged in my stomach and working like liquid bolts down my thighs—I managed a smile. "Then off you go. Rid the world of thieves and bad guys so it's safe for the rest of humanity."

I was careful not to place myself on either side of that equation.

Grant nodded and did a quick survey of the restaurant to make sure he hadn't forgotten anything before heading efficiently out the door. Predictably, it didn't make a sound as it closed behind him.

As soon as he was gone, I took a moment to make the same survey. The stucco walls, which had seemed so quaint and charming when we'd arrived, now looked dingy. A light in the corner flickered intermittently, and the mandolin music playing softly in the background picked up an almost country twang.

For the first time, I saw this evening as exactly what it was: a half-assed attempt at seduction, a cheap ploy to get information from a woman who was too stupid to know when she was in over her head.

Then the door flew open again, revealing Grant's dark, impressive profile against the evening sky. He crossed the restaurant without a word and pulled me into his arms. My head tipped back, my lips parted in anticipation, and my body lit up where it touched his.

"Fuck it. End of the date or not, I'm kissing you."

Grant's mouth crashed over mine in the arrogant, masculine sweep of energy that characterized everything he said and did. I toyed briefly with the idea of feigning outrage or chiding him for going back on his word, but what was the point? I wanted this as much as he did.

Who was I kidding? I wanted it more.

He firmed the kiss, his lips moving insistently against mine until I opened up and let him in. I lost all sense of my surroundings when our tongues brushed together. My world shrank to the four walls of that restaurant and then to the cage of his arms, his *mouth*. The only places I existed were where he touched. He was hard where I was soft, powerful where I was weak.

He was in charge—and never more so than when he released a deep groan and pulled away. His breathing was ragged and his skin flushed, but there was no denying that the decision to end that kiss was all his.

"Well, shit," he said, watching closely for my reaction.

I laughed. There was nothing else I could do. It was a giddy, reckless sound, but it was the only way to cover my dismay.

I knew, going in, that the touch of Grant's hands on mine was a dangerous thing. But nothing could have prepared me for the touch of lips and tongues and full-thrumming bodies.

That was catastrophic.

THE ESCAPE

14

(Present Day)

YOU MIGHT THINK THAT BEING TIED TO A CHAIR FOR HOURS on end would bring a calm reflection about one's life choices. After all, there's nothing like the passing of time to put things in perspective and force a little worldly wisdom on your head.

Wrong. The longer I sit here, struggling against Grant's damnably tight bonds, the further I get from calm and wise. I've spent more than enough time inside air ducts and kitchen cupboards to know that reflection time is rarely good for me. I don't get philosophical. I get annoyed.

And I'm *very* annoyed right now.

My fingers twist at an odd angle, working a knot near my side. I've almost got it to the point where I can nudge the jagged edge of my fingernail under the loop. I may end up with bloody nubs for hands when all is said and done, but I won't care as long as I can still use those nubs to wring Grant's neck.   —

Before I can rip the rope—or my fingernail—to shreds, there's a knock at the front door.

"Oh, sweet baby Jesus." My cry is half surprise, half relief. For all my illegal and hard-edged ways, I didn't really relish the thought of bleeding my way out of this situation. "Hello? Who's there?"

"Don't be stupid, Pen. You know who it is. Let me in."

I didn't know who it was *before*, but that irritated shout could only belong to one man. "Sorry, Riker—I can't let you in. I'm a little tied up at the moment."

I can't help it. I snicker. Now that the cavalry has arrived, I'm turning giddy.

"Not amused. I have about three thousand other things I should be doing right now. Either let me in, or I'm going home."

I kick my legs in a panic before I remember that no amount of kicking is going to loosen these Boy Scout knots. "No, I'm being serious. Don't leave—don't go—wait."

The following pause goes a long way in turning my stomach to—what else?—knots, but Riker's weary voice eventually picks up again. "What's going on?"

"I'm literally tied up. As in, to a chair, with real rope. You'll have to break a window."

"Any window I want?"

He makes it sound as if he's thought about this before. "Don't get too excited. I'd prefer if you could avoid drawing attention to it. You might be able to get in through the kitchen one."

He doesn't respond right away, and I'm afraid he's

going to leave me here as punishment for not taking the necklace when I had the chance, but the sound of shattering glass in the kitchen soon puts those fears to rest. Not *all* my fears, since the string of curses Riker releases indicates that he, too, might leave me here to stew in my life's mistakes.

"Goddammit," he mutters, taking his sweet time on his way to the living room. "I sliced open my jacket trying to get in. It's brand-new Italian leather. Look."

I do look, but only because that's the direction my head is pointed and I don't have any other choice. The jacket is sleek and cut close to his body, as most of his clothes are, but I'm not in the mood to admire it. "You look like a bargain bin mobster."

"What are you talking about?" He frowns at himself. "Jordan said this cut is very classy on me."

"Jordan is the queen of conciliation. She'd say you look good in the actual skin of a cow if you asked."

It's only then that he glances up to see me. His surliness and irritation disappear in an instant, and I know he'd have taken a knife to his precious leather coat himself for a chance to enjoy the sight all over again. "Holy shit, Pen. You're tied to a chair."

"Am I really? How odd, when that's exactly what I told you five minutes ago."

He responds with a crack of laughter that causes Grant's stupid red-and-orange abstract painting to tilt even more from where it hangs askew over the open safe. I'm really starting to dislike that thing.

"Laugh it up, my friend. Get it out of your system. I'll give you this one time, and then we're never speaking of it again."

"Oh, we're speaking of it again. We're speaking of this every day for the rest of our lives. What the hell happened here? Why aren't you gagged, too?"

I tactfully ignore the second question and nod at the safe. "We were robbed, that's what happened. Now, would you get me out of this chair, please? My thighs are chafing."

Riker's mouth opens, about to spout a thousand questions, but his eyes light with understanding as he takes in the crime scene. Considering how much energy we've spent arguing about that safe lately, it's no wonder he takes this moment seriously. Flipping out his switchblade, he begins sawing through the rope.

He works deftly and silently, freeing my limbs much more slowly than I'd prefer. It's probably for the best, since my hands and feet lie limply as they prickle back to life. My skin is raw where the rope rubbed against me, but there doesn't seem to be any blood. Which is disappointing, in a way. I want battle wounds, scars, physical signs of my captor's cruelty.

All I get is one sore fingernail and a few sleeping limbs. Go figure.

"Okay," Riker says. "Grab a bag and start tossing what you'll need in it. Clothes, shoes, any personal items you don't want to leave behind. If there's money somewhere—an emergency fund or jewelry we can hawk—be sure you grab that, too. What else?" He takes a slow turn, eyes roaming over every horizontal surface. "Is it worth going through Grant's office? Any papers that might come in handy for blackmail purposes? A gun he keeps in a locked drawer?"

At the mention of a gun, I stop massaging my foot.

We're not ones to resort to armed violence, and we never have been. With the right amount of planning and foresight and safely controlled explosives, there's no need.

"Whoa—slow down, Riker. It's not like that. There's no need to make a run for it."

He looks at me as if I'm the stupidest person on the planet, which, to be honest, I feel like right now. "I know you think you can bend the mighty Mr. Romance to your whims, but not even the best blow job of your life is going to get you out of this one. The second he comes home to find that necklace gone, you're culprit number one."

Um… "Actually, that's not true. This is the one time in my life he'll believe I had nothing to do with it."

"Forgive me if I don't stick around to find out if you're right."

"Oh, I'm right." I can't help it—I'm a little smug as I deliver the next part. "He's the one who stole it."

Riker's mouth opens and closes again. This has to mark the first time in our long history that I've ever rendered Riker speechless, and I take a moment to bask in it.

My triumph is short-lived as I try to get to my feet. My nerve endings are still firing up, and the adrenaline of my capture is ebbing away, leaving me shaky. I have to sink once again into that stupid chair to avoid another maidenly swoon. No way am I fainting twice in one day.

"You're kidding me, right?" Riker asks.

I know my sense of humor can be dark sometimes, but I don't joke about my husband running off with a two-million-dollar necklace. I don't think I *could*. "I wish," I say.

"Grant really stole it?"

I nod.

"Which means Grant also tied you to that chair?"

I nod again.

"But that doesn't make any sense." The scowling side of his mouth takes over, but I can tell he's not angry. He's perplexed. "Why would he do that? He's the one who called me to come get you."

I'm stunned for all of five seconds before realization creeps over me, slow at first and then gaining speed. It leaves a fiery path of indignation in its wake. "Oh, hell no. What exactly did he say?"

"Not much. Just that you might need a friend right about now."

"That motherfucking bastard." I make a vain attempt to reattach my bonds, but Riker did too good of a job cutting them. "It would serve him right if I died in this chair. Withered away and left him nothing more than my dusty bones."

"What are you doing?"

"Tie me back up. Make it even tighter this time."

"I'm not tying you back up."

"Then I'll do it myself." I know I'm working myself up for no reason, but I can't stop. What I feel isn't just anger. Anger is hot and explosive and makes my head feel tight. This is a full-body emotion, fury taking up residence in every nerve ending I possess. "He knew the whole time he was going to send you to free me. The stupid jerk. He wanted me to think I'd be stuck here forever so I'd do something drastic like gnaw through the ropes to escape."

Grant had been *laughing* at me. I'd been betrayed and

abandoned and overwhelmed, and he had the audacity to turn it into a joke.

"I'm going to end him," I say. "I'm going to kill him. I'm going to impale him with a stick and carry him through town for everyone to see."

"I don't understand most of what you're saying right now, but I like that last part. Let's do it."

That's when the laughing starts. It's mostly hysteria, the sound of hundreds of tangled threads working into a knot and slamming into my gut, but once I get going, I can't seem to stop. Grant, Tara, the necklace…it's too much.

After a minute, Riker joins in, which just goes to show what a good friend he is. He has no idea what's going on, but that won't stop him from breaking down right alongside me. That's solidarity, right there.

"Okay, Pen," he finally says, laughter fading. "What really happened today? Maybe you better start this story from the beginning."

"I will, but the beginning goes a lot further back than you think. Before today, before me and Grant, before me and you, before everything."

Riker's jaw doesn't fall, but it does tighten. "Back to your dad?"

"Back to my dad," I confirm with a nod. "And a certain someone I once called stepmother."

THE 15 PLAN

WE DECIDE TO SET UP A BASE OF OPERATIONS AT JORDAN'S apartment. My house is too hot, especially since we aren't sure what plans Grant has with Tara and the FBI, and Riker took over my apartment lease when I got married, so you already have an idea about the quality of living space there.

I'm not sure where Oz lives. Which is weird, now that I think about it. I wouldn't put it past him to sleep in a new location every night—a drifter without ties, a man on the run. The drama is nice, but he probably just crashes on Jordan's couch. It's pretty comfortable, and she has about eighty throw pillows, so it always feels like falling into a cloud.

I could use a cloud right now. Clouds and rainbows and an ironclad plan of vengeance—in no particular order.

Actually, there is a particular order. I'm starting with vengeance.

"When we find Grant, I'm the one who gets to punch

him. I know there are some here who maybe want to take a swing"—I shoot a very obvious gaze toward Riker—"but let's get that out of the way right now. I call dibs."

"You can't call dibs on hitting someone," Riker says, though he's not nearly as upset at being denied first blood as I'd expected. "There could be extenuating circumstances. What if I have to take him out from behind?"

"Then you tackle him, pin his arms back, and hold him for me. Let's not argue over details. The point is that I want to be the one to hurt him. Agreed?"

Riker nods. "Fair enough."

I feel better now that we have everything settled, but Jordan coughs discreetly. "I hate to ruin this moment, but is there an actual plan for *finding* Grant? You know, before we start tearing him limb from limb?"

"Um, that's where things might get complicated," I say. I have no idea where Grant is or where he might be heading with Tara. The obvious answer—somewhere inside the Federal Bureau—doesn't make sense, because the necklace was in their possession to begin with, and he could have taken it to them at any time.

Which means, of course, that it's time to face reality. It's cold, it's hard, and it's been staring me in the face far too long to feign ignorance any longer.

Grant has finally discovered the whereabouts of my dad's fortune. It's the one thing he's never bothered to hide his interest in, the one thing he values more than his stupid job, and the one thing that's kept him married to me all this time. Unfortunately, I have no idea how the necklace or Tara tie in to his plans. Believe me—if

Tara knew where that money was, she'd have ferreted it out years ago.

"Complicated as in he's hiding behind a government desk, or complicated as in you don't know?" Jordan asks.

"The second one," Riker answers for me. It's not a very *helpful* answer, especially since I don't hear him offering an opinion of his own, but Jordan accepts it in good form.

"So what happens next?" she asks.

"Easy," I say. "We just need to consider all the possibilities and get rid of the least likely ones."

That's another one of my dad's favorite maxims. *If you can't figure out the best way in, find all the worst ones instead.* It's a fancy way to describe the process of elimination, but then, he liked to make things a lot more complicated than they really were.

As the current situation attests. Like it would have been that hard for him to hide our money in a Swiss bank account like normal thieves.

Riker frowns. "Sure thing, Pen. We'll work our way through every possible hiding place in New York and work outward from there."

That makes for a second not-very-helpful answer, and I'm starting to get sick of it. He's been like this since I outlined the whole sordid tale back at my house. I was prepared for triumph and gloating—this was the ultimate opportunity for him to lay on the *I told you so*—but this brooding sarcasm is a bit much, even for him.

"It's not like we're without resources," I say. What we need right now are plans, not arguments. "Riker, you have all your secret underworld connections—surely someone saw or heard something about Tara in the past few days. She's the least inconspicuous person of all time. Start asking around to see where she's been and who she's been talking to. If she's on the trail of my dad's money, you can bet someone has noticed."

Oz and Jordan nod their agreement, but Riker maintains his stony front. I choose to ignore it.

"Oz, you should start hanging around the Whiskey Room under one of your aliases. See if you can pick up any chatter from the feds about Grant or Tara or the necklace. Something this big isn't likely to go unnoticed, and you know how much those guys talk once they've had a few drinks."

Oz, ever the trooper, nods in agreement. All that's left is Jordan's expectant air. Her willingness to follow me to the earth's ends is evident in the gentle arches of her brows. "And me?"

"You and I are going to take a little trip to Paulson Jewelers."

Her eyes drop to the infinity necklace that's still against my sternum. I almost ripped it off and tossed it out the window on the way over here, but I couldn't make myself do it. I needed that particular piece of jewelry. Not because I was feeling sentimental about Grant—God, no—but because it gave me strength.

This is the lie he told you. This is the promise he never meant to fulfill.

I would need to hold onto that anger until we caught him. Maybe even longer. *Something* would have to keep me warm at night once this was through.

"Remember the day I came over to ask if Grant could poison me with this chain?" I ask, waiting only for Jordan's nod to keep going. "How I said it felt like he was toying with me, like he was actively trying to get me to take the diamond necklace from the safe?"

I wish I'd done it, now. We might be banished to a tropical island somewhere, on the run and wanted by Interpol, but at least I would have been safe in the knowledge that *I* was the one inflicting pain on my spouse.

If wishes were diamonds and all that... I shake myself back to attention.

"I think it's because he *was* trying to get me to steal the necklace. He said something along those lines back at the house—about how his first choice refused to take the bait, so he was forced to turn to Tara as a backup plan. *I* was the first choice. He wanted me to do his dirty work, taking the necklace and leaving a trail of evidence behind. He was throwing that necklace at me every chance he got."

"But his backup plan for what?" Jordan asks. "If he wanted us to have it so bad, he could have let us get away with it in the first place."

"That's what we need to find out," I say. It doesn't make any sense to me, either, but one thing I know for sure: I won't rest until I have all the answers. "I'm wondering how much Paulson's might be in on it. Maybe they arranged the introduction between Erica Dupont and the FBI in the first place. Maybe Grant had them put a tracker on the necklace."

"It doesn't have a tracker." Riker is perfectly rigid. Usually, when Riker's overcome with emotion, he detonates with it. This quiet internalization, this turning off, is unlike him.

"It doesn't?" I ask. "Did you inspect it?"

The shake of his head is so small it's almost imperceptible.

"Was it a trap to arrest us, then? Catch us red-handed so we're forced to tell him what we know?"

That doesn't make sense, either, because Grant's had countless opportunities to do that over the past year and a half. So why this? Why now? What is it about that stupid necklace that causes the men in my life to act like incomprehensible beasts?

I ask a milder version of that last question out loud, but Riker just shakes his head, unable to meet my eyes.

"What aren't you telling us?" I ask. My voice grows sharper as I fall further out of my depth. "Was there a clue in that necklace about where my dad hid the treasure?"

"Not exactly."

If my voice was sharp before, it's like a dagger now. "What do you mean, *not exactly*?"

He sighs so deeply, it feels as though he's dredging up the very bottom of his soul. "The necklace is just a stepping stone, Pen. It's a bribe."

Bribes are something I understand, but not necessarily in this context. "Okay, so it's a two-million-dollar bribe. I still don't understand what that has to do with him trying to get me to steal it. It's not like he can bribe *me* with it."

Jordan's hand on my arm stills me from saying more. "What did you do?" she asks.

Well, for starters, I was born. From there, it's a choose-your-own-adventure of mishaps and questionable choices.

But she isn't talking to me.

"Riker," she repeats gently. "What did you do?"

The quiet internalization is done. He stands up with a twitchy jerk of his legs, and his eyes cast over the room—couch and table, lamps and chairs, anywhere but the three of us. "It's Pen's fault. It was her decision. Her choice."

I want to get up and start twitching myself, but I'm not sure my arms or legs will work the way I'd like them to right now. There's too much going on inside my body—cold and hot, foreboding and anticipation. All of it jumbles up and renders me immobile. What, exactly, is going on here?

"None of this would have happened if she'd just grabbed the necklace when she had the chance. I gave her the opportunity. I told her we could make a run for it."

The fact that he's talking about me in the third person, as if I'm not here, isn't doing much to make me feel better. Then his gaze zeroes in on mine, making me the complete focus of his attention and anguish, and I realize that I much preferred the Riker who couldn't look me in the eye.

I'm not sure I've seen him this angry before. At me, at himself, at a world that doesn't seem to care what becomes of us.

"I told you I had a buyer lined up for that necklace—I told you he was keenly interested in that particular piece and that he was willing to pay so much, no questions asked." His voice rises in pitch. "You didn't ask any questions, either. Remember that?"

He's mad at me because I trusted him to tend to the details? "I don't understand."

"I do," Oz says, though he doesn't bother to fill in the gaps.

"It was supposed to be a surprise, Pen. I didn't want to get your hopes up, because I know how much this means to you, but Blackrock offered more than money for that necklace." He winces, and a similar pain clenches my heart. "I told you he's powerful. He is. He's also connected. And he *knows* things—about the failed heist, about your dad, about you...information no one could possibly have access to."

Oz's grunt of confirmation is the only thing that pulls me back from the swirling black in my periphery.

"He told you about my dad? He knows what happened to him?"

"It looks that way. When I cut the deal, I made that information part of the payout. All we had to do was hand over the necklace, and he'd tell us everything he knew." Riker swallows heavily. "There's no way Grant could get anywhere near Blackrock on his own, not even with the necklace, but with you or Tara to grease the wheels..."

My world isn't black now so much as it's an explosion of colors—blocks of red and orange. I'm on my feet, dizzy with outrage, tempted to tackle Riker to the floor and demand justice.

I thought, a few hours ago, that I couldn't feel any worse than I did when my husband betrayed me.

I was wrong. Grant is my enemy, my foe, and I've always known that our life together has an expiration date. It's the only reason I've been able to stay married as long as I have. Knowing he's going to leave, knowing he's only on loan to me until life inevitably rips him away, is all that's saved me from losing my head and my heart.

But Riker? He's my friend. He's my family. He's the one constant in a life that's been anything but.

"And you never told me? You never thought that might be something I'd want to know ahead of time?"

It's hard for me to make sense of everything right now, but the underlying cadence is loud and clear. *Your father, the failed heist, your father, the failed heist.* It's the only thing I've ever wanted—to discover what happened, to understand how things fell apart so tragically.

Riker *knows* that. He knows, and he was in the same room with someone who has answers, but his need to be the Man in Charge is so strong that he didn't even mention it to me.

"You bastard. You selfish, single-minded, goddamn—"

"No." He whirls on me, and I can tell that his anger doesn't just match my own—it exceeds it. "You don't get to be mad at me for this, Pen. You had the necklace, you had the opportunity to take it, and you decided not to sully yourself with what I had to offer. And now Grant gets to sell the necklace instead. He gets to find the answers in your place."

"Riker, maybe now isn't the time..." Jordan attempts to intervene, but not even her diplomacy can save us. There's no coming down from this moment. Not even if you tossed us into a bomb shelter and let us finish each other off once and for all.

I cross the room in a flash, and my hands are against his chest—hitting, shoving, trying to make a dent that equals the one inside *my* chest. "You had no right to keep that information from me. You did it on purpose. You wanted to hurt me. You hate that I might have found happiness without you."

Riker grabs my wrists—the poor wrists Grant has already weakened—and I'm forced to stop. He pulls me close, within hugging distance, but this embrace contains no affection. His rigidity equals my own, his anger intertwined with mine.

"No. I stepped back and let you choose, just like you asked me to. It was the necklace or your fancy new life. It was me or him." His voice is so quiet that I have to strain to hear him over the rush of blood through my veins. "But you picked him. You always pick him. You always have."

He lets go so suddenly that I catapult backward and hit the floor with a thud. I'm dizzy with the fall and emotion, with outrage and something more. But Riker doesn't make a move to help me up, and neither does Jordan or Oz. For over a year and a half now, I've chased Grant in the pursuit of answers, and this is what happened. I'm broken down. I'm alone.

I rub my wrists—more in a symbolic gesture than actual pain—and Jordan softens. She extends a hand.

"Oh dear," she says. "What do we do now?"

Neither Riker nor I are able to look at each other, which is just as well, because there's nothing I could possibly say to him that would capture a fraction of what I'm feeling. Because even though I'm mad at Riker— *furious*, actually, more than I was when Grant tied me to a chair—I know he's right.

I did pick Grant. I did turn my back on our friendship. And, if given the same opportunity again, I'm not sure I'd choose differently. Even with Grant just on loan to me, even with our lies the only thing holding us together, I've found more contentment in the life we share than in all my wanderings with Riker.

I always wondered if Riker was aware of it. Now, I'm sure.

I slump to the couch again, no longer feeling the clouds' embrace. The couch is just fabric and wood and cushions, perfectly ordinary materials lumped together to hold me aloft. For the first time, I can see everything that way. Not as metaphors and wishes, not as what-if scenarios and dreams. My life is exactly what I made it.

A mess.

Silence threatens to hold us in place for hours, but none of us makes a move to break it. Which is why it makes sense when Oz is the one who finally speaks up. The man who rarely speaks is the only one who can.

"I don't see what the big deal is." He shrugs. "There's information to buy and a necklace to buy it with. All we need to do is steal the necklace back."

THE COUCH

16

(Seventeen Months Ago)

RIKER'S FAVORITE PLACE TO PLAN A HEIST WAS ON THE outer decks of the Hudson River Ferry. I never knew if he was afraid of being bugged or if he just really liked boats, but nine times out of ten, we conducted our plotting on the familiar waterway between New York and New Jersey.

Most of the time, I didn't mind. I liked a fresh river breeze as much as the next claustrophobic girl, and I was long since used to accommodating Riker's whims. But on a day like this one, with a bitter fall wind whipping along the water and a sky so overcast that the clouds weighed heavily on our shoulders, Riker's whims weren't at the top of my priority list. I mostly wanted a blanket.

"The job should be straightforward after that." Riker spoke directly into the wind, which meant Jordan and I had to strain to hear him, even though we brushed shoulders. Oz was, as usual, hiding somewhere in the distance. I figured he had equal chances of being the man reading the newspaper just inside the window or the captain of this vessel—they both looked enough like him to pass. "The key will be rigging the rooftop explosion in perfect alignment with the delivery driver's schedule."

"And we're sure Pen can make it up the laundry chute in that amount of time?" Jordan asked, glancing at me.

"I can't feel my face," I replied.

Jordan wrapped her hand around her ear and leaned closer. "What was that?"

"My face," I repeated, louder this time.

"What about it?"

"I can't feel it." If you've ever wondered how difficult it is to hold a conversation in forty-degree wind and sideways rain, the answer is *very*. "It's numb. Are my lips moving right now? It's hard to tell."

Jordan hid her smile behind a discreet hand, but Riker turned to me with a scowl. "No one cares about your stupid face. Can you or can you not handle your part?"

"I'll be fine."

"Are you sure? Because the last time we tried to use a laundry chute, you slipped two stories—"

"I'll get a pair of those grippy socks. No big deal." I wasn't as confident as my tone indicated—they must oil laundry chutes to try and make them unnavigable— but if we didn't wrap this up, Riker would make us ride the entire length of the river again to hash out the details. Not only was my body temperature unamenable to this plan, but I didn't relish the idea of reaching the terminal looking like a drowned rat. "We're about to dock. Can we finish this later? Somewhere with heat or a roof, maybe?"

"Oh, I'm sorry. Is my once-in-a-lifetime opportunity to steal a Civil War coin collection getting in the way of your comfort?"

"She has a date," Jordan informed him and turned to me to adjust my windblown hair. I wished her luck with that endeavor. I'd spent quite a bit of time that morning attempting to make myself more presentable than usual—lipstick and everything—but I doubted there was much she could do to salvage me now. "Grant's picking her up at the terminal."

I didn't have to look at Riker to know he wasn't pleased by this information—he was so hot and angry, my hair practically steamed flat again. "Oh really? You're meeting your FBI boyfriend at the place where we regularly conduct business? How nice. Would you also like to give him a list of the crimes you've committed in the past year?"

"I'm ninety-nine percent sure he already knows," I said. "I told you before—it's not us he's after. It's my dad's fortune."

"How can you be so sure?"

"Call it a woman's intuition."

"I'd rather call it a woman's infatuation."

That, too. "If you're so convinced I don't know what I'm talking about, why don't you come with me?"

Riker jolted so much, he almost pitched himself over the side of the ferry. "Come with you? Like, on your date?"

"Sure. Why not?" I shrugged with a nonchalance that was largely faked. I wanted Grant and Riker on a date with me the same way I wanted to dine with a bear and a wolf at the same time, but I wasn't sure what else to do. Riker wasn't going to be happy unless I made him see for himself that I could handle Grant.

Our guard dog was clever, yes, and he knew things about us that indicated months—if not years—of careful surveillance. And, okay, any more of those dangerous kisses from him and I was likely to give up the whole show, but I was taking just as much as I gave away. Riker wasn't the only one who could plan a perfect deception.

"You obviously don't trust my judgment, even though he's met Jordan and refrained from slapping her in irons," I said. "So come along. I'll introduce you. You can buy furniture with us."

As usual, he latched on to the least important part of that statement. "He's buying you furniture already? Let me guess. It's a bed."

I glared at him—ineffectively, I might add, as my eyes stung from the rain. Not only was Riker being offensive, but he was putting an innuendo on my relationship with Grant that didn't belong there. To need a bed, Grant and I would have to participate in activities of a carnal nature. Unless you counted the unholy thoughts that made up basically all of my waking—and sleeping—hours, Grant and I had done nothing of the sort.

Oh, we'd kissed plenty. I could tell you exactly how he preferred to hold a woman while his lips devoured hers, describe in detail the way he tasted when he was at his most demanding. I knew the contours of his body through his clothes so well, I could draw him from memory—and let me tell you, my memory liked what it saw.

Even though I'd always known Agent Grant Emerson was a strong man, nothing could have prepared me for the strength of his resolve in stopping each kiss before it got too heated. He licked and nibbled, taunted and teased, groped and groaned. But he never, ever took a bite.

He was a gentleman through and through. It was killing me.

"It's not a bed, Riker, and he's not buying me anything. He's just taking me to a store where I can trade my own hard-earned cash for worldly possessions. I'm thinking about getting a lamp."

Riker's scowl was replaced by a normal, everyday frown. "A lamp, Pen?"

I blushed despite the numbing cold. Riker could lay out all the insults he wanted without affecting me, could yell and scream and bluster until he lost his voice, and he never hurt me in the slightest. But that simply worded question spoke volumes.

See, my apartment wasn't a sad, empty space because I was broke. The reality was that I'd never felt an urge for furniture ownership before. I didn't want roots. I didn't want ties. I didn't want to grow attached to anything that could be taken away from me again.

To most people, a lamp signified nothing more than a convenient way to see after dark. To me—and, in many ways, to Riker—a lamp was a heck of a lot more. It was investing in the future. It was paying down on a life you weren't sure would be there the next morning.

"It's dark inside my apartment," I said and left it at that.

As was often the case between us, Riker understood perfectly. He nodded once and turned to look out over the water. "Okay. I'll come. But you'd better go inside with Jordan and have her do something with your hair first. You look like a drowned rat."

———————— ◆ ————————

Years ago, I took a class on manners. A *finishing course*, the fancy people of the world called it—one of those weeklong affairs where young ladies go to learn things like which fork to use and how to walk around with books on their heads. We'd been running a job that required me to make it through an entire five-course meal at a political fundraising dinner, and Riker was certain I'd do something to give away my roots, like shovel food in my face with both fists—which, let's face it, was a real possibility.

I don't remember much about the class except that I wasn't very good at being a gracious lady. For one, a gracious lady wouldn't have pocketed the silverware before she left. For another, a gracious lady would have walked away knowing how to skillfully manage the introductions between two men predisposed to loathe one another.

I only got as far as, "Grant, this is my good friend, Riker. Riker, this is Grant," before I ran out of things to say.

"It's nice to finally meet," Riker said stiffly and extended a hand. "I've heard so much about you." Most of the people standing around the glass-paned terminal could probably tell he was lying through clenched teeth, but Grant stepped up with all the good breeding and manners that no finishing class could ever give me.

He took Riker's hand in his own giant paw and shook, his smile deep and seemingly genuine. "You have the advantage of me there. I haven't heard anything about you, but any friend of Penelope's is a friend of mine."

What a liar. But a *cute* liar.

"Riker and I sort of grew up together," I offered. "I don't have any official family for you to meet, but he's as good as the real thing. Better, probably. We used to date."

Once again, I appeared to have caught Grant off guard with the truth. His startled gaze flew to mine for the briefest of moments before appreciation settled over his expression. Riker's startled gaze, on the other hand, stayed intensely *un*appreciative.

"I didn't care for her sense of humor," Riker said. Grant had yet to relinquish his hand, so they stood at an impasse, clutching one another as crowds of people streamed by. "In case you were wondering why we broke up. She thinks it's hilarious to pitch her friends into uncomfortable situations against their will."

Right. Because he never pitched me into uncomfortable places. Like boxes. Or laundry chutes.

"She does seem to have an unusual levity about her," Grant agreed. "I can see how that might get exhausting after a while."

"Hey, now—" I started.

"She's also surprisingly ambitionless," Grant continued. He finally released Riker's hand, turning so they walked shoulder to shoulder, leaving me no choice but to trail ineffectively behind. "You'd think a woman with so many talents would want more out of life."

"I want things out of life," I said. "Lots of things. Lunch, for starters, wouldn't be a bad idea."

"She's always been like that," Riker said, ignoring me. He still sounded sullen, but I could tell he was warming to the idea of discussing my flaws with an understanding ear. "You try to give her something nice—a present or a compliment or an opportunity—and she immediately wonders what the catch is. It's kind of sad."

"You guys know I'm still here, right?"

The look Grant tossed me over his shoulder indicated he was well aware of that fact and enjoying himself all the more because of it. "It's probably her daddy issues," he said.

Riker started, but he kept walking. "What do you know about her dad?"

"Not nearly as much as I'd like to. But I've always found that women who weren't properly cherished by their fathers have a hard time accepting the idea of unconditional affection."

"You think?"

"I *know*. And when you add abandonment into the mix…"

I gave up and allowed them to ramble on as we walked, torn between amusement at Grant's attempts to mine Riker for facts about my past and fear at how easily Riker slipped under his spell. Was that what I was like? Grant turned on the charm and chatted away, and I lost all control over my flow of information? If I spilled half the things Riker did, Grant must have my whole backstory by now.

Fortunately, any fears I had of Grant and Riker becoming best friends ended as soon as we reached the antique shop where I planned to make my first foray into responsible adulthood and lamp ownership. This was where Grant made his first error of judgment where

Riker was concerned—a mistake I have yet to see repeated, but one that made such a deep impression that it didn't matter how many heart hugs Grant offered later.

"Well, are we ready to head in?" Grant turned to me with a smile, indicating the large wooden door with a jerk of his head. "The sooner you pick out a lamp, the sooner we can head to lunch."

My stomach growled at the prospect. "You cruel manipulator. With an offer like that, I'll probably buy the first one I see."

He turned to Riker next, his hand extended. "It was nice to meet you—Riker, right? I appreciate you delivering her to me. I'll take care of her from here."

I was unable to hide my wince at Grant's unfortunate choice of wording, and both men saw it. They also both turned to me to see how I'd handle the situation. Riker clearly expected me to bristle and show my teeth—my standard response whenever *he* was the one trying to tell me what to do—and I didn't blame him for it. I normally hated it when he got all possessive and domineering, treating me like I was incapable of doing anything without him directing my actions.

But this was different. First of all, I couldn't lash out at Grant while we were still in the heady early days, or I risked upsetting the entire balance of our relationship. Perhaps more importantly, I didn't *want* to. There was a part of me—a long-dormant part, now sitting up and taking notice—that loved the way Grant's words wound up and down my spine, binding me to him.

I'll take care of her. A threat and a promise. Challenge and seduction. A bad idea that only made me want to play along even more.

So even though Grant made the first mistake—putting me in a position where I was forced to choose between them—it was me who made the second one.

I chose.

"I'll see you later, okay, Riker? You can come over and admire my new furnishings with Jordan."

"Sure thing, Pen." He pulled himself jerkily away from the door and out onto the street. "You do that. We'll just sit around waiting for your call."

"Your friend doesn't like me very much."

I whirled from where I'd been contemplating a lion's statue on a pedestal—the least practical item in the antique store and the one I wanted most. I'd already named him Horace.

"Who? Riker?" I tried not to let my alarm show. We'd been doing so well since Riker stormed off in a huff, the pair of us carefully avoiding the clunker of a cluster we'd made in handling him on the street. "Don't worry about it. He doesn't like anyone."

Grant didn't move from his position on the vintage floral couch he was trying to convince me to buy. He sat as only a large man on paisley flowers *can* sit: completely at ease, one leg propped on the opposite knee and his arm across the back, hugging the empty spot next to him. *Come sit by me*, that spot beckoned. *It's so warm and comfy here in this space we've created for you.*

I could picture it already, the way our thighs would press up against each other from hip to knee, how our hands would slowly wander into hidden seams to frolic together. He was clearly trying to entice me to buy that couch with hidden frolics, but Riker was in enough of a mood that the lamp was already pushing it. If I came home with a whole couch, I wasn't sure he'd ever forgive me.

To tempt me even further, Grant patted the seat next to him. He seemed to be on friendly terms with the proprietor of the store, a young, pretty brunette who dressed like she was about eighty years older, complete with the baggy sweater and glasses perched on top of her head. We could spend as long as we wanted, er, testing the springs.

In the grand scheme of life decisions, this one hardly ranked high enough on the scale to matter. It was like balking at a lie when you were caught hawking someone else's gold watch; refusing to share a big take when you didn't know how to spend what you already had. Sitting on a couch in full public view hardly mattered when I'd happily, willingly, all-too-carelessly let him knock my boots right off.

So I did it. I gave up and gave in and plopped my ass on that couch. And Grant caught me, even though I wasn't falling.

With a squeal, I found myself ensconced in his lap—which wasn't a bad place to be, all things considered, but I hadn't been prepared for that level of physical intimacy. Thighs touching, fingers brushing, maybe his hand on my face again as he leaned in for a kiss... those were the only places my daytime imagination was allowed to go.

This? This was strictly nighttime fantasy territory. My ass fit perfectly in the curve of his lap, my softest parts and his hardest ones nestled together, my legs swung sideways over his so that he could easily run a hand along my outer thighs, inner thighs, or any other part of my thighs he fancied. My arms had nowhere to go but around his neck, which they did, shamelessly and of their own accord, which meant my breasts pressed up against his chest. The areas where our bodies touched grew hot and heavy, and it was impossible not to notice the blood coursing through my veins.

It was a little like someone telling you not to picture an elephant, actually. I wanted to play it cool, act as though sitting in an insanely strong and attractive man's lap in the middle of an antique store was just another day in Penelope-land, but all I could see and feel and hear was that stupid elephant.

It was a big elephant.

"He doesn't like me," Grant repeated. The arms he had shackled around my waist twitched in a way that made me think they wanted to start roving. Not that he indulged. "And I can't say I blame him."

"He's incapable of smiling. It's because of his weird lips. He can only scowl or smirk. It makes him look a lot angrier and meaner than he really is."

I thought it was a good way of explaining Riker's attitude, but Grant shook his head. "Smiling wouldn't have made a difference. I told you I'm good at reading people. That man was prepared to dislike me before we met. I wonder why?"

Because you're an FBI agent and he's a thief hung unspoken in the small space between us, and I thought it was silly of him to ask when we both knew the answer. But Grant tightened his hold on me and locked his gaze on mine, forcing me into this weird and highly alluring staring contest where I couldn't escape the dark tunnels of his eyes.

Fortunately, I was used to cramped, dark places.

"He doesn't trust you," I said.

"Neither do you."

"Yes, but I find you incredibly attractive, so it doesn't count. I don't think you're Riker's type. He prefers brunettes."

The hold that was already crushing my waist grew intense enough to shoot pangs of hot, liquid longing between my legs.

"You find me incredibly attractive?" Grant asked.

"Is it that hard to tell? Here—let me help." I twisted as much as his grip allowed me, my squirming movements sending jolts of pleasure through us both. "Agent Grant Emerson, you are one strapping beast of a man, and even though I know it's a mistake, I can't stop thinking about you. About you taking me to bed." I lowered my voice, upping the ante. "About you taking me, period."

I didn't kiss him, showing a rare moment of restraint, but there was no mistaking the way he grew hard beneath me. *Strapping beast* was right. It was all I could do to bite back a low moan of my approval.

But if I thought being in his lap and outlining my desires was going to lead to something more, I was strongly mistaken. Grant seemed to take no pleasure in his body's reaction. He actually frowned, his muscles rigid.

"Are you two together?"

It took me a moment to realize he was still talking about Riker. "What?" I shook my head. "No. I told you. We dated a long time ago."

"How long ago?"

Was this another ploy to get information? I couldn't tell, what with the arousal and his grip on my waist and the fact that I'd never seen Grant like this before. He'd been playful and mocking and amused and suspicious... but never angry. This was angry.

"I don't know? Seven years? Eight? Does it matter?"

"Yes. No. I'm not sure." He stood then, almost tossing me out of his lap, heedless of the fact that a man in his current condition might not want to strut around so voraciously. I mean, I could watch an ex-football-player-turned-FBI-god strut around hard—because of *me*—for hours, but we were in a public place, after all.

His hand brushed through his hair as he turned to me, the tunnels of his eyes transformed to black holes. "You aren't lying about this?"

"Of course not."

"This isn't another one of your tri—?" He stopped himself before he finished, but it didn't take much imagination to fill in the blanks. *Another one of my tricks.* So much more than lying about the books in the library, he was talking about toying with his affections for the sake of the job. Selling myself for answers to my father's past.

I couldn't even be mad at the implication, because I wondered the same thing myself. Just how far was this man willing to go to insinuate himself into my life? Just how far would I let him?

I thought he'd turn the playful charm back on, afraid of having said too much, but he crouched in front of me and took my hands in his, perfectly earnest. "I really want to kiss you again, Penelope. More than is good for me."

My mouth grew dry, and I licked my lips to keep it running. The way his gaze followed the path of my tongue, as if he'd do anything to make that journey, almost robbed me of speech.

"Then why don't you?" I asked hoarsely. "I find it hard to believe a man like you would let anything stand in the way of what he really wants."

He swore and moved in. His hand cupped the side of my face, his lips prepared to devour mine. "You're a brat, you know that? Does anything unsettle you?"

If he'd waited a few seconds, I'd have given in to the folly of answering his question, but his patience gave out as quickly as my resolve. I was in his arms before I knew what was happening. And *then* I knew what was happening—the world was spinning, and my heart was flooding my veins.

I was also pinned to the couch by a man determined to unsettle me through any means necessary. Those means included wrapping a hand up into my hair and tugging on the strands until my head was exactly where he wanted it. The pain was slight but the meaning clear—*I am master here, and you will do as I command*.

I didn't have the heart to correct him. When it came to his groaning, possessive mouth on mine, I *was* his to command. He could press me into these cushions and demand anything of my body, and I'd have given it willingly. Skin and sweat and tangled limbs were his for the taking.

But he was not now and never would be my master. I could give as good as I got.

So I did.

My hands found their way under his shirt—an action

he seemed to appreciate, if his growl of approval was anything to go by. In retaliation, he increased the pressure on my hair, tilting my head back so he could continue claiming my mouth with his own. His tongue swept a determined path, twisting against mine in an explosion of taste and sensation. Since I couldn't move, I bit the side of his mouth and scraped my fingernails down his back, lightly scoring his skin.

His hips jerked forward, and I saw stars.

I have no idea how long we would have continued like that, falling deeper and deeper into the couch, the hard line of his erection pressing into the juncture of my thighs, but a discreet cough yanked us back to reality before things got out of hand.

Well, before they got *more* out of hand.

The cough was followed by a gentle query. "I assume you'll be purchasing that couch, then?"

Grant pulled away, dazed, as I took stock of the grand-motherly young woman struggling not to smile at us.

"Um, yes." *Dammit.* I knew this was going to happen. Fornicating in public was going to cost me a fortune. "It's very pretty."

"And comfortable," Grant said with a mischie-vous glint.

I smacked him on the arm, lingering a little too long on the hard swell of his biceps. Comfort and looks not-withstanding, that couch—and that arm—signaled a shift I wasn't sure I was ready for. Which was why I recklessly added, "And the lion statue, too, please."

Grant looked a question at me.

"To guard my domain," I explained. "Now that I have something worth protecting."

"Perfect. And I'll take the record player from the back room."

As far as I could remember, Grant hadn't even *been* in the back room, which was why I shot him a surprised look. He shrugged. "I figure it's high time you listen to that record your father left you. Nine years is a hell of a long time to wait."

I nodded vigorously, hoping the action hid the confusion of emotions swelling up and spreading through me. The kissing and the antique store, the jealousy over Riker—it was impossible to tell how many of Grant's actions were a planned seduction and how many were real.

It also didn't matter. Not now.

Because the truth was, nine years *was* a hell of a long time to wait, and it was sweet of Grant to extend this effort on my behalf...except that not once, in all our conversations, had I ever told him how long it had been since I'd last seen my father.

He was slipping. Agent Grant Emerson, man of determination and gentlemanly morals and oh-so-persuasive hands, was slipping.

With the taste of his lips still lingering on mine, the pounding of my blood drowning out any ancillary warnings, I had a few ideas about how I could get him to slip even more.

THE KISS

17

(Still Seventeen Months Ago)

"There. It looks almost homey in here, doesn't it?" Grant stepped back and surveyed my apartment, now adorned with the guard lion and a couch. He looked overly satisfied with himself for having wrangled me into temporary domesticity, but considering he basically hauled the couch up here on his own, I let him have his moment. "I like it," he added.

I squinted in the encroaching darkness of our midafternoon rainstorm. "Oops. I forgot to get a lamp."

"No matter." Despite the darkness, I could make out his wolfish smile just fine. "I'm sure we can find ways to entertain ourselves with what we've got."

I was all over that idea—and would have happily been all over *him*—but that wasn't the entertainment he had in mind. He rubbed his hands together and crouched next to the record player, which he'd had to put on the folding chair. It was as close to a table as we were going to get.

"Jeanine said she tested it a few weeks ago, so it should work fine. Where's the record?"

I didn't move to fetch it right away. Watching him get all sexy and down-to-business in my apartment was entertainment enough for me. "I distinctly remember being promised lunch first."

"I ordered takeout when you were in the bathroom." He checked his watch. "It should be here in about fifteen minutes."

Oh, how well he knew me, despite a dating record of just two months. I gave a squeal of delight and launched myself at him, fully expecting to be caught and twirled or at least embraced by the time I landed. But he stopped me with a hand on either side of my waist, holding me at arm's reach.

"Before you get too effusive, I should warn you that I won't be able to stay and have it with you."

My disappointment was a palpable thing, impossible to hide.

One of his fingers came up to stroke my cheek. "Sorry. Duty calls. I'm already pushing things with my section chief as it is."

Since I technically *was* his duty, I was starting to find that excuse wearying. Maybe if I'd played harder to get, he would have been ordered to spend more time in his pursuit of me. Penelope Blue would be his one and only concern.

I almost laughed out loud at the thought—it was far too late for that. I was hooked, and we both knew it. The only thing to do now was turn that weakness to my advantage.

I stuck out my lip in a pout. "Is that why you won't kiss me again? Because of work?"

The hand on my waist flexed. "No."

"Is it because you're still upset about Riker?"

Tighter still. "No."

"Is it because you don't find me attractive?"

I willed the words back as soon as they escaped. Not only did the question make me sound needy and pathetic, but there was a good chance it was the truth. I'd done enough meaningless flirting in the line of duty to know that sometimes, you had to fake interest in order to see results.

But then his hold on me reached even higher levels— the level of desire, the level of *need*—and he refused to let me budge. "Don't say that. Don't ever say that. Whatever else happens between us, know that this, at least, is real."

"Is it?" I couldn't help asking. How could he possibly know?

He didn't answer right away—at least not in words. With a low, rumbling growl, he dropped his head to mine for a kiss unlike any other we'd shared. Uninterrupted, private, and fraught with a passion so intense it couldn't be feigned, the feeling of his lips moving intently over mine was one I'd never be able to forget. It wasn't just that he was good at it—though he was definitely good, his tongue flicking expertly into my mouth, tasting and savoring and demanding I do the same in return. It wasn't even that he kissed with his whole body, holding me so firmly against his hard muscles that I was practically absorbed into his skin.

The gentleness is what undid me. Back at the store,

our kiss had been more challenge than anything else, the pair of us pushing and pulling to determine a victor. I'd wanted to force him over the edge, make him go beyond the boundaries he'd set for himself, get him to admit that he wanted me as much as I wanted him.

There was none of that urgency here. I don't know what I did or said to change things, but the way Grant held me—as if I were something precious, worth cherishing—shook me in ways I was unprepared to face. His arms crushed me to him, his kiss deepening until he was the only thing I tasted, breathed, knew.

In that moment, I felt eternal. Danger could come. Circumstance could rip us apart. The world could fall away beneath us. And still, Grant would hold me close and kiss me like I was the only thing that mattered.

For that brief space of time, I *mattered*.

By the time he pulled away, my breath was shaky and uneven, my entire body rattled. He pressed his forehead against mine, but the action didn't do anything to settle my pulse. If anything, the intimacy of the gesture only made my heart take flight all over again.

"That's how I know it's real." His words were a groan. "You could ask anything of me right now, and I'd do it. Any question, and I'd answer it. Any promise, and I'd make it. You know that, don't you?"

I did. Partly because of the way he looked at me, with stars overtaking the darkness in his eyes, but mostly because I felt the same way. I'd give up everything I had and knew if only he'd kiss me like that again.

"Why don't you try to sleep with me?"

My question startled us both. He blinked and shook his head as if trying to clear it. "I beg your pardon?"

Now that I'd spoken the words out loud, I couldn't take them back. I could only commit, so I swallowed heavily and tried again. "You said I could ask you anything. Why don't you try to sleep with me? What's stopping you from taking a kiss like that to its natural conclusion?"

He pushed me away, laughing without humor. His hands raked his hair in a gesture that spoke of the same desperation I felt. When he looked up, I could detect genuine pain mirrored back at me. "You don't want to know why I have to leave and go to work this afternoon?"

I shook my head.

"You aren't curious what caused me to run out on our date at that Italian restaurant last month?"

I shook my head again.

"You honestly don't care about anything else I may see or do as part of the U.S. internal intelligence network?"

Oh, I cared. I wanted to know. I felt the urge to turn the key to this man's soul and climb right in.

But I would never do it like this—not when I had him at a disadvantage. Not when it was unfair. I could be accused of many wrongdoings throughout my life and career, but I always, always played fair.

I shrugged. "We all have secrets."

His laugh that time was more assured—and warmer. Richer. As if he'd just found out the world wasn't such a terrible place, after all.

"Then I have one very easy answer," he said.

"Yes?" I leaned in, unable to help myself.

He pinched my chin, stopping me before I got too close. "Because I'm trying to woo you, Penelope Blue. The good, old-fashioned way. The way you deserve."

After a declaration like that, it was no wonder I grew mushy as I pulled my dad's record out of the kitchen cupboard.

Grant sat cross-legged next to my new record player, fiddling with the dials as he waited for me to return. It was such a normal and boyfriend-like thing, that relaxed jeans-clad pose of his, and I felt another pang of regret that my life was so far out of the realm of ordinary.

I wanted to deserve this man and the gentle wooing he'd undertaken. I wanted to be the kind of woman who could make him happy. Instead, I was awkwardly clutching a record worth a grand total of fifty cents to my chest. It was, at once, the most and least valuable thing I owned.

"Is that it?" He looked up, his lopsided and crinkly-eyed smile as familiar to me as my own. "Remind me to buy you a few more so you don't wear that one out."

That was it. That was all it took. A kind word and a seductive hint of the future, and I padded across the room to hand over the only thing left of my father—to the only man with the power to use it against me.

"It's not worth anything," I warned, lest he get any funny ideas about it being an original signed copy or something. "Just memories."

The crinkles around his eyes softened. "Memories are worth something."

Not nearly as much as he thought. A girl couldn't spend memories, couldn't eat them, couldn't curl up with them during cold winter nights without a roof over her head. "Then I should be living like a queen," I joked.

It was everything and nothing and all I could say in that moment. Grant seemed to understand, pausing as he waited for me to place the record in his waiting palms. When I finally did, his pupils went wide for a fraction of a second before they flared back to normal.

I pointed at the record's case, which was not the traditional psychedelic image associated with the album. I'd spilled milk on it when I was a kid, so my dad had been forced to store the record in an alternate sleeve, which he'd carefully covered in plastic so it wouldn't get ruined again. "I told you it's not worth anything. I actually made that cover."

One of his brows came up as he appraised the colorful scribbles of the makeshift cover. If you squinted and held it at arm's length, you could almost make out a face in the middle. "You painted this? That's some talent right there."

I gave him a gentle shove. "Don't be mean. I was little."

He looked curiously at me. "How little?"

"Oh, I don't know—four? Five? I can't remember." I ran my fingers over the familiar image. Clearly, I'd never been cut out for a career as an artist. "I'm not much better now, to be honest. I can only do stick people and clouds."

A smile touched his lips. "It just so happens that stick people and clouds are my favorite."

Grant Emerson was *my* favorite, though I wouldn't have dared to say so out loud. He pulled the record out almost reverently, careful as he blew off the dust and placed it on the turntable.

It was a waste of energy. As soon as the needle hit the vinyl, we heard a rip and a stretch. I glanced down, alarmed, to find that either time or mishandling had caused a scratch to form around the outer rings of the record. It was unplayable. Useless. Another memory turned to dust.

I sat back on my haunches and started to cry.

I tried my best to hide the welling tears and raw ache in my throat—the last thing I needed was for Grant to see how sentimental and weak I was capable of getting over my father—but he took one look at my quivering lower lip and swore.

It was a violent curse—a harsh and guttural sound that seemed out of place, given the circumstances—but I could only be grateful for it. It was the sound I wanted to make, the sound that had been lodged deep inside me for so long, it had become a part of my soul.

"Oh fuck, Penelope. I should have realized—" He didn't bother finishing his statement, choosing instead to crush me against him, his hold so tight, I could barely breathe.

Not that the wracking sobs threatening to overtake me qualified as breathing anyway. His hand moved in a soothing pattern over the back of my head, and his heart beat against mine in time to his words. "Shh. Don't cry, my love. I'm so sorry. Please don't cry."

I was so upset, I barely registered his words or the implication they contained. All I knew was that I *felt* them, felt the reassurance of his presence in ways I didn't know a human being could.

"It's not as bad as it seems," he continued, still petting and soothing, a man who knew he held a wild and dangerous creature in his arms. "I can get it repaired, I swear. We have tech experts who'll have it back to new in minutes. You'll never know it was damaged in the first place."

I sniffled, not yet ready to give up the comfort of being held like this. In all my life, I couldn't remember anyone holding me tight and rocking away my pain. Of all the jewels I'd stolen and all the high-class places I'd broken into, nothing could beat the pure luxury of this moment.

"Really?"

"Really." He leaned in and pressed a soft kiss against my forehead, his hands heavy and reassuring where they rested on my shoulders. "This one is easy to fix. This one I can do."

I didn't ask which ones he wasn't so confident about.

"I'll take it in with me now, if that's okay?"

I nodded, getting ready to wipe off the last of my tears, but he kissed them before I had a chance. If I thought it was pleasant to have someone hold me when I was about to break down, nothing could have prepared me for the vast extravagance of Grant's lips brushing away my pain.

My throat was tight and the jagged edges of my heart raw as Grant pulled me to my feet again, but there was no time to do anything more than wonder at how quickly things had turned around. A knock at the door signaled the arrival of my takeout, and Grant went to answer it, the record and its sleeve tucked securely under his arm.

Since I could hardly sit there crying forever, no matter how much I might want to, I managed a watery smile. "Food will help," I said. "For some reason, I always get emotional when I'm hungry."

"That's good to know," he said with a quirk of a

grin. "I'll remember that. In times of trouble, food is the answer."

"Preferably pizza." I sniffled.

"Noted."

"Especially from that place on 44th."

His only reply was a warm laugh and a promise to write it down.

THE
INTERR18GATION

18

(Present Day)

TRACKING DOWN A ROGUE FBI AGENT AND HIS CAT burglar cohort isn't nearly as easy as it sounds.

In the movies, all it takes is a few taps on the keyboard to access surveillance cameras or the lucky timing of a GPS tracker placed surreptitiously in a shoe. We are, unfortunately, without cameras or trackers or any other technological advantage that might give us an edge. What we do have, however, is a whiteboard. It's the one Jordan uses to keep her highly organized lists of grocery items and complex chemical equations, but I've taken it over.

Man Hunting Task List, I scrawl at the top. Now that I know Riker has been arranging clandestine meetings with criminal overlords behind my back, we need to act quickly. We don't have a lot of time to root around for information—the second Grant lifted that necklace from the safe, the countdown began.

We started this race a year and a half ago, standing near a sewer grate. Two people not exactly meeting for the first time but doing a heck of a good job pretending we were. Now that the finish line is within reach, I'm ready for the final sprint.

My heart might be broken and my best friend a traitor, but never let it be said that Penelope Blue gave up without a fight.

"As far as we can tell, we have three leads," I say. I tap the marker on the top of the board and start by writing Blackrock in bold letters. "We know they're going to try and sell the necklace to Blackrock in exchange for information, so Riker, you should start there."

He looks up from where he's slouched in the corner. "Why me?"

I don't have the time or the energy to placate him right now. "Because you're the only one who knows what he looks like or where he is. Find him, tail him, and see if Grant and Tara are skulking around. You might be able to intercept them before they can hand the necklace over."

"It doesn't work like that," he mutters. "He's not just sitting around an office taking appointments. He doesn't check in on Foursquare."

"But you've met him before, and you had a plan to deliver the necklace, right?" Jordan asks, much more gently than I was about to. "Can't you find him that way?"

"You don't find Blackrock. He finds you."

I wish he'd stop acting like we're too stupid to understand the intricacies of criminal relationships. The four of us understand nothing *but* criminal relationships. It's all we know, all we're good at. Just ask my husband.

"So they don't have any way to contact him either,

right?" I ask. The effort to remain calm stretches my smile thin. "We have time?"

"They have the necklace. That's enough—especially since you said Grant had Tara leave fingerprints behind." He looks at me, a cold, hard chip of ice on his shoulder. "There aren't a lot of things that would get the attention of a man like Blackrock, but an FBI agent tying his wife to a chair and running off with both his mistress and government property is one of them."

"She's *not* his mistress."

"Oh, I'm sorry. The woman he betrayed you with in every other possible way. He's a real prince."

Jordan stages another timely intervention. "Can you think of any other way to contact Blackrock, Riker? Side routes, a friend of a friend, a bribe?"

"I can try, but I'm telling you—he's not an easy man to find. The one time we had an actual face-to-face meeting, it was in the back of an unmarked van with a gun pointed at my head." He looks at me again, as cold and angry as ever. "He's as dangerous as he is powerful. It's why I was trying to keep you out of it."

I'm not sure whether I can believe him anymore, so I ignore the comment and start writing again. "Okay, that brings us to number two on the list—Paulson Jewelers. Jordan, I think you should follow through with our original plan by making a visit and poking around. Take Oz with you and pretend to be looking at engagement rings or something. The staff might let something slip about Grant or Erica or anyone else who might be involved."

"What are you going to do?" Jordan asks.

That's the two-million-dollar question. I turn my back to the group and slowly write out the last item on the list. Three careful letters—letters I've become hauntingly familiar with over the years.

"FBI." The marker screeches as I finish. "One of us is going to have to report the theft and see how deeply the authorities are involved."

Jordan sucks in a sharp breath. "Are you sure that's wise?"

Not at all. I cap the pen and survey my board with something approaching triumph. I might not have Riker's flair for planning a flawless heist from start to finish, but it's not bad.

"It has to be done," I say. "Either the feds are in on this scheme, which means they know where Grant is right now, or he's using them just as much as he used me."

"Which means…" Jordan doesn't have to finish. If he's using the FBI as a way to get to my dad's money, then Grant is even more dangerous than we suspected. That's a whole different level of treachery.

"Simon isn't going to be happy to see me, but I have to talk to him. He knows Grant better than anyone." Better than me, even. "Fair warning, though—he's probably going to slap me in handcuffs and throw me in a dungeon. There might be torture involved. That man has wanted to waterboard me since the day we met."

"What is it you're always saying, Pen?" Riker asks. "If they haven't arrested us by now, they're obviously not going to?"

"That was before my husband ran off with a two-million-dollar necklace that was supposed to be in their safekeeping," I say, but there's no use painting it in any other light. It's off to the gallows I go.

"Well, well, well. If it isn't the illustrious Mrs. Emerson."

I stiffen at the sound of Simon's voice mocking me from behind, but I don't turn to face him. First of all, I'm not Mrs. Emerson. Grant made the offer of his name when we got married, but I politely declined. And by politely, I mean that I told him the only way I'd ever cease being a Blue is if we swapped last names entirely.

Unsurprisingly, he didn't take me up on the offer. Seems his idealized view of being absorbed into another person's identity only goes one way.

Second of all, I'm not about to give Simon the satisfaction of subservience. I came in prepared to play nice, but that was before he had me detained and thrown into an airless interrogation room for eight hours while they went over the crime scene. If he wants to talk to me now, he can face me inside the interrogation room like a good little federal agent.

"Have anything to say for yourself?" he asks.

That I want nothing more than to climb into the mail cart and hide there until it's safe to leave? Too bad. I'm not giving him that ammunition. Instead, I smile sweetly and lift my wrists. "Are the handcuffs really necessary? I walked in of my own free will, if you recall."

Now that his pecking order has been established, Simon takes the seat across the wood-grain table from me. He's wearing his customary noose-like tie, his brown hair weighed down with enough product to set the entire room on fire. His nostrils pinch once he sees how unruffled I am, but I'm not sure how else he expects me to react. This is hardly the dungeon of my worst nightmares. Some air conditioning would be nice, but it turns out FBI interrogation rooms are a lot nicer than the inner city ones they show on cop dramas. I feel like I'm inside an accountant's office more than anything else.

Well, an accountant with a BDSM fetish, maybe. These handcuffs are tight.

"Let's call them a precautionary measure." Simon pauses until I lower my wrists again. "Your fingerprints *were* found at the scene."

"Of course they were. It's my house. I live there. I occasionally touch the things inside it."

"Including the safe?" He tosses a manila folder in front of me, and an arc of photographs of my living room fan out in an artful arrangement. "There seemed to be an awful lot of fresh prints all over it."

"I don't know if you remember, but I came in to these exact offices to drop off Grant's passport last week—you can check that with your security log. As it happens, we keep the passports in the safe. I had no choice but to open it. Mine's probably still in there, if you guys haven't already bagged it up and sent it off to forensics."

Simon looks as if he doesn't want to believe me—his face screwed up like a child being denied an ice cream cone—but he doesn't have any other choice. It's the truth, after all.

"Okay, fine," he concedes. "You have an excuse for that one."

"Let me stop you right there—I have an excuse for *all* of them, and I'm not afraid to use them." I lift my wrists and shake them at him, the metal rattling like old prison chains. "Take these off, and maybe I'll be willing to give you information that'll help your investigation."

"Do you *have* information that will help my investigation?"

I cock my head at him. "Did you happen to notice a few restraints on the chair in the living room? The ones that made it look like someone was tied up there for a while?"

"We noticed."

"Well, that someone was me. I was there when they took the necklace. I saw the whole thing."

He sits back, clearly surprised by my candor and unsure what to do about it. I should probably be more insulted that he thinks me incapable of telling the truth, but it's no worse than Grant's reactions over the past year and a half. I can almost picture my husband in the room with us, leaning against the door, his eyes crinkled in amusement as I make no attempt to fool him.

Something inside my chest snags. Whatever his faults, Grant has always been prepared to accept me for who I am. Lying, telling the truth, wasting precious government resources with wild goose chases…I like to think he takes pleasure in them all.

Then again, I also like to think he'd never betray me when it comes to the important things.

"So you saw the theft take place?" Simon asks.

"Yep."

"And you didn't report it right away?"

"Nope."

He makes a strange grunting noise, not unlike a pig crossed with a crow. "And you have the audacity to ask me to undo your cuffs? It sounds to me like you were an accomplice. You're not going anywhere."

I shrug. "Suit yourself, but I think it's only fair to

give me a pass on this one. The reason I didn't report it is because Grant is the one who stole it."

Simon's reaction is immediate. He leans sharply across the table, his face inches from mine. "You lie."

"I wish. Look me in the eyes. Give me a polygraph. Torture me. It'll still be what happened, even after you take out your frustrations on me." I don't look away from the icy gaze he has locked on me. "I know you don't like me, Simon. You never have, and I don't blame you for it. But that doesn't make this any less true."

"You were in on it, weren't you." He doesn't phrase it as a question. "You made him do it."

"No. I walked in on him in the middle of the job—and believe me, I was just as surprised as you are." Just as surprised, just as outraged, just as hurt. "But he did have an accomplice, if that makes you feel better. Once you finish running the prints, I'm sure you'll find a match for her."

"Who is it?"

"Her name is Tara Lewis. That's T-A-R-A L-E-"

"I know who Tara Lewis is," he snaps. I can tell the exact moment his brain makes the connection—Tara Lewis and Penelope Blue, related by marriage, bonded by loss—because there's an almost-human glimmer in his eyes. "It was really her?"

"Oh, it was her. The pair of them had been cooking it up for days, if not longer. They were on pretty intimate terms, if you know what I mean."

He looks suspicious at that, eyeing me slantwise, but he makes a fastidious motion with his hand that I assume means he wants me to keep going. Unfortunately for him, this isn't a free-for-all. I've learned everything I need to know. The FBI is no more aware of Grant's whereabouts than I am.

"So, there's your mystery solved," I say. "I gave you the names you wanted. Now, will you please let me go? Since you don't seem to be doing anything to find him, I'd really like to get back to searching for my missing husband. There are a few words I'm saving for his ears only."

Simon holds my gaze for a moment longer before pulling out his phone and stabbing the buttons. "Shit. Shit, fuck, damn."

It's the most discomfited—and human—I've seen him, and pity moves through me. He and I don't have so many differences, after all. We both want nothing more than for Grant to walk in and look us in the eye. We both want to know how something as meaningless and empty as money could have turned him rogue.

But then Simon glances up at me, and I can tell that any human feelings he has aren't going to last. "I knew this was going to happen. I knew you were pulling him in too deep."

I brace myself for what's coming next—the accusations and the fury, Simon pulling out the handcuff keys and swallowing them so I can never walk free again—but I'm saved by a knock on the door. Simon begrudgingly calls for the visitor to enter, and I'm greeted by my lawyer, arrived to uphold my rights.

By lawyer, I of course mean Oz.

He's in an impeccable costume, as always, a sort of scrambled together, absent-minded professor look, with his button-down shirt untucked on one side and a coffee stain down the front. He fumbles to make it through the door while balancing his briefcase, but his eyes are alert behind wire-rimmed glasses.

It's so perfect, I almost want to give him a standing ovation. If he'd come in sharp and polished, the kind of lawyer that accomplished jewel thieves are expected to keep on retainer, Simon might have dug in his heels and refused to let me go. But this? It sealed my innocence in ways that a thousand truths could never do.

My friends are seriously the best. I knew they wouldn't let me disappear into this building for so many hours without sending an extraction team. We could teach Simon and Grant a thing or two about loyalty.

"I'm here on behalf of, ah, Penelope...Blue, is it?" Oz consults one of the papers in his hand, which shakes just enough to give the impression of a drunk who's not as drunk as he'd like to be. "I'm sorry I'm so late. I just got the call a few hours ago, and the subway was a mess. Is this the right room?"

"It's the right room." I cast a meaningful look at Simon. "I'm being unlawfully detained in here."

Oz blinks at my handcuffs. "Are you? That can't be right."

"She's free to go," Simon mutters. He scoops up the file with one hand. "But don't leave the area. We're not done with you."

I feel pretty confident they'll *never* be done with me, but that's beside the point.

"Simon—" I call out before he has a chance to leave, raising my hands to show he still has to physically release me.

He doesn't want to do it—draw nearer to me, be close

enough to actually touch my skin—but he pulls the keys out of his pocket all the same.

I use the moment of intimacy, strained though it is, to ask the question that's nagged me since I walked in here. "Will he be in a lot of trouble for this?"

Simon stops in the middle of turning the key.

"It's just…" I bite my lip and try to think of a way to phrase my question without giving anything else away. "I know I'm the last person in the world you want to share government secrets with, but is there something I'm missing? Can you think of a reason he'd go out on his own like this?"

"I might ask the same thing of you, Penelope Blue." Even though he rhymes as he says it, the phrase holds none of the singsong quality of Grant's playful tone. He's stark and cold, and he bites off the syllables like they cause him pain.

He's not the only one. My heart pitters once, patters twice, and then fizzles to a stop. In that moment, I realize I'm done. With lying, with pretending, with tiptoeing around like I have something to hide.

"I refuse to believe it," I say. "Not even *he's* willing to go that far to find my dad's fortune. He wouldn't just throw everything away like that."

"Are you sure?" Simon yanks the handcuffs from my wrists, the edge of the metal leaving yet another painful mark. "As far as I'm concerned, he threw everything away the day he married you."

◆

"Thank you for rescuing me." I stretch on my tiptoes to plant a kiss on Oz's cheek as soon as we round the corner and escape the watchful eyes of the FBI building. "Your timing was perfect. I got all I could out of him—it was like talking to a particularly uninformed wall."

It's kind of ironic, saying that to a man who is a particularly *well*-informed wall, but Oz just shrugs it off.

"The worst part is, I'm not any closer to the answers. The authorities weren't even aware of the theft until I reported it. If they have any idea where Grant is or what he's doing, it goes a lot higher than Simon's pay grade."

"No need."

"For thanks?" On the contrary, I don't thank Oz enough. He's silent and capable in the background, always there when I need him. "There is too a need. I'm pretty sure Simon was prepared to keep me there until Grant himself came to save me."

"No. For answers. We've got him."

Cryptic though the remark may be, I understand Oz in an instant. There's no need to continue feeling Simon out for information because the team managed to track Grant down on their own, bless every last one of them. Poor Oz has to physically restrain me as I tug on his arm, peppering him with questions. "Where is he? What is he doing? Can I talk to him? Please tell me Tara died in the crossfire."

That last one makes him break out in a smile. I was wrong before when I said that Oz has no distinguishing marks. When he smiles to reveal charmingly crooked teeth and a near-dimple in his right cheek, I'd spot him anywhere.

"No one has killed anyone yet," he says. "We thought you'd want to go first."

THE CHALLENGE

(Sixteen Months Ago)

"YOU MEAN HE LITERALLY HELPED THE OLD WOMAN across the street?" I released an unladylike cackle and sat back in the corner booth of the Whiskey Room, where I currently held court with Simon and two other agents from their department. "As in, stopped the protesters, took her arm, and escorted her through an armed militia?"

"On my honor." The smallest of the trio—a techy guy in plastic-rimmed glasses named Nathan who I was developing a minor crush on—held up his hand. "To this day, it remains one of the most surreal feats I've seen performed on the job. He was like Moses parting the Red Sea. And I've seen some crazy stuff, so you know that's big."

I wanted to ask him what some of those feats might be—just out of curiosity—but although liquor had loosened this group's collective tongue enough to share

Grant's more impressive exploits, they were still a federal-looking bunch. And, yes, people can *look federal*. It's all in the shoulders. Even Nathan, who clearly spent most of his time hunched over a keyboard, looked like he could handle himself on the mats.

If their impressive statures weren't convincing enough, you only had to listen. In all my time among the men in black, one of the things that stood out the most was the way they paused a fraction of a second before speaking, running their entire dialogue through some kind of official internal checkpoint first.

"Okay, but that doesn't really count," I said. I turned my brightest smile toward the man on the end—Paulie, his friends called him, though the best I could tell, his name was actually Bernard. He looked more like a Paulie, with a calm air and a Hawaiian shirt I was pretty sure wasn't regulation uniform. "That's the kind of story a guy's friends are prepped ahead of time to tell his girlfriend so she gets all swoony inside. I want to know the dirty stuff. The stuff he wouldn't want his mother to know."

"It's classified." Simon, who'd been characteristically silent until that point, narrowed his eyes at me. "We couldn't tell you even if we wanted to."

I was fast learning that an FBI agent and his partner forged similar bonds to those between a jewel thief and her cohorts. The two men worked together, sparred together, shot at targets together, pitched themselves into life-and-death situations together. They were understandably tight. And protective.

Just as Riker and Grant had never warmed up to each other, so too did I have a hard time sharing a room with

Simon without feeling the urge to squirm and check my teeth for diamonds. I had the feeling he knew as much about my life as Grant did…and had about one-tenth as much appreciation for it.

"Well, I already know he'll abandon a girl out in the sticks of New York the second one of you idiots call." I smiled to show there were no hard feelings. Nathan, bless his bow tie–wearing heart, blushed. "I know he's habitually late meeting his girlfriend for dates, and I know he sometimes works for so many hours straight, he actually slurs his words."

I tapped my chin coyly and tried to come up with more seemingly innocent facts about Grant's professional life, but they were surprisingly difficult to conjure. Most of the things I knew about his past had been gleaned the unethical way, via Oz and Riker and a search through the deepest, darkest parts of the Internet, and I didn't care to share the things I knew that weren't work related.

Call me sentimental, but I wanted to keep the wooing to myself, clutched to my heart and cherished in ways that would have shamed the Penelope Blue of a few months ago. Riker and Oz knew almost nothing about the dates Grant took me on, and Jordan got the blacked-out version, but there was fodder for a hundred journal entries, complete with swirly lines and googly-eyed hearts.

So far, Grant had taken me to eighteen dinners, seven lunches, one long, romantic walk along the docks—the ones of the near-drowning wharf job, in case you were wondering—and spent an entire afternoon teaching me to shoot ducks in a carnival game at Coney Island. I was a terrible shot, a fact that had afforded him infinite amusement, and he solemnly vowed to protect me from any and all future gunfire, since I was clearly useless on my own.

He'd also returned my dad's record in mint condition, as promised. He'd hunted down the original cover and presented it a few weeks before with a shiny red bow. I didn't cry or anything embarrassing like that, but I came close when he put the record on and twirled me around my apartment floor, the pair of us dancing beneath tangerine trees and marmalade skies.

In short, he was perfect. Ever since that day at the antique store, he'd been attentive, interested, and not the least bit pushy. It was starting to freak me out. He didn't push for information about my dad, he didn't push me to stop stealing things, and he didn't push for anything more than the occasional knee-knocking kiss before sending me on my way. It was like he was on a lengthy stakeout, and I was the building he needed to watch.

Not *enter*, mind you. Just watch.

I meant that as euphemistically as possible. There was no entering happening in this building at all—and the building was seriously gagging for it.

I chose my next words carefully. "I also know he's like a dog at a bone when it comes to certain cases. Especially cases that have grown *blue* from being out too long."

The men's reactions told me everything I needed to know about them. Paulie nodded, agreeing with me. Nathan looked sheepish in the way of men who always feel they should apologize for the general shortcomings of their sex. And Simon—oh, Simon—he pokered up so much, I was surprised he didn't turn to stone.

So there it was. Paulie and Nathan didn't know anything about me beyond the cover story, but Simon was clearly in on the ruse—and he was none too happy about it. I almost felt like I should introduce him to Riker. They'd have so much to talk about.

"There's nothing wrong with being diligent," Simon said.

"There's diligent, and then there's obsessed."

"He's not obsessed."

"You sure about that? It looks a little like obsession from where I'm sitting."

Everything that wasn't already closed up on Simon's body tightened to black-hole levels of impenetrability. His nostrils became pinpricks, and his eyes narrowed to serpentine slits. "I'd watch myself, if I were you. Don't presume to understand his motivations—or how far he's willing to go to get what he wants. You have no idea how long he's been tracking y—"

His eyes opened again, as if suddenly noticing that we were in a bar and that Paulie and Nathan were looking at him with something approaching concern.

"How long he's been tracking certain cases," he amended. Poorly, if you asked me. It seemed that not all FBI agents were the close-lipped professionals they ought to be. Grant would have never let that slip—not even if I did everything I could to provoke him, not even if I started stripping off my clothes in an attempt to break him down.

A strange feeling of pride filled me at that thought. *My boyfriend might be killing me with chivalry, but he's a way better agent than you.*

"Would you look at that? It's four of my favorite

people in the whole, wide world." Grant approached our booth with a smile on his face and the top two buttons of his shirt undone. No combination of things could cause a flustered distraction as much as that. He had a marvelous chest—I saw it once when he was changing shirts, a brief flash of tawny skin and a smattering of hair. Those two buttons were like a peep show reminding me of what I couldn't have. "I would have said my four absolute favorites, but I'm not sure my mother would forgive me. So I'll cap it at five."

Grant wasn't close enough to give me a proper greeting, so he dropped into the seat across from me and nodded instead. It was enough—a nod from Grant wasn't like a nod from mere mortals. Every action that man took carried a hundred hidden meanings. That nod said, *hello*. It said, *I see you sitting here pumping my friends for information, and I think it's cute*. It said, *I also hope you discovered something good, because it's all the satisfaction you're getting from me today*. It probably could have kept going, but Simon intervened.

"How is Myrna, by the way? I haven't seen her in a while."

"Oh, she's fine. Busy at the hospital, as usual. I'll tell her you asked about her."

"You do that," Simon said and smirked. "What does she think of Penelope? I bet she's ecstatic to hear you're finally getting serious with someone."

I saw through Simon's ruse in a flash. He was baiting me. He was baiting me with Grant's *mom*.

I tossed my head and refused to let it get to me. Of course I didn't care that they'd been best friends for decades and that they had some kind of childhood tie that would forever bind them. Of course he had more insight into Grant's personal life than I did. And of course I hadn't met the woman who'd raised him. We'd been seeing each other for three months. There had been no talk of exclusivity. He'd only grazed my nipple once, and that was entirely by accident, even though I'd done my best to recreate the series of fortunate events that led up to it.

I was no expert on traditional male-female relationships, but I was pretty sure nipple play came before meeting the parents.

And if my throat hurt a little at the thought of how far out of the realm of possibility meeting the parents was, what of it? It wasn't like we were dating for real. This was still part of the game of pretend we were playing. Cops and robbers. Good guys versus bad guys. Make-believe.

"She doesn't know about Penelope yet, to be honest."

"Ah, I see." Simon's gloating look was so intense, it practically gave me a third-degree burn. "I guess she wouldn't, given the circumstances."

A heavily shod foot nudged against my calf, and I didn't have to look to know it was Grant's size thirteen snaking across the distance to comfort me. Then his other foot did the same thing, and I realized I wasn't being comforted so much as I was being pinned in place.

"I know," Grant said and winked at me. Holding me forcibly down with his feet and then winking about it—that was the man I currently called my boyfriend. "Which is exactly why I've decided to take Penelope on a road trip to my hometown for Christmas."

"*What?*" Simon cried.

I wasn't far behind with the theatrical outrage, but

resistance was futile with Grant's enormous legs holding me in place.

I settled for a glare instead. "What do you mean, a road trip to your hometown?" I asked.

"You. Me. A rental car. Miles of highway stretching before us." Grant reached across the table to cup the side of my face. "You'll come, won't you? I can't think of anything I'd like more than for the two most important women in my life to meet."

Wow. It took a low kind of man to make an offer like that in public, to foist a challenge in front of his friends, thereby making it impossible for me to back down. The crinkles around his eyes deepened, and that was when I realized he'd done it on purpose. He wanted me to say yes, and he knew very well this was the best way to get me to do it.

At any other time, in any other place, I'd have flatly refused the offer. But Simon was gawking and flustered beside me. Paulie and Nathan had smiles on their faces. And Grant's feet still held me down, forcing me to meet him on the battlefield.

Oh, I'd meet him. I'd meet him and his sweet old mother if it was the last thing I ever did.

"That sounds lovely," I lied.

The gleam of appreciation in his eyes almost made the sacrifice worth it. His thumb came up to trace my lips, and we might as well have been alone in the bar after that. "Perfect. I know she's going to love you."

THE 20 HOLIDAY

(Fifteen and a Half Months Ago)

WEST VIRGINIA WASN'T THE REMOTE WILDERNESS I'D imagined, but it was a far cry from New York. I'd left the state before—gone to New Jersey and Connecticut, picked up the occasional odd job in Washington, D.C.— but this was the farthest I'd ever strayed from home.

It was pretty, I'd give it that much. I could stand in the middle of Central Park and squint my eyes enough to believe I was surrounded by nature, but it took the rolling foothills of the Appalachians and snow deep enough to reach my knees for me to realize how far off the mark I was.

Grant's mom lived in a semiremote location. From where we stood on the freshly plowed driveway, all we could see was the cozy split-level house where he'd grown up, complete with smoke chugging out the chimney, as well as the six or so acres of land that surrounded it. We weren't isolated, exactly—we'd passed several houses on the way in—but I was pretty sure no one would be able to hear me scream.

A girl could disappear out here. Be murdered. Or—

Thunk.

Have snowballs thrown at her back?

"Hey!" I ducked before Grant had a chance to land a second missile—this one aimed neatly for my head. "That's not fair. You have to warn me first. I like to know when I'm being attacked."

He stopped in the middle of scooping up another handful of snow. He wasn't wearing gloves, which didn't seem to affect him in the slightest. "If you insist. Penelope Blue, light of my life, girlfriend extraordinaire, general pain in my ass—"

"The compliments aren't necessary."

He paused long enough to smile at me, the sight of it more blinding than all those acres of snow. "I'm going to throw snowballs at you until you beg me for mercy."

"Never."

Fast—so fast I thought it must be a supernatural trick—he flicked the handful of snow and caught me right in the face with it. The flakes melted on my skin almost immediately, but a few clung to my eyelashes, rendering my vision a blurred white.

Relying on instinct rather than sight, I ducked to the right, narrowly missing another well-aimed projectile. I paused to form one of my own. "You play dirty, don't you, Emerson?"

"Absolutely." With a flying leap, he dove out of the way, rendering my poor snowball null and void. I'd had really good aim, too. "If there's one thing you should know about me, it's that I play to win. Every time."

"I've always thought that was such a stupid statement," I said. Now it was my turn to dive, and I gave him a glimpse of my criminal derring-do with a tuck and roll that had me safely ensconced behind the wheel of the oversized Jeep we'd rented to drive down. Snow nipped down the collar of my jacket, and I could feel the damp seepage of my jeans pressing against the packed ground below, but I didn't care. Especially when the sound of two snowballs on the other side of the vehicle meant they missed me by a huge margin. "Everyone plays to win. Otherwise, why would they bother starting the game at all?"

He didn't respond right away, so I dared to look over the top of the car's hood. He wasn't in sight, which immediately put me in a panic. Already, I was coming to learn about his catlike grace, the way he could sneak up on people out of nowhere. Arming myself with a well-packed snowball, I crept along the side of the car, my eyes scanning for any sight of him.

I didn't get far. A hand grabbed my ankle and yanked, sending me—and my trusty snowball—sprawling. Before I had time to react to the sight of Grant wriggling out from underneath the SUV, he had me pinned to the snow.

Being overpowered like that, so easily and thoroughly and without a moment's hesitation, was exhilarating. The ground was hard and cold beneath me, but that hardly seemed to matter with such a hard and *hot* body on top. Grant wasted no time pushing the knit cap off my forehead and claiming his victory kiss.

What a kiss it was. If I'd had any questions about whether we'd indulge in public displays of affection at his mom's house, he laid them to rest with the force of two lips and one persistent tongue. Both of them pushed deeper and demanded more. Not that my lips and tongue were passive participants in this display, mind you. I might have lost this particular battle, but there was a long and fruitful war yet to be waged.

There were layers of winter clothes between us, but we might as well have been naked for how my body reacted to his touch. This marked the first time Grant and I had kissed horizontally—and if you think that isn't a distinction worth noting, then you've never been kissed horizontally by someone like Grant before. See, he didn't just kiss with his mouth. With him, it was a full-body effort, every muscle working hard to achieve its aim.

Vertically, this meant he constantly pushed me into things. Walls, tables, the side of his car—anything that would allow the press of my breasts against his chest, the hard lines of his muscles seared against me in ways that tormented me long after we said good-bye. Technically, we never did more than lock lips, even if the frantic way our bodies molded against each other signaled a need for more.

Now that we were on the ground, it was impossible to keep things at that level. I wanted to crawl inside the warm culvert of his body and burrow there. I wanted to open my legs and let him settle firmly between them. I wanted him inside me so badly, it had become more than a physical ache—it was a physical void, a phantom limb, the searing pain of knowing that I was missing a vital part of myself.

I probably would have done it, too. Had sex with him right there on a snow-covered driveway, my ass a block of ice, his mom a few yards away baking Christmas cookies in anticipation of our arrival.

Fortunately, Grant released a soul-deep groan and pulled himself away. Well, the top half pulled away. The bottom half only ground into me harder, reminding me how easy it would be for him to maneuver a few zippers and answer all my prayers.

"You're terrible at snowball fights," he said. "Did you know that?"

"I do now." Unable to help myself, I wriggled against him, eliciting another one of those rugged groans and making me feel like the most powerful woman in the world. "Do you want to know what I *am* good at?"

Contrary to my expectations—and my hopes—he didn't ask me to provide an answer. He didn't even smile. He just remained on top of me, his desire still very much a presence between us.

"I wasn't kidding before, you know," he said.

I blinked up at him, confused. What wasn't he kidding about? That he wanted to decimate me with handfuls of snow?

"I play to win, and I don't always fight a fair game to do it." His voice was rough, and it grated against my heart. He wasn't talking about the snow at all.

"Well, I wasn't kidding either," I replied.

Now it was his turn to look confused, though it was more of an adorable wrinkle of his brow than actual perplexity.

"I hate when people say that," I explained. "It's a humble brag, minus the humble. Name me one person who plays to lose. One."

That got him to smile a little. "A boxer who's being paid to throw the game."

"Okay, with the exception of *that*." Since I wasn't

quite sure what he wanted from me, I allowed the moment to settle back into solemnity. "I'm not afraid of things getting rough, Grant, if that's what you're asking."

"Oh, I know you're not afraid. That's the problem." He sighed and wrapped his hand around the back of my neck. His fingers were freezing against my flushed skin, but I didn't draw away. "You said you wanted to be warned before I attack. Well, I'm warning you now."

My heart picked up. "You're declaring war?"

"Not exactly. I'm declaring my intentions." Feeling me shiver, he rolled over on his back, his arms wrapped in a bear hug to bring me with him. The position we landed in was even more sexual than the previous one—I sat astride, my legs parted over the top of his. Both of us panted from something that wasn't exertion, but I knew this moment was about a whole lot more than sex. "I'm crazy about you, Penelope Blue, but I don't know how much longer I can be a gentleman about this."

My lips spread in a smile. I liked where this was going. "Then don't be one."

"I mean it." His hands spanned my waist to hold me still as I made a tiny—infinitesimal, really—movement against the hard length of him. Even that tiny jolt flooded my body with pooling warmth. I thought it might do the trick for him, too, but all he did was tip his head back with a ragged groan, drawing deep breaths like they were his only lifeline. When he finally spoke, his voice was strained with the efforts of immobility. "There are two guest rooms inside my mother's house, and I have every intention of using them during our stay."

"Why? Is she old-fashioned, like you?"

His eyes crinkled despite his best intentions to remain

in control. "Brat. You enjoy tormenting me, don't you?" He continued without waiting for my response. Which, to be fair, was a firm *yes*. And why not? He was tormenting me right back. "I didn't bring you down here to seduce you on my childhood bed, and nothing you say or do is going to goad me into it."

"Then why did you bring me here, Grant?" I'd promised myself I wouldn't ask that question, but there was no stopping it. I had to know. I had to leave here with an understanding about what was going on inside...if not his heart, then at least his head. "What am I doing spending the holidays with you and your family?"

The fact that he didn't hesitate was more unsettling than all the rest. "Easy. I wanted to show you where I grew up."

"Pen, would you be a dear and move the tree a little to the right? The glare keeps flashing off the window. I think it's giving me a migraine."

I paused at the top of the stepladder where I was putting the final touch on the Christmas tree—an angel topper, no less—and stared at the tiny scrap of a woman who had somehow managed to give Grant life.

"You want me to move the entire tree?"

"Would you?" She tipped her head back against the couch and sighed. "I don't know why I bother decorating anymore. It just comes right back down again."

It was a good thing her eyes were shut, because it took me a solid twenty seconds to recover my bearings. I cast Grant a supplicating look—he was trying to get flames to emerge from smoldering logs in a black-sooted fireplace—but all he did was twinkle up at me, laughter in his eyes.

"I'd offer to help, but it takes a lot longer to burn the water out of wood than you'd think," he said. "I could be here all night."

Mrs. Emerson didn't open her eyes or even look up as she said, "Laugh it up all you want, but I'm not feeding either one of you until it feels merry in here. This family Christmas was your idea. I'm supposed to be in Hawaii right now."

Grant's eyes only twinkled more. "Sorry, Mom. Pen promises to move the tree right away." He went back to throwing so many crumpled pieces of newspaper onto the grate, it was a wonder we weren't all asphyxiated.

There was nothing for me to do after that but get off the stool and move the tree. I wouldn't get any help from either one of the Emersons, that was for sure. I don't know what I'd expected Grant's mom to be like— I'd had one or two visions of a *Psycho*-like scenario in which Mrs. Emerson was revealed as Grant in a dress—but I should have known better. Mrs. Emerson was small—smaller than me, even—but other than a diminutive stature and a few strands of gray hair, she was exactly like Grant. Stubborn and charming and not the least put out by me at all.

The angel was slightly askew at the top of the tree, but I decided that even Christmas angels deserved to go a little crooked now and then, so I left her like that. I was still on the fence about whether or not Mrs. Emerson really expected me to move a fully decorated, eight-foot blue spruce on my own, but I knew Grant was watching me out of the corner of his eyes to see how I would handle things.

In other words, it was a test.

Yet another twist in a game I didn't know the rules to and, frankly, no longer cared to play. Had I been anyone else, my mocking suitor's vows of chastity and constant scrutiny might have upset me, but protocol was for other women. Softer women. Women who cared about whether they impressed their annoyingly perfect boyfriends in front of their mothers.

I marched over to where Mrs. Emerson sat reclining and dropped to her level with the crouch of my knees. She hadn't lied. From that angle, there was a reflective glow from the large bay window at the front of the house, and it flashed in an intermittent light that could quickly grow annoying. Which was exactly why I grabbed an engraved wooden screen posing ineffectively in a corner and dragged it over. A few minor adjustments, and it formed a barrier to the light without impeding her view.

I was examining my handiwork with triumph when I heard Mrs. Emerson break out in laughter. The sound of it was one hundred percent Grant, that signature deep-throated chuckle that practically forced its way out.

"You were right about this one, Grant." She didn't stop laughing as she spoke, merely forming her words in the spaces in between. "She doesn't take any crap, does she?"

"Nope." Grant glanced at the fire poker in his hand and back at me. "Since the day we met, I haven't been able to get anything past her. And believe me—I've tried."

Since it would have been impolite to glare at my hostess, I settled one on Grant instead.

"That's rude," I said. "Instead of constantly trying to provoke me, maybe you should just be nice for a change."

Mrs. Emerson answered for him. "What would be the fun in that?"

———————◆———————

"Okay, it's the moment of truth. Do you want to sleep in my boyhood room or the guest room?"

Grant stood at the bottom of the stairs, blocking the hallway and making it impossible to move past him without brushing my entire body against his. Mrs. Emerson had already gone to bed, leaving us alone in this part of the house, which would make it a perfect moment for stolen kisses and body brushes of that sort.

So of course, neither one of us moved. I had the feeling even the slightest touch right now would send us both reeling. Me, because I couldn't have more. Him, because he *wouldn't*.

"Boyhood room," I said.

"I should point out that the guest room has an adjoining bathroom."

"Still boyhood room."

"It also has a queen-sized bed and real goose-down pillows."

"That's gross. I only sleep on chemically manufactured fillers that have never touched a live animal's skin."

"But you eat animals all the time," Grant said. He heaved a mock sigh. "Forget I asked. You're planning on snooping through all my childhood treasures, aren't you?"

"Without question," I said and marched past him to what I assumed was his room, if the faded G.I. Joe stickers on the door were anything to go by.

I hadn't been wrong about how much space he took up in that hallway. In order to get around him, I had to shrink myself down, force that hard body to move just enough to make room for me, and squeeze past his massive thighs and chest. It was a pretty good analogy for everything this man did to me, actually. He never budged. He never gave. He never strayed from his position.

God, he was annoying. It was a good thing I was just using him. The poor woman who ended up with this man would have a hell of a lot to put up with.

Those same massive thighs and chest pressed against me a little too hard as I popped out the other side, and I felt a momentary twinge of regret. It made a nice companion to the other twinges my body suffered in Grant's constant looming presence. The poor woman who ended up with this man would also have a hell of a lot to enjoy. There were times when going head-to-head with a powerful and arrogant man had its perks.

Or so I assumed.

"I'm hoping there are old copies of *Playboy* between the mattresses and trophies of all your childhood triumphs on the walls," I said with a glance over my shoulder. "Maybe even a framed jersey from your winning touchdown."

He grinned. "Which winning touchdown? There were so many, I can hardly be expected to remember them all."

Oh geez. He probably meant it, too. "You know, one of these days, someone is finally going to take some of the wind out of your enormous, billowing sails. All I can say is that I really hope I'm there when it happens."

His hand caught mine and held it. "Believe me, Penelope—you already were."

I stopped, and my heart stopped with me. *This is it*, I thought. *This is the moment it all comes tumbling down.* I'd never seen a man look so earnest, so intent, so *real*—and yet things between us were exactly the same as they'd been the day we first met.

He was still a federal agent, and I was still the jewel thief he was tracking. That truth would never change. And the longer I stood there staring at him, the pressure of his fingers like claws around my heart, the harder it was becoming to remember that.

With a bright, false smile that fooled no one, I turned to his room for a much-needed distraction. Fortunately, it provided all the wonder I needed to transform my brittle smile into a genuine one.

"You lie," I said, my eyes wide. "This isn't your room."

He coughed. "You don't like it?"

Like it? I loved it. It was a history museum crammed into three hundred square feet, from the glass-framed corkboard on the wall holding various pinned bugs to the cracked vase in one corner that looked as if it had been glued together by ancient Greeks. There were no girly magazines, no trophies, not even a dumbbell set gathering cobwebs in the corner. It was books and old maps as far as the eye could see. It was too good.

"Oh my God. This isn't the nesting place of a virile youth with a football scholarship." I whirled on him, not bothering to hide my glee. "This is where a kid with no friends lives. This is the childhood room of Indiana Jones."

"Are you finished yet?"

Almost. "I can forgive you for a lot of things, but I'm not sure I'll ever get over the fact that you didn't tell me you were a *nerd*."

He grabbed me around the waist and pulled our bodies flush, threatening me with his strength and proximity, with the massive biceps taut as they held me against him. "I was not a nerd," he said.

He could flex all the muscles he wanted. I wasn't giving up this easily. "What was your grade point average?" I asked.

"Irrelevant."

"Were you, at any point, a member of a group that played chess and/or debated for fun?"

"I had a lot of interests."

I squealed—half in delight, half because he'd moved one of his hands to pinch my chin. It was his favorite move when he wanted to show his dominance. Or, you know, kiss me. Those two things often intertwined.

"You can abuse me all you want, but it's not going to change the fact that I know all your secrets now," I said. I smiled up at him, practically daring him to drop his lips to mine. "You had the audacity to mock my sad and empty apartment for being juvenile, when all along, you were hiding a museum of nerd relics in your mom's house."

"They aren't nerd relics. They're an *explanation*—which I'm not sure you deserve anymore."

He kissed me. It was fast and hard, as if he was afraid lingering too long would lead to something more, but it was effective all the same. For the moment, I forgot what we were talking about or why I needed an explanation, so caught up was I in the sensation of his delicious mouth moving over mine.

"That"—he pulled away and pointed at the vase in the corner—"was the first treasure I ever found. It was at an antique shop in town. The owner was tossing it out, because he'd dropped it on the sidewalk, and it cracked into a hundred pieces. He told me I could have them if I hauled them out on my own."

"It's...lovely?"

He ignored me. "And that"—this time, he pointed at a desk in the corner, which I'd overlooked in my earlier glee; it was rickety and unstable, chipped in ways that made it look about a thousand years old—"is an authentic seventeenth-century gueridon I found at an abandoned farmhouse about a mile up the hill."

I didn't tell him it would have been kinder to leave it there. "Um. Also lovely?" I said instead.

His eyes crinkled even as he sighed his exasperation. "And this"—he reached for a box on top of the fancy French table, opening it to reveal dozens of rocks and gems in various states of decrepitude. He pulled out a cameo brooch straight out of a Victorian movie—"I found under the floorboards at a school I helped renovate one summer in high school."

"Oh, that one really is lovely." I reached out to trace the woman's profile, but he yanked the brooch back quickly—almost like a reflex—before I made contact. A ringing silence filled my ears as we both realized what he'd done.

"Here, you can hold it," he said, but the mask had already slipped. For a few seconds, he'd unwittingly admitted the relationship between us—FBI agent and jewel thief, good guy and bad. A flush of color diffused his face, and he pressed the pin into my palm. "I found it in a box of old bills and jewelry, but I ended up giving those back to the woman they belonged to."

I still had a hard time registering the shift, so he had to force my fingers closed around the brooch as he elaborated. "The box of stuff was stolen about eighty years ago. It was a kind of local mystery, a string of robberies in one of the affluent neighborhoods not as badly affected by the Depression. According to the police records I found, they arrested a traveling salesman in the area after they found most of the stuff in his suitcase. But they never found these."

I swallowed heavily, unsure what to say. Something flippant about him holding on to women's jewelry seemed pertinent, but I didn't feel flippant. I felt angry, to be honest.

I might not have been the smartest woman he'd ever dated, but I could read subtext when it was being applied with a trowel. *Criminals bad. Police good.* Was he hoping I'd transform my way of life because he'd once found a box of buried treasure and returned it to its rightful owner? Did he think I took my position lightly, that I'd just woken up one morning and decided to embark on a life of crime for shits and giggles?

I made a motion to give the cameo back, but he wouldn't take it. "I want you to have it," he said.

As my response was to goggle furiously at him, he dove in to the rest of his story. "When I found this box, the town hailed me as a sort of local hero. I'd solved the closed case after eighty years, found the missing loot and all that, but I had a hard time accepting it. It didn't make sense to me that this one box would turn up under the floorboards after all this time, so I dug around in the county records department. It turns out there were some carpenters doing repairs on the school that year. I think one of them must have been a copycat—someone who took advantage of the other thefts to try and line his own nest."

"Maybe he needed it to feed his starving family."

Grant had the nerve to smile at me. "I'm sure he had a heart of gold and planned to give it all to charity. Unfortunately, he never got around to performing his good deeds. He died first."

"Oh? Did you find his ancient skeleton fingerprints all over the ill-begotten goods?"

"Not quite. But one of the carpenters died of natural causes a few weeks later. My guess is that he took the money and jewels, buried them, and then passed away before he had a chance to recover the box. Since he didn't tell anyone, it stayed there for all those years." His eyes had taken on an almost glazed, euphoric look as he spoke. "The woman's granddaughter was delighted to get the jewelry back. A lot of it had been in her family for centuries. She gave me the cameo as a gesture of thanks."

Once again, I wasn't sure what to do with that information, other than swallow it bitterly. "Let me guess—that was your first solved case, and you won't be able to rest until all of the world's wrongs are righted again. Is that it?"

"Something like that." His finger came up and stroked me on the cheek, his expression soft enough to lift some of my bitterness away. I suppose it wasn't his fault I was more like the dead thief than the sweet old lady he stole from. "I like antiques. I like mysteries that have gone unsolved for decades. I like holding something in my hand and knowing it has an entire history I know nothing about."

He grew quiet and pensive. So did I.

"I like even more that if I work hard enough, I can uncover that history. In all my years at the Bureau, one thing I've learned for sure is that nothing disappears without leaving a trace. Nothing and no one. Do you understand what I'm saying?"

Oh, I understood all right. He wasn't censuring criminal activity, and he wasn't telling me my entire life was wrong. He was admitting that his goal was—and always would be—my father's treasure.

I almost laughed out loud, giddy and desperate. My senses whirled. *Good luck with that, my friend*. If he thought I could give him even a little clue, he was headed for the disappointment of his life.

"So what are you going to do, Penelope Blue?" he asked, watching me.

I opened my mouth and closed it again. I had no idea. As far as I was concerned, he could spend the rest of his life in a never-ending search for a fortune that wasn't there. Not even he could find something that didn't exist. But if that was the only reason he kept me around...

He smiled and shook off the cloak of solemnity that had taken over, returning us to a place where I could at least feel the ground beneath my feet. "Do you still want to sleep in here tonight, among all my junk and boyhood dreams, or are you going to take the guest room after all?"

I could have kissed him for giving me such an easy out. He wasn't asking me to make a decision about us. I just had to understand two things: he played to win, and he wanted my father's treasure. Full stop.

"Oh, I'm staying right here." I flopped onto his bed,

laughing at his expression of dismay. "I refuse to believe there isn't at least one picture of a naked woman hidden somewhere, and I'm going to find it if I have to search all night."

THE PROPOSAL 21

(Fifteen and a Half Months Ago, Christmas Eve)

I KNEW WHAT GRANT WAS GOING TO SAY AS SOON AS he appeared in the kitchen.

"Oh no," I blurted. I didn't bother to hide my disappointment; my shoulders slumped, and a groan escaped my lips. I was pretending to help Myrna roll out cookie dough on the counters, my main contribution to eat the scraps that fell off the sides of her snowman-shaped cutters. "Are you kidding me right now?"

Myrna didn't look up from her work. It was almost impossible to get that woman up from her chair, but once she was, it was one hundred percent focus and action. I bet she made a killer nurse. "What's that, dear?"

"Grant has to leave," I said and mustered up a smile for his benefit. "I'm guessing he just got the call. Sterling Simon needs him."

He returned my smile with a slight upturn of the lips,

guilt and gratitude in equal proportions. "I knew you were too smart for your own good."

"Alas, we all have our crosses to bear," I said.

Myrna brushed her stomach, leaving a trail of floury fingerprints across the frilled red apron that covered her robe. "I can't say I'm surprised," she said. "Criminals never seem to take federal holidays off to be with their families."

I couldn't help but meet Grant's eyes at that, but if he passed judgment, he did a much better job of hiding it this time.

"I'll just, ah, leave you two alone for a moment?" Myrna said. She didn't wait for a response, but she reached up to place an affectionate kiss on Grant's cheek before she bustled out of the kitchen. There was an equal chance she was going to collapse on the couch while the cookies magically baked themselves or head out to plow the entire street using only a shovel and pickax. She was capable of either one.

"It gets worse," Grant apologized as soon as the door closed behind her. "I'm booked on the next flight out."

"Does this mean you're asking me for a ride to the airport?"

"Yes, unfortunately. It also means you'll have to drive back on your own to return the rental. It's terrible timing, I know. I'm sure this isn't how you pictured spending your holidays."

I paused a beat too long. He noticed.

"If it helps, Simon's even more upset than I am," Grant said. "He loves Christmas."

"He does?" I had a hard time picturing uptight Simon spreading cheer and getting tipsy on eggnog. I assumed he went around handing out lumps of coal.

"He's a regular jolly old soul."

I could tell Grant wanted me to say something more, either fly out in anger or reassure him that spending eight hours in the car by myself on Christmas was my favorite thing to do, but I was never that kind of liar— the ordinary, white-lie kind.

"Well, I won't pretend I'm not disappointed, but I understand. The job comes first."

"The job doesn't—" He grimaced and shook himself off. "No, you're right. It does come first. In our line of work, it has to."

I appreciated that he wasn't the white-lie kind, either—and that he used the term *our*. It placed us on equal footing. We were just two people, dedicated to work, sacrificing human relationships for the sake of reaching our goals. No biggie.

Equals we might have been, but I was still hesitant to get out the next part. I rolled a piece of cookie dough between my fingers, worrying it into a ball before popping it in my mouth. Mrs. Emerson made fantastic cookies. "If it's okay with you and your mom, I'll stay here for the rest of the weekend rather than drive back right away."

He didn't respond, once again staring at me in that surprised, penetrating way of his, making me wonder if I was about to make the biggest mistake of my lifetime. Again.

"I don't want to be a burden or anything," I rushed on. I wasn't a woman given to fits of self-consciousness, as my life story attested, but there was something about commandeering someone's mother that put me at a disadvantage. "But since she canceled her whole vacation for our visit, it seems cruel for us both to abandon her. If she wants the company, I'm happy to stick around. I like her."

There was no immediate end to my agony. I tried not to let it upset me—after all, overstepping boundaries was an everyday affair with me—but it was hard. Large, intently staring men are more difficult to shrug off than you think.

Then Grant's face broke into a smile, lighting up the room and flooding my body with warmth. That wasn't just relief I felt, let me tell you. There were feelings that would have frightened the little snowman cookies.

"You want to stay here with my mom?" he asked.

"Only if she wants me to," I added hastily. "I know some people prefer their solitude to a strange houseguest."

"She'll love it," he said.

"Maybe you should ask her first."

"She'll love it," he repeated.

"You don't know that."

"I do know it." He crossed the room and grabbed me, the expression in his eyes so tender, I almost couldn't look at him head-on. "She'll love it because *I* love it."

Not wanting to be alone on Christmas seemed like a strange reason to be moved to the extremes of passion, but that was the exact effect it had on Grant. Even though we were vertical—always so damnably vertical—he showed me exactly how he felt about my offer. Hard and strong and determined to suffocate me.

But then, who needed air at a time like this? I'd have gladly given up my lungs altogether if he held me like that forever.

"You never cease to surprise me, you know that?" he said.

I squirmed under the intensity of his regard. "Maybe I only want to stay here without you so I can keep snooping through your stuff."

He just smiled.

"Or maybe I want to rob the place," I added. "You know what they say. While the cat's away..."

"...the mouse is welcome to do whatever she wants," Grant finished. "The cat likes her too much to care."

Damn. My stomach and heart merged into one.

Grant touched my mouth, one fingertip where his lips had just been, and I felt the rest of my organs give way. He had to know how that undid me, the pressure of his hands against the sensitive and swollen skin that belonged to him alone.

"I should probably warn you, though," he said.

I knew there had to be a catch. There was always a catch. "Uh-oh. What is it?"

"When you get back to New York, I'm going to ask you to marry me."

The edges of my vision went black, and the only thing that kept me standing was Grant's arm around my waist.

"I just wanted to get that clear, right from the start." He echoed the words from our first-ever real date, unconcerned that he held what amounted to a limp rag doll. "If you have any objections to that plan, for any reason whatsoever, now's a good time to let me know. There's no telling what I'll do once this thing gets underway."

I blinked up at him, waiting for the punch line, but it didn't come. Apparently, he was done using his mouth for words.

And I, unable to form any of my own, didn't bother fighting it.

THE STAKEOUT
22

(Present Day)

"I CAN'T TAKE IT ANYMORE," I ANNOUNCE. TOSSING THE binoculars that have branded permanent rings around my eyes, I unlock the car door and leap out. The air smells like the back alley we're currently parked in, but I embrace it as I might a fresh ocean breeze. "I have to know what's happening in there. I'm going in."

Riker tries to reach across the console and pull me back into the passenger's seat, but I'm fueled by energy drinks and boredom—a lethal combination under the best of circumstances. And these circumstances definitely aren't the best. I've been sitting in this car since yesterday afternoon, performing what can only amount to a stakeout in front of a seedy New Jersey motel, waiting for Tara and Grant to make their move.

As it turns out, there are some things I enjoy less than being crammed inside an air vent for hours on end.

Sitting in a car with a man who won't even *look* at me is one of them.

"I'll just burst in to room 283, wave a gun, and demand that they give me the goods," I say, being careful to keep my glance at least a foot above Riker's head. I made the mistake of eye contact early on in our adventure, and he punished me by not talking for a full five hours. My ears are still ringing from the silence. "They do it in movies all the time. How hard can it be?"

He snorts his derision. "Considering Grant is probably packing and knows how badly you shoot? Very."

I kick the tire, but it doesn't make me feel better.

"Get back in the car," Riker says. "They'll see you."

"No, they won't, because I don't think they're in there. We haven't even seen a curtain move."

"Maybe they're busy doing…other things."

I kick the tire again, this time hard enough to send a jolt of pain up my big toe. "Don't start, Riker. I'm not in the mood."

"Yeah, well, neither am I. It's not like I asked you to come with me in the first place. I wanted to do this alone."

I allow my gaze to drop the twelve inches necessary to look at him and immediately wish I hadn't. The long day and even longer night of sitting in stiff agony beside me have taken their toll on him. His hair is greasy and hangs limply in his eyes. Dark circles give him a haunted, hunted look. He's a mere shadow of his sharp, cocky self, and there's no one to blame for it but me.

"Riker—" I begin, but I don't know what to say.

Riker does, though. He sticks to business—always business. It's the only thing we have left.

"Jordan and Oz should be here to relieve us within the next few hours," he says, his tone clipped. "If there hasn't been any movement by that time, we can talk about a new plan."

I won't last a few more hours. Grant and Tara are within arm's reach, and the necklace with them, but instead of marching up to their room and demanding answers, I'm forced to sit here and simmer in hostile silence. We can't move until we know what we're dealing with, and we can't find out what we're dealing with until they move.

The inaction is killing me. Or maybe the tension is. At this point, I can't really tell.

A glimmer of movement across the street catches my attention, and I latch onto it like it's a safety line. "Hey—I think I see someone."

At first, I assume the familiarly tall and gaunt man lurking near the bulletproof motel clerk's booth is Oz in yet another flawless disguise, but the figure rounds the corner and disappears as quickly as he arrived. I'm disappointed, but not for long, since a matronly woman in scrubs pushes a cart by a few seconds later.

"There's a cleaning lady!" I snap my fingers to get Riker's attention.

He leans his head across the console. "So?"

"She's making her rounds."

"I can see that."

"You know who does a really good job of coming and going inside a motel without getting noticed?"

He jolts up in his seat, all his sullen severity gone in a flash. "Absolutely not. Don't even think about it."

"But that cart of dirty linens looks awfully roomy..."

"No."

"You could distract her with your charm to give me enough time to hop in."

"Pen, *no*."

"I won't even try to get out to investigate, I swear. It'll be strict recon only, in and out with no one the wiser. Even if Grant and Tara turn her away at the door, it'll at least give me a chance to confirm whether they're in there."

Riker's lips form the word *no* again, but then he stops. "Actually, that's not the worst idea you've ever had."

"It's not? I mean—of course it's not. If your information is wrong and they're not in there, we're wasting our time. It's only logical. We should have done this hours ago."

"Don't oversell it," he says dryly. "I already agreed."

I immediately clamp my mouth shut and do my best not to set him off in another downward spiral. I don't think I could survive another one.

He slides out of the car and surveys the situation across the street. The lone cleaning woman seems to be the only one working, so her progress is necessarily slow, giving him ample time to concoct a plan of action.

Riker has always been good at this part—seeing the big picture before breaking down a scene into its constituent parts—and today is no different. "Okay. This should be pretty straightforward. I'm going to pull her away by asking her to check out a flooding issue near the ice machine. That should give you time to sneak up from that ledge above the garbage."

I see at least four other ways I could access her cart, including walking up the stairs like a normal human being. But it's obvious that Riker wants to punish me by making me climb on top of garbage cans, so I nod.

"You'll have to empty at least half of the towels before you jump in." He casts a cynical eye over me. "She'll notice the added weight. You haven't been running."

This time, nodding and playing nice costs me the top layer of enamel on my molars. It's true—I haven't put in my requisite three miles in days—but in case he failed to remember, I've been dealing with the necklace and infidelity and being tied to chairs.

"As soon as you get to the end of that hall, I'll pull her away again so you can get out," Riker continues. "Under no circumstances will you leave that bin any earlier, understand?"

Oh, I understand all right. There will be no overreacting to events beyond my comprehension. No trusting my own instincts to see me through. Never mind that the cleaning lady was my idea; when it comes to the details of the job, it's Riker's way or no way.

"I mean it," he adds firmly. "No matter what's going on in there, you stay put. I don't care if the necklace is sitting on the floor within your reach. Leave it there."

If it's sitting on the floor within reach, then Grant and Tara are obviously not to be trusted with it for any length of time, but I don't say so out loud. That's not the point Riker is trying to make. The point is loud and clear and ringing in my ears.

He doesn't think I can do anything without him standing a few feet away, directing my every movement. He treats me the same way he always has—like a lost, wandering fifteen-year-old who can't take a step without him.

I'm suddenly exhausted by it—by all of it: walking a tightrope whenever he's around, struggling to gain his approval, carrying the weight of my choices around my neck as some kind of penance I can remove only with his blessing. In many ways, Riker became my whole world when my dad disappeared, the only person I could rely on to stand by me when everyone else erased me from their memory.

I love him for that, and I think a part of me always will. But I haven't liked him—not in the way a friend should be liked—for a lot longer than is fair to either of us.

"You know what?" I say. "No. I don't agree to those terms."

He just looks at me. His right-side scowl is in place, but his eyes are more hurt than angry.

"I'm going to head up there and make an assessment based on my experience and intelligence. I'm going to hide in a laundry basket to gather data, and then I'm going to use that data to make an informed decision about whether it's safe for me to exit said basket."

He snorts. "Right. An informed decision."

"Jesus Christ, Riker. Can you even hear yourself right now?"

"Yes. I have ears. I sound like a man who's trying to help a friend. A friend who, I might add, doesn't appreciate it in the slightest."

I know he's hurting. I know he's been through a lot these past few weeks. And I know he could easily start the car and drive away, leaving me to deal with this mess on my own. It's a testament to his value as a human being that he doesn't.

But I'm hurting, too.

"Do you know *why* I always choose Grant instead of you?" I ask. "Here's a hint—it has nothing to do with the sex."

The angry red flush that covers his face isn't much of an answer, but I run with it anyway. See, the problem with Riker and me is that we never moved past being angry kids together. Everything between us has been drama and angst, emotions left to simmer until they boil over. We never learned to interact as adults, and we never got to see each other grow up. We've been too busy running laps around this Neverland of our own making.

"From the day I met him, Grant has treated me as an equal," I say. "*His* equal. It doesn't matter that he's an FBI agent and I'm a thief. He doesn't care that I lie and cheat and steal to get my way, because he'll lie and cheat and steal right back. That's what equals do."

Riker raises a hand as if to keep the words back. "He's walking perfection. I get it. You don't have to keep going."

But I do. Now that I'm going, I'm not sure I can stop. "I know it seems wrong, to think that an FBI agent could respect me, but he *does*—and that's something you've never done, not even when I bail you out of debt or pull off incredible heists. He sees me as his enemy, yes, but an enemy worth engaging. An enemy worth his time and effort—an enemy he'll tie to a chair to keep from getting in his way, because he believes in me enough to know I can."

"You want me to tie you up, Pen? Is that it?"

In that moment, he probably would. But it wouldn't

be for the right reasons, as strange as that sounds. He wouldn't tie me down to stop me from stealing a necklace or going up against him in battle—he would hold me down, keep me back, prevent me from growing enough to stop needing him the way he needs me.

"I've always been a sad, scared little girl to you," I say. "All alone in the world, able to steal anything you ask but without a lick of common sense."

That gets me a ghost of a smile, so thin it's almost transparent. "You never did have any."

"I know."

"I was just trying to protect you."

I know that, too. "I appreciate what you've done for me over the years, Riker. I really do. There were times…"

But I don't need to tell him. He was there. He knows how many times he was the only thing keeping me alive.

I soften. "At some point, we have to accept that we're not kids anymore. We're not fighting for survival, and it's not us against the world. There's nothing to protect me from anymore. You did it. You won. You saved me."

I've never said the words out loud before, and the truth in them causes my throat to tighten. Riker is—was—my salvation. That fact will always be the basis of our past, but it can't be the basis of our future. That wouldn't be fair to either of us.

"You saved me," I echo, quieter this time. "Now don't you think it's time we focus on saving you?"

Riker doesn't move. He continues looking in the distance, his attention concentrated across the street. But I know he registers my comment, because I hear him say, "And how do you suggest we do that?" in a low voice.

I don't have the answer, so it's just as well that he

nods toward the cleaning lady. "If we don't move soon, we're going to miss our window of opportunity," he says. He takes a deep breath and faces me. "I hope you know what the hell you're doing, Pen."

"I don't," I say truthfully. And that's going to have to be good enough for us both.

After today, I'm going to have to add musty, used towels to my list of Unpleasant Smells to Be Trapped With. Based on the aesthetics of this particular motel, it doesn't cater to a high-end crowd, and that fact shows in the linens forming my cocoon. The one underneath me is wet enough that it leaves a trail of drips behind the cart, while one wedged uncomfortably near my nasal passage seems to have been used to wash a skunk.

But I'm in, and other than an, "Oy, this is getting heavy," the cleaning woman hasn't noticed an extra passenger on her journey.

Based on my count of stops along the way, we should be approaching room 283 now, and I can feel the wheels bump over a crack in the sidewalk just outside the door. A knock and the sound of "housekeeping" send me into a deerlike state of immobility—which is just as well, because Grant's rumbling voice is enough to set any woman running.

"We don't need any cleaning—" he begins before cutting himself off. Panicking, I wonder if he can see my human-shaped lump inside this bag and plans to wheel me on a short path down a dark stairwell. Then I remember that he laughed outright at the idea of me hiding underneath our bathroom sink, and this is a much smaller space. "Actually, we could use a quick run-through," he amends. "Come on in."

She hesitates before pushing the cart over the threshold. "I could come back later," she says.

Oh God. Is it because she's facing a den of vice, a love nest among the bedbugs? Is the cleaning woman of one of the most squalid motels ever to grace a dirty street horrified by the depravity spread out before her?

"You're already here. We'll do our best to stay out of your way."

"What's that?" Tara's voice sounds over what must be a blow-dryer.

So. Showering has happened in some form or another. That's not troublesome. Not troublesome at all.

"Housekeeping is here," Grant says.

"Oh, good. We need more towels."

The cart rattles as I presume the cleaning lady hands a stack of fresh towels to my stepmother. I really hope Tara's wearing more than one at the moment. I bet she looks fantastic in a towel.

"How can you possibly need more?" Grant asks. "They stocked the bathroom with twelve."

"Um...I just took a shower?"

"And you used all twelve?"

"I used my half of the twelve, yes. So now I need more."

Grant's grunt of irritation penetrates my canvas walls. Since his mom is a nurse, he has this thing about putting an additional burden on women who spend all day working on their feet. "Can't you just hang them up and let them dry? We won't be here much longer."

"That's what you think. I warned you how it would

be. You can't expect these guys to trust you immediately. This situation has 'sting' written all over it." A pause. "You know, you *could* just give it to me and let me handle the transaction for you."

"No."

"I'm sure Blackrock won't object to seeing me alone."

"No."

"I'm not going to take it!" Tara insists. "I want to find out where Warren hid that money just as much as you do."

Warren. *Thunk*. My heart turns to lead inside my chest, and I'm suddenly suffocating underneath these disgusting towels. The one nice thing about being abandoned as a teenager and finding your own way in this world is that few people want to talk about your parents. The people who raised you have no bearing on the harsh realities of street life, so they're rarely mentioned. And anyone who *did* know about my dad usually had professional ties, so they referred to him as the Blue Fox rather than by name.

Hearing it now is like having him conjured in front of me. Warren: a fox, burrowing inside dark and warm places to avoid being caught. Warren: a man so obsessed with his own talents, he ended up dying in pursuit of the next big thing.

Warren: a father.

The cart rolls deeper into the room, which I assume means our cleaning lady has moved on to the bathroom. For a moment, I'm afraid—and almost grateful—that this will take me out of earshot, but even though the cleaning lady seems to have disappeared, I'm closer to the conversation. I think I might be wedged between them.

"I already told you how this is going to work," Grant says. "You follow my lead. You go where I say. And maybe, just maybe, I'll see that you get fairly compensated."

Tara makes a huffing noise that perfectly captures her displeasure. *That's* the Tara I remember—the one who liked things her way or not at all. "Technically, I'm the one with the most rights to that money. I was his wife."

The sudden pressure of Grant's leg against my hiding spot is the only thing that prevents me from springing out of the laundry basket and pulling out all her hair. That tiny bit of contact—my husband so close, I can feel him—works as a balm on my soul. It's corny, but there's no other way to describe it.

Grant soothes me. Grant makes me feel like there's more to life than bouncing frantically between jobs in search of something that doesn't exist.

"Forgive me if I disagree," he says. The pressure increases, though this time I suspect it's building inside my chest. "*Penelope* has the most rights."

Tara laughs, but it's a forced, unnatural sound. "Of course she does—that's what I meant. We can split it three ways. I've always wanted to do more for her."

"Why didn't you?"

"What?"

"Why didn't you do more for her?" Grant repeats carefully. "To hear her tell the story, you walked out on a fifteen-year-old who'd just lost the only person she had. Seems a little cold, if you ask me."

I squeak. I can't help it. Since the other reaction bubbling up inside me is a rallying cheer, the squeak seems like a reasonable alternative.

The cart rattles in reply, and I feel pressure from

above, heavy and consistent. Grant is leaning on it—on me.

"It wasn't that simple," Tara says.

"No?"

"No." Her voice is defensive, stiff. "I don't know if you've noticed, but Penelope can be...difficult to live with."

The cart shakes with his laughter. "I noticed," Grant says.

"It might be funny to you, but remember, I was little more than a kid myself at the time. Irresponsible and fun-loving and yes, I know it's hard to believe, but in love. I grieved over his loss, too."

Bullshit. The only grief she felt was the loss of my father's income.

"I had no idea what I was supposed to do with her after Warren died," Tara continues. "Or before, if I'm being honest. That girl hated me—right from the start, with the kind of hatred you can *feel*, deep down—and of course she blamed me for his disappearance. He was supposed to retire after we got married, did you know that? We were going to settle down, find a place where we could lay low and figure out how to be a family together."

A family? *A family?*

"Wouldn't that have been something?" She releases her signature low-throated laugh, but it's brittle around the edges. "Me, a mom. Sometimes, I think Warren did us all a favor by dying when he did."

At that, Grant's knee pushes harder into me, deliberate and focused where it lands. With a barely stifled jerk, I realize he knows I'm in here. The nearness, the touching, the comfort—it's on purpose. I'm not sure whether I did something to give my position away or if he simply knows me too well, but there's no doubt in my mind that he's having this conversation for my benefit.

He wants me to hear this. He wanted me to find him.

Understanding grabs hold of me, clenching my stomach from the inside. Everything that's happening is part of his plan. It's why he tied me up and taunted me, why he set up the necklace scam in the first place. Whatever he's trying to do, I'm meant to be a part of it.

"I begged him not to go after that stupid necklace in the first place," Tara adds.

"You did?" Grant's surprise equals my own. I'd always been sure it was her greed that drove him to take the unnecessary risk. "You weren't in on it?"

"Not at all. Warren didn't want me to help, since he was getting it for Pen." She pauses long enough for me to think that's the end of the conversation, but she keeps going. "It's not like he needed money or anything. It had to do with her mother, a legacy he felt she was owed. Penelope was having such a hard time adjusting to us being married, to the idea that she wasn't her dad's one and only anymore. He thought having a physical tie to her mom would help."

"Huh. Penelope has always made her mom seem like a big mystery. I wasn't aware she knew anything about her."

I didn't. I *don't*. I can't breathe in here, and I think I might have just grabbed Grant's leg through the canvas.

"Well, I don't know anything, either, so stop looking at me like I'm the bad guy in this story. I did the best I could under the circumstances. If you want to blame someone, blame Warren. The Dupont mansion has so many security cameras and alarms—it's practically a fortress. The Mint was easy by comparison, but he wanted Penelope to have her mother's necklace, so he went against all advice to get it. And then he disappeared, leaving me with a surly teenager who couldn't stand the sight of me. I know I should have done more and tried harder to take care of her, but I didn't know how. She wouldn't let me. If it helps, Penelope is ten times the thief I'll ever be, even back then. I knew she'd be fine."

"Wait a minute—backtrack there a second," Grant says. He leans over the cart, but I barely register the movement. I'm too afraid to shift, even more afraid to breathe. I'm not fine. I'm not fine at all. "Are you saying it was her *mother's* necklace?"

"Yeah, it was some kind of family heirloom. The Duponts disowned Liliana when she married Warren, and they blamed him for her death. They wouldn't have anything to do with Penelope unless he relinquished his paternal rights and promised never to contact her again, which, of course, he'd have never done. He adored that girl."

"Are you telling me Penelope is related to the Duponts?"

There's a thump from a few feet away, and the sound of footsteps signals the cleaning woman's return. I'm horrified that I might miss this next part—wheeled out before I have a chance to hear the ending to this awful tale—but Grant commands the woman to wait in that stern, authoritarian voice few have the guts to withstand. He turns it to Tara next.

"What exactly is her relationship to Erica?"

"She's her granddaughter. I assumed... Didn't Pen tell you? I always thought it was odd that she didn't turn to Erica for help after Warren disappeared. I assumed it was part of her prickly nature. That girl has never been happy unless she's plunged in the middle of a convoluted mess."

The pressure of Grant's leg disappears even as my mind screams in protest. Turn to Erica for help? I was supposed to have been saved by a woman I didn't know existed?

"No," he says, his voice distant. "No, she never said."

"That's Pen for you. God forbid she forms an actual connection with another human being. Well—with the exception of that delicious little friend of hers. What's his name? Biker? Striker?"

"Riker." Grant's voice is colder than I've ever heard it.

"That's it! Riker." She laughs. "Uh-oh. I see that's not a subject you care to talk about. I'll stop."

"They're just friends," he says flatly.

"I'm sure they are."

"He was all she had when you and her dad left."

"Not *all* she had," Tara reminds him. "He must be something special if she gave up the Duponts for him. You know what they say. Like mother, like daughter."

She's wrong. She's *wrong*. I didn't know Riker at the time. I didn't know my grandmother. The only person I gave up was Tara, and based on this conversation, it's a decision I'd make a thousand times over again.

Grant releases a violent curse. "She promised me there was nothing between them. She said she didn't have anyone else."

"And of course Penelope has never lied to you."

I never lied about the things that matter, I want to cry, but I can't. Not because I'm hiding, but because I'm not sure it's the truth anymore. Not about whether I lied—there's no denying that—but whether the things I lied about mattered. It was supposed to be harmless, all those games Grant and I played. Keeping secrets, tiptoeing around our true motivations, pretending to be happy together. As long as we were both in on it, no one could get hurt.

But I hurt. I hurt so much, I can feel my chest cracking open, lies pouring out like blood. They trap me on all sides—my lies and Grant's, Riker's and Tara's, my dad's most of all. He never told me why he wanted to go after the necklace. He never mentioned how far my mother had fallen for love. He never saw fit to disclose that I had a grandmother who actually wanted to know me.

Those things matter.

Grant matters.

I matter.

I know, at this moment, that it's time to end the game. I'm probably going to give the cleaning woman a heart attack when I pop out of the laundry basket, but I'm not sure I can go another minute without telling Grant the truth.

I love him. I always have.

From the moment he turned that crinkly-eyed smile on me and picked up the gauntlet I tossed his way, from the second he declared his intention to woo me the way I deserve, I was done for. Marrying him was the only brave and decent thing I've done in my life, and I don't want to spend another minute on this planet without him knowing that.

It seems I have to. A loud *BOOM* reaches my ears, followed by the sound of splintering wood as someone smashes in the motel door. A hissing smoke canister rolls underneath me, but the damp towels serve as thick enough barrier that I don't inhale it right away.

That's when the shouting begins.

"Get down. Stay back. Hands behind your head."

My heart thumps sickeningly. It's the FBI. Did they follow me here? Did I lead them straight to Grant? I don't think I could bear it if he was arrested for my mistake.

There's a bustle of movement around me. The cleaning woman mutters a prayer on repeat, and I feel the whomp of a body hitting the ground next to me. A few clicks and a grunt are enough to convince me that Grant has just been stripped of his artillery.

I feel the loss as keenly as I'm sure he does. *He needs that gun.*

"Grant Emerson?" a low, rough voice asks.

"That's me," he says. He's nearer than I expected— almost within reach.

"We heard you're interested in meeting with a certain someone."

"You heard correctly." Another grunt from Grant, more pained this time. "I assume this is our pickup service? It took you long enough."

"Sorry to keep you waiting. Blackrock doesn't take kindly to ultimatums from the feds."

"Ah. So you picked up on that part, did you? But I have a criminal associate and everything. Surely that makes us equals."

"Just get up."

"I would, but your knee is in the middle of my back."

The reply is another sickening whack. It sounds like metal against flesh, solid as only true pain can be, and I almost cry out.

"Funny guy, huh? We'll see how long that lasts when you're eating the barrel of my gun. Let's go."

"Your wish is my command," Grant says and staggers to his feet. I use the term *staggers* because I feel him lean on the laundry cart to stabilize himself. He lingers with his lips against the canvas, right next to my ear.

For a moment, I think he's going to issue an order, tell me where to go and who to contact for help, but he chooses his last words with more—or less—care than that.

"You could have trusted me, Penelope," he says. "All I've ever wanted is to make you happy."

I do trust you. The words are close to escaping and giving up my position, but he's yanked away before I have a chance to get them out. Amid the crashes, grunts, and hysterical shrieks of the cleaning woman as she's left behind, Blackrock's associates force Grant and Tara out the door. I can only assume the screech of tires peeling out of the parking lot belongs to them, but it can just as easily be Riker's arrival, which he performs in a frenzy, scaring the poor cleaning woman even more.

"All right, Pen," he says and yanks the towels off my head. "What the hell did you do this time?"

THE 23 LAMP

(Fifteen Months, One Week Ago)

FOR CHRISTMAS, I GOT TWO LAMPS.

There were plenty of other gifts in my holiday haul—Jordan got me a subscription to a delivery service that drops off a box of snacks every week, Oz surprised me with a fantastic sneak photo he took of me and Jordan with our arms around each other, and Grant's mom wrapped a stack of paperbacks with cupcakes and kittens on the covers. They were thoughtful gifts, making me feel unworthy of so much affection all at once.

I also got the lamps. The first was from Grant. It was hideous, and I loved it. The cast iron base was shaped like a lion cub—to match my guard lion at the door—and it had a fringed lampshade that I suspected was one of his antique finds. There was history in that lamp, both ours and his. There were also strong implications of a future.

The second lamp was, of course, from Riker. It was waiting in my apartment when I got home from West Virginia, taking over the far wall with its five fully adjustable arms. It had no bows and no tag, but I didn't need to be told who dropped it off—or why. I also didn't need that many lamps shining lights into the corners of my apartment. In the semidarkness, it had always been a comfortable enough place to lay my head at night. Small and underwhelming, perhaps, but *mine*.

So much illumination meant I could see every chip in the floor, the uneven paint on the ceiling, the spidery cracks reaching up the wall. I saw my life in bright light for the first time, and I wasn't happy with what I found.

"We need to talk," I told Riker over the phone as soon as I had enough time to absorb the implications of both gifts. "Something happened in West Virginia that I think you should know about."

Jordan would have been a more ideal choice for a play-by-play breakdown of my romance, Oz would have grunted and nodded and done whatever I needed to make sense of it all, and I had two new lamps that would have made a willing audience. But what I really wanted was my best friend and ally, the man who'd been there during the lowest point in my life and had walked by my side ever since.

He was understandably upset.

"You have to end it." Riker paced through my apartment like a wild animal, eating up the floor with his long strides as I outlined a bare-bones version of my holiday. "You have to break up with him. This has gone too far."

"Okay, but if you think about it, this might actually work in our favor. If I say yes—"

He stopped. "Are you fucking kidding me right now? You're actually considering marrying this guy?"

"It's not like that."

"I can't believe you're saying this to me right now. He's an *FBI agent*, Pen. You're a criminal. In no world does that relationship make sense."

I raised my hands, supplicating and holding him back at the same time. "Hear me out for a minute."

"What for?"

I knew, going in, that this conversation with Riker wasn't going to be easy, but nothing could have prepared me for the way it split me down the middle. Half of me wanted to tell Riker that of course he was right, of course I wouldn't marry a man he hated, of course it was time to walk away. The other half was still in West Virginia with Grant, lying next to him on his twin bed, our fingers intertwined as we talked about everything and nothing.

"It's not as bad of an idea as it sounds. He admitted something over the holidays—about his motivations, about what he's trying to do. I'm pretty sure he'll keep tailing us, regardless of whether or not he and I are in a relationship. He's…I don't know how to put it. Obsessed? He's going to keep looking for my dad's treasure, and nothing I do or say can stop him."

"So?"

So indeed. That was no reason to commit matrimony, and we both knew it. But I didn't know how else to make Riker understand when I couldn't begin to understand it myself. I was balanced on the top of an iceberg that went so far down, it touched the ocean floor.

"My best bet is to keep him close," I said. "I can

watch his movements, see if he makes any progress in his investigation, intercept incoming information. He thinks he's being clever and sneaky, preying on my emotions like this, but it only works if I'm not aware of him doing it. And you know it's good for business to have an FBI ally. He won't let us get arrested if he thinks we still have value."

"You're serious. You're actually considering it."

"No, I'm not. I—"

I didn't have a chance to finish my sentence. Without another word, Riker grabbed one of the arms of his lamp. He pulled it so hard that the cord came out of the wall, sending the whole thing crashing. Glass from the bulbs shattered around him, and one of the lights gave an intermittent buzz before plunging into darkness.

All I did was stand there in the wreckage, mouth agape. Of all the types of anger I'd seen Riker exhibit over the years, he'd never been physical before. He was mean, sarcastic, a wounded animal snarling at anyone who got too close—but he'd never crossed the line to violence.

Until now.

"No, you're not considering it, are you?" He stepped over the broken glass, heedless of how he sent it flying. "You've already decided. The guard dog takes all."

I was on the phone with Grant within minutes of Riker's departure.

My feet crunched over the broken shards, but I was too shaken—too shaky—to make the attempt to clean them up. I was also too shaken to be alone, which should have been my first clue that I was in over my head.

Being alone was the one thing I was supposed to be good at. It was a thief's default state.

"Sit tight. I'm on my way," Grant said as soon as he heard my voice. I don't know what I said to tip him off, but I only got as far as *Riker was here, and he broke my lamp* before all the background noise dropped. "I'll be there in ten minutes."

"But how can you—" I began before I thought better of finishing that question. There was one very good reason why he was only ten minutes away, and it had more to do with me being a thief than with me being his girlfriend. "Okay. Thank you."

I clicked the phone off and stood surveying the mess, wondering what I might have in my apartment that could work as a broom. One of my older T-shirts could probably be sacrificed to move the glass off to one corner, but there wasn't anything approaching a dustpan in the place. Cleaning was just another task I never mastered and never cared to. What was the point? When one place got too bad, I could always just pack up my three belongings and move.

It was that thought, more than anything else, that set me off again.

Riker was right. I don't have any common sense. I'm not good at ordinary things.

I had no roots, no ties, and no dustpan. Who was I to think I could live a normal life with anyone?

"Penelope?" Grant didn't bother knocking. The door was already half-open from Riker's abrupt departure, and he pushed through with an urgency that bordered on the frantic. "Are you here? What happened?"

He skidded to a halt as soon as he saw me standing

in front of the wreckage. Without asking any questions, he picked his way carefully to my side. It was the first time I'd seen him hesitant to approach me, unsure of his welcome or how I would react to him. Maybe it was because we'd left things hanging so open-ended back at his mom's house, or maybe it was the fact that there were large and dangerous shards of glass within arm's reach, but he didn't try to touch me, didn't even try to speak.

"He gave me that lamp as a Christmas present," I said.

Grant paused. "I see."

"I liked it."

"I see."

I turned to him then, wondering if he was aware how close to breaking down I was, how close to sobbing in his arms, but his gaze was trained straight ahead, as inscrutable as always.

"I take this to mean you told him?" he asked, as nonchalant as if we were talking about the weather. "About what I said back in West Virginia?"

I snapped. There was no way I could talk about West Virginia while Riker's anger was still a palpable presence in the room, no way to admit to Grant how much the shattered lamp meant without giving myself away. So I didn't try. Heedless of the glass or of the fact that Grant was in full FBI regalia, complete with a closely cut dark suit and his gun holster, I launched myself at him.

He was so taken aback at first that he didn't respond, accepting my twining arms around his neck and my lips pressed against his without demur. In fact, his body responded before he did. His lips parted to accept my kiss, a groan of pleasure escaped his throat, and I thought for a full thirty seconds that I might get away with it.

But then my hands moved down his back and grazed that holster, and he jerked back. His expression was one of agony, his breathing labored.

"Wait, Penelope. Wait." He took a wide step, arms up, backing away as if afraid I might attack again.

It was a good instinct. I wanted to do just that.

"I'm not going after your gun," I said, an angry undertone to my voice. Always, always, that stupid gun got in the way—at least metaphorically speaking. There was nowhere we could go, nothing we could do, where the gun and the badge didn't follow.

"I know you're not," he said. "That's not why I stopped you."

"Oh? Do you have somewhere else to be?" I asked. "A big case that needs your attention?"

"No," he said slowly, watching me. "I'm free if you need me."

I did. I needed him in ways I didn't understand, ways that would ruin me if I brought them to light. "Good," I said. "Then come here."

He didn't.

"Let's get this mess cleaned up first." He shrugged out of his coat and unclipped his gun, setting it carefully on the kitchen counter before efficiently rolling his sleeves. As usual, he was a man on a mission, and he made that mission look good. "Where are your supplies?"

"I don't have any," I said flatly.

His lips moved in a smile. "Why am I not surprised? Do you at least have any grocery bags lying around? That should do the trick."

I rustled around beneath the sink and handed over the plastic bags with a sullen expression on my face. It shouldn't have bothered me that my boyfriend rushed over in the middle of the workday to clean up broken glass in my apartment, but it did. He was so freaking perfect all the time. Always kind, always generous, always the gentleman.

Just once, I wanted to see him as rattled as I felt inside. Just once, I wanted him to pick up a lamp and smash it in anger.

"There," he said as soon as he was finished. "As good as new. You okay?"

I nodded. The broken shards were gone and the lamp pushed aside, my apartment returned to the sparse warehouse it had always been—with the small addition of *his* couch, *his* lamp, *his* record player. He was everywhere inside this place.

He was everywhere inside me. And oh, how good he felt in there.

This time, when I launched myself at him, I didn't give him a chance to slow me down. That man might have been stronger than me, and he might have had the willpower of an ox, but I had something more. With one quick, efficient movement, I stripped off my shirt. His eyes flared—in alarm or appreciation or more likely a combination of the two—and I used his momentary distraction to push my leggings over my hips.

"Penelope, before you go any further, I think we should talk about what I said—"

"*No.*" I spoke so forcefully, I almost shouted. "No talking. You said you have some free time if I need it, right?"

"Yes, but—"

"I need it, Grant. I need you." *I choose you.*

More than anything else in that moment, I needed him to choose me back. Throughout the course of our relationship, stare-down challenges like this had become a regular occurrence. No matter where we were or what we did, there was always a chance that one of us would pull out a dare and wait for the other to accept it. We were good at that, he and I—playing the game, following the rules.

But for once, this was about more than just two people going head to head. We were going heart to heart.

"He broke my lamp," I said. "Please don't break my heart along with it."

I knew I'd won when he released a string of curses that would have done a pirate proud. Well, that and when he started to undo the knot of his necktie and the line of buttons down the front of his shirt. Finally, I was getting a glimpse of the marvel of his chest, and I couldn't even appreciate it properly through the rapidly forming tears in my eyes.

"I promised myself it wouldn't happen like this," he said as the last button came undone and he kicked off his shoes. It was a daring maneuver when there might still be glass on the linoleum, but he didn't heed the dangers as he crossed the floor to sweep me into his arms. "I promised myself a lot of things where you're concerned."

The skin-on-skin contact sent a reverberating shock through me. Even though I knew it was ridiculous—and physiologically impossible—I could have sworn our heartbeats synced the moment we touched.

"Oh yeah? How's that working out for you?" I asked, breathless as his hand slid up the side of my neck and tilted my face toward his.

He swore again, but this time, there was a smile on his lips. "Like shit, and you know it."

"Good."

His lips crashed down on mine, preventing me from goading him further. Not that I wanted to about twenty seconds into the kiss, when it became clear that Grant intended to take things horizontal in the best possible way.

My new couch was the only comfortable horizontal space in the apartment, and he nudged me in that direction with the kind of efficiency that proved he was capable of casing a room the second he walked in. He knew exactly how many backward steps it would take me to get there, understood the specific force required to lower me to a lying-down position. He also timed my descent perfectly so that he undid the clasp of my bra before my back hit the cushions.

"Jesus. You're so beautiful." He swallowed heavily. "I might have stood a chance, if only you weren't so goddamned beautiful."

That confession—the idea that he was as powerless to stop this as I was—undid me more than the fact that I was half-naked and supine on the first real piece of furniture I'd ever owned.

"I feel even better than I look," I said—still challenging, still playing. Mostly, I was hiding the fact that I didn't know what else to say. I'd never been this nervous over a sexual encounter in my life. "Want to find out for yourself?"

He hesitated a moment, and I was afraid he was going to try and introduce the topic of West Virginia again. I couldn't let that happen and was about to do something drastic like rip his pants off, but when he spoke, it was on a different topic altogether.

"I didn't come over here expecting this," he said.

"I know, Grant. You've made it very clear that you're only doing this out of a sense of duty."

His eyes grew dark, kindling a warning. "No. What I meant was I didn't come expecting this. As in, I didn't stop to grab condoms."

Oh. *Oh*. "The medicine cabinet. Top shelf."

He was gone so long, I was afraid I'd scared him away or he'd found a secret stash of jewels I'd forgotten about, but he eventually returned with the promised prophylactics. He paused in the bathroom doorway, clad only in a pair of black boxer briefs that outlined every shape of his anatomy.

I'd never seen such a beautiful man—not before that moment and never since. It wasn't just the muscles, though they were impressive enough where they dipped and swelled above his waistline, leading up to a body designed to bear the weight of the world. No, it was the expression on his face as his gaze found mine that caused my heart to skip a beat.

If I didn't know better, I might have said it was the look of a man in love.

"Before we do this, I need you to tell me why you called me over today."

I blinked, my heartbeat erratic. "What?"

"It wasn't duty that brought me here, and it's not duty that's going to carry me across the room. So tell me."

I wasn't sure how to respond, so I didn't.

"Why did you call me?" he repeated. Although his look still said affection, his stance was growing rigid at my lack of response. "What were you hoping I'd do when I picked up the phone?"

"I don't know," I said with perfect honesty. I felt exposed in more ways than one, but I didn't make a move to cover myself. It wouldn't have been fair. "I was just sad. I was sad, and the only thing I could think of was how much I wanted to hear the sound of your voice."

He crossed the room in three strides.

From that moment on, Grant's strength was no longer a thing of conjecture. He lifted me off the couch and placed me in his lap, his hands everywhere at once. In my hair, stroking my face, cupping my breasts—if there was a patch of skin on my body, he found it and explored it until I was reduced to nothing but nerve endings. I wanted to return the favor, but he made it impossible for me to do anything but accept his long, slow kisses and then his harder, faster ones.

He held me on top of him. Pinned me underneath him. Showed himself to be dominant and in control in every possible way.

That is, until the moment we were both naked and breathless, his body poised to enter mine. The hard length of his erection was so close that I could barely hold my body still. I wanted him on top of me, inside me, moving with the same assured and agile grace that characterized all his movements.

But of course, he wasn't going to make this easy.

"You're sure about this?" he asked, his words a

whisper spoken into the side of my neck. "This is what you want?"

My body had never been wetter, my limbs never more pliable. Unless I took a short break to announce my ecstatic consent from the fire escape, I wasn't sure what other clues he needed.

"What if I said no?" I whispered back, mostly to be contrary. "What if I said I changed my mind? What would you do then?"

"I'd wait," he said, and with such calm assurance, I knew he meant it. "Until you were ready, until you decided you wanted to try again. Forever. That's how long I'd wait for you, Penelope Blue."

I don't remember giving him the go-ahead to continue, but I do recall crying out. I cried my pleasure and his name, my satisfaction at finally feeling the full throbbing weight of him inside. I might have cried other things, too, things I'd be ashamed to look back on, but he was too much of a gentleman to mention them.

He was also a gentleman when it came to taking his pleasure. My own orgasm came swift and powerful, the result of long months of waiting for this man to claim me as his own, but he took his time with his. Not content with a quick release, he returned his attention to all my secret, hidden spaces, exploring with fingers and then lips, treating my body as though it was the first—and last—time he'd ever hold a woman in his arms.

In fact, he waited until I was a quivering, blubbering mess before he entered me once again. By that time, I was so far gone that all he had to do was reach between our bodies with his strong, capable, ex-football player hand to send me over the edge. With one flick of his thumb he had me crying out in ecstasy all over again, his own body shuddering as he finally let himself go.

I was, naturally, exhausted by the time we were through. Grant was, naturally, not. He pulled me into his arms and held me there, hands stroking my hair and my back, tracing the line of my waist, for what could have been hours but felt like minutes.

And then he ruined it.

"I know you've been trying to avoid it, but I think we need to talk about West Virginia."

I stiffened in his embrace. "I had a good time. Your mom and I got along really well without you there."

His laughter was low but still managed to shake us both. "My mom isn't the person I want to talk about while your thighs are entwined with mine."

"It's getting late, isn't it?" I asked. "Don't you have to get back to work?"

"Penelope."

"I mean, you must have been working on something big if you had to cut your holiday short to get back here. I wouldn't want to keep you any longer than necessary."

"Penelope." More firmly that time.

I decided to turn it back on him. "Grant," I said, my tone brooking no argument. "Thank you for coming over here today, and thank you for what is unquestionably the greatest sexual experience of my life—"

"I asked you to marry me. You can't just ignore that."

I jolted out of his arms. Ignoring it was exactly what I planned to do—and for as long as I could get away with it.

"Technically, you didn't," I said, frantic. Rushed. "You only said you intended to. There's still time to take it back."

I don't know why I thought that would work, but of course, it didn't.

"I have no intention of taking it back," he said. His eyes were dark, devouring mine. "In fact, nothing would make me happier than for you to—"

The shrill sound of his phone prevented him from finishing that disastrous sentence.

"Goddamn Simon and his goddamn sense of timing." He reached for his pants and extracted his phone, his stare daring me to make a move in any direction.

Despite my strong urge to do just that, I stayed put.

"What?" he barked. "This had better be good."

I couldn't make out the conversation on the other end of the line, but I could tell from the way Grant's expression went from annoyed to full-on outrage that it was plenty good.

"Yeah. I know, but— Yes. I can, but—" With one long, lingering look at me, he groaned. "Fine. I'll be right there. Don't move from your position."

Never had I been on friendlier terms with Simon than I was in that moment.

"Duty calls?" I asked brightly.

"Please don't," he said and sounded pained enough that I didn't. His movements were rough as he found his clothes and got dressed, looking very much like a man who'd shirked his professional duties all afternoon to indulge in the pleasures of the flesh. I wanted to point that out to him, but there was a serious air about him that caused hard knots to form in my stomach.

Ever since that semiproposal in West Virginia, I'd done everything I could to convince myself that it was another game, another trap. Agent Grant Emerson was just trying—and succeeding—to get under my skin. Even the fight with Riker had been me convincing myself that marriage was an impossibility.

But watching Grant get dressed, seeing the way he struggled to keep it all together, made me question everything.

Maybe he meant it. Maybe what he offered was real.

He shoved his feet into his shoes and shrugged back into his holster, running a hand through his hair as he surveyed my apartment for signs of anything he missed. But the only thing remaining unattended was me, naked and unsettled and raw.

When he spoke, however, it wasn't to press me to give an answer I wasn't prepared to give.

"Are you okay?" he asked. He drew close enough to run his hands up and down my arms—a gesture of affection, a gesture of comfort. "Is there someone else I can call to keep you company? Maybe Jordan?"

My eyes swam. The man had just been cut off mid-proposal, called back to duty while at his most vulnerable, and the thing he was worried about was *me*. "No. I'm good."

"Are you sure?" He crouched so we were on eye level. I was sure he could see the tears forming in mine, so I nodded vigorously.

"I'm better now, I promise. The mess is gone, and I've calmed down. Riker won't—"

I didn't know how to finish. Riker wouldn't what? Return? Blow up at this new turn of events? Throw more lamps?

"Riker won't bother me," I said. "Thank you for coming when I needed you."

"Anytime," he said and dropped a kiss on my hairline.

From the way he looked at my lips and down to my bare breasts, I felt sure he wanted to kiss more of me, but Simon was waiting. Duty called. It always would.

"I have to run, but think about what I said, okay? You and I are not done talking about this."

I nodded and managed a smile to send him off. Had he lingered a few seconds more, he would have seen that smile transform into a frown, watched me sink to the floor in a slump that showed just how *not* okay I was.

That was the second time Grant had almost proposed to me, the second time he turned my world upside down with just a few warm words.

One more, and I wasn't sure I'd have the strength to turn him down again.

THE RESCUE

24

(Present Day)

"Pushing your feet against the floor isn't going to make the car go faster." Riker cuts off a taxi amid an outpouring of honking and curses. The other guy's curses—not his. "We're not that far behind anymore. I can see the van up ahead."

"They're going to shoot him, aren't they?" I ask. Even though I'm trying not to move my feet, I can't help them from straining against the Road Runner mats Riker has in his car. "Because he's a fed? Because he'll be able to identify them now?"

"Don't be ridiculous. Of course they won't shoot him."

I cast an anxious look at Riker's profile, but he's concentrated on the dark van currently weaving through traffic. "Are you lying to me?"

He seals his lips in a tight line. "Yes."

I must have released a wail or something, because he

indulges in a quick glance my way. "I'm sure he's fine. It's not like he isn't trained for this kind of thing. He knew what he was getting into the moment he took that necklace and cast it out as a lure."

On a cognitive level, I know that. None of us has chosen a safe path in life, and there's always been a chance things could go wrong, especially where Grant is concerned. He often works on cases—big cases, scary cases—where shoot-outs are a real possibility, and he sometimes comes home after a long day with bruises he won't explain.

But in all my catastrophic visions, *I* was the one heading to a jail cell for the rest of my life. *I* was the one being shot by a vigilante Samaritan with justice on his side. Grant is the good guy. He's supposed to win.

"I'm not so sure about that anymore," I say.

"That he didn't know the stakes?" Riker laughs, but there's no joy in it. "Oh, he knew. That man always knows."

He doesn't. The genuine shock in his voice when he heard that Erica Dupont is my grandmother—my *grand-mother*, for crying out loud—is proof of that. Whatever it is Grant thinks he's buying with that necklace, it's clear he doesn't yet have all the puzzle pieces. At this point, I doubt any of us do.

But he's the one with a gun to his head, probably mouthing off and daring them to shoot him. He's the one sitting in the back of an unmarked van, believing I don't care if he only has five minutes left to live.

I know, now, what I'd say to him in that moment. It's not *I promise to wear black* or *I'll put on a veil*. It's not even *I love you*. It's nonsense words I'd kiss into his skin and hair until there was no more life left in either of us.

"You were the one who said Blackrock isn't a man to cross," I point out, my voice wavering. "You said he's dangerous."

"He is." The tight line of Riker's lips thins even more. He swerves to the right as a pedestrian fails to wait for the crosswalk signal. We're headed out of Jersey, which means we might cross into Manhattan soon, or we might bypass it entirely. The destination doesn't matter to me so much as this journey. We can't lose Grant.

"Just how dangerous is he?" I demand. "Why were you doing business with that kind of maniac in the first place?"

"I don't know what you want me to say," Riker snaps. Predictably, he's angry, but for once, I can't blame him. It's a lot to undertake, chasing after a man he despises, putting his own life on the line for someone he'd rather see dead. "Is there a chance Grant's life is in danger? Yes. Is Blackrock dangerous and unpredictable enough to take us all down? Of course he is. They all are."

"They?"

He hits the steering wheel with the palm of his hand, but I can't tell if the action is directed at me or the person who just cut him off. Me, probably. His next words confirm it.

"*They*, Pen. The men who pay us to steal things. The buyers who don't care where something comes from or how it was acquired so long as it makes them money. I know you think I'm a big, condescending jerk for hogging the driver's seat all these years, but I only did it to protect you."

Protect. There's that word again, but I don't find it as unpalatable as I might have a few hours ago. There's something to be said for hiding your head in the sand while someone else takes care of everything.

"You did?"

"There's a reason I kept you away from that side of things," Riker says. "Yes, some of it was because I liked picking the jobs and planning the heists, but it's also because you wouldn't have lasted ten minutes with most of those guys."

"Hey—" I protest, but Riker isn't moved.

"Possibly less," he amends. "You're one hell of a jewel thief, no one disputes that, and your dad's legacy might have helped you out of a few tight spaces, but you have no idea what these men are capable of when they see a beautiful, unprotected woman who doesn't even know how to shoot a gun."

I bristle. "I'm not stupid. I wouldn't have done anything careless."

"You're also not mean."

I don't understand, and Riker knows it. He glances sideways at me. "You're a nice person, Pen. A *good* person. I know you like to think you're this badass criminal up to all the tricks, but you've never belonged to this world the way I have, the way Oz and even Jordan do." He draws a deep, shuddering breath. "Before you and I met, there were things I saw, things I did... No one should go through that kind of hell, and I won't apologize for trying to shield you from it."

"What did you—?"

He shakes his head, refusing to say more. "When I found you on the street, this sad, lost girl with more courage than common sense... *Fuck*, Pen. Of course I never wanted you to descend as far as I did to survive. I knew I could spare you from the worst of it by making myself responsible for your safety, so that's what I did. And if you think Grant didn't do the exact same thing by throwing the mantle of his badge over you the first chance he got, then you're being purposefully blind."

"What are you talking about?" I demand.

Riker slams on the brakes, propelling me against the seat belt as we come to a stop. "He didn't marry you to get at your father's treasure, you idiot. He married you so he could protect you from guys like Blackrock. He married you so he could protect you from guys like *me*."

"Riker…" There are no words to capture the way my heart breaks for him right now, all those shards slicing my lungs open.

"Don't. It's done now, and I wouldn't change things even if I could." He stares straight ahead, unwilling—or unable—to look at me. "You were right back there at the motel, you know."

"About which part?" I ask hesitantly. Riker doesn't admit to being wrong very often, and I'm almost afraid to hear what he has to say next.

"All of it. Everything. When you said we were done. When you said there was nothing more you needed from me."

No. That's not true. That will never be true.

"Riker, look at me."

He doesn't comply.

"Look at me," I repeat, my tone sharp. All I get is a slight tilt of his head in my direction, but I take it. "You will never say that to me again, do you understand? I know I haven't always handled things with you and Grant well, but I do need you. I'll always need you."

He releases a soft snort. "Oh yeah? What for?"

"To be my friend."

His head turns the rest of the way, facing me head-on. He's wearing neither smirk nor scowl, his expression open and honest in a way that magnifies his good looks tenfold. Someday, that man is going to realize his value and leave a trail of broken hearts in his wake.

"Thank you for protecting me all those years," I say softly. "Thank you for protecting me even now, when it's the last thing you want to do. I don't know what I did to deserve having you in my life, but it must have been something amazing. There aren't ten men in a million who would sacrifice as much as you have for me."

He groans. Sentiment has never been his favorite thing.

"I mean it," I say and reach for his hand. He lets me, which says a lot, and even suffers through my meaningful squeeze, which says more. "I couldn't have done any of this without you."

"Maybe not, but you sure as shit would have tried." Something approaching a smile lifts the left side of his lips. "I know this is probably hard for you to believe right now, and I'm not saying I *like* the guy or anything, but I'm glad he makes you happy. You deserve to be happy. Now can we get out of this car and finish the job? I don't know if you noticed, but we're here."

I glance up, surprised to find we've stopped about a block from the van. It's parked in front of a ten-story office building, which stands discreet and understated against the Jersey City skyline.

"We'll get him back, Pen." Riker nods at the van, his eyes locked on the doors as he makes assessments and counts bodies. It's the look of calculating determination

I've seen echoed on Grant's face in the middle of the job. "You have my word on that. If he's what you want, you know I'm all in."

Oz taps a few keys on his laptop, his expression grim. Instead of interrupting him to ask what kind of horrible visions he's getting from the security feed across the street, I look to Riker, who's perched over his shoulder.

"That's not good," Riker mutters.

I reach for Jordan's hand.

"We're sure those blueprints are accurate?" Riker lets out a low whistle and points at the screen. "Is that—?"

Oz nods.

"Shit. There's no way we're getting around that."

I can't take it anymore. "What? What are they doing to him?"

"No idea," Riker says, his brow furrowed. "We can't see anything on the tenth floor. The rest of the building is financial offices, but as soon as you hit the top? Nothing. No cameras, no elevator access, no emergency exits. It's a dark floor."

"A dark floor?" I ask.

"Yeah. That's where you go to do the stuff you don't want anyone to know about."

My lower lip quivers. While I'm grateful for our sudden attempt at honesty and transparency, I wish Riker would paint his words with a few more rainbows. Tara and Grant have been inside that building for several hours now—enough time to sell a necklace and be on their merry way ten times over. Something is wrong.

"So what now?" I slump to the floor. We're holed

up in an empty apartment across the street. There was a huge pile of newspapers on the doorstep and several days' worth of mail in the box downstairs, so we decided to break in and make it our base of operations. This place has all the signs of an owner on vacation.

"As far as I can tell, we have two options." Riker is almost apologetic as he slips into his usual role of command. I want to tell him it's okay—that I appreciate his ability to take charge in ways I never realized before—but there isn't time. We have to get in there and save Grant before it's too late. "Option one: we involve the feds."

A collective groan fills the air, and mine is the loudest. I can't think of anything I'd like to do less.

Riker raises his hands. "I know, I know. It's not ideal. But we may have to face the possibility that they're better equipped to handle this than we are. The men I saw go into that motel room were heavily armed."

"But if Grant is breaking protocol or—God forbid—the law, he could get into a lot of trouble," I say. I can't just hand him over to the authorities like that. Given how many opportunities he's had to do the same to me and my friends over the past year, I owe him that much. "We're talking substantial jail time. And like you said before, he's trained for this sort of thing. He wouldn't appreciate us calling this in if he has everything under control."

"And if he doesn't?" Jordan asks gently.

I crush her hand. There is that.

"How about we call it our last resort?" I say. "Riker said he had another option. Let's hear that one." I look to him expectantly, and I think there's a smile taking up residence on the left side of his mouth.

"Option two: we do what we do best." There's no groan this time, just a spark of excitement, that collective sense of anticipation we all get when a new plan looms on the horizon. "We break in, take what we want, and get the hell out of there."

"Yeah, but how?" I ask. I hate to be the one to usher in the doom and gloom, but we usually spend months planning a job. There's reconnaissance, contingency plans for our contingency plans. We don't have time for that now. "If you can't even break in to look at security cameras on that floor, how are we supposed to get inside and extract two human beings? It's not like I can squeeze through a vent and pull them out. Tara might fit, but Grant would get stuck at the first turn."

"I don't know," Riker says.

This has to mark the first time he's admitted to not having all the answers. It's been a long time coming, and a part of me wants to cheer at how little fuss he makes over the confession, but this must be the worst case of bad timing known to mankind. I *need* Riker to know what he's doing. I *need* his confidence and edge.

He drags a plush armchair across the floor, settling it so the four of us make a circle—me on the floor, Jordan leaning on the windowsill, Oz typing maniacally on his laptop in hopes of finding a back door.

"Okay, guys, this is it." Riker leans on his knees and steeples his fingers. "We've got one hour to come up with an ironclad plan, or we have to call the feds. There's a ten-story building across the street packed with dangerous, armed men, insanely high levels of security, no underground access, and the love of Penelope's life trapped inside. How do we get in?"

We sit there a moment, silent and transfixed as failure waits on standby. The stakes have never been higher, but there doesn't seem to be an easy solution to this problem. We don't have the manpower or the artillery. We don't have the intel. There's no getting in without...

An idea hits me. Dazzling and brilliant and planted by Grant himself the day we met.

"We need a hazmat suit," I say, starting to laugh. "And about six levels of clearance."

THE FIGHT

25

I STORM THROUGH THE FRONT DOORS OF THE OFFICE building, assessing the interior as quickly as I can without giving anything away. In the manner of busy offices everywhere, it's sleek and modern, with a cavernous entryway that doesn't invite loitering. A reception desk sits near the elevators; a waiting area showcases two uncomfortable-looking chairs and nothing more. In fact, if it weren't for the man at the desk, who looks about ten times meaner than your average security guard, I'd feel like I'm at the dentist.

"Where is he?" I shout, doing my best imitation of a woman in hysterics. Thankfully, it's not that much of a stretch, given the state of my nerves. "Where is that cheating bastard sneak?"

Again, not much of a stretch. I'm still holding onto some emotions about the whole Tara thing.

The man at the reception desk jumps to his feet. He's at least six and a half feet tall, and he doesn't look happy to see me. "Ma'am, I'm going to have to ask you to stop right there."

"Are you covering for him? Is that it?" I make a pretense of looking around the empty waiting room. "Did he put you up to it? Manfred! Manfred, get out here this minute!"

"Ma'am, you need to calm down."

I whirl on him, fixing my glare in the center of his forehead. It's a long way up, and I try not to gulp when he moves away from the desk to showcase a physique that makes Grant look like Tiny Tim.

"*You* calm down," I tell him and almost lose my steam in a fit of nervous giggles. "And tell that man-whore to get down here where I can see him."

"I think you might—"

Another woman marches through the sliding glass doors at the entryway, her finger pointed at me like a fury. Jordan is barely recognizable in a miniskirt that makes her legs look about fifteen feet long and a pair of hoop earrings that rival Saturn's rings, but one could say the same of me. These fishnet tights aren't exactly my normal attire, and I'm wearing one of Jordan's push-up bras, which means I can almost lean down and lick my own boobs.

"You bitch," Jordan snarls. She launches herself at me, fingernails and teeth bared. "I told you to stay away. I told you what would happen if I saw your Little Orphan Annie face sniffing around him again."

It's all I can do to hold her back and not laugh at the same time. I love that Orphan Annie is the biggest insult she can come up with. She's too nice to call me anything that might hurt my feelings. Fortunately, following the plan becomes easier when she pulls my hair in earnest.

"What are you doi—?" I begin, but then she jumps me—as in, actually jumps me from behind, knocking us both to the ground for the most glorious of catfights—and there's no need to finish my sentence. I know what she's doing. She's making this count.

"He loves *me*, you ginger floozy," she says.

"Oh, you did *not* just call me that, you long-legged prude." To cover another laugh, I fight back with everything I have, slapping and pulling and rolling her underneath me until she's pinned against the cool marble tiles. Jordan's in pretty good shape, but she has nothing on my daily running and dancing regimen, even if I have been slacking lately.

"You two need to take this outside," the guard-slash-receptionist says. He grabs me around the waist, ready to yank me off Jordan and end the fight. "You have the wrong place. There's no one in this building named Manfred."

"What's going on out here?" Another gruff voice joins the fray, but I don't have time to assess the second guard's threat level. Instead, I catch a flash of movement near the front doors. Oz needs just enough time to slip in and dump Jordan's failed chemical experiment from last week—the one that smelled like poison but did no harm—into one of the elevators. If it's half as bad as I remember, the plan should work perfectly.

But only if the security guards don't notice him, which means there's only one thing to do. With a silent apology for Jordan's pretty purple camisole, I reach down and rip hard enough to give the guards a free peep show.

Her gasp of outrage is mostly laughter, but the trick works like you wouldn't believe. The man holding me lets go and quickly steps back, allowing the fight to continue unabated. Jordan tears at my clothes in retaliation, but I fend her off with a tube of lipstick, which she gleefully smashes into my forehead. We could probably go on like this for hours, but we still have a job to do, so I fall back in a pant and a groan of feigned agony.

There's no sign of Oz, which means his job is done, and we need to get out of here before the toxic smell takes hold. Jordan says it takes about ten minutes to neutralize and reach its full potent scent.

"You can tell Manfred I'm done," I say, climbing to my feet with as much dignity as I can muster. Her hair and makeup are a mess, her clothes askew and a trickle of sweat dripping down her cheek—but I can see her trying to hide her smile with an appropriately angry face. "He's all yours. I hope you have hundreds of skanky babies together."

"You wish your babies could be as skanky as mine."

One of the guards coughs and grabs me by the arm. He hauls me to my feet and enjoys himself a little too much in the process, if you know what I mean. I make a good show of digging in my heels and protesting the treatment, but I'm happy to find that the other guard busies himself lifting Jordan. His eyes never leave her exposed cleavage as he forces a similar retreat.

"I repeat, there's no one in this building named Manfred," my guard says. He flashes me a toothy smile that's missing two incisors. "But if you ladies want to tussle over me…"

I yank my arm away. "As if. Manfred could crush you with one hand tied behind his back."

"Manfred is ten times the man you'll ever be," Jordan adds with a jeer.

And then we hightail it out of there before they get it into their heads to challenge Manfred—or us—to a duel.

We're suited up and ready to head in on cue. Jordan and I have shed our trashy trappings—though I'm keeping the push-up bra until further notice—and we now swim inside matching yellow rubber suits and masks. Neither of us thought to question Oz on the procurement of these, but they sure look like the real deal. Riker is similarly attired, but we plan to leave Oz on the outside to intercept any authentic emergency personnel who might show up to assist.

For what we can only assume are extreme security measures, the elevators in the building don't go up to the tenth floor. According to the blueprints, however, the elevator *shafts* do. Which means we just need to shimmy up to the tenth-floor access panel and break in from there. With the toxic smell doing a convincing job of scaring the security guards at the reception desk, we should be able to have them turn the elevators off and leave us alone with our hazmat suits and carefully concealing plastic walls. Riker and I can spend as much time as we need on the top floor while Jordan gives the appearance of industriousness below.

It's not a foolproof plan—mostly because neither Riker nor I know what we'll find once we reach the top—but it's the only one we have. Just knowing I'm in the same building as Grant, making an effort to reach him, is a step in the right direction.

Toward him. That's where I'm headed. Not hiding

behind some stupid black mask, and not pretending a wedding ring is all that's needed to make a relationship work.

I hope I'm not too late.

"Are we ready?" Riker asks as he secures his mask. I flash him a falsely confident thumbs-up, and that's all the sign we need to get going. He taps Jordan on the shoulder, and she floors the white van we've skillfully "borrowed" for the afternoon. She tears around the corner to the office building so we can pull to an impressive stop out front—which is exactly what we do.

I've never actually *seen* a hazmat crew in action before, but I doubt any of them have been as terrifying as us as we hop out of the van to unload supplies. We didn't have time to pull together an authentic set of tools, so it's mostly old buckets, tarps, and an air compressor with *Danger: Hazard* stickers plastered on it. It's all we need. Grant was right—no one looks at you very closely when you're decked out in full hazmat gear. They mostly turn around and run for their lives.

Riker motions with his hand for us to head inside. With a nod he probably can't see, I pick up a bucket with one hand and something I'm pretty sure is an amp with the other. It's heavy, and it looks good, so I'm going with it.

My enormous security guard friend is at the door when we arrive, looking relieved to see us, which goes to show you how noxious Jordan's compound is.

"You guys are fast," he says and jerks his head toward the elevators. "We shut down the north elevator and put up a sign directing everyone to the stairs for now."

"Good. Has anyone gone in there since the substance was first detected?"

"No, but the lady who found it is pretty shaken up." He points to the reception desk, where a matronly woman in a red cardigan coughs heavily—and, if you ask me, unnecessarily. The second security guard, Jordan's peeper, is doing his best to calm her down. It's not a job I envy, and I'm the one about to climb up an elevator shaft. "She was coming down from the sixth floor for her lunch break. Is she going to die?"

"There's no saying," Riker says. He moves toward the elevator, his steps wide and sure. He almost never takes on these roles—the kind in the trenches—and I forgot how convincing he can be when he puts his mind to it. "If the spill is contained, we should be able to seal off the area without interrupting your regular business."

That's my and Jordan's cue to start taping up the plastic walls that will conceal our movements. We roll out the supplies and get to work, grateful the gas masks hide our faces. In the background, Riker continues to issue orders.

"Tell anyone who asks that it's routine maintenance—or that someone got sick inside the elevator. That usually does the trick. The woman needs to be kept quarantined until we identify the substance, and it's probably best if you minimize your contact with people. You washed your hands?"

We don't hear the guard's reply, but we can guess what it is when Riker issues a curt, "Do that first, and don't eat or drink anything until you hear from us. Try not to worry. Nine times out of ten, it's just someone who spilled nail polish remover in their bag. I'm sure it'll be nothing."

I don't know if allaying fears is the best way to

guarantee us the privacy we need to get to the top floor, but it works. The guard accepts Riker's calm assurance as a sign that he knows what he's doing and leaves us to finish taping off the plastic walls around the elevator doors.

The second our area is sealed, I whip off my rubber mask and breathe the sweet, nontoxic fumes of Jordan's genius. The first part of the plan has gone off without a hitch, which means we're that much closer to getting where we need to be.

Riker does the same, quickly unzipping his suit and stepping out of it so he can unscrew the emergency panel at the top of the elevator. He pauses for a moment to catch my eye, his left-side smile bigger than I've seen it in a long time. "This was a pretty good idea, Pen. Time to work, privacy to work in, and a security guard eating out of our hands. We might have to try it again sometime."

It's almost more than I can take. Grant is still trapped upstairs with scary, gun-toting men, and he may never forgive me for all the lies I've told, but for the briefest moment, I feel like everything might be okay.

Because that man right there? Fearless, confident, and prepared to journey to the depths of hell by my side? I've missed him even more than the father who disappeared ten years ago.

He's my ally. He's my equal. He's my friend.

And I know with absolute conviction that he's not going to stop until my husband is safe in my arms.

THE BREAK-IN

FROM A LOGICAL STANDPOINT, WORMING MY WAY UP AN elevator shaft should cause less anxiety than sitting inside a ventilation system. This metal tube is substantially bigger, and I can feel a cool breeze whistling up either side of the elevator car. I'm also more active in this scenario, my feet searching for each foothold in the metal framework as my hands grip the cable like my life depends on it.

Which, technically, it does.

Ten stories might not seem like much when you take the stairs, but let me tell you, when you gain every inch by the force of your strength and willpower alone, it's a heck of a long climb.

"Do I need to include a weight-lifting regimen in your workout?" Riker jokes as he leaps from one wall of the shaft to another. In all our time together, I've never seen him in action like this before, and I can barely believe my eyes. He's like Spider-Man, putting me to shame with how easily he manages to scale the passageway.

"I can make it," I say through gritted teeth. Upper body strength might not be my greatest asset, but determination *is*. "I haven't met a back entrance I can't handle yet, and I don't intend to start today."

"Good girl," Riker says, genuine encouragement in his voice. "Just think of the prize waiting at the end."

If he'd have dangled Grant as an incentive a few days—heck, even a few hours—ago, I wouldn't have believed he wanted me to make it. But I know that he means it now. We have to keep going to get to the end. The prize. My husband. A man who may not love me but who I love with everything my black, thieving little heart possesses.

Which, as it turns out, is quite a lot.

"Race you to the top," I call. "Last one up has to lure out any guard dogs."

Riker responds to my challenge by swinging impressively from one side of the shaft to the other, but he's got nothing on me. His fancy tricks might look good on the outside, but I've been doing this sort of thing a lot longer than him. When it comes to breaking and entering, the motto is always *slow and steady wins the race*.

That would be another of my dad's maxims. No matter how tempted we might be to look for shortcuts or blast through walls, it's always better to let patience rule the day. Crack the safe's code with a stethoscope and painstaking care. Sit in the air vent for eight hours before you strike. Put one hand over the other and pull yourself up all ten flights of the elevator shaft.

Which is why I make it to the top first.

"You cheated," Riker grumbles but with a good-natured air. "I want a rematch."

"Sure thing. I'll just need about two weeks to recover from that climb first."

Panting only slightly, I extract a multi-tool from my belt, which Oz had the foresight to acquire along with the hazmat supplies, and start removing the bolts to the access panel. I've done this enough times that I'm able to make short work of it, carefully tucking each bolt in my pocket in case we need to replace them later.

I lift the panel away and hand it to Riker, poking my head out just enough to make a quick initial assessment.

"It's clear," I say, dropping to a whisper, "but we'll have to be careful about cameras. I wouldn't be surprised if they have a separate closed video feed just for this floor."

"Or lasers," he adds.

I stare at him. "Lasers?"

"You know, alarm lasers?" he says. "The ones that detect movement?"

"Those aren't a real thing. In all our years of breaking and entering, have we ever seen security lasers?"

"Well, no," he admits. "But we will someday, and when we do, you'll be glad I know what I'm doing."

Feet first, I swing through the panel, landing in a silent crouch on the other side. From there, I make a survey of our surroundings.

The elevators are located at one end of the floor, in an alcove that shields us from the main hallway. Beige carpeting silences our footsteps, but there isn't anything to hide behind, which makes the silence a moot point. There are no large potted plants, no conveniently located snack machines, not even box windows with a few inches to spare. The second we round that corner, we'll be in plain view of whatever awaits us.

To make matters worse, there's a slight shadow shading the carpet near the wall, and my heart sinks at the sight of it. That shadow looks decidedly human, which isn't a good sign. We'd have a better chance getting past lasers.

I turn back to Riker with a finger on my lips. "I think there's a guard posted at the end of the hallway. We'll need to find a way to distract him."

"Distract him how?" he asks.

I don't know. My mind runs over a list of possibilities, but we didn't plan for a distraction. We can't cut the lights, and we don't have any of Jordan's smoke bombs on hand. Equally out of the question is running screaming into the hallway to divert his attention, as that would alert any other guards to trouble.

I'm still mulling over the problem when Riker steps forward.

"Make some noise," he whispers.

"What kind of noise?" I whisper back.

"Any kind."

"Why?"

"Because I know how we're going to get past him, that's why." He cracks his knuckles and crouches against the wall. "Now."

"Riker, are you sure you can—?"

"Just do it."

"But what if you can't—?"

He glares at me. "I might not be a heap of brainless muscles like your husband, but I'm not without my uses. Trust me."

It seems like people are asking me to do that an awful lot lately.

It also seems like maybe I should heed their advice. If I hope to get out of this hole I've buried myself in, I'm going to have to take someone's hand. One fortifying breath and a wordless prayer later, and I shake the panel Riker removed. The wobbling clang of the metal sounds too loud to my ears, primed as they are for any sort of movement, but Riker nods to show his approval.

I press myself as flat against the opposite wall as possible, tempted to close my eyes against the inevitable. Unlike that day at Paulson's, however, I keep my eyes wide open.

I'm not hiding anymore.

It's over so fast, I barely see it happen. The guard rounds the corner to investigate the noise. Riker's hand shoots out, and the side of it catches the guard in the throat to silence him. The man gives a strangled gurgle and reaches for the gun strapped to his waist, but Riker knees him in the stomach with an alarming show of efficiency. Sympathy pains weaken my knees as the man doubles over, at which point Riker brings his elbow down on the back of the man's head.

That's it. The guard, who is easily forty pounds heavier than Riker, crumples to the ground with a barely audible groan, knocked out cold. Grabbing the man's gun and sticking it in his belt, Riker jerks his head for me to follow.

"Holy shit," I whisper. "Where did you learn to do that?"

His sharp look is all the answer I need. Riker, it seems, goes a lot deeper than I've given him credit for.

"Stay behind me. I don't think there's anyone else in the hallway, or they would have investigated. It must be clear."

I nod and take a few tentative steps around the unconscious man, prepared to follow Riker and his mad ninja skills to the ends of the earth.

As it turns out, the end of the earth isn't far away.

With a seemingly endless hallway of doors to choose from, it might have taken us hours to find out which one contained the treasure we were looking for. But just a few doors down, slumped against the wall with her arms wrapped protectively around her knees, is Tara.

At first, I think she must be hurt, because there are tears in her eyes and her face is a mess of running mascara. All jokes about being caught in the crossfire aside, I don't actually want anything bad to happen to her. I make a motion to go to her side, but Riker stops me with a hand on my shoulder.

I can't imagine why until Tara notices us. She doesn't seem surprised to see us, nor does she seem particularly excited to be rescued. In fact, she looks as though she's seen a ghost. Her face glows white against the charcoal trails down both cheeks.

"Don't go in there, Pen." Tara's voice is strangled, and I think it might be the end of us both. "Whatever you do, don't go in there."

Riker flings out a hand to stop me, but it's not enough. Death, danger, a trap set to destroy me... Nothing beyond that door scares me as much as the idea that Grant might not be on the other side of it anymore.

Heart pounding, I push my way inside.

THE 27 AGREEMENT

(Fifteen Months, Six Days Ago)

GRANT WASN'T EXPECTING ME.

I stood nervously on his front porch, out of place in his neighborhood of picket fences and carefully sculpted lawns north of the city. It said something that standing on this nicely kept street made me more uncomfortable than I'd ever felt trapped inside a box or vent, but there was no turning back. I'd already knocked.

He pulled open the door, looking incredibly gorgeous in his at-home attire—low-slung track bottoms, a shirt that clung to all the ripples and valleys of his torso, and bare feet. His expression registered that brief flash of almost-surprise unique to him. It lasted a second and then disappeared, replaced by the smile that had the power to crush my heart.

Except I was the one about to do the crushing.

"I can't marry you," I said.

Damn. I'd intended to ease into it, but that smile had me flustered. I don't think anyone had been that happy to see me before.

He blinked, his hand still on the doorknob. "You can't, or you won't?"

I blinked back. "Um. Does it make a difference?"

"More than you think." He jerked his head toward the interior of his house—a house I hadn't seen before and wasn't sure I cared to. He'd been very gentlemanly in always picking me up at my place for our dates, even if he had to cut half of them short for work. His home, like his heart, was still a mystery to me. "Come in."

I hesitated. Even though I'd been to his mom's house and sort of shared the holidays with him, it felt strange to cross that line. Into hearth and home. Into the space where the job ended and *he* began.

He saw my reluctance and swore. "I knew it was a mistake leaving your apartment before I got a firm yes."

"How do you know I was going to say yes?"

His voiced dropped to a sexy rumble, and his hand reached for me with its big, warm palm and promises of tenderness. He rested it on my cheek, his thumb running its familiar path over my lips. "You were going to say yes."

I bit.

Not hard enough to break the skin, mind you, but enough so he knew I meant business. He pulled his hand back with a louder curse and a sad smile.

"We're going to do this the hard way, I see," he said. "Come in. I think there are some things we need to talk about."

I shook my head, eyes wide and heart fluttering, prey

caught in the wolf's snare. If he reached for me again—if he kept touching me and saying sweet things—I wasn't going to be able to fight this.

And I needed to fight it. I needed to fight *him*. After he left my apartment yesterday, I should have been over the moon—after all, I'd finally won, finally gotten him to break his self-imposed restrictions on making our relationship a physical one.

But I'd never felt less like a winner in my life. I'd been vulnerable and alone, my apartment echoing with a cavernous silence it had never contained before he pushed his way inside. If one sexual encounter with this man could do that to me, what would a lifetime of them do?

"There's nothing to say. I thought about it, and I'm flattered by the offer, but I think it's time we break up."

He didn't move, not even to blink. "Come inside, Penelope."

"Why? What are you going to do to me in there?"

The etched lines of his frown went soul-deep. "You think I'm going to hurt you?"

No. I *knew* he was going to hurt me. Nothing beyond that door would bring me anything but pain.

"Grant." I was pleading—something I almost never did, but I didn't know what else to do. If I entered his home and he turned the full force of his charm on me, there was a good chance I'd tell him everything he wanted to know. That wasn't going to do anyone a favor. Not me and certainly not him. If he knew about half the terrible things I'd done in my lifetime, it would break his heart.

"Can we please just call this what it was—a good

time? A fling?" I hesitated over the next one, but I had to say it if I planned to get out of there alive. "A mistake?"

"You and I are *not* a mistake."

"But—"

He cut me off before I even knew what I was going to say. "Do you know how difficult it was for me to leave your apartment yesterday?"

I blinked at him, wondering where this was going, wondering if I really wanted to find out. "No," I said slowly, not sure which question I was answering.

"I've done plenty of difficult things in my life before," he said. "Physical challenges, psychological ones. I've been Tasered and maced, forced to go days without sleep, fought men two times my size and won."

Yes, I thought, staring at this flawless, infallible man. *As Riker would call him, a real prince.*

"And you know what? None of it took more out of me than putting my clothes back on and saying goodbye. Nothing hurt as much as walking out that door knowing you might still need me." He lifted a hand toward me, dropping it only when he saw how close I was to bolting. "I could get kidnapped tomorrow, face down ten firing squads, claw my way through deserts and mountains, but leaving you would still be the hardest thing I've done."

"But you did," I pointed out, my throat tight. He always would.

"Then *marry* me, dammit." The ferocity of his words took me by surprise. "Marry me so I won't ever have to leave you again."

Yes.

My body answered for me, drawing me forward until

I was in his arms. It wasn't the direction I wanted to go, and my mind recoiled at the thought of how easy it would be to give up everything for the sake of his embrace.

Nothing felt better than this man's heart beating against mine. Nothing made me happier than hearing him speak my name.

"Does this mean you'll do it?" he asked, the words spoken directly into the sensitive skin at the base of my earlobe.

I stiffened almost immediately.

"I've got a whole speech planned, if that helps," he added.

It didn't help, and I twisted to get out of his grip. "You don't want to marry me, Grant. I'm a horrible person and I don't get along with others and you'll regret it. You'll regret it every minute you're stuck with me."

He held firm—both his obstinacy and his arms. "I think that's for me to decide, isn't it?"

"I'm dangerous."

"Not to me, you aren't."

"That's because you're overly confident in your skills. I could become dangerous. I could ruin everything you've worked toward."

He paused long enough to toss me aside, but, of course, he didn't. He devoured me with that stare of his instead. "That's a risk I'm willing to take."

Before I could come up with any more excuses, he pulled me toward the living room. Now that I paid attention, I could see that his house wasn't what you'd expect a hot bachelor FBI agent to call home, but exactly what you'd expect a deceptively gentlemanlike mystery collector who loved antique stores and flea markets to mark as his own. I saw the painting he'd talked about before. It was perched on the living room wall, the colors as bright and vivid as he'd promised.

This wasn't just a place he put his head down for the night before he went to work the next day. This was his *home*. And I wanted to share it with him so much, I almost couldn't bear it. It was like looking directly into the sun.

He placed me on the couch, and my body slid along his as I fell into a sitting position. He sat next to me, and I thought he might use the moment to his advantage, pressing me against the cushions and kissing me until I capitulated, but he maintained a decorous distance, my hands clasped in his.

"Look, I think we should—" he began, but I shook my head and refused to look up. I couldn't.

He was about to confess all and destroy everything: his position, our relationship, *my life*. The moment he admitted out loud what he was doing—that he'd been assigned to watch me, that I was part of an elaborate plan to uncover the Blue Fox's fortune—the future I'd pictured inside this house was gone. More than anything else, I wanted a chance at that future. For the first time in my life, I wanted hope.

"Don't say it. Not yet," I said. My words slurred as I tried to make sense of what I was about to ask, and my head felt heavy and hot. "If I agree to marry you, can you promise me something?"

"Anything," he said so fiercely, I almost believed him.

"That day we picked out my couch together—do you remember what we talked about?"

"Of course I do. I picked you up at the ferry terminal,

and you looked like you'd just stepped out of a hurricane. You were beautiful." Then he stiffened, his fingers turning to stone in mine. "Wait a minute—is this about Riker?"

Riker, who'd been there that day. Riker, who'd met Grant for the first time and didn't hesitate to show his displeasure. Riker, who would never get over the fact that he wasn't my number one choice anymore.

What I was about to say *wasn't* about him, not even a little, but I must have delayed for a second too long. It was an important second—a life-changing second— because part of Grant withdrew in that moment, retreating behind a wall I'd constructed myself. If I didn't know him as well as I did, I might not have noticed, but this man was already so much a part of me that it felt like a slash to the heart. It was a reserve, a hesitance, a too-quick smile that burned like fire. And it stayed there for much longer than I ever realized.

More than a year, in fact.

"No. It has nothing to do with Riker," I said, but it was too late. Even saying his name gave Riker power. It told Grant that he wasn't the only man in my life I cared about, the only one who cared about *me*.

Not that Grant would admit as much out loud. He was too far committed to retreat now. He'd admitted as much at his mom's house. *I play to win.*

As if there was any other way to play. As if we'd ever be anywhere but on opposite sides of the equation.

"I see," he said slowly.

That time, *I* took *his* hands, pulling them into my lap and worrying my fingers over the rough skin of his palms until it felt safe to continue. It took longer than it should have, my courage flagging at the idea of laying so much of myself on the line.

Bravery was easy when it meant putting yourself in physical harm's way. It was the emotional stuff that really scared me.

"I was actually referring to the conversation we had at my apartment, when you told me I could ask you anything," I said. "Remember?" I did. I'd played it over and over inside my head—that feeling of power I had over him, the precious way I still held that power, close to my heart. "After we kissed, you said you were so flustered, you wouldn't be able to help but tell me the truth. Government secrets and everything—they were mine for the taking."

"I meant it, Penelope."

No rhyme that time. Just my name. Just me.

"I felt the same way," I said softly, toying with his fingers. "I still do. When your lips touch mine, when your hands are on my skin and your body is next to mine, I know there isn't anything in the world I wouldn't confess. All you have to do is ask."

He opened his mouth to say something, but I stopped him. I squeezed his hands so tightly, he couldn't mistake the urgency of what came next.

"You can't ask, Grant," I said. "You have to promise me that no matter how much you might want to, you won't ask. You can never ask."

He wanted to ask—he'd never wanted anything that much, I was sure of it. The struggle I saw in his eyes was the most clearly his thoughts had ever been revealed. He wanted to kiss me right then and there and demand answers. He wanted to push me to the couch and extract every last one of my secrets.

Oh, how I wanted to let him.

I almost took back my words—almost gave him everything—but then I pictured all the terrible things I'd done in my life, all the terrible things I still planned to do. There were so many parts of me that belonged solely to my dad and to Riker, to the dark, dishonorable places that would make Grant look at me with loathing instead of desire. So I held firm. We played the game this way, or we didn't play at all.

He waited just long enough for me to say something more, to surrender to the overwhelming force of his personality. When I didn't, he cupped my face and forced my gaze to lock on his so I could see how much he didn't like this request of mine.

I saw.

"This is what you really want?" he asked.

No. "Yes."

"This is the only way I can have you?"

Never. "Yes."

"Then I accept your terms."

Holy shit. Was I engaged? "Really? Just like that?"

"If that's what it takes to get you to marry me, I'll do it." He issued it as a challenge. He was ferocious in his words and bearing, daring me to contradict him. "I might not like it, but I can't think of anything I wouldn't do to make you mine—and there are things I've done in my lifetime that no man should admit to. That's how much I adore you, Penelope Blue."

My heart lurched into my throat. *Adore.* Not as big as love, but not as small as desire. It would have to be enough.

I wasn't familiar enough with the protocol for

marriage proposals to know what was supposed to come next. Chances were good that the standard reaction wasn't to burst into tears, but that was exactly what I felt like doing. I had no idea *why*. I'd gone into this situation with my eyes wide open. I knew what the stakes were and still chose to play—but there it was. I wanted to curl up in Grant's lap and cry like a baby until he made it all okay again.

Which was why I did the opposite. I did the only thing I could think of that would take this ache away, the only thing between us that I knew was one hundred percent real.

I kissed him.

With my arms around his neck and my body pressed to his, I kissed him so hard, he couldn't deny me any longer. I kissed him so deep, I still haven't come up for air.

THE END

28

IT'S A STRANGE THING TO KNOW YOU'RE A WIDOW.

I've seen good, decent women react to that news before, falling to their knees and screaming in agony, a part of their soul ripped away. I've also seen Tara react to that news before, in a huff of irritation and outrage, her bags packed and the cab waiting before it had time to settle.

I feel neither of these things. Standing outside the room that contains all that's left of my husband, I have neither voice nor body. I'm only numb.

"Pen, don't—" Riker tries to prevent me from twisting the doorknob, but I have to know. I have to see.

I notice his body right away, a huddled lump near a desk on the far side of the room. It's almost funny how much one man's body looks like another when the life has been extinguished. From here, it looks like he shares several characteristics with the man Riker felled over by the elevators—the same tilt to his head and slack jaw, the same eyes closed against the world, fluttering to wakefulness.

Wakefulness?

With a cry still lodged in the base of my throat, I take stilted steps toward the body. It isn't dead. *He* isn't dead. I'm not too late.

I stop before I get far into the room as the man groans again and rolls onto his back. I don't recognize the pug nose or the pointed chin, and I would never have fallen for someone who could so casually wear that shade of green. Not only is the man on the ground not dead, he's also not Grant. I cast a wide-eyed glance around me, scanning for the familiar dark-blond curls that run like silk through my fingers.

I see more slumped bodies, groaning bodies, huddled bodies...none of which are his. Nor is he the man standing behind the desk, the one with his arms raised as if there's a gun pointed at his head.

"Penelope, you're blocking my aim." Grant's voice sounds from behind me before I can make sense of my surroundings. "Do you think you could move about two feet to your left?"

I turn and release the scream that the good, decent woman inside me has been holding hostage—and for once, I'm not ashamed. I'd scream a thousand times if it meant I could capture this moment forever.

"Grant!" Even though the gun is now technically pointed at me, I don't hesitate in throwing myself the remainder of the distance and burying my head in his chest. I've always loved the smell of him—soap warmed by skin and sweat, the fabric softener all our clothes share—but I'm not sure I've ever appreciated it as much as I do right now. "You're not dead. You're here. You're alive."

"Of course I'm not dead," he says, amusement in his voice. Amusement and something more—something that catches in our throats, binding us. "I'm incredibly hard to kill. I hope you weren't looking forward to cashing in on that lovely insurance policy just yet."

"But Tara is crying out in the hall, and there are all these bad guys..." I'm pretty sure I'm getting tears and snot all over his chest, but I don't care. I burrow deeper until he's forced to hold me awkwardly, one arm around my shoulders while the other grips the gun. "We broke in to come rescue you."

"I can see we might have saved ourselves the trouble," Riker says from behind me. The cock of another gun—the one he took from the hallway guard—fills the room. "Don't worry, Emerson. I'll cover him while you two have your little reunion. My aim's a lot better than Pen's."

At the sound of Riker's voice, dry enough to turn this room into a desert, Grant stiffens. I hate that he stiffens, hate even more that he went up against this room full of scary men believing I didn't love him. Even though his arm drops from around me, I cling tighter.

We can't both let go. We can't both give up.

"I'd rather not lose my advantage, if you don't mind," Grant says. "In case you haven't noticed, I went to considerable lengths to secure it."

Riker laughs. "I noticed. Do you mind if I ask why we're holding Blackrock at gunpoint?"

"I'm deciding whether or not I want to kill him."

"I see," Riker says, which makes one of us.

"I don't suppose I get any say in the matter?" Blackrock's smooth, clipped, *familiar* voice weighs in. It comes from the other side of the room, which means it must belong to Blackrock. "A few years ago, I might've told you to have at it, but I'm suddenly discovering I have a wealth of things to live for."

I drop my arms slowly from around Grant's waist, and the room makes dizzy revolutions around me as I turn.

Blackrock's face comes into focus. It takes me a moment—and several deep breaths—before his features register. Eyes and nose, mouth and cheeks. The tall, thin form. All the parts are there, as familiar to me as my own, but aged ten years and lined with the kind of worry that only a decade of hard usage could bring.

"Daddy?"

Despite the pair of guns pointed at him, Blackrock lowers his hands. "Oh, baby doll. You have no idea how much I've missed you."

THE FALLOUT

29

FOR REASONS I CAN'T FATHOM AND DON'T CARE TO, GRANT and Riker turn their guns on each other. I can hear them argue in the background—*You mean Blackrock is really the Blue Fox? Are you telling me you didn't know? How was I supposed to know? I never met Pen's dad*—but I don't pay them any heed. I'm too busy staring at the man I once called father, trying to assemble my jumbled thoughts.

"I don't understand," I say. Though not the most intelligent, that remark seems the most apt. I *don't* understand, not any of it. My dad hired Riker to steal the necklace he failed to get ten years ago? My dad missed me? My dad is alive? "You can't be my father. My father is dead."

The smile that threatened to split Blackrock's face— familiar and strange at the same time—wobbles. "I'm not dead, baby doll. I'm right here."

He moves around the desk to approach me, but

I back away, my body in strict recoil. I don't know what's going on, but I do know I don't want this man to touch me.

"No. Stay back. I don't know who you are."

Without a word, Riker and Grant turn as one, their guns once again pointed at Blackrock's head. They also move closer, automatically flanking me on either side. I take comfort in the dual presence of these men—my best friend and my husband, two people I don't deserve, two people I've done everything in my power to push away. I'm secure in the knowledge that no harm can come to me if they're near.

Why had I ever thought that was a bad thing?

"Don't come any closer, asshole," Grant says. I only know Grant is the one speaking because of the direction of his voice. Otherwise, he's completely unrecognizable. I've never heard that cold, steely hatred from him before. "You heard my wife. After what you've put her through, you don't get to do anything without her permission."

"So it's true," Blackrock—my father—says. "You *are* married to a federal agent."

I don't see what business it is of his, and I'm about to say as much when Riker speaks up. "If you think you're safe because he's not allowed to shoot an unarmed man, think again. I'm not bound by the same rules."

"And here I was worried you might not have anyone to take care of you," my father says. Even though a spasm of pain moves across his features, he releases a soft chuckle. "Put the guns down, gentlemen. I won't come near her again. Not until she wants me to."

Neither one of them follows his orders. They stand

rigid and at attention, unwilling to step down despite my father's commanding presence.

My heart gives an odd lurch. Blackrock may not have the power to stop these two men, but I do.

"It's okay," I say. "There's nothing he can do that will hurt me any more than he already has."

My dad's face falls the rest of the way. "Penelope—"

I ignore him and turn to Riker. "Riker, will you please make sure Tara is okay out there? She seemed really upset."

"But—"

"I'd like a moment alone with my dad, if that's okay. I'm not scared of him."

He looks as if he wants to argue, but something about the calm, even way I hold his gaze convinces him I mean business. "Sure thing, Pen."

I nod my thanks before turning to my other protector. "And Grant, can you make it down to the bottom floor and pull the hazmat team away from the elevator?"

His eyes flash as they meet mine. "Hazmat team?"

"It was really hard to find a way up here," I reply with an attempt at a smile. There's so much I want to say to him, so much I need to know, but I'm too overwhelmed to offer more than that small gesture. "Security is crazy tight around this place. Jordan will be happy to know we're still alive."

"Is Oz down there, too?" Grant asks.

Riker and I turn to him as one. "You know about Oz?"

Grant holds up his hands and backs away, laughter on his lips. Oh, how I want to capture that laughter, taste it, hold it close. "Don't hate the player. Hate the game," he says. "If it helps, it took us six months to figure out he was only one person."

"I *knew* you saw a lot more than we realized!" Riker says triumphantly, leading the way out the door. He casts me a gloating look before he makes it all the way out to the hall. "Pen was sure you suspected almost nothing."

"Pen has always held my intelligence in low esteem."

Pen thinks the sound of them amicably bickering is one of the best things she's ever heard, but she doesn't have time to dwell on that now. As soon as they close the door tactfully behind them, I'm standing alone in a room with my dad...and four of the semiconscious thugs he hired to kidnap and abuse my husband.

"Was she crying?" my dad asks.

It takes me a dizzy second to realize he's talking about Tara. Even now, he places her emotional well-being above mine. He doesn't ask how *I'm* doing or if *I* feel like crying.

Terrible. And yes.

"Yes, Dad. She was crying. Did you expect a different reaction, appearing out of nowhere like that? She thought you were dead."

He notices the *Dad* slip in there with a tight smile. "She always had a soft heart."

"Yeah. She's a real sweetie."

"*Still*, Penelope?" My dad shakes his head. "I thought for sure you would have gotten over your antagonism by now."

I stare at him, looking for a clue in the deep, weathered lines of his face. While the past ten years have done great things for Tara, my dad looks tired and old. He looks his age, which must be pushing sixty by now.

"I might need more than a few days of her shacking up with my husband to manage that," I say coldly.

"Maybe you haven't heard the story yet, but I haven't seen Tara for over a decade. She left me shortly after you did."

"Well, she could hardly go with you, could she?"

"To live on the streets?" My incredulity is strong enough to crack the room in two. Now that I don't have Riker or Grant to calm me by proximity, I feel myself starting to unravel. How dare my dad be alive? Doesn't he have any idea what I went through? "Yeah. I guess that would have been asking a bit much of her. My mistake."

"What do you mean, living on the streets?" Now it's my dad's turn to look incredulous. "I meant she couldn't go with you to your grandmother's house. I always regretted not being able to provide better for her. *You*, I knew, would be fine. But Tara..."

I'm out the door so fast, my vision blurs. I don't know where I plan to go or what I intend to do once I get there, but all I know is I can't be in the same room with that man and his hired thugs right now. I almost wish Grant had left a gun with me or gone ahead and shot him to begin with.

I always knew my father was no saint—a god, maybe, but no saint. He put work first and treated me like a partner instead of a child. He stole from the rich and gave to himself. But this went beyond everything—to worry more about Tara than me, to regret the way he'd treated her but absolve himself of guilt for my pain...

"Penelope Marianne Blue, you stop right there."

My heels dig into the carpet, stopping me in my tracks. Some things are impossible to forget, and that terse rebuke is one of them.

"You are *not* walking away from me now, young

lady. I've spent months following you—trying to figure out whether you're a thief or a fed, wondering whether it's safe to contact you. You're not leaving until I get some answers."

Months? He's talking about a sacrifice of *months*?

"I waited for you for *years*," I wail. I don't turn around, fearful of what he'll say once he realizes I'm crying. "Years, Dad. On my own, with no idea what happened to you, wondering why you'd leave a teenager all alone without a safety net. If anyone deserves some answers, it's me."

He lays his hands on my shoulders and spins me around to face him, but I can't look him in the eye. I hate him and I love him and I'm so tired of those two emotions coexisting inside my heart. "Are you telling me your grandmother never contacted you?" he asks.

The tears suspended in my lashes spill over, surprisingly warm. "No. Until a few hours ago, I didn't even know I *had* a grandmother."

"And you didn't take the savings?"

"It really exists? It's not just an urban legend?"

He pulls me to him in an awkward hug, an embrace between two strangers who used to mean something to one another. But then he holds it—just like Grant's heart hugs, forcing me to stay there and *feel* it—and I slowly unwind. Bit by bit, the layers peel away—the anger and the outrage, the questions and the fear—until all that's left is my raw, exposed emotions. I'm pretty sure I'm sobbing by the time he's finally ready to let me go.

But if I think I'm going to escape, I'm sorely mistaken.

"I think it might be time for you and I to have a talk,

Penelope," he says. "It sounds like I have some explaining to do."

———◆———

Sitting in a diner with my dad is one of the most surreal moments of my life. I've held millions of dollars in my hands, broken into places most people only dream of, stood next to a federal agent and pledged my eternal devotion...but this plate of French fries and cup of coffee feel so strange that my hands shake.

I wrap those shaking hands around my mug in an effort to still them. My dad sees the action and moves to place his hand over mine, but I'm still too upset for that kind of physical contact.

He sighs and takes his own cup in hand, though I notice he doesn't drink. We chose the diner because it's around the corner from the office building, not because either of us is particularly thirsty. We just needed to get away from the carnage and the hazmat suits, so we snuck out the secret back entrance like the villains we are.

I'm sure the FBI will know how to find us if they want to. Persistent bastards, those guys. I wouldn't put anything past them.

"I didn't intend for any of this to happen," my dad says. Under the bright lights of the restaurant, he looks older than he did before. His hair is thin on top, showing the shiny pink scalp below. "If you don't believe anything else I say, know that much. All I've ever wanted is to make you happy."

"Why does everyone keep saying that to me?"

My dad pauses as he brings his coffee cup to his lips, a question on his face.

"You. Grant. Even Riker," I say. "Every time something in my life turns to shit, you guys pop up out of nowhere and tell me you only wanted me to be happy—as if that means you don't have to take responsibility for your actions. *Well, at least I had her best interests at heart. Time to move on.*"

"It's not wrong to care about you."

"It's also not right to assume you're in control of my happiness. I might have needed you ten years ago, but I've moved on. I've made a decent life for myself."

"Is that what you call this?"

I don't answer right away. Okay, so that decent life might be a bit of a mess right now—a tangled web of good and bad, right and wrong—but at least I don't abandon people when things get tough. The one thing I've always done well is own up to my mistakes.

"I did the best I could, given the circumstances," I say. "Tell me, Dad—was the necklace really worth it?"

He puts the cup down carefully. "Do you know *why* I went after it?"

"Because you're greedy and narcissistic and wanted to prove you could?"

He laughs silently, carrying a wave of nostalgic memories over me. Oh, how I remember that silent laugh of his. Laughter, outrage, surprise…when you're a jewel thief whose success depends on stealth, all human emotion is stifled. I've always known I'll never be as good as my dad, if only for that reason.

"Well, yes, that was part of it," my dad says, losing the laugh as quickly as it came. "But it was also because your mother wanted you to have it. It was the only thing she regretted leaving behind when she gave up her family for me. The big house, the full bank account, the high society lifestyle…she never missed those things. She never had time to."

Because she'd died only ten months into her disinheritance. Because her life was the first thing I ever stole.

"It was a tradition in her family to give the necklace as a birthday gift whenever a new generation of women was born. Her grandmother gave it to her mom, her mom gave it to her, and she wanted more than anything to pass it on to you. Not having it weighed heavily on her throughout the pregnancy, and I offered to steal it for her countless times. Of course, she wouldn't hear of it."

See? I told you. My mother had been beautiful and funny and *good*. Not like the rest of us.

This time, when my dad reaches for my hands, I let him make contact. His fingers are long and tapering, like Riker's. Like mine. *A thief's hands.*

"I know I did a lot of things wrong, raising you to follow in my footsteps, but it's the only life I've ever known. Without your mom there to keep me in check…"

I squeeze his hand. I know exactly what he's trying to say. Marrying honest people seems to be the only thing the Blues do right.

"It was a stupid, risky heist, and I knew better than to try. I was too emotionally involved and made too many mistakes. You remember what I always used to say?"

I do—of course I do. "Never steal anything you can't turn around and sell the next day."

I can almost feel the hands of time tugging me backward at the smile that spreads across my dad's face. So many maxims, so many rules.

"You always were a good student. It's too bad I didn't take my own advice."

"So you got caught?" I ask, finding the idea difficult to digest. You didn't catch the Blue Fox. He was infallible. That was the point of him.

"Red-handed." My dad grimaces, remembering. "I didn't realize it at the time, but they'd left her bedroom as a shrine. Pictures, clothes, perfume—it was all exactly as she'd left it. I should have hightailed it out of there the second I lifted the necklace from her jewelry box, but I couldn't make myself leave after that. Erica's security team found me sitting on her bed, staring at the rose wallpaper."

"You were in *jail* all this time?"

The look he gives me yanks me even further back in time, to a time when this man's approval meant everything. "Of course I wasn't in jail. I don't know how much you know about your grandmother, but she's not an *easy* woman by any stretch of the imagination. She made me promise to disappear from your life in exchange for not going to the police. I hated to do it, and I can't tell you how many times I've regretted it over the years, but it seemed like the best thing at the time. She promised to take good care of you in my absence."

"She didn't."

He looks at me queerly. "I figured there was always a chance you'd stubbornly refuse her overtures and head out on your own, which was why I left all the money behind and started fresh. I wanted you to have options."

Even though I want to stubbornly refuse *his* overtures and head out on my own, I can't move from this spot. My need to understand the truth is stronger than my urge to hide behind my usual lies.

"Dad, none of that happened. Not one bit of it. I don't understand why everyone keeps thinking that my living on the streets was some kind of choice. There was no magical rich grandmother swooping in to save me, none of your secret cash to fall back on. It was just me and Tara and a hotel bill we couldn't pay. We were out within the month."

"That's not possible. I took care of it. She promised to pick you up and explain everything."

You didn't take care of it, I want to cry. *You didn't take care of me.*

Suddenly, though, I'm not so sure that's true. Seeing my dad like this, hearing Tara talk about what went down in those dark days after his disappearance, is like being transported back in time. Usually, I fight that pull as hard as I can, determined to look ahead, only ahead, always ahead. This time, however, I give in and let the memories come.

I can easily picture the hotel room, the check-patterned carpet and silvery wallpaper, the coffeemaker that bubbled and clicked every time it turned on. Less easy but still present is the bewilderment and shock I felt as hour after hour passed with no word from my father. Most difficult of all, I can remember entering the lobby a short time after the failed heist, mostly needing space from Tara, but also on the hunt for any easy marks that might provide a distraction. There was a woman there, older and well-dressed, seething with cold fury as she informed the clerk that she would bring in the police to search every room in the place unless he helped her find what she was looking for. I'd assumed she was after something stolen—maybe something *we* stole. It never occurred to me that she was really after...

Me.

Oh God. She'd been looking for *me*.

And I, hearing the dreaded threat of authority I've been trained since birth to fear, snuck out a side door and didn't return until it felt safe again.

"I didn't know," I say, dazed. "I didn't know I had a grandmother, didn't know she was there for me."

"Someone has always been there for you, baby doll," my dad says. "Always. Sometimes, I think you refuse to see it on purpose."

"But where did you go all those years?" I ask, my voice sharp. His words cut too close for comfort, and I need another distraction. Abandonment has been my default for so long, I'm not sure what to do if that, like everything else, turns out to be a lie. "Why did it take you so long to come find me?"

"I went overseas, tried Prague. After a while, one city is much like the next."

"And then?" I prompt.

"Does it really matter, Penelope?"

"Yeah, Dad, it matters," I say. I need to know what he went through. I need to know that I'm the only one who makes mistakes and suffers from them.

He sighs. "For the first year, I was so devastated and humiliated that I mostly wandered around, taking what jobs I could find. To be honest, I don't remember much from that particular period." The subtext—that drugs or alcohol or other available vices played a role—isn't lost on me. I don't remember much of the first year, either. "After the initial shock wore off, I decided I should probably try to find Tara—at least attempt to explain why I had to leave so suddenly. I found her pretty easily. She's never been one for keeping a low profile. But she'd... moved on by that time, and I didn't think it would help either of us to get in the way."

Oh. I don't say anything. The last thing I want to do is hear anything remotely sexual related to my father and Tara. If she found herself a man to replace him when he abandoned her, all I can say is: *Good for her*.

"As for you, well—I waited until you were eighteen to make contact again, per the agreement I made with your grandmother."

Eighteen. Seven years ago. Almost a quarter of my life ago.

"But you'd *disappeared*, baby doll. There was no sign of you still living at the Dupont residence, no record of you attending school in New York or abroad, no passport or driver's license in your name. You were untraceable."

Yeah. That happened when you lived on the street. People forgot you existed.

"That is, until about a year ago, when I got a hit on a marriage license between a Grant Emerson and a Penelope Blue in West Virginia, of all places." He pauses. "An FBI agent, Penelope? Really?"

I flush. "It's complicated."

"I'll say it is." He shakes his head and releases a reluctant chuckle. "I wouldn't want to go up against him in a fistfight. He took out all four of my armed men without breaking a sweat. I thought I was done for."

I'm not sure how he wants me to respond. I've always known Grant is an amazing agent and an even more amazing man—having proof only makes my stomach feel leaden.

"But that was a year ago," I say.

"I know. I spent a few weeks in West Virginia trying to track you down, but you two had left by then. I eventually followed the trail back to New York. You were easy to find after that, and I've been keeping an eye on you since."

A blurred memory jars me out of the story. "Wait—were you outside my house pretending to be a gardener a few weeks ago?"

"You saw me?"

"And at the motel earlier—skulking outside the office?"

He nods. "Yes, I was there."

I cast my memory over all the other times I thought I'd seen Oz over the past year—so many days, so many sightings—and I can only slump back against the vinyl booth in wonder. My dad had been close all that time, watching me, unaware how desperately I missed him.

"I can't believe you never said anything," I say.

"I didn't know if I *could*. Even with all that watching, it was impossible to tell whose side you were on. Half the time you were breaking the law with your friends, and the other half, you were hand-in-hand with the feds. When I heard that the FBI convinced your grandmother to get the necklace out of storage as part of a sting operation, I saw my chance to put you to the test."

"You hired Riker to steal it."

"It seemed a golden opportunity," he says. "I had to see for myself where your loyalties lay. I was afraid your grandmother had succeeded in turning you against me. I had to know if you wanted to find me as much as I wanted to find you."

Oh, the irony. If only he knew the lengths to which

I'd gone to find out what had happened. But then, seeing me now, seeing the ring on my finger, I guess he did.

He pauses. "You did good, by the way—with the air vent at the jewelry store and finding your way up to my floor. If you got rid of that husband, you could become one of the best thieves out there."

I can't help the flush of heat to my cheeks or the sense of pride that fills me at those words. I don't think I've been the best at anything before.

"But what I don't understand is what happened to the painting," my dad says. "Even if you weren't sure who to sell it to, Tara had more than enough connections to set herself up comfortably with the proceeds. What did you two do with it?"

My hands are finally calm enough for me to lift my mug without splashing all over the table, so I take a sip of my lukewarm coffee. It still tastes good.

"What painting?" I ask.

"Are you trying to be funny?"

"Um…no?"

My dad leans over the table, his voice low. "You know what painting I'm talking about, Penelope. The one I invested all our savings in. The de Kooning."

I end up spilling the coffee all over my hands anyway. "*What de Kooning?*"

"If I told you once, I told you a dozen times—if anything ever goes wrong, you'll always have our song. You should have been able to get a hundred million for that album cover."

The sounds of the diner pick up around me, the volume rising and swelling like an ocean wave about to crash overhead. I let go of the coffee altogether, and the cup drops to the table with a wet thud as my fingers grow numb.

"Are you trying to tell me those scribbles and smears of paint contained your entire life's fortune?" I ask. It's impossible. It can't be. Not even Grant has that kind of audacity. "I assumed I made that when I was a kid!"

He tosses napkins at me, but I can't grip the paper to help him clean the spilled coffee. The rest of my body is growing numb now, too. Numb and cold.

"I swear, baby doll, sometimes you have zero common sense. Of course you didn't make that—it's one of the rarest and earliest examples of de Kooning's gestural development. We studied it at the museum together right before my friend Lionel lifted it. Please tell me the painting is at least still in your possession."

"No." I sit back with a thump. My limbs are too heavy for anything else. "No, I don't have it. Someone replaced that cover as a gift to me. It was one of the happiest days of my life, actually."

A cough from somewhere above my head interrupts us. I somehow find the energy to peer up at the person who has the audacity to approach *now*, of all times.

I'm unsurprised by who I find.

"You two didn't make it nearly as far as I thought you would." Despite his light words and half smile, Grant's stance is squared at the edge of my booth seat, making it impossible for me to flee. Simon does the same on my dad's side of the table. "We expected you to be at the border by now."

I bet he did.

"You bastard," I say, my voice a snarl.

Grant's eyes widen in a flare of surprise, but he

doesn't move or lose the smile. "Well, maybe the border is a stretch. But I did expect you to at least *try* to escape. We have roadblocks posted from here to Maine."

Even though there's no way for me to stand up without brushing against him, I do it anyway. I meet Grant toe to toe and chest to chest, refusing to let those brushes of physical intimacy fill me with anything but rage. It's much easier than I anticipate.

"You jerk. You son of a bitch. You sneaking snake of a man."

His smile falls away in an instant. "Look, Penelope, I know you probably have a hundred questions, but—"

I push him. Hands flat against his chest and shoving with all my might, I *still* can't get him to budge, but that doesn't mean I stop trying.

"You've known this whole time," I say. "About my dad, about that painting, about the best way to manipulate me to get your hands on it." He moves a fraction of an inch backward. "You played me from the very first day. You played me from the very first day, *and I let you.*"

He tries to grab my arms, but I'm too fast, pummeling against his chest in a way that's both satisfying and ineffective. I'm like a cat trapped in a corner, hissing and clawing and venting my rage, when he stops me with just a few gentle words. "It's not what you think, my love."

I freeze at that endearment. "Don't you *dare* call me that. You never get to call me that again."

He casts a pained look at Simon, whose flat expression displays nothing but disgust for such an obvious show of emotion.

"She's not wrong. You did play her," he says. "You played all of us."

Grant releases a low curse. "I already apologized about leaving you out of the loop. Orders from the director—besides, I had to in order to gain Blackrock's trust. Do you think you could—?"

"Sure. *Now* you want my help." Simon turns to my dad with a click of his heels. "Warren Blue, you are under arrest. Anything you say can and will be used against you…"

It's my breaking point. I know Grant has to arrest my father and possibly the rest of my team, and that I'm the one who led us into this trap. I also know Grant is a manipulative bastard who will stop at nothing to see justice served. But to have it confirmed before my eyes, to see my father being handcuffed and led away after I finally found him again, is more than I can take.

I do the only thing I can think of in that moment. I hold out my own wrists in a gesture of surrender.

"Congratulations, Grant," I say, my voice razor sharp. "You win."

His expression turns pained. "I'm not going to arrest you, Penelope—you or your friends. You can put your hands down."

His pain, his gentleness, only fuels the red-hot rage pricking at my eyes. Now is not the time for him to try to get back on my good side.

"Why not?" I ask. "I steal. I lie. I hurt people." The implication of those particular sins forces me into a startled laugh. "Then again, I guess you do those things, too. Did you scratch my dad's record on purpose so you had an excuse to take it in?"

He shifts uncomfortably. "Yes, but I—"

"And did you know he was still alive?"

"Yes, but we—"

I refuse to soften. "And have you been planning to use me as bait to find him this whole time?"

He doesn't answer that right away. Whether from fear of retaliation or out-and-out cowardice, he can't seem to form the words that will rip me in half.

So I do it for him.

I push him aside. This time, he gives way easily, staggering on his feet. I reach up and remove the infinity necklace from around my neck, dropping it to the table in a serpentine coil. "I want a divorce."

THE 30 WEDDING

(Twelve Months Ago)

THE BRIDE WORE WHITE.

I didn't want to, of course. I'd always been much more comfortable in black, and to don the color of purity and innocence on a day like this one seemed sacrilege of the highest order. Besides, Grant and I were getting married in a West Virginia county clerk's office with all of four people in attendance. Going full bridal seemed like overkill.

"Oh, Pen. It's perfect. *You're* perfect." Jordan put to rest any fears I might have had that the dress made me look like a meringue. She put her hands on my shoulders and spun me, causing the skirt of my short, party-style gown to flare. "I think I'm going to cry."

"Please don't," I said, mostly out of a sense of self-preservation. Weddings had never caused me to start welling up before, but there was something about this one that had me teetering perilously close.

Oh, right. *Because it was mine.*

The fact that I was standing in a public restroom and my bridesmaid was rummaging through her bag to find a lipstick that wasn't a plastic explosive in hiding didn't change any of the surreal factor. This was really happening. I was going through with it.

"Aren't you so glad I made you get this dress?" Jordan asked as she made a few minor adjustments to my ensemble. Tuck a strand of hair here, wipe a smudge of mascara there—I couldn't tell if she was keeping busy to distract me or herself.

Either way, she stopped when she hit the cameo brooch pinned to my neckline.

"Holy smokes, that's gorgeous!" She leaned in for a closer look. "Real shell, from the looks of it. Is it your something new or your something, er, borrowed?"

I laughed. For once in my life, nothing on my person was *borrowed*.

"It's my something old," I said, fingering the delicate carving. "Grant gave it to me a few months back."

Jordan's eyes met mine in a look of swift understanding before she lowered them again. Jewelry had never been something we held onto for very long, for obvious reasons. Why wear what you can hawk? A valuable piece like this—appraised at four grand, according to Riker's best guess—would have gone a long way in helping us plan the next big heist.

"Well, the man has good taste, that's for sure," she said. "Though I guess that was never in question. He picked you, didn't he?"

It was a nice thing to say to an anxious bride-to-be, but there was too much forced joviality to make either of us comfortable. Unfortunately, hiding in the bathroom for the next few hours wasn't a viable option, and there weren't any windows to escape out of, which meant my comfort had to take a backseat to reality.

"Is he out there?" I asked.

"Yes, and he's more nervous than you, if you'd believe it."

I didn't believe it, and I was pretty sure she knew I wasn't talking about the groom. "No, not Grant. Riker."

Jordan nodded. "Yeah. He's right outside."

"I better go talk to him." I gave myself another once-over in the mirror, but there wasn't anything to fix. Jordan had attended to all the details, made sure there wasn't so much as a smudge of lipstick out of place. Whatever the knot in the pit of my stomach might say to the contrary, I certainly *looked* the part of the blushing bride.

As Jordan promised, Riker was waiting for me in the hallway. Like me, he looked his role to perfection. Although the ceremony itself wasn't much—just a courthouse room and the traditional marital vows— our attendants were dressed to the hilt. Grant brought his mom and Simon; I had Riker and Jordan. Just four people in this whole vast world to witness our union, but at least Riker did that tuxedo justice. He looked like a rock star with a hangover.

"Hey," I said.

He didn't offer a response, not even a blink at seeing me standing there with a veil.

"Okay, you have five minutes."

He was slouched against the wall opposite the bathroom, but other than a slight lifting of his head, he didn't change his posture. "What?"

"Five minutes." I gestured at the clock above his head. "Say what you need to say. Get it off your chest. I'm giving you five minutes of repercussion-free time to outline why I'm about to make the biggest mistake of my life, and then I have a wedding to attend."

He pushed himself to a standing position. "No."

"No?" Was he saying that about the five minutes or the wedding?

"No," he echoed, clarifying nothing. But then he offered me the crook of his elbow and stood perfectly rigid until I placed my arm on his. "Your betrothed was afraid you might bolt before the ceremony, so he tasked me with the job of making sure you get there in one piece. Lucky me, huh?"

Oh man. That sounded exactly like a challenge Grant would offer...and exactly like a challenge Riker couldn't refuse.

"He's either the smartest bastard on the face of the planet or the stupidest," Riker said, his sentiments echoing mine. "I'm getting tired of trying to figure out which. Are you?"

I blamed all the lawyers and cops milling around the hallways for my lack of understanding. "Am I tired of trying to figure him out?"

"No, going to bolt?"

"Of course not. We've talked about this, Riker. It's what's best for all of us."

"Sorry. My bad. I keep forgetting how you're doing this for my sake."

I didn't say anything. Not because we were done with this argument—far from it, especially given how many times we'd repeat it after that day—but because we approached the heavy wooden courtroom door where I was supposed to meet my groom.

Supposed to being the operative phrase.

"He's not here?" I whirled, looking for signs of the wide, capable shoulders that were supposed to carry me through this thing. "Oh God. He's not coming, is he? It's a trap. He lured us into a courthouse, and we'll never be able to get out in time."

"Relax," Riker said, unable to keep the annoyance from his voice. "He's waiting for you inside. He wanted to make it a big old thing with you walking in on a cloud of pillows and light. Where's Jordan?"

"I'm coming!" she called, a bouquet of English daisies in her hand as she jogged to catch up. I'd always liked English daisies—to most people, they were an obnoxious, difficult-to-eradicate weed. I thought they were pretty. "Here you go. Flowers, check. Veil, check. Dress, check. I think you're ready. You've got everything you need."

"Don't forget: Jordan, check," I said, smiling at her. And then, my smile not quite as wide, "And Riker, check."

"Riker, check," he echoed.

No one made a move to open the door or head inside, our sudden silence heavy with meaning. Just when it seemed we'd stand there awkwardly until the courts closed for the day, a bailiff rounded the corner to escort us inside. The tan uniform added an air of authority to the proceedings, only serving to make me more nervous about our possible escape routes, until the man paused and cleared his throat.

"Oz, check."

I almost burst into tears at the sight of him.

"You came!" I cried, fighting the urge to throw my arms around his neck. Only the knowing press of his finger against his lips stopped me. "I'm sorry, but I can't help it. My whole family is here now."

"You ready?" Jordan asked, her own eyes suspiciously moist.

I nodded, not trusting myself to speak. Truth be told, I wasn't ready—not even close—but if I didn't go through with this ceremony now, I wasn't sure I'd ever be able to.

"Then it's go time."

The groom wore black.

He looked good in it, too—all those muscles of his packed into a tuxedo that molded to his body, outlining his handsome physique. His hair gleamed, his crinkly-eyed smile was pointed right at me, and there wasn't a single part of him that wasn't perfection in shirtsleeves. Still, none of it floored me quite as much as the single daisy tucked into his lapel.

He must have stolen it from my bouquet or asked Jordan for a spare. It looked wilted from his body heat and lonely without the rest of my bunch to keep it company, but the message was the same.

He wore it for me. Sad and scraggly and pale in comparison to his splendor, that flower was nonetheless nestled next to his heart.

"Hey," I said for the second time that day. I was really killing it in the moving speeches department.

His response couldn't have been more different from Riker's. There was nothing sullen in his posture, nothing lacking in the way he lit up at the sight of me. Despite the fact that we were in a court of law and his mother was present, he pulled me into his arms and crushed every last finishing touch Jordan had made on my coiffure.

He also kissed me in a way I was pretty sure was supposed to be reserved for *after* the ceremony.

"Hey, yourself," he said, his lips moving against mine. "I sure am glad to see you here."

For the second time that day, my eyes welled up with tears. Poetically speaking, it was hardly the stuff of legends, but no words had ever sounded sweeter to my ears.

"I sure am glad to see you here, too," I managed.

The judge who was marrying us, a kindly-looking woman in sober black robes, cleared her throat. "I take this to mean we're all present and accounted for?"

I cast a quick look around the room to confirm. Everyone I wanted was there. Grant's mom, wearing a floral dress and a hat straight out of a horse derby. Simon, looking dour and uncomfortable among so many thieves. Jordan, beaming at me as she sniffled into a tissue. Oz, feigning professional indifference over by the door.

And Riker, of course.

I was half-afraid Grant was going to say something to set him off—send him on another errand or comment on his sullen expression—but instead, he nodded once. Riker waited a full ten seconds before moving, but when he finally did, it was to return the gesture with a quick nod of his own.

And that was it. Without a word being spoken aloud, the ceremony was underway.

I barely heard any of it—not the vows the judge asked

us to repeat, not Grant reciting after her, not me reciting after him. Everything moved so quickly and swept along without any help from me, it was almost as if I was sitting in the defendant's chair, watching someone else's story being told.

I did, however, feel the constant pressure of Grant's hands on my own. I couldn't bring myself to look up in his eyes, but that touch, that reassurance, was all I needed to make it through.

Until, of course, the judge released a soft chuckle. "I apologize for this next part, but it has to be done. Is there anyone here who knows of any legal impediment to this marriage? If so, now would be a good time to bring it up."

Although Jordan and Myrna offered an obliging laugh, the rest of us froze. Legal impediments abounded on all sides—they boxed us in, trapped us, built a cage that no amount of kisses and soft words could break down.

I didn't even know if an FBI agent's alliance with a known criminal was *allowed*. There had to be some kind of rule in place about this sort of thing, an escape clause so Grant could arrest me, prosecute me, and testify against me all in the same day. Maybe our marriage certificate would be a lie committed to paper. Maybe he could turn around and annul it at any moment, with no more pretext than a list of my sins.

Maybe this entire day was nothing more than a sham.

"I can't think of a single reason why I wouldn't want to make this woman mine," Grant said. "Legal or otherwise."

I glanced up at him, surprised at how confident he sounded, how sure.

"There are no impediments," he said. "You may proceed."

"But—" I began.

He turned to me, his expression melting into one of inexplicable tenderness. "Not a single reason, Penelope. Not now, and not in the next hundred years. I'm ready to do this thing. How about you?"

There were literally hundreds—no, thousands—of reasons why it made sense for me to turn on my heel and run, not the least of which was the fact that this man stood, upright and honorable, for everything I didn't. Yet, as I stared up at him, falling into the affection of his gaze, I couldn't think of one.

Not a single one. Not now, and not in the next hundred years.

I nodded.

It was all the consent the judge needed. With a triumphant shout, she formally announced us husband and wife. "And *now* you may kiss your bride," she said.

Grant was all too willing to comply. He swept me up into his arms, crushing my daisies and my mouth with a single movement. For the longest time, I couldn't breathe, so caught up was I in his embrace. But it didn't matter, because I didn't need to. In that moment, surrounded by the people I cared about most in the world, air was only a secondary consideration.

I was happy.

"You won't regret this, my love," Grant said, pulling away just long enough for the words to settle like a blanket over my heart. "I can't promise you much, but that's the one thing I'll always make sure of."

Yeah, right. That turned out to be the biggest lie of all.

THE PROMISE

31

(Present Day)

THERE AREN'T MANY PLACES YOU CAN HIDE FROM AN FBI agent who also happens to be your husband.

I come up with at least a dozen destinations that are immediately discarded for being too obvious. I can't go home, since his name is on the deed. I can't go to the rare books room, because I'm pretty sure he has the librarians there on payroll. My friends' apartments are probably being watched, and the rec center is closed today. The obvious answer—to find a small, dark hole I can wedge myself into until the world stops spinning—is the worst option of all.

Grant always knows I'm in there. He's seen me—seen *through* me—right from the start.

That's my excuse, anyway, for why I end up casing a bank in the middle of a busy downtown street. There's a sewer grate at my feet and an apartment building about two blocks away that I could theoretically crawl underground to.

Not that I will, mind you. There'd have to be someone I love an awful lot waiting for me at the other end.

"The first thing I'd do is get Oz in as an employee," I say aloud. A few passersby look startled to hear me speaking to thin air, but this is New York, after all. Stranger things than a tearstained and disheveled woman standing on the street corner talking to herself happen all the time. "Not as a security guard, because that would be too obvious. A teller, maybe, or the custodial staff."

I nod once, liking the sound of that last one. He'd need to get on early in the planning process so we could use his input to inform future decisions. The layout of the bank, employee protocols and habits, any weaknesses in their daily routine...in order to pull off a job of this caliber, we'd need all the eyes we could get. If we got Jordan in there, we might even be able to plant explosives that would rip the safe door right off its hinges.

For all of five minutes, I entertain myself planning a heist I have no intention of performing. It's soothing, this familiar act of what-if and what-next. We could go back to the way things used to be—me and Jordan and Riker and Oz—taking on the world and winning.

But, of course, that's impossible. I took that option away from us that day in the courthouse.

There was never any coming back from that, I realize now. Optimism, arrogance, naïveté—call it what you will, but the truth is that I let my feelings for Grant blind me to the reality of my situation. I am and always have been a thief. A *good* one, if what my father says is true. *One of the best.*

My spine straightens as I replay my father's words in my head, hearing him this time with perfect clarity. No tight spot was ever too tight for me, no escape so difficult I gave up and let the authorities take me in. I might not be the fastest or the smartest thief out there, but the one thing I've always had in abundance is determination.

Penelope Blue doesn't give up easily.

"Casing the bank again, I see."

I don't turn at the sound of Grant's carefully casual voice by my ear, though my pulse leaps. I wish I could say I'm surprised to find him here, but Grant Emerson doesn't give up easily either.

We've always been evenly matched that way.

"A girl's gotta eat," I say with a shrug. "Especially since *somebody* took the only thing of value she had."

"Oh, I'm not worried about Penelope Blue being able to land on her feet," he replies and nods across the street. "She's got at least half a million dollars stored in a safety deposit box over there."

I release a short, bitter laugh. "You know about that, too?"

I'd opened the account in a fit of perversity a few days before our wedding—an attempt to ensure he wouldn't stumble onto my ill-begotten goods, my last-ditch attempt at holding onto something of my own. A safety net, I realize now. A safety net against the inevitability of despair.

"Wait, what am I saying?" I add. "Of course you know about it. In the past year and a half, I haven't done or said a single thing that you weren't aware of ahead of time. My dad, the painting, Oz, Tara, the first place I'd run to get away from you…you know everything."

His lips fall at the corners. "That's not true."

Something about how sad he seems—how *betrayed*, of all unfair sentiments—reminds me of how upset he was at the motel before my dad's thugs whisked him away.

"Oh, sorry," I say. "You didn't know about Erica being my grandmother. Well, that makes two of us, so that doesn't count."

"That's not what I meant."

"What, then?" I turn to him, anger pricking at my eyelids. I want to play it cool and aloof, become the devil-may-care jewel thief who always has an escape route, but it's hard. Mostly because for the first time in my life, I don't *want* to get away. The place I want to be most in the world is right here with him. "What could possibly be left for you to know?"

"You have no idea, do you?" he asks.

I shake my head. I really, truly don't.

His voice drops to a low rumble. "No matter how hard I try, no matter how many hours I spend by your side, I've never been able to figure out if you love me even a fraction as much as I love you."

My knees wobble and grow unsteady beneath me. I want to clutch his arm to hold myself up, fall into him and let him catch me, but I don't.

"I don't understand," I say. "You were using me as bait. You admitted as much back there at the diner."

"Not *only* as bait." He runs a hand through his hair, tugging at the tawny strands in what looks like desperation. "Did I know about your father being alive? Yeah, of course I did. A man like that doesn't just disappear. Did I know he put all his money in the de Kooning painting that went missing fifteen years ago? You bet your ass I did. He was my thesis at Quantico."

"He was?"

He drops his hands and casts that stricken glance my way, ensnaring me like prey in headlights. "I told you all this. That day at Christmas, at my mom's house, I told you that nothing and no one disappears without leaving a trace. I promised I would find him for you."

He didn't. He hadn't. I would have remembered something like that.

"Why? So you could turn around and put him in prison for the rest of his life? Forgive me for not being grateful."

Grant releases a short, bitter laugh. I don't like the way it grates, so far from the genuine joy I've seen in him in the past.

"He won't be there for long," Grant says. "When I checked in with Simon, they were already working on the negotiations."

"Negotiations?"

"I told you that, too. Like you, like Riker, like Oz and Jordan and Tara, your father is more valuable as a resource than a prisoner."

He doesn't need to elaborate, as I remember all too well his description of my kind of people: *slightly shady but useful enough for the good to outweigh the bad*. For the first time, I start to detect a glimmer of hope on the horizon, see the shape of a future in which a life with this man isn't impossible.

"There are quite a few suits at the Bureau who would

like to see him behind bars, but he has some valuable contacts we'd like to get our hands on. Half of his known associates are wanted by Interpol, and I'm willing to bet the other half are wanted by the CIA. As long as he's willing to cooperate, I should be able to get him a light sentence in exchange for information." He settles a heavy glance on me. "Especially since he has such a good reason to stick around now."

"So you knew you might be able to get him a light sentence this whole time? But that means—"

His laugh is short and bitter again. "That I never set out to hurt you or your family? That I would do everything in my power to keep you out of harm's way? That I would run interference between the FBI and your friends for *years* to ensure their safety as well as yours?"

I can feel my lips start to wobble along with my knees. "You did that?"

"Of course I did," he says roughly. "There were times—so many times, so many temptations—when all I wanted to do was slap a pair of handcuffs on Riker and drag him into the twisted depths of the justice system. It would have been so easy to separate you two that way, to get rid of my competition with the snap of my fingers and a day's worth of paperwork."

"But you didn't."

Grant draws close, strength radiating off his body. "That man will never be my favorite, but as long as your happiness depends on his, I promise to protect him. It kills me every time you look at him with that unquestioning love and loyalty in your eyes—that unquestioning love and loyalty you can't seem to give me—but I will protect him. You have my word on that."

"Oh, Grant."

The hard edge of his anger ebbs away at the sound of my voice, but he still doesn't reach for me. He's watching, waiting, a man who knows that moving too soon could result in a loss of the prize.

He's not too different from me in that regard. He might have a badge in his pocket and a gun at his hip, but this man has lied and cheated and stolen since the day we met. And he's been good at it, too. Better than me.

He'd make a hell of a jewel thief, if only he'd put his mind to it.

"I know you may never be able to forgive me for taking that record cover from you, but you have to understand that the way I handled it has always haunted me," he says. "I had to act fast. I didn't expect to find the painting in your apartment that day—I'd long since given up on it by then. I only planned to find your dad."

"But you did take it," I accuse. "You took it and you kissed me and you made me cry."

He winces. "I'm so sorry. If it's any consolation, it was the record that made me realize I'd fallen in love with you."

There's that word again. *Love*. Not adoration, not devotion, not obligation. Love.

"The moment you claimed to have painted a hundred-million-dollar de Kooning as a five-year-old child, I knew you were just as naive and wonderful as you seemed."

"I'm not naive." Or wonderful.

"I knew that even though you were a thief and a liar and a beautiful, magnificent tease, the anguish you felt for your father was real. That vulnerable girl, the one who opened herself up to me even though she fought it every step of the way, was the end of me. I'd already fallen in love with you, but that was the first time I allowed myself to admit it."

"You lie."

"Not this time. And not next time, either. Not ever again, if I can help it."

Any attempts I might have made to continue holding him back crumble in that moment. I should have been angry that he stole a hundred million dollars from me and angrier still that my father was being forced to compromise his position for the sake of government intelligence. I should have been panicked at the thought of giving up my life of crime for something as silly—and as wonderful—as a man.

But looking at him, knowing how guilty he feels for the role he played, knowing full well he'd do it all over again if he had the chance, I only feel admiration.

This is *exactly* why I married this man in the first place. To keep my friends close and my enemies closer, to be near the intel and the action, to live in a fast-paced game of cat-and-mouse where every day is a new opportunity to win.

And also because I can't imagine my life without him in it.

"Penelope, I know I promised I'd never ask, but I can't do it anymore. I can't wake up to you each morning without telling you how I feel. I can't make love to you every night without showing you how much you matter to me. Since the day you jogged into my life, so full of courage and fire that you'd confront your biggest enemy head-on, I've been entranced by you. Every day that goes by, I fall further under your spell."

"Grant, I—"

"I know you don't necessarily share my feelings, but is there a chance that might change? Do you think, if given time, you could love me even a little? That's the only thing I need to know—the only question I have to ask. I have to know if it's all been a game for you or if at least part of you feels the same way."

"Of course I love you," I say.

He doesn't register my words right away, brushing over my barely audible response as he continues to plead his case. "And if you can't reciprocate my feelings, please know that you have people you can turn to for help. I haven't had much time to talk to Erica—your grandmother—yet, but it sounds like she had as much trouble tracking you down as your dad did. Apparently, that's why she let us use the necklace as bait in the first place. You and Tara left the hotel before she could find you, and it's weighed on her ever since."

"Grant, I said I love you."

"And if you need space or time or a divorce—"

"Grant!" I speak sharply enough that several people turn to stare, but that's fine with me. Breaking down in public has never stopped me before. "I freaking love you, okay? I love your nerdy childhood relics and your strange relationship with your mother and your determination to beat me at my own game. I love that you're sneaky and underhanded and that you'd go to these lengths to protect the people I care about. I even love that you know everything about me and somehow still want me."

I realize, as I say it out loud, that they're the truest words of all. "You *see* me," I add. "You accept me. You always have."

That's when he reaches for me. I know what happens next. He's going to cup my face. He's going to run his fingers over my lips. And I'm going to let him.

Of all the embraces this man and I have shared, it's that one—simple and sweet, a gesture of love that says everything our words can't—that undoes me the most.

He knows it, of course. He always has.

"I've never felt about anyone the way I feel about you," I say. "Riker might have saved me from the darkest parts of my past, and I'll always love him for that, but *you*..." I offer him a tentative smile. "You're my future, Agent Grant Emerson. You're the one I want to spend the rest of my life with. You're the one I'd do anything to keep."

"Anything?" he asks in a rumbling voice.

"Anything," I say. I turn into his embrace like a cat.

"Then I want you to marry me all over again." He replaces his fingers with his mouth, a sweep of a kiss that leaves me breathless. "And this time, my love, you better mean it."

EPILOGUE

AS USUAL, GRANT GETS HIS WAY. THE OFFICIAL celebration of our one-year anniversary takes shape as the big family wedding we never had the first time around. I know, it's pretty excessive to renew your vows after only twelve months of marriage, but he was adamant that we do it the right way.

By *right way*, he means with my father here to give me away and everyone we know in attendance. This is no small ceremony in a dark room—every cousin and acquaintance was pulled out for the event, and there are even caterers buzzing around in the background of the courtyard we've hired for the day. My side of the seating arrangement is pretty sparse, but I've got Riker, Jordan, Oz, my dad, and even my grandmother, which seems like an abundance of love and support from where I'm standing.

Of course, we're also doing the marriage a little differently this time. We've promised no more lies about who we are or what we want out of this relationship. Grant even got me a new ring to celebrate our fresh start. This one has an infinity knot to match my necklace. Paulson Jewelers is going to see a lot of our business over the next few years. I think he feels guilty for all the trauma we put them through.

He looks gorgeous, of course. He's decked out in a tuxedo, filling it in all the right places. He cleans up the way most rugged, dashingly charming FBI agents do— like James Bond on his best day. I know I'm supposed to listen as he recites the vows he wrote for me, but he already whispered each word into my neck last night. And this morning. And about ten minutes before our guests arrived.

They're good vows, I'll give him that much. Incredible vows. Vows I won't mind enjoying later tonight, if you know what I mean.

He hasn't heard mine yet, so when I hear my cue, I turn to him with a smile. My dress is beautiful—it's a long, flowing satin gown with an open back that Grant can't stop touching—but most people are fixated on the jewels around my neck. The Dupont necklace is quite a crowd-pleaser, and I promised Jordan she could try it on later. It's only on loan to me, my grandmother's first attempt to heal the breach that opened when she failed to hold her end of the bargain with my dad. I think she's half convinced she's never going to see this necklace again.

I'm only half convinced she will, too. There's an energy crackling around Riker I don't trust.

Unfortunately, any plans of his to take the necklace will just have to wait. I've got a long speech planned about how Grant works too much and too hard, about how I'll always be second in his heart next to Sterling Simon, and about how even a second-tier space in his heart is worth it. I don't know what a claustrophobic jewel thief like me did to deserve a spot in there, but I do know that I'll fight like hell to stay.

Blues don't give up easily. We climb in and hold on. We live and love with everything we've got. And sometimes, when we're lucky enough, we find someone who makes it worthwhile.

After that, I hope everyone gets good and drunk so Grant and I can sneak out early for our second honeymoon. We're going antiquing in Vermont. He's got his eye on this rolltop desk that some president or another used to write love letters to his wife, and I'm pretty sure he's going to use some of my hidden cache of cash to bid on it.

As for my professional life? Well, let's just say I'm on a temporary sabbatical—emphasis on the temporary. These vows might have me promising to love and cherish, but there's nothing in there about obeying.

Not even a man like Grant could make me do that.

Dying to see more of Grant and Penelope's courtship? Want to hear Grant's perspective on their emotional game of cat and mouse?

Please enjoy this EXCLUSIVE BONUS SCENE from the early days of *STEALING MR. RIGHT*!

GRANT

(Sixteen months ago)

"IF YOU'RE GOING TO SUCCESSFULLY SHOOT THE bastard, the first thing you need to do is firm your stance."

Although I knew it was dangerous, I placed my hands on Penelope's hips and nudged her thighs apart with my knee. Her body responded to my directions the way I knew it would—gracefully and with suspicious compliance.

Legs open. *Check.*

Hair tossed back. *Done.*

Ass pressed firmly against my groin. *Fuck.*

This was going to be a lot more difficult than I'd expected.

"And don't hold the gun like it's going to bite you," I said. My voice came out gravelly, but I was too happy to find it worked at all to care. "I swear, Penelope. Haven't you ever had one of these in your hands before?"

"No, never," she replied and gave her head another toss. Her reddish-blond locks whipped backward, scoring my cheek and leaving the unmistakable scent of raspberries behind. "I'm not a fan of violence."

This time, I had to struggle to keep the laughter at bay. Penelope Blue: world-famous jewel thief, insouciant girlfriend to a federal agent, pacifist. The unlikely combination of attributes made zero sense, yet here we were.

"I don't see what the big deal about shooting wooden ducks is, anyway," she added with a glance over her shoulder. There was challenge and laughter in that glance—another pair of remarkably attractive attributes that belonged to this woman and this woman alone. "If I really wanted one of those stuffed bears, I could just ask that man to give me one. I'm sure I could convince him."

The man in question stood watching us from the other side of the Coney Island carnival booth, his red-and-white striped apron clutched in his hands. His indulgent grin was all the proof I needed to agree with Penelope. There were few people in this world who could resist her when she chose to put in the effort. I sure as hell wasn't one of them.

Besides, if she couldn't charm a bear out of him, she'd come up with an elaborate scheme to steal one instead. Knowing Penelope, it would involve at least one explosion, a mad climb up the side of the Wonder Wheel, and a handoff from where she'd no doubt be hidden inside the hot dog vender's cart at the park's entrance.

But no guns. The lady disliked violence.

"This isn't about a stuffed bear," I said as sternly as I could. "This is about protection. How can you expect to survive in this world if you can't shoot a moving target?"

"By my wits, of course," she replied with a laugh. "But I guess your way is fine, too, if you don't have any of those."

"I have plenty of wits," I growled.

It was true. Wits were a must when dating a woman like Penelope Blue—wits and a sense of humor and an infinite reserve of patience. The gun helped, too. Two months into this relationship, and I was still shocked I hadn't had recourse to shoot her yet. She'd done more than enough to warrant it.

"Of course you do," she cooed. "So many wits."

"Thank you," I said, taking the high road by ignoring the provocation. Then, because the high road and Penelope Blue were two mutually exclusive entities, I added, "You know, some girlfriends would appreciate a boyfriend who pulls out all the stops for a date like this."

As expected, my casual use of the terms *boyfriend* and *girlfriend* held her in momentary check. Poor Penelope. She could scale skyscrapers and laugh in the face of law enforcement, but talk of romance paralyzed her.

Especially when it came to *me*.

"Fine," she finally said, recovering with a mock sigh. "Your barbarism wins for today. Let's murder some wooden ducks."

Although I could have stood there for hours, verbally sparring and basking in her proximity, I released my hold on the tantalizing curves of her hips and focused on the task at hand. "Put your pointer finger on the trigger, but just barely," I instructed. "You want to hold the gun firm but your finger limp. You'll avoid any premature misfires that way."

BANG.

Penelope's whole body tensed as the gun went off and the blast of air went wide, but she didn't scream or jump as I could tell she wanted to. She had far too much control over her reflexes for that. It was the cat burglar in her.

"I hate to criticize, but that wasn't what I'd call limp," I said.

Her response was to bump her ass against my groin playfully. "Neither is that," she teased.

Penelope spoke no more than the truth—my body's response to hers was a palpable, physical, damn near painful thing. But as I always did in situations like these, I ignored it and her. It was the only way I'd managed to make it this far in this strange relationship of ours. I had to ignore her strongest provocations, subdue the various…emotions she gave rise to, and focus on my end goal: complete and utter victory over the enemy I was steadily falling for.

"If I didn't know you better, I'd think you were lying about being a terrible shot just to mess with me." I lifted her arms to the proper position once again.

Her body was small but strong, and she held the gun perfectly parallel to the ground. The yellow wooden ducks marched in their well-timed procession back and forth across the booth, daring her to knock them over.

"How do you know I'm *not* lying about it?" she asked archly.

I knew. With my hands moving firmly over hers, I pushed the gun to the right. This time, I was in control. Stance firm, arms steady, a quick press of my finger over hers, and BANG. The duck farthest away fell over flat.

"There are some things you can't hide from me," I

said, chuckling at the tension that had filled her at the sound of the second shot. I'd been around enough guns and enough training exercises to know when someone was faking it, and Penelope was faking it big time. The recoil on these air guns was practically nonexistent— only someone truly uncomfortable with artillery would find them alarming. "No matter how much you might want to, your body always gives you away."

"It does not!" she protested and yanked the gun from my grasp. "You're making me nervous, that's all."

She then proceeded to take aim and fire the remaining three shots.

BANG. Miss.

BANG. Miss.

BANG. Miss by a mile.

"I wonder if I could," I mused as she shook the gun in exasperation.

Distracted, she didn't pick up on my meaning. "You wonder if you could what?" she asked.

I hesitated, timing my response carefully. Penelope might have become adept at physically torturing me, but I was playing a different kind of game—a mental one, an emotional one. Even more, I was playing for keeps.

I waited until her full attention was on me before clarifying. "I wonder if I really could make you nervous."

As expected, this was one blast she didn't recoil from. She turned on me, the gun dangling from her fingertip. "That's not a very romantic thing to say," she pointed out, syrupy sweet. "Why would you want me to be afraid of you?"

"I don't," I said—that wasn't the kind of *nervous* I meant—and waited.

Just *what* I was waiting for, I couldn't quite say. For Penelope to admit that she felt a fraction for me what I felt for her? For her to say I *did* make her nervous, that when I was around her heart raced and her blood rushed and her head was so full of ridiculous hope she could barely stand it?

Or maybe more than anything, I just wanted her to tell me the truth—about her life, about her past, about the fact that she was probably carrying stolen jewels in her pockets right now… But of course that would never happen. She didn't trust me enough for that. I wasn't sure she ever would.

As if to prove my point, she continued with her slow, careful seduction, refusing to respond to my gentle push for *more*. "Oh, but maybe I *am* scared of you. What with you so big and strong and manly. What's a poor girl like me to do?"

"You could learn a little self-defense," I said, giving in for now. "Starting with duck hunting. I don't like the idea of you sauntering around out there unprotected."

Her lips spread in a wide and dazzling smile—the smile had been my undoing from the start. How a person who had seen the things she'd seen and done the things she'd done could still be filled with such easy joy was one of the many mysteries I had yet to solve. "Aw, Grant. You really think I can't take care of myself? A street rat like me?"

I *knew* she could take care of herself. That was part of the problem. She was self-sufficient and fearless and determined to prove it to every man, woman, and child who crossed her path. As a general rule, I found over-confident criminals to be the easiest ones to trap, but

Penelope Blue was anything but easy. Her confidence, unlike that of so many others, was borne of competence, which meant she'd earned every scrap of it.

In other words, she didn't need me. Not the way I needed her. And if she finally grew tired of stringing me along, I wanted to make damn sure she *continued* to keep herself as safe as possible.

"Just hand the gun over already," I grumbled. "I'm going to teach you how to do this if it takes us all afternoon."

The park was filled with its usual mixture of tourists and truant teenagers, but few of them were interested in the overpriced duck hunt that had been my sole plan for today's date. Part of my plans had arisen from an honest desire to teach her how to handle a gun, but I'd have been lying if I didn't also admit to a perverse desire to show off.

I could hardly be blamed for it. Getting the better of this woman—in life, in love, in *anything*—was virtually impossible. No matter what kind of a curveball I threw at her, she caught it and tossed it right back.

If I found her out in the middle of a lie? She'd keep lying until she was out again.

If I paraded her in front of a team of federal agents? She'd smile and laugh until each one was putty in her hands.

And if I told her how I felt, as though the ground was shifting underneath my feet, crumbling my previously unshakable foundation of good and bad and right and wrong? Hell. I had no idea. *She* might have infinite reserves of courage, but I didn't. I wasn't ready to hear her admit that I was nothing more than a game to her.

"All right, Agent Emerson," she said as she handed over the gun. "Show me how this is done. Save me from the bad guys."

I tossed the man another bill and nodded at him to set the ducks going. I waited just long enough to get a feel for the cadence of the thing—they vary the ducks' speed with every game in an attempt to throw you off—before popping off my shots.

BANG. *Thump.*

BANG. *Thump.*

BANG. *Thump.*

A warm, tantalizing curl of air wrapped around my ear, causing my fourth shot to go awry. In preparation for the fifth, I could feel Penelope's entire body, lithe and ready, by my side. Nowhere did she touch me, nowhere did she allow her long, dexterous fingers to brush against my skin, but the damage was already done. I couldn't fucking *concentrate*.

"We're not going to win any stuffed bears this way," I warned. "I only have one more shot."

"Then let me help," she said in a low, beckoning voice. Before I could stop her, she assumed the position that had been mine only a few minutes earlier, her body bracing mine from behind. As if that weren't bad enough, she nudged her leg between my thighs. My stance was impeccable, but she wanted me to suffer.

And suffer I did.

From there, she let her hands linger on my hips, holding me in place while she adjusted her posture so that every soft, round part of her rubbed against my back. As if I needed a reminder how her body felt against mine, of all the promise contained in five feet three inches of gorgeous, playful jewel thief.

"Don't hold the gun like it's going to bite you," she said, echoing my orders from before. I could hear the

laugh in her voice as she lifted her arms to support mine.
She took her time with the task, fingers trailing up and
down my forearms, her hands coming to rest on the gun
in a way that had even the carnival hawker flustered. "I
swear, Grant. Haven't you ever had one of these in your
hands before?"

"I can't help it," I said, driven to full honesty. "You
make me nervous."

That startled a laugh out of her. "Me?"

"Yes, you." I gave up all pretense of shooting the
gun. Fuck the ducks. Fuck the stuffed bear. Fuck all the
people passing by, wondering at the man in shirtsleeves
unable to pull the trigger and seal the deal. I whirled
so that we stood face-to-face, her gaze dragged up into
my own. "You have no idea how much you shake my
resolve—how much you shake *me*."

As always, any sign of affection—of sincerity—startled her. She tried to pull back, but by that time, I had
my arms around her and held her close.

"You have more power over me than you realize," I
said. I didn't allow my eyes to stray from hers, but I did
adjust my posture so that I stood sideways, perpendicu-
lar to the duck booth. Without looking, I lifted the gun
and fired off my last shot.

BANG. *Thump*.

"The gentleman wins a prize!" the man in the apron
called, but I paid him no heed. The prize I wanted wasn't
even close to won yet.

"Good thing I know how to take care of myself, too,"
I told her. "This round goes to me."

Her eyes were big at the showy success of my shot,
bigger still with the realization that I wasn't going to

let her off the hook so easy. Especially when I brought my lips to hers and claimed my victory kiss—loving the way she went pliant and welcoming at the first taste. How a woman so physically soft and yielding could be so damned hard in every other way was beyond me.

But then, a lot of things were beyond me. Including the fact that as Penelope's mouth opened to let me in, I realized there was no way I could let her slip out of my life as stealthily as she'd slipped in.

Penelope Blue was a terrible shot and a lying thief, but she made one hell of a delightful adversary. It was almost enough to make a man not dream of all the *more* there could be—to make him content with what he had.

Almost.

Penelope and Grant's story is far from over.
Read on for a glimpse of what's coming next in

SAVING
MR. PERFECT

COMING AUGUST 2017!

THE 1 HEIST

INFILTRATING THE FBI IS A LOT MORE DIFFICULT than you might think.

The seventh-floor waiting room in the New York field office is one I'm intimately familiar with. There are no windows to penetrate from the outside and no air vents big enough to squeeze through, which means it's impossible to access this floor unless security clears you first. The fifty-something woman at the desk *seems* nice, what with the glasses perched on the end of her nose and the fresh flower pinned to her chiffon blouse, but she'd shiv you sooner than let you through the door.

I know this because in addition to the gun she carries, Cheryl also has a letter opener that doubles as a throwing knife strapped to her upper thigh.

And I know *that* because I'm the one who gave it to her.

"Hey, Penelope," Cheryl says with a smile that welcomes me and warns me not to make any sudden movements at the same time. "It's lovely to have you visit us today."

Loosely translated, this means: *I know you're a thief and I'm packing. What do you want?*

"I'm so happy to be here," I reply. My own smile stretches wide and full of meaning. "How are the kids? And Dan?"

In other words: *I'm not scared of you. Also, I know where you live.*

"They're good, they're good. Dan got that promotion he was after, so that's been pretty nice for us. We finally bought that gun safe we've been eyeing."

Meaning: *We keep extra weapons at home. Don't even think about it.*

"Safety is so important," I agree.

"Do you want me to let him know you're here, hon?"

"If you don't mind. He's not expecting me."

"Oh, how lovely," she says. You'd think, from the way she beams at me, that she means it this time. She doesn't. "Is it a surprise lunch date?"

It's a surprise *something*, that's for sure. But all I do is offer her a bland look and say, "In a manner of speaking."

"I'll buzz him."

And with that, I'm in as far as I'm going to get on my own. Only once in my life have I made it past Cheryl's desk, and that was in handcuffs. It's not an experience I'm keen on repeating.

To pass the time until my husband's arrival, I settle into one of the austere metal chairs set against an even more austere white wall and struggle to suppress my air of expectation. A buzz of adrenaline is common before a big job, and since it's been more than six months since

I've so much as *looked* at a lock the wrong way, my expectations and my buzz are flying.

The fact that things are progressing exactly as planned only helps my high. I haven't always loved the FBI—what with their spying on my every move and the arrest of my father earlier this year—but I can always count on their love of protocol.

To Cheryl's credit, she doesn't make excuses as the minutes tick by and there's no sign of my husband. To *my* credit, I don't let my anxiety at his delay show. There's a small window of opportunity for this particular job, and I need him to appear before Riker—my best friend and coconspirator—gets things started down below. In about five more minutes, I'm going to have to do something drastic (like fake a seizure) to get Grant out here.

Fortunately, my acting skills aren't put to the test. A shadow appears in the doorway before I hear the impressively faint sound of footsteps, and I know it must be Grant. No one moves as silently—or as deadly—as my husband.

"You're here!" I cry. All six feet two inches of him fill the room—and my heart. Even considering what I'm about to do, I'm honestly happy to see him. He didn't come home last night until the wee hours of the morning, and he left for work while I was in the shower—a schedule that's been on repeat for much longer than I like. The occasional late night is par for the course when you're married to an FBI agent, but tacit avoidance has become our default mode as of late.

In any other marriage, such a thing might indicate waning sexual interest or a general lack of communication. In *our* marriage, it means one of us thinks the other has started stealing again.

I'll let you guess who.

Grant accepts my proffered hug warily, one eye on the door, the other on his watch. I'm tempted to tell him it's exactly two-thirteen in the afternoon, give or take thirty seconds, but that might give too much away. I only pay such close attention to the passing of time when I'm up to no good—a fact he knows from personal experience. I want to throw him off-guard, not set him on high alert.

"My sweet darling, how I've missed you!" I say instead, dialing my beaming smile up to twelve. "I've been waiting for the chance to wrap my arms around you all day."

He doesn't miss a beat. "Okay, who are you and what have you done with my wife?"

"That's unfair." I feign outrage with a flick of my ponytail, my more-blond-than-red hair pulled back in the lifelong style I can't seem to shake. As my role in the breaking and entering circuit used to involve squeezing into tight spaces, I grew accustomed to minimizing the amount of space I took up—hair included. Nothing is more disastrous than squeezing yourself inside an air conditioning duct only to have your hair sucked into the blades. "Can't I be happy to see you?"

"You could be, but you're not."

I fake a pout. "How can you tell?"

"For starters? Not only have you never called me *my sweet* anything before, but your skin is flushed and your pupils are dilated. What are you up to, Penelope Blue?"

I bite back a laugh. His air of distrust is offset by the familiar playful rhyme. It's always been one of my favorite sounds—that combination of suspicion and adoration in Grant's voice. I like to think it's how he shows his love.

"I'm not up to anything." At least, I'm not up to anything *yet*. The action isn't set to start until two-twenty, which means I've got about five more minutes to keep his attention focused by being suspiciously charming and wifely. "Maybe I'm flushed because I'm happy to see you. Did you ever think about that?"

"Once. Maybe twice. Then I learned better."

His eyes narrow as he continues assessing me from top to bottom. I attempt to keep my breathing mostly even and my posture just a little too relaxed—I want him to be suspicious, but I don't want him to *catch on* that I want him to be suspicious. It's harder than it seems under his special brand of scrutiny. Grant is very good at his job.

He's so good at it, in fact, that his face doesn't register even a flicker of surprise when he reaches my feet and catches a glimpse of my footwear. Normally, I'm all about functional flats and comfort soles, but this is a special occasion. Today I've paired my black skinny jeans with bright red peep-toe heels that threaten to topple me with every step.

The shoes were a gift from Grant—a gift *and* a reminder, and a large part of the reason I'm here today. It's a thing with him, a tradition of sorts, to give double-edged presents. The habit goes all the way back to our early courtship, where each date could end with an arrest as easily as a kiss. Instead of confronting me with his suspicions like a normal man, Grant likes to toy with me to see if I'll break.

I'm on to you, Penelope Blue, he all but said with

a few shiny pieces of patent leather. *The Peep-Toe Prowler better not strike again.*

Which is totally unfair, by the way. Even if I was the burglar currently working her way through a string of Upper East Side homes—which, for the record, I'm *not*—I wouldn't wear heels while I did it. I prefer to make my getaways quick and painless, thank you very much.

"Well? Am I a threat to national security?" I ask when it appears he's finished his assessment. I even give my foot a sassy kick for good measure, but I elicit no response and almost lose my shoe in the process. "Do you want to place me in one of the interrogation rooms until you get the all clear? I'm partial to the one Simon uses. Such fond memories I have of being held there against my will."

Grant sighs, his exasperation causing a crease to form down the middle of his forehead. Don't get me wrong— my husband is and always has been annoyingly handsome, and no amount of annoyance can change that. His hair is the blondish-brown you typically find on frat boys and surfer dudes, and he has these huge brown eyes that exude sleepy innocence and puppy-dog friendliness. It's the perfect look for lulling unsuspecting cat burglars into falling in love and spilling their secrets.

"This better not be one of your tricks, Penelope."

"It's not!" I lie.

"You said you were having lunch with your grand-mother today."

"She had to cancel," I lie again. "I never see you any-more, that's all." I run my finger up the line of his suit jacket. It's loose and crumpled, which says a lot about his current state of mind. He usually wears his suits like they're made of neoprene. "You've been spending all your free time at work lately, and even when you come home, it's like you're not there. I miss you."

"Stop batting your eyes at me. I'm not falling for it."

"I'm blinking. You want me to stop blinking?"

"I want you to tell me why you're really here."

"My profound love for you isn't good enough? Thanks a lot."

His lips twitch in amusement, though I wouldn't go so far as to call it a smile. When Grant really smiles, he does it with his whole face. His eyes crinkle at the edges in a way that sets my heart skittering and makes me wonder what I did to deserve such a gorgeous, strapping beast of a man in my life.

"I mean it." He places his hands heavily on my shoulders. "I'm in the middle of something at the moment. There's been a new development in the case I'm working."

Aha. Now we're getting closer to something interesting. By *new development*, I can only assume he's talking about the ruby bracelet that went missing from New York's elite inner circles last night. This makes half a dozen pieces in all, each one worth more than the last. They're saying this one clocks in at over a million bucks.

I almost feel sorry for Grant having to head up this investigation. With such high-profile victims as the CEO of a chain of hospitals and an energy tycoon known to contribute in presidential campaigns, he must feel the pressure to find the culprit before any more rich people are outraged.

But the thief—again, *not me*—is a good one. According to the newspapers, there have only been two clues worth note. The first is a bathmat bearing the imprint of a woman's size seven shoe. The other is a maid who claims to have seen a pair of peep-toes poking out under a curtain in the same room where a diamond watch later went missing. It's not much to go on, but I assume Grant has dozens of theories and facts he's not sharing with the world.

Theories and facts that appear to be pointing to yours truly.

"What kind of development?" I ask.

"Nice try. I know I've been distracted lately, but I'm not *that* distracted." He squeezes my shoulders again, and there's a finality to it that lingers long after the pressure is gone. "I'm sorry, love. I appreciate you coming all this way to see me, but I need to get back. I'll have Cheryl show you out."

"I wish you wouldn't." And not only because I need to keep him distracted for a few minutes longer. The truth is, I don't like feeling shut out of his life—of *our* life.

But all he does is sigh in frustration. "Why don't you go home and enjoy the rest of your day? Aren't you supposed to be finishing that novel for your book club?"

"I tried, but it was about zombies. It gave me nightmares."

"What about your plans to overhaul the garden?"

"Too many bugs." I give a delicate shudder. "They also give me nightmares."

"There's always that volunteer gig at the rare books room you were talking about..."

I let him trail off, refusing to pick up the bait. Of all the book clubs and garden plans and volunteer opportunities Grant keeps dangling in front of me, that one is by far the most appealing. I've always loved the New York Library, and that room, in particular, has personal meaning for me. But the larger issue isn't about how I spend my leisure time—it's about how he doesn't trust me to find a productive way to fill it. To him, the succession of long, empty days I've faced since renouncing my life of crime are nothing more than an opportunity to get in trouble.

It's sweet that he's so concerned for my well-being and all, but it's almost enough to make me want to give the real Peep-Toe Prowler a run for her money.

"You're such a man sometimes," I say with a *tsk* of real annoyance. "You just have a thing for the sexy librarian look."

He tilts his head, playing along. "Hmm. Maybe I do, now that you mention it. A pair of glasses here, a tight skirt there…"

Oh, he's good. A tight skirt and its immediate removal does have its appeal. I can feel myself faltering already. "I am *not* volunteering at a library so you can get off on your weird, repressed fantasies," I say.

My insult, neatly aimed, goes wide. He laughs. "Nice try, but there's nothing repressed about the things I'd like to do to you, Penelope Blue."

"Don't look at me like that," I say, though not very convincingly. I happen to adore that particular dark-eyed stare of his. "I'll have you know I'm more than a pair of legs."

"True. But you have to admit they're very nice legs."

Sure. *Now* he looks, his gaze intense as it moves from my toes along every curve of my calves and thighs. Dammit. That's not what the shoes are there for.

I put them on this morning to take the lead in the cat-and-mouse game of our marriage, not to get sidetracked by seduction.

"Stop it," I warn, "or you're not getting anywhere near these legs again."

His smile only curves wider. "Oh, really? Is that a threat…or would you rather call it a dare?"

"Let's call it a promise."

"Excellent. A promise." His voice comes out in a low rumble as he takes a predatory step toward me. He's ostensibly letting a woman in a black suit and oversized handbag by, but I know better. Grant is an excellent tactician, and he's using his environment to manipulate the scene.

And me. Oh, how he loves to manipulate me, often in the best of ways.

"In fact," he continues, "I *promise* to do everything in my power to appreciate your legs to the fullest."

No, no, no. I refuse to be swayed by his hot, raking glances or the lulling heat of his proximity. Playing Grant's mind games—however much a thoroughly enjoyable staple of our marriage they may be—is not on the menu today, and none of the pistons firing between my thighs will change my mind.

I'm going to be strong. I'm going to prove my innocence. I'm going to show this man what I think about his underhanded tactics.

I'm not feeling particularly strong or innocent as he edges even closer with a determined gleam in his eye, so it's for the best that we're hit with a sudden blast of toxic air. My eyes sting and my lungs recoil and all thoughts of seduction reach an end.

Good old Riker. His timing hasn't always been impeccable, but he's managed it this go around. That smell means one thing and one thing only.

It's showtime.

The smell of Liquid Evacuation (patent not pending) is difficult to nail down, but most people who encounter it say it smells like a deadly cocktail of a dozen different chemicals—a sulfurous tang you do *not* want anywhere near your lungs.

In reality, it's perfectly harmless…much like the group of thieves currently breaking into the FBI to have a look around.

The chemical made its way into the building thanks to the woman who slipped past on her way to Cheryl just moments ago. Riker planted a few drops in her bag while she snagged her daily coffee from the cart out front of the building. With a delayed reaction of about ten minutes, the timing of the chemical's release was perfectly planned to allow her inside and past all security checkpoints before it hit.

Grant smells it as quickly as I do. His first instinct, as always, is protective, and he propels me to the far side of the room so fast I barely have time to register what's happening. His hand presses my head against his chest, where I feel his heartbeat pick up and his muscles coil in preparation to hoist me over his shoulder and carry me to safety, fireman-style.

My own body experiences something akin to a swoon. Oh, how I love this man. There's so much nobility in him it scares me sometimes.

His next instinct isn't so sweet. It takes two seconds for the scent to register, and two more for him to sift through his memories until he recalls where he's come across it before. His arms drop as suddenly as they came up.

"Oh no. Oh, hell no. That better not be what I think it is."

"What do you think it is?" I ask all-too-innocently. "Is it anthrax?"

"Don't be ridiculous. Anthrax doesn't have a scent. That smells an awful lot like—"

Three agents burst through the back door, cutting Grant's sentence short. Not that I need to hear it to know what he's thinking. The way he looks at me—as if he'd like to tie me to the metal chair so I can't escape—says it all.

You did this. You're attacking the FBI.

Yes. Yes, I am, sweet husband. Deal with it.

"Emerson, there you are. We've shut down the ventilation system." The largest of the agents is clearly in charge, and he has the enormously wide chest to prove it. He looks like a Saint Bernard carrying a cask of ale around its neck. "We're isolating the floor and evacuating the rest of the building. Cheryl, make sure no one comes off those elevators."

He stops, as if only now noticing the diminutive woman Grant is inches away from murdering with his bare hands. "Is she with you?"

The *she* in question schools her features to give nothing away. For all this man knows, I'm nothing more than an innocent bystander. A victim of bad timing. A poor, put-upon wife.

Hey, stranger things have happened.

"Don't evacuate." Grant's voice is tightly controlled, a slice of cold, hard steel coming to the surface. "Don't isolate the floor. Don't shut down the elevators."

"But they're saying it could be something lethal—"

He doesn't even blink. "Call it off, and call it off *now*."

"I don't think we can ignore—"

"I'm not asking you to think. I'm asking you to call it off. Anything that's standard protocol, any action we'd normally take. Don't do it." Grant turns to me, his dark eyes flashing. "And make sure you get those ventilation fans back on as fast as possible. We don't want anyone taking advantage of the downtime to sneak inside the ducts."

Please. As if FBI vents are big enough for that. Even the lowest-level thieves know they're impossible to navigate.

"I think the smell is already starting to go away," I point out—which, indeed, it is. Jordan, our chemist and explosives expert, worked out a new formula recently. This one has a delay activation of ten minutes, an active smell for half that, and then all trace of it disappears. It's a toxic smokescreen. *Poof* and then it's gone. "Maybe someone had gasoline on their clothes. That happened at a movie theater I went to once, in Jersey. Some lady spilled gas all over herself at the pump and had no idea she was carrying it around on her clothes. We thought the entire place was going to blow."

Agent Barrel Chest listens to my story with interest, taking me for the innocent that I'm pretending to be. Grant, however, grips me by the elbow, the clasp tight enough to warn me what thin ice I'm on.

The other agents sniff tentatively, noticing for themselves that the air is starting to clear.

"See?" I say. "It must have been an accident. Someone probably stepped in a weird puddle."

"It does seem unlikely…"

"I wonder if an air-conditioning unit went out…"

"They're not reporting anything on the other floors…"

One by one, the agents begin doubting their senses. Their shoulders relax and their guards lower inch by inch. Only Grant remains unconvinced, refusing to let go of my arm—bless his suspicious heart.

"Not good enough," he says. "I want to know if anyone's had any unusual visitors or received unexpected deliveries today." He glowers at me. "Also, the names and IDs of all independent contractors we've hired in the past three months. No job is too big or small—even some guy filling in for the window washing staff. Got it? I'm especially interested in males between the ages of twenty-five and fifty, about five-eight, nondescript in every regard."

That would be Oz, the fourth member of our team. A master of disguise, he can sneak in anywhere undetected.

Well, anywhere except this building. We might be good, but we're not *that* good.

"There's no need," I tell Grant truthfully. Knowing he won't believe me and loving the irony of it all. "He's not here."

Agent Barrel Chest perks up at that, but Grant yanks me a few paces out of his range of hearing. "If you know what's good for you, you won't open your mouth again."

"But I have to breathe!"

"Not for much longer."

"Oh dear. This is because I called you *my sweet darling*, isn't it?"

The stifled choke of his rage-fueled laughter is a sound I won't soon forget. It's like a werewolf being forced to swallow his howl and finding he rather likes the taste.

"Uh, Emerson?" Cheryl coughs discreetly, intervening before Grant can respond.

"Yes?"

"When you say you want to know about visitors, are you counting Blackrock?"

His head swivels in her direction so fast it leaves *me* dizzy. "Blackrock is here? *Now?*"

She scans her computer before nodding. "Sterling had a meeting set up with him at two. I haven't checked him out yet, so I assume they're still back there. Do you want me to notify him?"

I could kiss Cheryl for her perfect timing, and I make a mental note to get her an even deadlier concealed weapon next Christmas. Maybe a lipstick grenade or something.

"Goddammit!" Grant swears. "So that's what this is. Make sure Simon has backup and get a man posted at every exit. Blackrock doesn't leave until I personally search him, got it?"

"Do you know what's going on?" Agent Barrel Chest asks as he steps forward, ready to set his impressive physique into action. "Who's Blackrock?"

"I don't know what's happening yet, but I'm going to find out," Grant says. He's careful to ignore the second half of the question, but I don't mind because I already know the answer. Blackrock is the code name for Warren Blue, a thief-turned-FBI-informant who's done miraculous things in helping my husband and his partner, Simon Sterling, put bad guys behind bars.

He's also my father, the man who taught me everything

I know about breaking into highly secured government facilities. So you can imagine Grant's concern.

"As for you…" Grant finds himself at a loss, gazing around the lobby for the best place to stash me while he tends to his duties. From the look on his face, I get the feeling he'd like to knock me unconscious with a potted ficus, but that's frowned upon, even by the feds.

"Why don't I stay here?" I motion to the metal chair, knowing the mere fact that I'm suggesting it will force him to reject the idea out of hand. "Then I won't be in your way while you go about your business. It sounds *super important*."

"Oh no," he says, distracted enough to take the bait. "You're not going anywhere." He yanks me closer, holding me against the hard wall of his side. When the other agents look at him curiously, he adds a lackluster, "I want to be able to keep an eye on her until we know the danger is passed."

"Maybe you could leave me under Cheryl's protection," I suggest.

Cheryl lifts her hands. "No thanks. I'm not going anywhere near this one."

"I don't mind keeping an eye on her," Agent Barrel Chest says, but I can tell that option doesn't weigh much in Grant's opinion. There's no telling what I might get his coworker to do with a few smiles. Federal agents I'm *not* married to find me incredibly charming.

Time is ticking by, and Grant still has no idea what I'm up to, so he pulls me with him as he strides out of the room. "Fine. I guess you'll have to stay with me. Don't look at anyone, don't talk to anyone, and don't you dare try anything. Understand?"

"Yes, dear," I say meekly. I can't even pretend to be outraged, because I'm too busy keeping the smile from my face. In a few short steps, I've now breached the hallowed walls of the FBI—and with nary a handcuff in sight.

Of course, being manacled to Grant's side isn't conducive to finishing the job, especially since he doesn't slow down as he moves through the maze of hallways to the interview room where my father is being held.

We're halfway down a particularly gray corridor when Simon appears. A permanent frown carves into his face, his customary tie pulled so tight it's a wonder his head doesn't pop and send gallons of shellac-like hair product flying. His frown only deepens when he spots me. Despite the fact that my father's capture has done great things for his career, Simon isn't much of a Penelope Blue fan.

"What are you doing?" Grant demands. "Why aren't you with Warren?"

"He's waiting for me in the interview room. I heard there was a breach?"

"Get back there immediately—and keep an eye out for anyone who might be Oz."

Simon turns to me and levels a knowing glare. "What did she do?"

"I don't know yet," Grant says grimly.

"Want me to beat it out of her?"

There's a long enough pause to cause me momentary concern. I mean, I know Grant and I have our problems, but there's a line between tricking a spouse and torturing one. It's thin, but it's there.

"Can I get a raincheck on that?" Grant asks, his eyes fixed on me. "I'd like to keep the option open."

"Why, Grant Emerson, I think that might be the sweetest thing you've ever said." I nod back down the hallway. "I'll make this easy on both of you and go home. I know the way out."

"*No!*" both men yell at once. Grant releases a frustrated groan. "We don't have time for this. Simon, get back to Warren and don't let him out of your sight. I'll take Penelope—"

He glances at the door we've stopped outside, which I now notice has his name engraved on a metal panel. My heart picks up speed as I realize it's his personal office. *Jackpot.*

I'm afraid my rapid pulse is going to give me away, so I pull my arms out of his grasp and pretend to rub the sore spots.

"Lock her inside," Simon suggests and pushes the door open. "You don't have any windows or vents, and we can post a man in the hallway to make sure she doesn't sneak out."

Grant grunts his agreement. "It isn't ideal, but there's not much damage she can do in there." He turns to me with an expression that's difficult to read. Determined and professional, yes, but also pained. "We talked about this, Pen. You're supposed to be keeping a low profile, remember? Head down, nose clean. There are people here who would like to see you—"

He shakes his head, cutting his own words short. He finishes instead with, "I'm sorry to do this to you, but I can't have you wandering around the building. Not until I know what you're up to."

"I can't believe you think me capable of such deception," I say, playing up the role of wounded wife. It's not a stretch. My profile has been nothing but low for months—and it hasn't been an easy thing to maintain. A little credit would be nice. "After all we've been through together."

He's not fooled for a second. "And I can't believe you'd use Jordan's chemical again. You should have known I'd recognize it." I *had* known; that was part of the plan. Thankfully, all the late nights and overworked hours have thrown my husband off his game—he doesn't yet realize I wanted to be caught. "Now get in there. We'll deal with this later."

He gently-but-firmly nudges me inside his office, offering a curt command to Simon before slamming the door and turning the key.

I hold my breath and count to ten before I look around, fearful this might be too good to be true—or perhaps Grant is toying with me, coming out on top in our endless game of cat and mouse. But as I turn to face those four whitewalls—Grant's home away from home, the place where he's leading an investigation that some-how pinpoints his *wife* as the Peep-Toe Prowler—the heady realization sinks in.

I did it. I'm in.

I guess infiltrating the FBI isn't so hard, after all.

ACKNOWLEDGMENTS

This book is the result of hours of hard work from so many different people, all of whom deserve their own page of praise. Since I don't have that much space, I'll try to keep things brief. Elyssa Patrick was, as always, instrumental in keeping my spirits up and the words flowing. Nicole Helm has been this book's champion from the start. Thanks to my agent, Courtney Miller-Callihan, and Deb Nemeth, freelance editor extraordinaire, for helping to make this book the best version it could be.

A special shout also goes out to everyone at Sourcebooks. I didn't expect to find such an incredible team at my back, but you guys have made every step of this process a delight. To Mary Altman, Laura Costello, and the entire Riker Appreciation Fan Club—thank you, from the bottom of my heart, for loving these characters as much as I do.

ABOUT THE AUTHOR

Tamara Morgan is a contemporary romance author whose books combine fast-paced antics and humor with heartfelt sentiment. Her long-lived affinity for romance novels survived a BA degree in English literature, after which time she discovered it was much more fun to create stories than analyze the life out of them. She lives with her husband and daughter in the Inland Northwest, where the summers are hot, the winters are cold, and coffee is available on every street corner.